Praise for *The Humiliation Tour*

"I love this story and wish it for everybody."
BILL RODGERS, American Marathon Legend

"Recker showcases his story telling talent by crafting a humorous tribute to the angst of growing up that is both entertaining and heartwarming while capturing the spirit of running through generations."
JEAN KNAACK, CEO – Road Runners Club of America

"A fantastical coming-of-age running novel which will make you laugh, cringe, and cry."
JESSICA GRIFFITHS, *Colorado Runner Magazine*

"*The Humiliation Tour* is a Trials of Job story of a young runner suffering through an almost unending tragic-comic events on his path to adulthood. Even non-runners will find it a page turner."
BENJI DURDAN, 1980 USA Olympic Marathoner, 1983 USA World Championship Marathoner

"Hugely entertaining coming-of-age story of an endearing young man you will find yourself cheering out loud for. Billy's epic journey is equal parts hilarious, poignant, insightful and captivating. You don't need to be a runner to enjoy!"
MAUREEN CUSTY-ROBEN, Former #1 ranked US Marathoner

"Heartwarming and inspiring. It's a laugh out loud, what's going to happen next, page turner. My favorite read of the year."
KIRK APT, Former course record holder of Hardrock 100 Mile Endurance Run

"Writing comedy is an ultra-rare skill. Recker has it in spades."
GEOFFREY SIMPSON, Author of *The Slummer*

THE HUMILIATION TOUR

THE HUMILIATION TOUR

JEFFREY RECKER

Published by

BarkingBoxer Press

The Future of Sports Fiction

The Humiliation Tour / by Jeffrey Recker — 1 ed.
Published in the USA by BarkingBoxer Press LLC
Sheridan, Wyoming

Issued in print and electronic formats
ISBN 978-3-9822801-6-5 (pbk)
ISBN 978-3-9822801-7-2 (ebook)

FIC038000   FICTION / Sports
FIC043000   FICTION / Coming of Age
FIC016000   FICTION / Humorous

To Kathaleen

Always my inspiration

PART ONE

1

Soup
~ Arizona, 1993 ~

An eccentric pop-culture artist once said this about the future: Everyone will be world-famous for fifteen minutes.

Andy Warhol was a big deal in our house, not for his artwork—which my parents hated, yet owned—but for the simple fact that Andy's father was a coal miner from Pittsburgh, and that made him akin to family. A print of his Campbell's soup cans painting hung in a plastic frame in our kitchen. I've never understood art, and I certainly didn't understand this print. How could someone become so infamously rich by painting...this? And how could anyone who works for a living put more value on it than a ten-hour shift in a coal mine? I bet Andy's father hated him.

I also bet there weren't as many *that's my boy* praises in his house as there were in mine.

On the morning of the state finals cross-country meet, I woke early. Jet, our black Labrador who identifies as human, was curled at my feet, and groaned when I slipped out from underneath the covers. I quickly dressed and checked my pulse—elevated. Jet moved up to my pillow and plopped down. It was too early, even for him. I walked in circles until I heard Mom rustling in the kitchen. Then, I came out and sat down for breakfast, and—as moms do—she asked me if I felt like a winner. "You tell me," I said, agitated. I felt badly for answering her that way. But that's what teenage boys do. I hadn't slept well.

"I didn't sleep well," I offered.

Dad entered the kitchen in his pajamas and sat down at his usual spot on a dinette chair that whined under his weight and warned of collapse. He was a large man; six-foot-four, with a presence that matched his girth.

"How are you two related?" Mom asked, making light of our match. I appeared childlike sitting next to him. But, so did Mom. "Billy takes after my side of the family," she said, flatly. "It's why he can run so fast."

Dad ignored her comment. "How are you feeling?" he asked me.

"Not like a winner," I said.

"That's my boy."

Dad didn't listen well.

Nerves had the best of me, and my stomach growled when Mom filled my bowl with Cheerios. I couldn't eat. So, while my parents discussed the weather and the day's schedule, I sat staring at those Cheerios until the milk saturated the oats, turning them into bloated, decomposing bodies. I forced a spoonful down and then held the bowl beneath the table for Jet to finish.

"Jesus Christ, Jean," Dad said. "When are you going to stop feeding this kid? He's eighteen."

"Richard…"

"And Billy—goddammit," he continued. "Don't feed the dog under the table." Dad was not a religious man, but he cried Jesus Christ and God twenty times a day, which confused me as a kid, but I'd grown accustomed to it now, and some days even understood it.

The Cheerios did not settle well. I hurried to the bathroom and vomited. Through paper-thin walls, Dad shouted, "You okay?" When I came out, Dad was still sitting at the table, waiting for Mom to feed him. He never saw the hypocrisy in that. He smirked, remembering the athletic competitions of his own youth. "That's my boy," he said.

Mom, on the other hand, was concerned. She stood, arms crossed, framed by the soup can print. And this time, instead of asking me if I felt like a winner, she asked if I was ill. Before I could answer, seeing all thirty-two of those soup cans—tomato this and tomato that—made me do an about-face and return to the bathroom for another bout of nausea. When I emerged a second time, Dad asked if I was done, and said that I was ruining his appetite.

"I feel better," I told him. "Just nerves."

"Are you sure?"

I shrugged my shoulders. "I guess so."

Three words.

Like most teenage boys, I never had a lot to say to my parents. For their sake, I wish they'd had a daughter.

Dad, who'd barely advanced his vocabulary beyond the Xs and Os of high school football, stood up and pointed to the Warhol print. "Fifteen minutes today, Billy," he said, passionately. "Fifteen minutes and you'll be world famous!" He raised an open palm, and considered slapping the green Formica countertop for effect, but pulled back. Nothing in our cheaply constructed, ranch style home, was a match for him and his antics. And he knew it.

But oddly enough, he was perfectly right about the fifteen minutes comment.

Fifteen minutes—that's how long it takes me to run a 5k. Yes, I'm fast. Very, very fast. But it also depends on the course. Cross-country runs on grass, or winding golf course paths, or wooded trails, and in Arizona, the rocky, undulating terrain of the desert. And they hurt. They cause side-stitches, missteps, and falls, and if the terrain is hard enough, lesser runners might vomit in mid-stride. I'd seen it. Sometimes they cry like toddlers when they finish.

This histrionic teenage drama was on display at every meet across the country on fall Saturday mornings. They'd spill into the chute, moaning, holding their sides, leaning against each other for support, acting like they'd just been shot, sometimes passing out, and other such nonsense. Parents were horrified. Coaches were embarrassed.

In Tucson, the courses are particularly tough. It's common to race on cacti-covered trails that run atop granite ridges, and through sandy washes. It's here that the steep, sharp-crested, Santa Catalina Mountains dominate the skyline, rising thousands of feet above the valley floor, spilling into the foothills in a labyrinth of ridges and folds and valleys filled with boulder-debris flows.

But getting back to my dad's comment—yes, it was going to take me roughly fifteen minutes to dispatch the three-time defending state champion from his throne.

We live in a small town named Oracle that sits on the north side of the Santa Catalina Mountains. Here, the saguaro cacti are so tall they scratch and claw at the sky all day until it bleeds red at sunset. Tucson is just a thirty-minute drive to the south, and since it's so close, Coach gave us the option of riding in the school bus with our teammates, or not. I chose the latter, which meant that I'd be riding with my parents. I was thankful I wouldn't have to endure the irritating chatter of my teammates.

Those conversations would always go something like this: *I've been sick all week. I pulled a muscle. I just started my period. And my favorite one—I can't shit.* And I'd roll my eyes, and lean my head against the bus window, wishing I was not there.

On these bus rides, the boys and the girls sat apart. The girls up front, gossiping, braiding their hair. They'd paint our school colors onto their faces to look intimidating. I found this ridiculous because by the end of a race, their faces were a hot mess as those colors mixed with sweat and tears. The boys sat in back. They'd fart and tell jokes. But on the way home, we'd mix and flirt. Alcohol and weed would magically appear and pass between us. One time, Jack Ash peed into an empty Coke bottle and threw it out the window because Coach Jones refused to stop to let us relieve ourselves. Another time, he and Jenny Ledge went at it pretty hard in the last row of the bus.

I'd told Jack I'd take the bus home, but only if I won. And if that happened, my parents would have to wait to tell me how great I am—which happens often on race day. Mom loves to shower me with compliments, and often in front of my teammates. It is so embarrassing. She insists that I inherited my athleticism from her side of the family and wants everyone to know it.

At 9 a.m. we jumped into Dad's pickup truck, which has a bench seat up front and a smaller one in the rear. It's an older model that he only drives on special occasions. Jet was not happy about being left behind on this family outing, but he wished me good luck by barking incessantly from the backyard and waking Old Man Baldwin, our neighbor from across the street. He appeared on his porch shaking his cane at us.

When Mom got in the passenger's side, she slid closer to Dad, the way she might have when they were dating twenty years ago. Despite myself, I do notice these things, which proves that I'm not a horrible son. Whenever we rode in that truck, Dad reminded me that times were simpler back then, when vehicles moved slower, seat belts were optional, and drive-in movies were the preferred date night. It was nice to think about, and see the things that shaped Mom and Dad. I sat behind them, cramped in the undersized cab, my torso twisted right, and my knees tucked into my chest.

"Got enough room back there?" Mom asked, politely.

"Can't breathe," I said. I'd been telling her this since I was ten years old, when, even at my slight build, I had outgrown the space. "Why'd we have to take the truck?"

"It's a special day," Dad said.

"Yeah, but I've got a race to run and I can't feel my legs."

He didn't reply. Neither did. Perhaps they too felt the weight of the day, and a burden shouldered out of parental kindness or obligation. Parents are strange that way.

We pulled out of the driveway, and I sat staring out the window, lost in thought, wondering what the next few hours would bring, but also admiring the rising sun that kissed low-hanging clouds, turning them pink and muted.

"Don't forget to pick up Rigby," I said.

Rigby was a sophomore, and my girlfriend. We'd been dating for five months, which in high school meant we were long overdue to part ways. She played the clarinet and the whites of her eyes would bug wide if she blew too hard. My parents adored her. They'd likely talk the entire ride to Tucson.

She squeezed into the cab with me, my knees pinned fully against my chest now.

"Hi, ya'll!" She flipped her long, stringy, black hair, and flashed her perfectly white teeth. It was a common greeting she used, and each time I'd pull back, or risk being whipped in the eyes by her fine hair. As for the Texas accent, I don't know where she got it from. Nor had I ever asked. The shallowness of our high school relationship didn't beg to know. But it matched her effervescent character, her smile lively, brimming with excitement, even as I swallowed hard, not sharing that feeling.

Now, if there was one good thing about Rigby riding with us, it was that my parents didn't ask me another question during the entire ride to the race, which was staged at an elementary school adjacent to the state park where we'd run.

By the time we arrived, the venue was abuzz. Dozens of school busses parked uniformly in the lot. Kids stretched and ran sprints, while others huddled around coaches, looking for what—last-minute advice? Overhead, Mount Lemmon loomed like a granite hammer ready to crush the weak and the novice, and I laughed out loud about any last-minute advice that a coach might possibly give. Spectators found places to make themselves useless and mostly walked in circles bumping into each other, not knowing what to do or where to go and simply getting in the way.

I spotted the starting line beyond this chaos. There, a television crew was setting up, readying themselves for the most anticipated cross-country meet in state history.

When we parked, I busted out of the cab like Superman exiting a phone booth in my green polyester uniform with Bald Eagles written across the chest. And like all things issued by the school, it should have been retired years ago. The top had shrunk two sizes from hundreds of tours in the washer and dryer. The bottoms were nothing more than loose threads clinging mercifully together in a life extended far too long. But I loved them. They were light and lucky, and made me feel free and fast.

Mom wished me good luck, and Rigby threw me a kiss. I ignored both. Instead, I sped away and forgot to thank them for coming, for just being there to support me. I left them sitting in the truck to undoubtedly talk about what an ungrateful son and boyfriend I was.

I'd apologize later. I had too much on my mind for now. Like, where is Charlie?

Charlie was my lifelong friend and neighbor who had talked me into joining the cross-country team because I was awful at everything else. When we were kids, I'd chase her around the neighborhood and try to kiss her. I never did get that kiss. "I'm too fast," she'd say. And she was. Later, when she developed, I gave up the chase because that would have been way too weird.

I needed to see her now, to wish her good luck in the women's race. Likely, she was warming up on the course, studying every turn and dip and rise. Charlie Simmons was nothing if not headstrong and determined. She'd wear the stress of a race on her otherwise placid, freckled face, worry lines marking the corners of her gold-flecked eyes, and a look of consternation, so primal, intimidating, her rivals would look away. She also owned a vocabulary worthy of a miner's daughter. She used it often. Though, I knew other sides; softer sides. Today, she was hoping for a top-ten finish. Recruiters from the area's top universities were in attendance, and this race was everything to her.

In my quest to locate her, I bumped into an older, heavy-set man wearing a hat that said ORACLE THEATER. "Excuse me, Billy," he said. I asked if we knew each other and he said not really but that he knows my dad. Adults are strange that way.

Fortunately, Coach assembled the team as planned, and it was there I was able to wish Charlie good luck. "Screw off," she said. "I don't need luck. I need more miles!" That's the relationship we agreed upon as kids; one full of salt and vinegar and brutal honesty.

"You're not wearing the 'I'm With Stupid' T-shirt," I said. She'd worn it the first day of practice our freshman year. That day, I'd tried to put space between us, but she shadowed me for fun.

Now, she rolled her eyes. With both hands, she framed the words "Bald Eagles" on her uniform. "My one request fell on deaf ears."

"Budgets," I laughed. These uniforms will outlive us all.

"It's humiliating."

Unlike our men's team, our women's team hadn't qualified for the state meet, so it was just Charlie out there on her own, officially a representative of the district, not the school. I know this made her nervous, running alone without the support of Jenny Ledge and her other teammates.

But Charlie did what she does best, and ran a handful of girls down in the stretch and placed seventh, swearing as she crossed the line—likely at her mom, who couldn't bother to show up again.

Then it was my turn.

There are few things I remember about the start. I lined up and exchanged good-lucks, high-fives, and fist bumps with my teammates as well as competitors I did not know. Then I saw Christmas Day. Yes, that is his real name, and by virtue of his name, and that he was the defending three-time state champion, he had his own fan club, and was celebrated by the state's sports reporters. He made for great headlines, and articles praised him like the Next Coming. In these articles, sometimes I might get a mention that read something like this: "In a gallant effort, William Ball hung on for second place." Sometimes, I wasn't mentioned at all.

And today I figured the headlines had already been written. Most assumed Christmas was unbeatable. He lined up to my far right. He was easy to spot in his black uniform with a red stripe across the chest. He had a black tuft of thick, wavy hair and piercing blue eyes that, in that moment, locked on mine.

I mouthed, "Good luck, Christmas." Then, he lifted his chin as if he was about to return the wish. But instead, he spat.

The least he could do was say my name.

Then, a race official walked the length of us to ensure everyone stood behind the line, pointing at runners whose toes inched over it. "Get back," he'd say. When he stopped and pointed at me, I looked down to see if I was in violation, but I'll be damned if he didn't wink and tell me, "Good luck, son." He was one of only a few who knew I'd challenge Christmas.

The pistol fired and two-hundred of the best runners in Arizona shot onto the course. Collectively, we were hot-tempered, spirited like race horses, stampeding for position, agitated and hell-bent on making a name for ourselves. Behind us we left a cloud of dust that choked the spectators, leaving them coughing and spitting.

Coach liked to say we were lucky because running is not a contact sport like football, but I can tell you otherwise. In my peripheral view, a kid in a red uniform tripped and fell, curled and trampled. Coach never ran cross-country.

I stayed out of trouble in those early yards, running in the bubble of my teammates. Soon, I broke free and positioned myself up front with four others, including Christmas Day.

Christmas ran as if the outcome was already decided.

He floated above the ground like a saint, without expression and propelled by omnipotent forces. His long, sinewy legs seemed to reach all the way up to his neck, forgoing any hint of an actual torso, a weighted mass to be transported over distance, that say, a human might possess.

His gait, so smooth, so impossibly long. *Was he beatable?* I ran on his heels, wondering. And I gave no thought to the other three who ran with us. They were already panting like dogs.

Now, unique to running in the desert is having to negotiate cacti. I've returned home from runs with scratched, bloodied legs from sideswiping jumping cholla. They're short in stature, but nasty in disposition. As the five of us took a corner, one runner was squeezed to the inside and brushed up against one; its barbed needles broke away and tenaciously attached to his hip. I never saw him again.

Christmas pushed the pace, and we fell in line. I took up directly behind him. And behind me I heard the heavy footfalls of a kid running too fast for his own good, occasionally clipping my heels. I turned and yelled at him to back off, and considered the threat of going down on this course, falling into a giant saguaro cactus, quite possibly. The course was thick with these green-ribbed giants that sprouted inch-long needles from top to bottom. A solid hit on one of them could actually end in death.

But I knew the course well. I cut and weaved along with ease and precision, and before long it became a two-person race.

Christmas continued in front, while I was content to follow. He didn't look back. He didn't need to. He knew I was the only one in the field who could challenge him. But in the days leading up to the race, even he was quoted as saying, "Billy Ball is a fine runner, but I've beaten him three years in a row. That's not going to change."

Perhaps. But at the moment, I pulled alongside as we entered a sandy riverbed, the farthest point on the course where there were no spectators. It was eerily quiet except for the cactus wrens that called to us from the hollowed-out saguaros. We were running in concert, step for step, breath for breath. And for the first time, Christmas acknowledged my presence, if nothing more than a glance to his left to calculate my effort. I was breathing hard, but he was too.

I took a slight lead, checking Christmas as well as any other threat. But we had already gapped the field by nearly a minute.

Christmas pulled next to me and then surged ahead, and I sensed then that he was done playing around. Somehow, I managed to stay with him.

In the final half mile, the course opened up to a wide field. Here it flattened out. Fans appeared in the distance, though they cheered for Christmas.

And I thought to myself, every story needs an antagonist. Here I was, locked in step with him, playing it. I surged and pulled ahead with a quarter mile to go.

The sun was at our backs, and in front, leading the charge, our shadows melded as one. Our feet touched as we wheezed and grunted in unison. *Who would kick first?* A hard right turn was fast approaching.

This particular turn skirted a cactus patch that looked like a cornucopia of death. At its edge, a giant saguaro jutted out onto the course. A bed of jumping cholla and prickly pear grew behind it. But it was also the hot corner, meaning it was a popular spot for spectators. Locked in step with Christmas, I instantly knew my plan.

I'd slingshot around the saguaro, forcing Christmas to the outside, causing separation. The finish line was a fifteen-second sprint beyond that. But Christmas had a plan too, because when we approached the turn, he cut into me hard, causing me to compromise my gait, or risk being impaled by the giant saguaro.

We'd swept into that turn at a five-minute-per-mile pace, and the next thing I knew, all hell broke loose. Christmas clipped me from behind. I spun sideways, and my next step purchased nothing but air. Christmas yelled "Fu…" before his voice muffled. I could feel the weight of him passing over my body and I knew we were both going down in the cactus patch.

I know a lot about time. It has consumed my life for years. Einstein theorized that at top speed, time slows down. Athletes, in pinnacle moments, talk about the clarity of their surroundings and how everything plays out in slow motion. And that's how this moment played out for me.

Everything was blowing up. A tumbleweed of body parts and clothing spun in a vortex that shot me out, on my back, looking straight up at a crystal-blue sky. I hadn't hit the saguaro cactus, but I *had* fallen into the bed of prickly pear.

Dozens of needles had broken off and attached to my hip, where my skin abraded and puckered red. I rose gingerly and navigated through the cactus patch, an upheaval of dust, and back onto the course. Peripherally, I saw Christmas, also working to right himself. He was calling me something that was not my name. I loped into a jog, and the jog became a run. The finish line drew close, and I fought to run to it, but I was dizzy and the terra firma moved in waves beneath my wobbly legs. *How much time had I lost?* I could feel the presence of other runners descending upon me like a swarm of locusts. Soon I'd be swallowed up and passed if I couldn't sprint. But adrenaline kicked in, and I did sprint.

Behind me, I heard the fading claps and cheers from the bystanders who'd witnessed the fall. They were shouting for me to run faster and win the race.

And then someone yelled, "Fancy Pants!" Whatever that meant.

From the hot corner, they'd seen my approach, leading the race in my green shorts. What they saw as I ran away was my bare-naked ass, my beloved shorts left behind, ripped from me in the fall and stuck to a prickly pear.

In the heat of the moment, I had no idea this had happened. I'd gotten up quickly from the fall, assessed the damage to my hip, and took off in a desperate attempt to reach the finish line.

The waiting crowd was in a frenzy now, shouting as I approached. This was my moment, the one I'd dreamt about for four years. This was my fifteen minutes of fame. I'd finally beaten Christmas Day and was going to win my first state championship. But as I closed in, a very different thought entered my mind: *Why could I see my bare hip back there?*

As quickly as I knew the answer, the cheers turned to gasps, and I heard someone laugh, and another, and still another. But I did what came naturally in the moment—I threw my arms up in victory. A reporter from a local television station lowered his camera and mouthed the words "Oh, shit…" Then I spotted Mom and Dad. They didn't look celebratory at all. Next to them stood Rigby, who was wide-eyed, and Charlie, who had her eyes fully covered. Dad pointed at me, although his aim was low. My eyes followed. My rail-thin torso provided unobstructed views of my bottom half, and as I crossed the finish line and looked down, I saw my penis swinging freely left to right, right to left, with each step. Cameras flashed. Left to right, right to left. I stumbled, and reached out for something to break my fall. I grabbed a volunteer, who shrieked and slapped my hand away as I landed hard in a cloud of dust.

I bounced up and held one hand in front of my crotch, and the other in back, and looked for someone to throw me a towel to cover myself. Nobody did.

Forget the state championship. Within seconds I knew what would define me for years to come.

Andy Warhol also said this about fame: If you want to make a person miserable give them everything they desire.

I was now state champion. My reward was humiliation.

My legal name is William Ball. But I prefer Billy. My friends call me Billy Ball, because it rolls off the tongue easily and it's fun-loving. And Charlie prefers the simplicity of BB. But from this point on, my girlfriend, friends, rivals, teachers, administrators, and complete strangers would know me—or know *of* me—as Billy Balls.

Or simply, Balls.

2

Birthing Sucks and So Does My Inheritance

Mom says that birthing me was the most humiliating thing she's ever experienced. I've got to say it wasn't that great for me either. I came out early—a "pre-me" was the term she used, as if the child she delivered wasn't really me, but rather someone I might grow into. I was so preemie that nobody had even considered my entry into the world that night. She said it was the spicy Thai food that induced her, and that she'd gone to bed with a stomachache.

Meanwhile, Dad was wide awake, watching television and drinking beer in his recliner. Linus, our Beagle, tucked beneath him, scared by a fierce wind and driving rainstorm that sounded like it might rip the roof off our house. Dad found himself mildly entertained by a recap of today's Boston Marathon. An American was leading, and the announcer was rather animated about it. Just then, Mom burst into the room, shouting that her water broke and they needed to get to the hospital "now!" Like an upturned turtle, he fought to rise from the recliner, jerked forward, and, half drunk, tripped over Linus. He fell face-first, barely missing the television set on his way to the floor, dropping his beer. Dad had a history of dropping things—which I'd soon find out. Linus howled, and Dad clumsily got to his feet, now more panicked than Mom.

The storm worried him. He looked out the window and could barely make out a streetlight through the downpour. The roads, which dipped and ran through several washes, would be impassable.

Though it wouldn't matter. I was in a hurry to come out, and Mom shouted she was going to give birth right now and here.

"Where?" asked Dad. He saw her eyeing his recliner. "Oh, hell no! No, you don't!" But Mom moved quickly past him with razor-thin eyes, holding high an index finger that shut him up. Dad was no match for Mom, ever. Dropping into the recliner, she pushed down the lever. It pitched backward, and she assumed the most humiliating position of all: childbirth—legs splayed up and out, hollering at Dad and me, her unborn child, that we had caused this and she was going to die. It hurt so much. "It must have a square head," she screamed. Sadly, she'd be right. At this point Linus was cowering in a corner, as wide-eyed and frightened as Dad.

So, it was up to Dad to deliver me. He didn't know what to do or how to do it. In 1975, dads didn't know much about child birthing, and it was supposed to be that way, according to him. Mom guided him on what to do—which was to call somebody. But not even the doctor's answering service picked up that night. His second call was to 911.

He had the dispatcher on speaker now, and she was guiding him on what to expect. But when he saw that I was crowning he nearly fainted. My big, tough dad was wide-eyed and blue in the face and weak in the knees. Nature was taking over and about the only thing Dad could do now was fuck things up. And that's exactly what he did after Mom gave a final push and I burst into the world as blue as my dad.

He was waiting for me, crouched low, staring straight into Mom, hands positioned in a V, as if he was about to accept a football from under center. But I slipped through his hands and he dropped me on my head before I took my first breath. Mom shouted at Dad to pick me up, while the dispatcher told him to smack my behind, and he did that too, probably a bit too hard in all his panicked excitement. I breathed my first breath and let out my first cry. Dad located a pair of scissors and cut the umbilical cord. The blue in all our faces subsided. And then there was a quick moment of exaltation, as if the storm had passed and the heavens had parted.

How I survived that first night is still a mystery. As a preemie, there were complications and dangers that Mom and Dad knew nothing about, like not being able to regulate my body temperature. My skin was that of an onion, a blue network of veins visible beneath. The dispatcher said to swaddle me to keep me warm until they could get me to the hospital the following morning.

But for now, Dad shouted, "Kid's got lungs!" The dispatcher asked if I was a boy or a girl, and according to Mom, he looked down at my penis and said, "It's a boy!" He chuckled and added, "More or less."

Dad found humor in his sophomoric wit and smacked my behind once more. I cried. Mom screamed. Linus howled. The TV blared. Thunder clapped. Then, he held me above his head and did an endzone dance. Dad was impressed with himself. Delivering me in that recliner was the coolest thing he'd ever done. He was so delighted he'd forgotten about the dispatcher who shouted, "Hello? Hello!"

"It's a boy!" Dad said again. He was tongue-tied and searched to call me something other than *It*, but gave up.

I didn't have a name yet. Since I'd arrived so early, they hadn't decided on one. About the only thing they had decided on was that I was not going to take his given name. So, he just kept saying, "*It* this, and *It* that," as the dispatcher guided him on post-birth protocol.

But Dad's attention waned, and the dispatcher's voice melted away, lost in the noise and chaos of our small living room. The heavy rain drummed our roof and Mom begged to see me, telling Dad to stop screwing around. Linus howled again, excited and not sure what to make of me, the new chew toy.

All the while, the television announcer was excitedly calling race winner Bill Rodgers across the finish line of the Boston Marathon. "Billy! Billy! Billy!" shouted the TV. They locked eyes, then looked at me, and in unison said, "Billy." And that's how I became Billy Ball.

I've had to relive that day hundreds of times. Dad would tell my birthing story to family, friends, and clients. Sometimes he'd tell it to complete strangers while standing in the checkout lane at the grocery store. And if I did something stupid, as kids do, he'd start by saying, "It's okay—I dropped him on his head when he was born." His booming voice and jovial laugh would shake a room because that was the funniest thing that had ever happened to him, and one hell of an icebreaker. "That's my boy, Billy Ball," he'd affectionately say, patting the top of my head.

What's in a name, anyway?

For the first four years of my life, I thought my mom's name was Jesus Christ. Dad was fun-loving, but a bit ill-tempered, frustrated by life's responsibilities and a job as an insurance agent that didn't pay enough. He'd say to Mom, *Jesus Christ, I didn't know it. Jesus Christ, I knew that. Jesus Christ, I didn't do it. Jesus Christ, I did it.* Basically, anytime he addressed Mom, it started with Jesus Christ. And even worse, I thought *my* name was Goddammit. I don't know if he was frustrated with me for my stunted growth or shitting my pants well after I had been potty trained.

Once, when I was almost five years old, I was playing out front, pushed on a tire swing by Mom. A girl about my age, wearing a pink dress, and straight blonde hair that shot out beneath a pink princess helmet, rode past our house on a bike with training wheels. She turned around, stopped, and waved hello.

"I'm Charlie," she said. "I live three houses down. That's a cool tire swing. What's your name?"

I didn't understand how to respond. I didn't know that I was *allowed* to respond. Because at that age, I hadn't been asked much besides if I had to go potty. And this was a real question, from a real girl.

"I'm Goddammit and this is my mom, Jesus Christ," I said. "Can I ride your bike?"

At this, Mom, embarrassed and red in the face, corrected me. "Hello, Charlie, that's my boy just being silly! My name is Jean, and this is my son, Billy."

Charlie stood over her bike, expressionless. A long silence followed.

Mom added the punchline. "We're the Balls."

Names have always cursed our family on Dad's side. He was the fourth Richard in his family tree. Everyone called him Dick. As Dick Ball, he suffered immeasurably in high school at the hands of bullies, dicks, and, oddly, even other Dicks. But that's how inheritance works. Fortunately, when Bill Rodgers won the Boston Marathon, it was the end of Dick.

I'm thankful he didn't pass that name down to me.

Last year, I heard Mom in a spirited talk with Dad. She told Dad that the only things I inherited from him were a surname and an emerging shitty attitude. They were arguing because Dad was being an asshole. Her words, not mine.

As an only-child, I received constant and unwanted attention. These talks were about heredity and genetics, and discussed so frequently that it felt like they were in competition with each other. When I was really young, the back and forth was prideful, and laced with compliments. *He has your eyes, he has your nose, he has your feet, he has your toes.* No body part was off limits or went unnoticed. As I grew up, and developed less virtuous qualities, the banter became accusatory and never rhymed. *He has your shitty attitude. Where did he learn that from?* I didn't understand the point of these talks, good or bad, but they'd continue this never-ending analysis of my body and mind throughout my adolescence, and well into my adulthood, because I suppose…I'm all they've got.

So, here's my two cents: I don't think I inherited anything from Dad. He stands six-foot-four, and weighs north of 240 pounds. He has a barrel chest, deep and round, which pushes his arms out to each side, making them appear much shorter than they actually are and causing his hands to fall well short of his waist. When I was young, he'd chase me around the house pretending to be Sasquatch, moving side to side and grunting loudly. But he could never catch me. I was too quick, and second, if he did manage to corner me, he'd reach out with those short arms and purchase nothing but air as I slipped underneath them and escaped to play on. Sometimes, the quickest escape route was right through his legs.

Mom says he used to be much thinner when they met in high school, when Dad was a wide receiver for the Oracle Bald Eagles. I have no memories of his thinner self. I do know she's not lying because I saw a photograph of him leaping high in the air to catch an apparent game-winning touchdown pass. More about that later, because that was the *before* photo! But, in this way, he was athletic, and it's possible, buried deep within that meat cage he calls a chest, I inherited a great set of lungs. Though I'm still not convinced. I'm eighteen now, and I'm only five-foot-six. When I take off my shirt, people say I look like a drought-stricken saguaro cactus, thwarted by growth and nothing but dry ribs.

Mom says I inherited everything good from her. But I also doubt that's true. She's soft-spoken and polite, and that hardly describes the young man I've grown into.

Though, she's no pushover, so I suppose I can give her credit for my fighting spirit. But I think that has more to do with nurture than nature. Who knows? I've never been a good student.

The one thing I know I inherited from her side of the family is my speed. Mom's grandfather was a runner. He's buried at an abandoned mine, just ten miles outside of town. Once, they took me there to show me his headstone. On it was an etching of a runner, and I thought that was pretty cool.

I thought Charlie might like to see the runner too. So, I rubbed the image onto a piece of paper and gave it to her. I was always bringing her things that I thought were cool, like skin shed from a rattler, or a dead scorpion.

Mom told me to stop doing that, and said that pretty girls like pretty things. But I told her she didn't know Charlie, and that Charlie likes snakes and spiders. We'd even catch lizards in her backyard. Sometimes, when she had one by the tail and it escaped, she was left holding the detached appendage. Charlie would snicker and snort as it flopped back and forth in her palm.

"Well, she'll grow up," Mom said. "She'll like pretty things eventually."

"I hope not," I said, thinking of my own looks.

Mom was speaking from experience. She owned a pearl necklace, which she thought was beautiful. Unfortunately, the pearls weren't real. Once, at a fancy gala where my parents felt out of place, a well-to-do man pointed that out. "What a shame to see a beauty like you wearing costume jewelry," he'd said to her. She smiled at the well-to-do man like the fucking Mona Lisa and then poured a full glass of Cabernet onto his crotch.

That tells you a lot about Mom. She can take care of herself just fine.

Dad knows this too. "Never underestimate Mom," he says. "She's French and Irish." And when I asked what he meant, he said, "She can sit with perfect posture and speak to a wine's characteristics, but the next day, she'll drink beer in the back of our pickup truck while singing Irish songs and gazing up at the stars."

Dad loves that about her. He says that her fiery, red hair sets his heart ablaze like an Arizona sunset. It's weird to think about Mom this way, but those are Dad's words. To me, she's just Mom.

So, while my parents still enjoy the spirited discussions on whom I take after most, I just nod and smile, and play along, or maybe I cover my ears and disappear. I'm not big or loud like Dad. I don't have his black hair. I don't have the self-confidence of Mom. And I don't have her red hair.

Mostly, I think I'm just my own person, shaped by infinite and foreign influences that nobody, including myself, understands.

Did I mention I'm eighteen? I'm very, very confused.

3

Pittsburgh Escapades
~ Pennsylvania, 1933 ~

For the average citizen, living in Pittsburgh in 1933 was like living in Hell. But for a bootlegger, life wasn't so bad.

The City of Smoke was shrouded in smog so thick from the coal and steel industries that downtown streetlamps were often left on during the day. The rivers, the city's main water supply, were contaminated with raw sewage discharge that was poorly regulated. And while Pittsburgh was a poster child of the industrialized world, the Great Depression had hit hard. Factory jobs disappeared. Mining jobs disappeared. Houses of prostitution dotted the Hill District, and one-third of its 650,000 residents were unemployed. The booze business, on the other hand, was thriving, not because it was legal, but because of the very opposite—its illegality. Prohibition was the law of the land, but in this blue-collar city where drinking was a tradition, and a given right of the working class, people drank in thousands of illegal establishments that operated openly within city limits, turning up their noses at the law. Alcohol was in high demand.

Paddy O'Donnell prided himself on supplying this demand. He was a savior, a liberator, and a champion of the people. And as a result of his good deeds, he'd become a very wealthy man.

Despite his five-foot-six frame, a soft chin that melded like cheese on a toasted bun, and a body without form, he didn't lack confidence and moved with the flare of a peacock. Paddy O'Donnell relished the attention and graced himself with considerable accessories. He wore a diamond-studded watch, a six-carat diamond ring, and a pair of two-toned Oxfords that he shined each morning on his way to work. He drove a Cadillac, custom-painted green with bulletproof windows. Others in his trade preferred the Packard Roadster, a meatier, meaner-looking car of status and wealth, but Paddy considered himself a true gentleman, and opted for something more refined; something that an educated, gentile person would drive. He was a striking, conspicuous character who dressed in fine-tailored suits with exaggerated shoulder pads, making him appear larger than his frame. He slicked back his red hair with petroleum jelly that gave him sheen and nerve. He looked and acted every part of an educated businessman with a pedigree from a well-to-do family. Except he wasn't. He was an Irish immigrant and the city's most notorious criminal.

Each morning he met his lieutenant, Big Mike, at a coffee shop on Wylie Avenue, one of a few money-laundering businesses he owned in downtown where they'd discuss the complicated business of bootlegging. The business plan was simple—supply the illegal drinking establishments in Pittsburgh with beer and whiskey. However, the operations troubled him. There were negotiations with the moonshiners and brewers. Negotiations with the bar owners. Negotiations with crooks on the other side of the coin—the politicians and beat cops. And negotiations with other bootleggers that typically involved territory disputes and price-fixing.

The talks were ongoing and ever-changing, and frankly, exhausting and often messy. When rival gangs, especially the Italians, whom he considered ruthless savages, became too emboldened with aspirations too big, strong-armed tactics supplanted business negotiations, and sometimes the very removal of people occurred. Paddy had known of men shot, strangled, stabbed, and blown up. Because he had ordered it.

So, on this particular morning, when a wiry young man came into his coffee shop brandishing a pocketknife and demanding money from the cashier, he was wildly amused at the simplicity of it all.

The kid's hands shook as he tried to hold the knife steady. There was a forced toughness in his voice that shook and stuttered. "Ca-ca-c'mon now, hand it over," he said to the cashier. "Nobody ga-ga-gets hurt."

The amateurism that played out before Paddy was so funny, so nostalgic, that it reminded him of his own youth.

The cashier, an older man with a pockmarked, no-nonsense face, and a permanent layer of grease from working in coffee shops, was unfazed. "You're uglier than I am. And stupider." Johny turned to his boss. "You want to handle this, or should I?"

There were no customers this morning, and Paddy motioned to Johny to handle it. This was going to be a fun show.

"You just messed with the wrong person," Johny told the kid.

At that moment, the kid turned and recognized Paddy, whose face often appeared on the front page of the newspaper for his business dealings, arrests that never stuck, and, above all, his philanthropy. Paddy was beloved for taking care of his own and offering protection against the police and the in-power Protestants.

At this, the kid tried to flee, but Johny jumped him, taking him to the floor. In the scuffle Johny managed to dislodge the knife, which flung high into the air before skidding across the floor and stopping at Big Mike's feet. Johny had him pinned now, rabbit-punching the top of his head until the kid kneed him in the groin. Johny moaned, clutched, and reeled. The kid pulled himself to the counter, but Johny, still on the ground, reached up and managed to grab hold of his pant leg.

"We're not done yet!" he shouted. He had a firm grip of the kid's pant leg, while the kid held on to the countertop, kicking to free himself. And as he did this, his pants wrestled down and pinned at his shoes.

Meanwhile, Paddy and Big Mike were hollering like they were at a prize fight. Big Mike was rooting for the cashier, but Paddy, intrigued, found himself rooting for the kid. "I love underdogs," he said to Big Mike. "Ten dollars on the kid."

The kid kicked at the cashier, who lost his grip on the pant leg before managing to strip the kid's shoes. Then Johny found purchase of the kid's pant leg again, pulled, and swoop! Off they came.

But the kid was free now. Shoeless and pantless he escaped out the door, leaving Johny on the floor, holding onto nothing but a pair of empty pants and the humiliation of loss. "That kid was as slippery as a wildcat," he said to Paddy.

That would have been the end of it—all but a great anecdote for Paddy and Big Mike to tell over whisky and beer later that night—except too many people outside the coffee shop had witnessed the kid fleeing the scene. Including the police.

The kid sprinted south to Schenley Park, Frick Park, through Forest Hills, and onward to Wilmerding, his hometown, some thirteen miles from Pittsburgh. Coincidentally, it was also Paddy O'Donnell's hometown.

The run had become a game of cat and mouse with the police giving chase. And for them, it was mostly a comedy that starred a pantless, shoeless, failed robber who nobody actually wanted to tackle and apprehend.

The kid approached St. Aloysius Catholic Church. Mass had just finished, and the churchgoers poured out onto the sidewalk, saying their goodbyes and thanking Father McClary for a service that preached virtue and Mother Mary. There was no way around them as the police closed in. Navigating the crowd was his only choice, and it failed before the idea had come to pass. He slammed directly into Father McClary, and the two went down hard with the kid

31

resting on top. In the tangle, Father McClary shouted, "Holy Mother of Shit. Where are your pants, son?" His congregation watched on. Some hid their eyes; others crossed themselves and said Hail Marys.

When the cops finally pulled the kid to his feet, Father McClary recognized him at once. He had baptized him years ago. "James Flynn." Father McClary shook his head. "And I expected so much more from you."

With that, Jimmy Flynn, a fine young man from a fine Irish family, was cuffed and stuffed into the police car. Jimmy wore nothing but a sweat-soaked T-shirt and the guilt of his sins.

***

Paddy O'Donnell ran the most successful organization in Allegheny County. But few of his businesses were recognized as legitimate by the government. For this reason, he owned shares in every police precinct within the county, including Wilmerding, where one lieutenant and six beat cops were on his payroll. He was beloved by these cops, whose meager salaries could barely feed and house their families. When he entered the precinct, he was greeted with handshakes and pats on the back, and asked in jest about the robbery attempt. After he spoke with the arresting officers, he was escorted into a small holding cell where the kid sat.

Jimmy Flynn had a contusion above his brow and a busted nose. He'd clearly been roughed up. He wore a police-issued jumpsuit, and cloth slippers that were loosely tied around his feet, which Paddy assumed were bruised and swollen from the run. He sat alone behind a metal table, with a non-encased lightbulb directly overhead that hung on a thick, black cord.

Seeing Paddy enter, the kid winced, waiting for a blow that didn't come. He shielded his face with cuffed hands.

Paddy studied him from across the table. The kid was even thinner than he had appeared in the coffee shop. Yet, as Johny had pointed out, there was a fierceness about him like a rabid animal. He mashed his teeth so hard that his jawbone accentuated an already angular face. His hair was chopped and cropped, leaving nicks where blood had pooled and dried. His piercing, ice-blue eyes swept the room for an escape. But for this animal, there was none.

Paddy started...

"They tell me your name is Jimmy Flynn." He paused, circling like a shark around a wounded fish. "They tell me that you're nineteen and have no previous arrests, and that you were running home. Correct?"

"Yes, sir. I—"

"Shut up!" he continued. "They tell me you ran into Father McClary and knocked him on his ass, and that you embarrassed him in front of his congregation. Correct?"

"I—"

"Shut up! They tell me your father worked at Westinghouse Air Brake Company but was fired."

"I don't think he was fired. I think he was let—"

"Shut up!" They tell me you acted impulsively out of desperation."

By this time, Jimmy was afraid to answer.

"Is that true?" Paddy asked. "Is that what you did?"

"Please don't kill me," Jimmy said.

"Easy kid. I'm not going to kill you. This is a police station." He circled behind him and laughed sinisterly. "I'll wait until we get outside."

Fear, the kind that Paddy had seen a hundred times from weaker foes, flushed Jimmy's face. But Paddy let him down with a whisper. "Just messing with you kid. But I'd bust up your face if it wasn't already busted. Cops do that to you?"

Jimmy didn't answer. He cast his eyes downward until something startled him.

A bag dropped. "Thought you might want these things. Your shoes and your pants. I put your pocketknife in there too. It has your name etched in its side. Word of advice, kid. Don't ever leave a business card at the scene of a crime."

Their eyes locked.

"Besides," he continued. "I don't kill amateurs. I don't kill nobody!" *My soldiers do that.* "You're a celebrity. How many people have the balls to rob Paddy O'Donnell and run through the streets naked? By tomorrow you'll be a household name."

"You're not going to ka-ka-kill me?"

"You're going to be fa-fa-famous," Paddy mocked, rubbing his chin, thinking. Shifting now. "Jimmy—the Rabbit."

"What?"

"You run like a rabbit."

"I've been told."

"I ain't never seen nobody run that fast. For that long."

"Yes, sir."

"Rabbit. I like that. It fits you. Can I call you Jimmy the Rabbit? Or would you prefer Shit for Brains?"

"You can call me anything you want, sir. You can call me Shit for Brains. You can call me Jimmy the Rabbit. I di-di-didn't know it was your coffee shop."

"Shut up, Shit for Brains."

Jimmy sized up this most intimidating yet oddly short and colorful character, who toyed with him and confounded him with questions that wavered between patronizing and fearsome.

"Great, then. It's settled," said Paddy. "I'll call you Jimmy the Rabbit because you're scared like a rabbit. And besides, who can run like you do?"

"I like to—"

"You like to run? Who the fuck likes to run? And you just ran barefooted with your naked ass disrespecting the neighborhood, disrespecting Father McClary. Who does that?"

"I don't know, sir—"

"Mr. O'Donnell. Call me Mr. O'Donnell."

"Mr. O'Donnell, I was ru-ru-running for my life."

Paddy leaned close, menacing. They were face to face now. "I suppose you were, kid." Paddy sighed. "Aren't we all?"

***

After a long day, Paddy O'Donnell slipped away to his estate in a secluded, quiet neighborhood in Mount Lebanon reached by windy, lonely roads. Only his consigliere and a few others knew of its whereabouts. Any fear of retribution resulting from his profession slipped away in the Cadillac's rearview mirror. For all his success, the job of being a mob boss wore on him. The estate was his place of respite.

He pulled into a circular driveway, framed by tall hedges and a canopy of mature trees that still hung barren after a long winter. Once inside he locked the door and moved with tired steps to the kitchen. He felt much older than his forty years. There, a craft of bourbon awaited him, but he reached beyond it for a Cabernet. He poured a tall glass, allowing it to breathe before swilling it and watching its legs trickle downward. In compliment, he took a deep breath and exhaled slowly.

Making his way upstairs, he fought the gravity of a worn life. Stripping down, he changed into a bathrobe and ran the tub with hot water, emptying a bottle of bubble bath into it. A nice soak would do him well. Waiting for the tub to fill, he reached into a drawer and took out a casing of red lipstick. He applied it and stared at himself in the mirror for a long minute. He liked how it looked. He thought that it accentuated his soft features and lifted his tired eyes. In a different life, he could have been something, or rather, someone else. But he was married to the responsibility of his work—and the pageantry of his deception. He unrobed and eased his way into the tub, the water embracing him like a warm hug, soothing his aching muscles and cleansing and idling his troubled thoughts. Sipping the wine, he left an imprint of lipstick on the glass. He sighed and then smiled at the foolishness of it all.

Being a gay mobster was the most humiliating thing in the world—if anyone knew, that is. And those that had known were six feet under.

Life was good in Pittsburgh.

4

Fried Eggs
~ Arizona, 1993 ~

When we were thirteen, and in the clutch of adolescence, Charlie and I successfully fried an egg on the sidewalk in front of her house. The temperature hit 112 degrees that day, and she'd burned her feet walking shoeless on the concrete sidewalk, which prompted our little egg experiment. After what seemed like a failure, the egg started to hiss and bubble, then *pop pop pop*. Before long, the yolk started shooting off bits of its yellow self like fireworks on the Fourth of July. A piece flew onto Charlie's nose.

She pointed at the egg. "A dollar if you eat it. Two dollars if you keep it down."

Charlie and I would bet on anything. I accepted, and sucked it right off the sidewalk. My tongue singed and my esophagus burned as it slid down. I was not going to lose the bet.

"You've got to keep it down for a minute," she said.

"A minthut?" I tried, my tongue failing.

"A minute," she said. "I know you need the money."

This made us laugh. Needing money was typical for both of us. Which meant most of our lost bets had gone unpaid over the years.

When Charlie smiled, she revealed a gap in her teeth that parted her freckled face. And that's what she did now—smile. I told her I hoped that the gap would never close and she said not to worry because her mom couldn't afford braces. Then, her gold-flecked eyes sparkled like a pirate's bounty and I told her she should never cover them up. And she told me not to worry because her mom chose to buy more important things than sunglasses. "But this is Arizona," I said. "You'll go blind." And she said, "That's her problem." And I said, "Not really."

At thirteen I was starting to have strange feelings of things I knew nothing about. I felt guilty for stealing looks; her long legs and stringy blonde hair that fell straight to the small of her back; the blonde peach fuzz on her nape and arms. And of course, her scent. *Confectioners' sugar.* And just as I'd have these feelings, she'd do something in character for kids our age, like slap my sunburnt back, as she did now.

Her wallop left a palm print so clear she said she could read her lifeline. She thought this was funny, but the pain was so awful I hollered like the child I thought I'd grown out of years ago.

"Why aren't you wearing a shirt?" she asked.

"Too hot for a shirt."

She called me dumbass and raised her hand again, threatening. I cringed, readying for the slap. But she stopped short and laughed.

"Look," she said. "I'd give you the shirt off my back if it would help, but where would that leave me?"

In an uncomfortable place in my mind.

"Charlie, don't say things like that," I said.

But she couldn't understand why. To her, I was just a best friend, and yes, she *would* give me the shirt off her back.

So, it was no surprise that four years later, she was the first to help me when I stood pantless at the finish line of the state championship cross-country meet. Without hesitation, she removed her singlet and gave it to me to cover up, leaving her in just her sports bra.

My running shorts had been ripped clean off from the fall, and I stood there, exposed, as people stared and pointed. I looked to hide, but the chute was like a fishbowl. So, I covered my privates with both hands—one in front and one in back.

Just as I recognized the futility of this, Christmas Day shuffled past and called me an asshole.

"Asshole." This was the first race he'd ever acknowledged me in four years of competition. It warmed me.

"Love you too, Christmas."

Others were finishing behind him now; some seeing my situation but not comprehending exactly what it was they were seeing. They were being funneled through the chute and didn't stop.

Charlie had appeared at my side and handed me her Bald Eagles singlet, a very small polyester top that shielded

41

me no better than my hands did. So, I turned it upside down and stepped into each arm hole.

Clearly, I was not thinking straight. My genitals stuck out from the collar opening. Charlie stepped back and said, "Oh, fuck no." I'd subjected her to this awful sight that would likely stick with her for a lifetime.

Coach suddenly appeared at my side carrying a duffle bag. I hoped that he'd pull out a gun and shoot me straight in the head, but instead he pulled out a pair of sweatpants. I went to strip off the singlet, but the fabric snagged on the needles that still stuck out of my injured, bloody hip. I shuttered.

Where's Rigby? Did she see this?

I carefully managed to strip the singlet from my body. Coach and Charlie shielded me while I pulled the remaining needles from my hip and gingerly stepped into the sweatpants.

Eyes truly are the window to the soul. Because when I scanned the crowd, I could see sympathy, concern, amusement, and even fear. And in that moment, time stood still. Every wrinkle of an eyebrow, every grin, or pursed lips and words spoken, appeared in slow motion.

Charlie told people to shoo and to get away. Although her language was laced with expletives. The scene sparked chaos, with spectators, race officials, volunteers, coaches, and other runners scurrying around, trying to make sense of what had just occurred, asking questions, pointing fingers and yelling.

Coach had his arm around me now, and we walked some fifty feet away from the commotion to a big granite rock where I sat down.

Coach was celebratory, like he didn't care or notice that I'd just finished the race butt-naked. He patted me on the back, cheerfully, and told me I'd done it, that I was the new state champion and that I'd kicked Christmas Day's ass.

"You kicked Christmas Day's ass!" He spat in my face. "Just like I knew you would!"

This, I found interesting, because I don't recall Coach ever saying that. The last thing he'd said was to give it my best shot, which was hardly a vote of confidence. But he continued in his exalted state.

"You did it, Billy!" Coach didn't smile easily, but he tried now. With his hardened demeanor, the smile came unnaturally, offset, a crack in a cement foundation. He squatted, his eyes moist with happiness, goggling. "Tomorrow you'll be a household name!"

That's for sure.

Behind Coach, a messy scene played out. Charlie's finger was in some guy's face and the two were shouting at each other. He was an older man, wearing a black shirt with a Hawks emblem on it—Christmas Day's team. I couldn't hear what she was saying, but her body language was clear. Beyond her, my teammates—Jack Ash, Piper Cox, Henry Fly, and Tuba—were barking like a pack of dogs at runners from rival schools. Beyond them, a heated interaction ensued between a few coaches and race officials. Christmas was standing off to their side. He had his shirt pulled up and was showing his ribs to one of the officials. He was dirty and abraded from the fall. Blood congealed on his right leg as he picked cactus needles out of it. My dad stood behind him, trying to listen in, but was kept at bay by a race official who was half his size and holding both arms straight out like a traffic cop. Another race official, a heavy-set woman with a round, dimpled face, walked up behind Coach, tapped him on the shoulder, and motioned that they needed to talk.

"The Hawks coach is protesting," she said to Coach.

"For what?"

"He says Billy threw an elbow and impeded Christmas' line over by the cactus patch. You saw it."

"That's not what I saw!" Coach barked.

"We need to ask some questions before deciding who won the race."

Coach's eyes bulged. "There ain't nothing to protest! Christmas clipped him from behind."

"We just need to—"

"You can't change the outcome on account of these two getting tangled up!"

"We've got a handful of people who claim Billy misjudged the corner and overcorrected."

"Bullshit!"

"Sir, watch your—"

"Bullshit!" Coach yelled like he was back on the sidelines coaching football.

"We need to talk with Billy. We're talking with everyone who witnessed the fall. A lady named Ms. Sommers got it on her camcorder. We'll look at that too. We're not making any decisions right now."

"Because there ain't no decision to be made!" Coach was boiling now. "Billy won!"

This exchange went on for a long minute.

Then, the head official stepped in between the two. He was older and shorter and put his hand on Coach's back to settle him. "Coach, you're going to have to cool your jets or else we'll disqualify your whole team."

This shut Coach up. But he was sizzling like that egg Charlie and I had fried on the sidewalk four years ago, ready to *pop pop pop*.

"We'd like to speak with Billy." He turned and faced me. "You good to walk, son?"

"I got clipped," I told the officials, out of earshot from Coach. "I had the edge around that corner. The next thing I knew we were going down in the cactus."

"Can you show me the mark where he clipped you?"

I glanced down to my heel, but there was nothing to show. "He caught my shoe, not my heel."

"Got a couple of folks who say you initiated the contact," said Dimple Face. "They say that you deliberately threw an elbow."

"Well, yeah," I spat. "He was crowding me and steered me right into that big saguaro!"

"So, you're saying you initiated the contact? That you threw the elbow?"

"I was just fighting for position!"

The race officials looked at each other. Dimple Face raised an eyebrow and flipped through a rule book.

"Wait? What?" I was confused now. "I ain't saying that! I ain't saying that at all!" But even as I rescinded, I realized that I had said *exactly* that.

* * *

It didn't take long for the race officials to announce that I'd been disqualified. When cheers rose up from Christmas' camp, I pitched forward, the pang of loss kicking violently in my stomach.

My teammates, who knew this would gravely impact the team score, stomped their feet and shouted obscenities at the officials. Coach pulled us together and said he would protest the meet, but for now we needed to show good sportsmanship and behave ourselves because we were representing the school. He stood between us and the officials to keep the peace. But sure enough, when the team results were calculated and we failed to make the podium, obscenities launched like grenades.

At long last, Rigby showed up next to me. She hugged me before I let her arms fall away without reciprocating. I can be a real asshole at times. She turned and bit her nails.

Then, when the individual awards were presented, I could barely bring myself to look up as Christmas was recognized as the race winner.

I left without fanfare, walking back to the truck. My parents trailed me, keeping their distance.

I climbed into the back seat and we drove home. Rigby found a ride with one of her classmates. For this, I was grateful. I didn't want to talk about the incident. But with only my parents in the truck now, it allowed them to remonstrate and beat a dead horse ad nauseum. Even Mom, usually reserved, was outraged and matched Dad in a back-and-forth rant that lasted the entire thirty-minute drive, themed with unfairness and collusion and conspiracy and even corruption. From the cab, my head swiveled back and forth between them.

Charlie came over later that evening. My parents had flamed out and had taken their prone positions in front of the television. Charlie and I went out back to the patio and sat side by side on a double chaise that faced west with open views of the saguaro-spotted desert and the craggy base of the Santa Catalinas. Jet was quick to take his place at our feet and find her palm. Charlie petted Jet for a long minute. "I love you, Jet," she said. "You're such a good boy."

And he was. We'd had Jet for a few years after he showed up at our front door in the heat of summer. Either abandoned or lost, he appeared half dead. How he'd survived in the desert for any length of time was a mystery, but with no meat on his bones I suppose even the coyotes weren't interested. His ribs, corrugated metal. Charlie was over that day, and together we coaxed him to the backyard and washed the grime off him with a garden hose. He didn't object. He didn't try to run away. He just sat there under the pressure of the hose, looking up at me with crossed, pitiful eyes. I knew right then he was going to be my new best friend.

"Sorry, Charlie," I said. "I have a new best friend."

Mom and Dad came out. "Can we keep him?" I asked. At first, they objected, but they too felt something special for this dog. I think they missed Linus, who had passed several years earlier.

"Until we find its owners," Mom said, knowing the chances of that happening were slim.

I stroked his belly and noted his long legs. "I bet this dog can run," I said. And Charlie replied, "Let's call him Jet."

Then, we let him inside the house and he lifted his leg and urinated on the sofa. Mom screamed. Dad laughed. I said, "Bad boy." And Charlie said, "It's okay, boy." Jet had marked his forever home. He'd claimed us and our home in *his* fifteen minutes of fame. He wasn't going anywhere.

Charlie stroked his ears now, her eyes sparkling with praise.

Neither of us had siblings. So, as kids we spent a lot of time playing together, often hiding from our parents, but for different reasons. I complained that mine hovered over me like helicopters, and she complained hers barely paid her any attention, especially after they'd split up and her dad moved out.

Now, lost in thought, we watched the sun drop, which in Southern Arizona is like reading poetry. It was effervescent this evening, and it did the talking for us. It bled red and orange, leaving us content in its glow, leaving us enshrouded in the long shadows of the Santa Catalinas. Living here, it's impossible not to notice these things.

"Well, that was the bomb," Charlie said, breaking the silence.

"Kaboom!" I used my hands to mimic the explosion.

"You okay?"

"I'm good." I bounced the question back to her. "Bueno?"

"Muy." She added, "Hate my mom."

"I thought she'd show."

"She would have enjoyed it," Charlie said. "Not my show. Yours."

"Yeah. Some things will burn in our eyes forever. You want your singlet back?"

This made Charlie laugh. "Not after where it's been!"

"You had a great race," I said, turning the conversation to something positive.

"Thanks. A recruiter from Arizona said she'd be in touch." A thin smile lifted her eyes—and my spirits.

"That's great, Charlie."

Then, from her purse, she produced a bottle of tequila and two shot glasses. "I stole it from my mom's *medicine* cabinet."

We threw back the shots and laughed at our faces, pinched and contorted from the sting of the tequila and the burn in our throats.

"Again."

"De Nuevo."

Laughing now. On fire.

"Hey, how's your pumpkin patch doing?" I asked her. "Halloween is almost here." Charlie had been trying to grow a pumpkin since she was six years old.

"Another failed year," she said. "I water it. I talk to it. But not one pumpkin. They just die on the vine."

"Don't give up. It will be worth the wait."

"Well then, hasta luego," she said.

This time, when she reached for my shot glass, her wispy, fine hair brushed my arm, cool against my skin, earthy and fresh like the creosote bush after a desert monsoon. I was intoxicated in more ways than one. But I convinced myself, this was just the tequila talking. This was Charlie, and I didn't want to feel for her in that way.

But gap-toothed Charlie with the freckles, reached for my hand when she settled back into the chaise, entwining her fingers in mine out of pure habit and comfort, while Jet gnawed on a bone that he'd scavenged from the desert earlier that week.

***

Sunday was bad. I had difficulty getting out of bed. My head was cloudy from the tequila, but I was also stiff from the fall. The bandage on my hip had fallen off sometime during the night and the wound had reopened. Jet licked at the bloody sheet, and I pushed him down. When I came out, Dad was sitting in his recliner reading the Sunday paper.

"You got robbed." He was in a sour mood.

"That's what everyone keeps telling me."

"And Rigby called."

I ate some cereal and stared up at the Andy Warhol soup can print. Fifteen minutes of fame, my ass. I removed it from the wall and placed it on the floor, backwards.

I called Rigby, but her dad said she'd gone hiking with friends.

I went back to bed. Sleeping was the best way to escape and pretend yesterday never happened.

Monday was worse. A joint pep rally was planned to celebrate what we had anticipated would be a cross-country team state championship, along with the football team's march to the playoffs. It was a bad idea from the start. First, we didn't win the state cross-country championship. And second, you can never put the cross-country team on the same ticket as the football team. We would never be anything but a bad opening act for the main show.

Jack Ash was the first to greet me at my locker that morning. By the way, his real name is Jackson Ashworth, a name more worthy of his New England roots, but Jack Ash was better suited for our small desert town. His mouth had no filter, and his body moved with the unbridled speed of a rodeo bull. He was a smartass in every sense of the word, which is why we affectionately, and otherwise, called him Jack Ash.

"Apparently, you can't throw an elbow and break someone's ribs in a cross-country meet."

"He deserved it," I replied.

"Cost us the state championship."

That was true. My disqualification was a huge blow to the team. We were the odds-on favorite to win the state championship. Factoring in myself, our top five runners had scored a team-low 34 points, one of the best scores in state history. But when I was disqualified, and my first-place finish was thrown out, Tuba's sixth place score factored in. He had floundered and finished in 126th place. So, our team score rocketed to 159 points and pushed us off the podium. "Tuba eats too much," I said. "It was his fault."

"Tuba wasn't winning. You were."

"Sorry," I said. "I don't think I elbowed Christmas. I think he broke his ribs in the fall."

"Not according to the *Tucson Daily Sun*," he said. He held the sports section of the newspaper in my face.

Cross-country star Christmas Day culminates a stellar scholastic career. Broken ribs don't stop phenom from capturing his record-breaking fourth state championship.

Jack stopped there. "He's like a saint, that Christmas. The media loves him." He wiped his nose. "If there's any consolation I don't see any photographs of your bare ass in this article."

That much was true, and even appreciated.

Though, my classmates still mocked me throughout the morning. It was a collective opportunity to bully me; one of the better skill sets of high schoolers. Newspapers were left on my desk. A pair of shorts hung from my locker.

Later, Rigby was a no-show at lunch. Now, this bothered me. Since she was only a sophomore, and we didn't share any classes, we always made it a point to sit together at lunch.

So, instead, I sat with the cross-country team.

Collectively, they told me I'd been robbed.

Their words cemented our bond as teammates and friends, and I truly appreciated them, but they also felt empty because there was no way to reverse what had happened.

"Coach will appeal," said Tuba, eyeing my half-eaten sandwich.

"He already did," I said.

"I bet he gets it overturned," offered Charlie.

"We've bet on lots of things, Charlie. But that's not a good bet,"I said.

I had slim hopes of winning any appeal. When your rival's face is plastered on the front page of newspapers as the most beloved high school runner in state history, and adults have moved on to their Monday jobs, everything feels final.

At the pep rally, the team lined up on the gymnasium floor facing the student body and flanking Coach. The football team stood behind us and called us derogatory names that were not exactly unfamiliar, given our social status. We stood between them and four hundred classmates who yelled down from the stands the same derogatory names, and only shut up when the rally band began playing. With this, they stomped their feet and clapped.

When the band stopped playing, Coach introduced the women's team. Cross-country gets little recognition, and for the most part, we blend into walls. Few know us. But when he introduced Charlie, there were celebratory whistles. Charlie turned to me and mouthed, *This is ridiculous.*

But I was proud of Charlie.

Then I spotted Rigby, holding her clarinet. We made eye contact and she smiled affectionately as Coach began introducing the men's team.

He started with the freshmen, and then he introduced the Fly Five. Tuba stepped forward and did a little jig. He was known for this kind of spontaneity. The students applauded and some tossed quarters at him. He picked one up and shoved it up his nose to more cheers. Tuba was a kid of many talents. Piper Cox was introduced next. Dead silence. He was an awkward kid with stunted growth who kept to himself. I suspect few knew he was a classmate, much less part of this team. Henry Fly, a lanky kid with a forced swagger, stepped forward. He wore Ray-Ban aviator sunglasses and a bright orange Polo shirt with the collar turned up. He carried a certain smugness about him that was ill-received. When no applause came, he stepped back. Coach introduced Jackson Ashworth, who pumped his fists as the students shouted his name. With his handsome, wide grin, and wavy blonde hair, he was the one person on the team who had any popularity.

Then Coach looked at me, putting his hand on my shoulder. "I don't need to tell you who this young man is.

This is our team leader. Billy Ball was—" But Coach didn't get to finish.

A pair of running shorts launched and landed right in front of me, shot from high in the stands. Then someone shouted "Balls!" Another echoed. "Balls!" And still another. Soon, the entire student body was shouting "Balls" in concert.

Coach yelled back to shut up and sit down. My teammates came to my defense and engaged in the shouting match, holding up their middle fingers as they did so.

Principal Stevens took the microphone from Coach. "Show some respect!" he shouted. Then he motioned to our team to move off to the side so that he could introduce the football team. Oddly, we received some genuine applause as we exited stage left. As is often the case with high school students, there was no malice behind the outburst. When opportunity meets adolescence, these things happen.

But Charlie was hot, and said the students were assholes. Her words, not mine.

"Go ahead," I said to her. "Call me Balls. I can handle it."

"I will not!"

"Do it!"

"That was awful, BB."

"It's fine."

Charlie locked arms with me in support. This felt as natural as anything. But I suspect it did not settle well with

Rigby. When I located her again in the stands, she stared at me without expression, wondering.

Still, as I stood next to Charlie, the worst day of my high school life seemed to lift and pass, ridden out like a fierce desert monsoon that moves on, leaving behind a certain stillness. I could breathe now.

I had a bright future. I was being recruited by several colleges. Sure, there'd be questions, but I'd already built a fine resume of regional wins and other finishes that would carry me through this hiccup. And, I still had track and field in the spring to cement their interests. I managed a smile.

My spirits grew as I watched the football team accept accolades from their coach and applause from the students. The Cheer and Pom girls danced in uniform, the school band played our fight song, and the gymnasium was rocking with school pride now. *Thump thump* from the stands, reverberating on the wooden gymnasium floor.

But then my eyes gravitated to two cops who entered the gym. These weren't school security guards, but real police officers with thick black belts that held pepper spray, handcuffs, and handguns. They were being escorted by a school administrator.

"What's this?" I said to Charlie, motioning their way.

Before I dropped my pointed finger, I saw the barrel of the administrator's finger pointing directly at me. "What the hell?"

These three walked with purpose, and as they neared, my heart pounded.

"William Ball?" an officer asked.

"I'm ba-ba-Billy."

"Come with us, William." The other handcuffed me. "We're placing you under arrest."

I looked up to the stands hoping nobody had noticed. But Rigby and a few others were already pointing.

Coach stepped in and asked what was going on, and the cop told him to stand back. I told Coach it was okay and that we'd take it outside. I didn't want to bring any more attention to myself than I already had. I just wanted out of there. Charlie stood slack-jawed, perhaps for the first time in her life, not sure of what to do or what to say. And then, in front of the student body, I was humiliatingly escorted out of the pep rally, with Coach and Charlie in tow.

I felt like that fried egg from so long ago, ready to *pop pop pop*.

5

Echelons

The Sonoran Desert is anything but kind. Every living thing, plant or animal, is at the mercy of a relentless, baking sun and too little rain. If lucky enough to survive the elements, death still comes through natural selection and the food chain. It goes something like this: the tarantula eats the cockroach, the rat eats the tarantula, the snake eats the rat, and the hawk eats the snake. Teenagers are no exception. Somewhere, low in this echelon, I exist.

Jack Ash showed up at my door with a copy of the *Tucson Daily Sun*. "Check it out, Balls."

"Ball," I said. "No *s*." I wasn't in the mood.

An 18-year-old man was arrested after exposing himself to several children on Saturday. William Ball, of Oracle, Arizona, faces a misdemeanor count of public indecency, according to court documents. Police were notified by a parent of one of the said victims, just hours after the violation occurred. Ball was taken into custody without incident at Oracle High School on Monday, booked at the Pima County Sheriff's Department, and is now awaiting arraignment.

There was nothing mentioned about the circumstances that surrounded the incident. The article simply stated the facts.

But I begged for clarity—the real story—that would defend me in the court of public opinion. My booking headshot appeared next to the notice, and I appeared sinister and menacing; my eyes sunken and dark in shadows cast from the room's poor lighting, my wan face maligned in the moment.

"Turns out you can't get naked in the presence of kids," said Jack Ash. "Who knew?"

This made me laugh. "I kind of knew," I said. "After the race my dad got in a heated argument with the parent who pressed charges. The guy said I grabbed his kid and tried to use her as a shield to cover myself."

"Is it true?"

"I don't recall grabbing anyone," I said. "I'm not worried about it."

"You shouldn't be. Everyone saw what happened."

"That's why the charge was Public Indecency and not Indecent Exposure. I guess that's way worse," I said. "Honestly, I wasn't surprised when the cops showed up at school. The guy made it pretty clear to my dad."

"What an asshole," Jack said. "But look on the bright side. You're famous now."

"Fifteen minutes of fame," I said.

"Rockstar status, actually."

* * *

My arraignment was scheduled for the next day. It was a simple procedure. The Court would inform me of the charges, and I would enter a plea of innocent or guilty. I found this confusing since I was technically guilty but obviously innocent. My parents told me to plead innocent because, as my dad joked, the *naked* truth would get me thrown in jail. The judge would then enter my plea into the court docket and set a trial date. I figured a trial would never take place since the charge was so absurd and nobody wanted to waste each other's time with such trivial things. But I'd probably have to do some community service and pay a small fine—that's what the cops said when I was riding in the back seat of their car on the way to the booking, amused by the story I'd told them on how I came to be pantless at the elementary school.

I should mention that I do own a car. It's a two-door, 1976 Chevy Malibu. It used to be red, but the Arizona sun had turned it pink in recent years. Jack Ash said I should be embarrassed to drive it. But it only cost me five hundred dollars and it's a bit of a muscle car, unless you own a real muscle car, in which case you would not think it's a muscle car at all. The engine is loud, the muffler is loud, and when I drive it, I feel tougher than my 140-pound frame suggests, especially with Rigby at my side. She screams for me to go faster and faster. When I do, she sticks her head out the window and lets the wind catch and whip her hair.

I thought about driving it down to the courthouse in Tucson, but ended up taking my dad's truck since his gas tank was full. Like all teenagers, I take advantage of these things.

On the way out of town, I passed the entrance of Biosphere 2, a glass-and-steel terrarium that looked like a compound of Mayan pyramids. It was built as an experimental ecological laboratory that tested the human capacity for living in isolation. Four men and four women had recently lived there for two years and had grown their own food and survived without help from the outside world. The media called them Twenty-First Century Pioneers. But they were confined without toilet paper and beer. So, naturally, the experiment failed, and the group exited and went their own ways in search of toilet paper and beer.

My mom worked there now as a tour guide, educating tourists on factual tidbits about things like sustainability and Earth's ecosystem; things she thought they might find interesting. Some feigned interest by nodding, or smiling, but most were completely detached and shuffled through the tours with incomprehensible blank stares. They followed her from building to building, room to room, like ducklings, waddling and chirping, and mostly looking for the bathroom or gift shop. The tourists didn't get it, or didn't care, or would soon forget if they did get it, or did care. This much I knew because I followed a trail of discarded trash along State Route 77 for miles and miles on my drive into Tucson.

As for my dad, he's an insurance salesperson, and he says that he's always busy, but other than answering an occasional phone call I have no idea how he spends his time. Regardless, he didn't want to come to the courthouse with me. Perhaps he thought the experience would be a learning one and a natural introduction to that awfulness my friends and I refer to as adulthood. Honestly, adults confuse me, and I feel sorry for them because their lives seem so trivial, so solipsistic and made to feel important. I was never so sure of this than when I arrived at the courthouse.

Everyone there was dressed in character. Police officers dressed in neatly pressed uniforms, *insisting* respect and authority. Security guards dressed in wrinkled uniforms, *begging* respect and authority. Lawyers, dressed in neatly pressed suits, *negotiating* respect and authority. Plaintiffs, dressed in ill-fitting suits, begging for neither respect nor authority but for mercy. Judges dressed in black robes, symbols of their scholarly status, *commanding* respect and authority. And this much I bought into, because anyone who wears a robe at work definitely occupies the top rung on the ladder of success.

I have to say, all of this made me a bit nervous. The courthouse was a large brick and granite building without character that sat far off the street and up a long flight of concrete stairs that I assumed was designed to simply exhaust and subdue most criminals before entering. And when I entered, I had to wait my turn to walk through a metal detector. Then, when I was called to move forward, I put my wallet, my keys, and some loose change into a bucket and handed it to a small security guard, who then motioned for me to step through. On the other side stood a very large security guard—disheveled, unshaven, and brooding. He judged me and—I swear to God—growled. I walked through stiff-legged like I had to take a dump, avoiding his eyes, for fear he would turn me into a meat patty if I stepped out of line. Once through, he nodded his approval, letting me pass. I could sense his disappointment that I wasn't packing a weapon, that he wouldn't be able to take said weapon and shove it up my ass.

Then I had to find the courtroom where my hearing was to take place. I walked down a wide and long hallway with polished floors and neatly aligned portraits of old guys in suits, old guys in robes, a dead-guy senator, and a former President of the United States of America—a guy named Ronald Reagan—all meant to convey trust and faith in our judicial system and pride in our country. The message was simple: the truth will be served here, and justice will prevail. I was comforted knowing that Ron, America's gift to itself, had my back. But along this hall of fame, I also felt like the Cowardly Lion on his way to see the Wizard of Oz. My legs shook.

Inside the courtroom, I sat with a half dozen other delinquents while the judge perused the court docket. The room was quiet with the exception of an occasional cough and sniffle. The judge was dressed in a black robe that overwhelmed her small frame. She wore reading glasses anchored to the tip of her nose; a look of importance like she was presiding over cases that would ultimately shape and save the world. On her desk was a name plate: JUDGE

CAROL BELL. To me, this sounded like a nice name, a person who was supposed to hand out cheer and goodwill at Christmastime, not threats and sentencing in this stale building.

She opened the docket and began calling us, one by one, to approach the bench. The guy before me pleaded innocent to driving without a license, which I didn't understand because that seemed pretty black and white to me. The guy before him pleaded innocent for possession of marijuana. Again, that also seemed pretty black and white, and from the looks of him he appeared stoned right here and now. "Are you currently under the influence?" Judge Bell asked. When he asked her to define *under the influence*, she had the bailiff remove him. Judge Bell had darts for eyes and a scowl that reminded me of Dad when Mom burned dinner. Now it was my turn.

"The Court calls the case of the State of Arizona versus William Ball. Good morning. Sir, please tell me your full name."

"William James Ball, but you can call me Billy."

"Thank you, William. Your file indicates that you have been warned of your rights by a magistrate at the time of your arrest. Did you understand the warnings?"

"Yes, ma'am. I mean, Your Honor."

"Your file says you waived your right to have an attorney present. Do you still want to proceed without counsel?"

"Yes, Your Honor. I mean, this won't take long, right? I mean, it was just an accident. I didn't mean to—"

"William, this is not a trial. This is an arraignment. The purpose is to ensure you are the person charged, to inform you of the range of punishment for the offenses you are charged with, and finally, to take your plea. I shall now read the charges brought against you."

"Charges? As in plural?" I asked.

"Please, Mr. Ball. Let me continue. You are charged with the crime of Public Indecency. This is a Class A Misdemeanor. The range of punishment for this offense is a fine not to exceed one thousand dollars and confinement in the county jail for a term not to exceed thirty days." She paused to see if I was following. "Do you understand the allegation against you and the full range of punishment for this offense?"

"I do, Your Honor. It's just that I've never been in jail before and I—"

"Mr. Ball," she said. "There's more. A second charge has been brought against you for Child Endangerment. Since this occurred on school grounds, an elementary school, specifically, this has been upgraded to a Class A Felony. The range of punishment for this offense is a fine not to exceed ten thousand dollars and confinement in the county jail for a term not to exceed twenty-four months. Do you understand this allegation?"

There had been many moments over the last four days that had stopped my heart. But hearing the word *felony* topped them all. "Your Honor, I didn't do anything. I was running a race and my shorts got ripped off and I didn't know it and I just ran and ran and tried to run away but there was nowhere to run to and I got stuck by a cactus,

66

and I tried to hide but there was nowhere to hide and then Christmas called me an asshole and people tried to help and—"

"Mr. Ball. Again, you are not on trial here. This is a proceeding," she said, poignantly. "Do you understand this allegation?"

"I—I do."

"You may choose to plead guilty, not guilty, or no contest. How do you plead to the charge of Public Indecency?"

"I'm innocent, Your Honor. Not guilty."

"I will accept your plea of not guilty and enter it into the court docket." She paused to write it in. "Mr. Ball," she continued. "How do you plead to the charge of Child Endangerment?"

"Your Honor," I said. "This is bullshit. I didn't do anything!"

"Mr. Ball, please answer the question and refrain from the language or I will have you removed from my court. Sir, how do you plead to the charge of Child Endangerment?"

"I'm innocent," I said. "Not guilty, Your Honor."

"I will again accept your plea of not guilty." She entered it into the docket. "The Court finds that the bond previously set in this matter is sufficient to ensure your appearance before this court. Do you have any questions, Mr. Ball?"

I didn't know what to ask, so I asked the obvious and only question I could think of. "Can I still get a lawyer?"

"You may obtain an attorney of your choice at any time, Mr. Ball. If you cannot afford one, the Court will provide a public defender for you. Would you like the Court to do that?"

I nodded and cleared my throat. "Yes, I would, Your Honor."

"Very well, then. A date and time of a preliminary trial will be announced once we have secured a public defender for you, Mr. Ball. That is all for today. Bailiff, please see Mr. Ball out."

There's twenty miles of open desert that separates Tucson from Oracle. On the long drive home, I witnessed a coyote running alongside the highway at a full sprint. He had a rabbit in its mouth and still negotiated the desertscape with vivacious ease. The coyote was probably bringing it back to its pack in all his excitement. I couldn't tell if the rabbit was still alive, but I hoped it was not. What an awful way to exist, even for a moment, in the mouth of a monster that was not letting go until it ripped your limbs off and ate you for lunch.

6

Giddy Up
~ Pennsylvania, 1933 ~

Paddy O'Donnell saw himself as many things. However, he did not see himself as a bootlegger. The word itself labeled him criminal, something he strongly took issue with. The way he saw it, he was a man of the people and provided life's little pleasures to the hardworking folks of Pittsburgh. He also employed hundreds of men whom the steel mills, coal mines, manufacturing plants, and the U.S. Government had all failed during the economic meltdown. These men had families, with dogs named Spot and Buddy. They shopped, barbequed, went to Pirates games, dressed in suits, and kept the peace better than the cops.

No, Paddy did not see himself as a criminal. However, he did see himself as an opportunist. So, he jumped at the chance to bail Jimmy out of jail.

As he'd predicted, Jimmy Flynn became a household name overnight. Word spread quickly about this brazen, scrappy young man, who had botched the robbery of his coffee shop, fleeing the scene and running pantless thirteen miles home.

Then, when Jimmy's mugshot—a hapless, bruised face—appeared in the newspaper, he earned celebrity status. Written below the photograph was a story of a hard-luck kid and his economically depressed and emotionally spent family: an out-of-work father, a despondent mother, and his younger sister, who at age twelve ditched school occasionally to beg for bread and money. The article spoke of desperation and pulled on the heartstrings of the reader to accept and admire this kid for the courage to risk it all to help his family. He was no criminal. He was a hero, and a martyr of the less fortunate. "Like a good Catholic kid, he'd ended the police pursuit by 'willfully' running into the waiting arms of Father McClary, begging for forgiveness." All of this endeared him to the reader.

The article then pivoted to the kindheartedness of Paddy O'Donnell for not pressing charges. "I feel awful for the kid," said Mr. O'Donnell. "He had to resort to such desperate measures to help his family." It mentioned that Paddy paid the twenty-five dollars bail, and ended with another quote from Paddy. "I'm going to find this kid a job because he deserves a second chance at life."

Paddy asked Big Mike what he thought about it. "You *can* read, right?"

"If you weren't my boss, I'd take issue with that." The two had a punchy relationship. "It's great press for the coffee shop," he said, amused, sitting across from Paddy in their usual booth. "Joint is jumping this morning."

"Everyone flocks to the scene of the crime," Paddy agreed.

"The article is great, boss. It's like you wrote it." Big Mike laughed heartily, his belly rising and falling with each quick breath. "What'd you pay the writer?"

"Fifty."

"Fifty dollars? I'm in the wrong business."

"It's good public relationships," Paddy said.

"You mean relations?"

"Shut the fuck up," said Paddy. "You can't even spell your own name. Besides, the kid's parents were there at the jail house. Proud people. But ashamed. They couldn't afford bail. I saw the opportunity and bit. Then the newspaper guy showed up looking for the scoop. So, I introduced him to the kid's parents after we talked."

"Brilliant move, boss."

"I know. Look, everyone's pointing fingers at me because that Italian got shot up last week. Like I had anything to do with it." Paddy paused and sipped his coffee, smirking.

"He asked for it," Mike insisted.

"Shhhh!" Paddy put his finger to his lips. "We've got paying customers in here."

"Sorry. The article touched my heart," Big Mike said, back on point. He tapped his chest and laughed. Mike was jovial when he amused himself.

Paddy laughed at Mike's gesture. Big Mike was as indifferent to peace as he was to violence. For him, it was two sides of the same coin. And Paddy felt the same way. But he also knew that a good mob boss kept the peace, at least in the public's eye. Things had slipped recently with an upturn of street violence, the shooting of the Italian, and so he took any opportunity to remind the good folks of Pittsburgh that he was just one of them, a regular citizen, a humanitarian, and a philanthropist. The article was not game changing, but it twisted public opinion. Jimmy Flynn, for all his troubles, was a shot of medicine that in the moment inoculated Paddy from the sours of the public eye.

***

On an unusually warm spring day, Paddy O'Donnell removed his suit jacket and laid it next to him. He wore a white fedora, a white butterfly-collar shirt, and tan-colored slacks. He was a reflection of the vanilla ice cream cone melting in his hand. *Ice cream in Schenley Park.* It brought him back to his childhood and simpler times. Today he was seated in his private box at the Oval to watch the Saturday horse races. It was a splendid day; the maple trees, crab apple trees, and tulips were all budding and filled the park with scent and color. No longer did the gray skies and barrenness of winter loathe over the city like a damp rag. The air was unusually clear, and from his spot in the grandstands he could see the raked skyline of downtown Pittsburgh.

Surrounding him were hundreds of affluent, nicely dressed people. They were here to bet on the horses, but mostly to be seen and socialize. Paddy enjoyed mixing with them. The escape, the politeness, and the ease of conversation with this higher social class pleased him.

Nobody said *fuck you*, *asshole*, or *dumbshit*. Everyone finished their sentences. *It was fucking remarkable,* he thought.

Here, he could unwind, bet on the horses, and sometimes get lucky. And always laugh. Here, he was surrounded by people who, just ten years ago, would have seen him through the narrow lens of their Protestant lives, dismissed him as just another uneducated, Catholic mick. But things had changed since the beginning of Prohibition, when he managed his family's small grocery store and his customers came in fishing for liquor and willing to pay exorbitant prices. He jumped at the opportunity to meet the demand. That was a long time ago, a different, brash Paddy. So, he was always taken aback on days like today when he entertained some of Pittsburgh's most successful and influential men, all the while being served in his private box by the well-mannered Schenley Oval staff. Today, Paddy held the company of an executive from the Pittsburgh Coal Company, Charles Finick.

Charles wore the same white fedora, his silver hair bristling in the bright sunlight. His eyes lined with crow's feet. Despite the heat, he wore a white and gray harlequin sweater, and gray pleated slacks. He spoke in a mild, gentlemanly fashion, personifying his education at Carnegie Mellon, where he graduated magna cum laude. It bothered him greatly that the coal industry was failing. Charles and Paddy were an odd couple to keep each other's company, but success mirrors itself in strange ways.

Charles pointed toward another nicely dressed man, seated several rows to the side of them. "Mr. Rooney loves the horses. He'll bet big."

"Is that so?" Paddy said.

"That's so. He's also buying an NFL franchise."

"NFL?"

"National Football League."

"Here in Pittsburgh?"

"Ridiculous thought, isn't it?" Charles stoked a cigar. "It will fail."

"Perhaps," said Paddy. "Once Prohibition ends do you think I could sell beer at those games?"

"You, Mr. O'Donnell, are a great visionary with a thirst for money. Perhaps his NFL franchise will succeed with the promise of beer."

"That'd be something."

They turned their attention to the track where the first race was about to begin. Paddy took out a flask filled with whisky and offered it to Charles. "To horse number five," Paddy said. But horse number five, Pirates Bounty, lost by ten lengths. "Damn horse ran like it had a broken leg. Jimmy Flynn could have beaten it."

"Who?"

"Jimmy Flynn, the idiot who tried to rob my coffee shop last week."

"Yes, of course."

"The kid has wheels," Paddy said.

"Does he?"

"He fled the coffee shop a little after eight and the police apprehended him at nine-fifteen, about thirteen miles later. He wasn't even wearing shoes."

"You should stage a meet here at the Oval, featuring the kid," Charles suggested. "People will pay to see him. Do it while he's relevant."

A slight hand fell on the back of Mr. Finick. "Gentlemen, I hope you are enjoying this beautiful day. Is there anything I can do for you?" It was the manager of the Oval, a finely groomed gentleman with pleasing eyes and a mild disposition accustomed to kissing ass of the rich and privileged. He was tall and lanky and draped over the two.

"Your timing is impeccable, Mr. Hurley," said Mr. Finick. "Take a seat. You've heard about that boy who tried to rob Mr. O'Donnell last week?"

"I believe everyone has."

"Have you ever considered a human race, right here at the Oval?"

"I don't follow, sir."

"A running race, right here on the track, starring the kid."

"Sir, this is a horse racing track."

"It could be both," Mr. Finick suggested.

"That's not possible, gentlemen. These fine people come here to enjoy the horses. Are you suggesting they bet on humans? There is no precedent for that."

Paddy weighed in. "People will bet on anything. Baseball, boxing, horses. Humans too. Trust me. I know people."

Mr. Hurley was polite in his discretion. "I don't even know what that would look like."

"Who cares?" Paddy said.

75

"The Gaming Commission cares. I rather like my job."

"Well then, if you rather like your job you might want to fill the seats," Charles said. "The Board of Trustees will call you genius when they see the Oval's take."

Mr. Hurley glanced up at the half-filled grandstands, and for the first time in his position, he saw more than the affluent, happy-go-lucky patrons; he saw the empty seats. But he still balked. "I would not want to jeopardize the integrity of the track. Horse racing is a legitimate sporting event, Mr. Finick. It is not a circus. And this proposition sounds a bit like a circus."

"You see, Mr. Hurley, that's the problem," interjected Paddy. "Make it a circus. People love the circus. People pay to see the circus."

***

Only two weeks later, on a rainy day at the Oval, the circus they'd envisioned came to life. Jimmy Flynn, accompanied by Paddy, and fourteen other runners with their sponsors, were paraded in the walking ring like horses so that the betting public could view and evaluate them before wagering.

Jimmy, with deadpan eyes, and pronounced cheekbones, wore the number 5 and held his position in the ring, as instructed. Paddy had outfitted him with a matching black and white checkerboard shirt and shorts, and running shoes with a rubber sole that was glued to a canvas upper. Paddy said he got them from a science guy at a rubber factory and that they were a secret weapon. They were light and flexible, unlike the leather single-stitch shoes with spikes that the others wore. Leave it up to Paddy to gain the upper hand.

"Winner takes all," Paddy reminded Jimmy.

"What's all?"

"The purse—375 dollars. That's the combined entry fee."

"That's a lot of money," Jimmy said.

"That's only the purse. That doesn't include the bets."

With Jimmy's newfound celebrity status, and an expected draw of hundreds from his hometown, Jimmy would be the odds-on favorite.

Rain had come in fits that morning, and was now threatening again. Paddy pitched an umbrella, and he and Jimmy stood underneath it, smiling for the press. In that moment, Paddy recognized the symbolic gesture of holding an umbrella over the kid's head, and how that might look on the front page of the *Pittsburgh Gazette*, fulfilling his promise to help the kid out.

"What do you think about the other runners?" Paddy asked.

"I don't know any of them," Jimmy said.

"I do," Paddy said. "Mr. Hurley shared their registrations and bios. They're good, but they're old. They don't have your legs or your young heart." Paddy pointed to a runner wearing the blue colors of his alma mater. "That guy must be thirty years old."

"That sounds pretty old," said Jimmy, looking his way.

"It is. I'm surprised he's not dead by now. I hear running eventually kills you."

"You know a lot, Mr. O'Donnell."

"I do."

Nearly all of the runners gathered in the walking ring had credentials. Many ran cross-country at local universities. Some ran in competitions between local athletic clubs.

The media and odds-makers vetted them throughout the week. Besides Jimmy Flynn, the other favorites included Justin Thyme, who ran for the Pittsburgh Athletic Club. Randy Hand represented the Alleghany Athletic Club; Moe Jobs was sponsored by Charles Finick and represented the Pittsburgh Coal Company; and Colon Herts ran for a meat packing plant.

Although Colon had no race experience, he ran four miles to and from work every day, which the owner found astonishing, and brashly announced that his runner would win. The boast had helped Colon's early odds, but as he paraded in the walking circle his odds dropped. Colon was dressed in a blood-stained T-shirt and baggy trousers.

"Look at that bum," Paddy said. "Presentation is everything."

"It is?"

"You have to look the part," Paddy said. "What do you think of your outfit?"

"It's loud," Jimmy said, in his checkerboard uniform.

"Checkerboards represent winning," Paddy pointed out.

Paddy, himself, was dressed in a green pinstripe suit with a matching fedora, made special for the occasion. "What do you think about my outfit?"

Jimmy thought Paddy resembled a ripe watermelon, split in the middle with a red face. But he managed to smile. "You look great, Mr. O'Donnell. Very spiffy."

Over the loudspeakers: *"Six minutes to race time!"* Then "The Star-Spangled Banner" played, and Paddy asked a reporter to photograph him saluting the flag.

"I love this country!" Paddy shouted.

As the music came to an end, a thunderous cloud burst overhead, and the rain came down in pellets. Three minutes to race time. Paddy slapped Jimmy's ass, winked, and wished him good luck.

Jimmy walked away, then entered the gate corresponding with his number. Through iron bars, Jimmy looked left and right at each of his competitors, and wondered what *they* thought of this circus.

Humiliation comes easily with the promise of money. Did anyone else recognize how absurd this was?

The rain hammered him now. He couldn't wipe it from his eyes fast enough. It ran down his legs, pooling at his feet.

"One minute! One minute to race time!"

Above the drumming of the rain, the announcer's voice bellowed in a slow staccato that clung to syllables like words tracked through mud. "It's a sloppy track for this sixteen-furlong race. For those of you from Wilmerding, that's a mile. Two trips around the oval. Today's purse is 375 dollars. For those of you from Wilmerding, that's a lot of money. More than you'll ever see." He cupped the microphone at this, muting his laugh.

The announcer was a hairless old man with sunspots that dotted his head like a rotting banana. Gravity rounded his features. His ears hung low, and his nose lower, red and bulbous. Yet his voice was buttery and strong.

He was determined to have fun with this call. He'd have to. A horse could cover this distance in roughly one minute and forty seconds and so he'd become skilled at delivering the action quickly as it unfolded. But the world record in the human mile stood at four minutes and nine seconds. Given today's sloppy track, it would take much longer—a lifetime for an announcer to carry the excitement of the crowd.

"And they're at the post!" he shouted.

In the gate, the smell of urine and pungent horse shit rose up from the saturated soil. Jimmy looked out, toward the stands, and saw the dingers, reveling in the rain. Many were bare-chested, whipping their soaked shirts overhead. They shouted, "JIM-ME, JIM-ME, JIM-ME!"

They were the ones that Mr. Hurley counted on to fill the stands, yet loathed and feared, who came to breach the integrity of the Oval with proletariat persuasion. They were the ones who didn't know a furlong from a yardstick. They were the working-class Irish who backed their own, whose rank in society would elevate for the next six minutes, suspended in a liminal state as they became one with Jimmy Flynn.

Jimmy recognized this and knew he had to win.

The announcer shouted, "The flag is raised!"

Paddy, Big Mike, and Charles Finick stood tall trying to see through the pitched umbrellas.

The gates ratcheted open and the clank of metal-on-metal startled Jimmy. And when he jumped forward his shoes slipped in the mud.

"And they're off in the first running of the Humiliation Tour!" shouted the announcer, laughing at his own dim wit. *"Two laps of this sloppy track. This ought to be something!*

"Everyone is screaming for Moe Jobs as he takes the early lead. Randy Hand is on his shoulder. Then it's Colon Herts, followed closely by Jimmy Flynn, while Justin Thyme runs behind. That's your top five in the first furlong.

"Into the backstretch they go!

"They're settling in now. Jobs still leads. But it's a pedestrian pace for these fellows. The mud is wreaking havoc on them."

From the grandstands, the runners appeared barely moving, snail-like in the mud. In the barn, the horses were laughing.

"The frontrunners are bunched up on the backside. Colon is blocked, and Jimmy Flynn bypasses on his right.

"Wait! Randy Hand has pulled in front, as hope fades for Moe Jobs.

"And here they come to complete the first lap.

"Something's wrong with Jimmy Flynn. He's slipping away in the mud.

"One more lap of the track they go!

"Now it's Jobs again, shadowed by Hand.

"And look! Jimmy Flynn has pulled off to the side and is removing his shoes as Thyme passes him by.

"On the backstretch Hand is closing fast.

"And back comes the favorite, Jimmy Flynn, running in his bare feet, moving up on the outside and passing Thyme.

"They're approaching the final turn and INTO THE STRETCH THEY GO!"

Chants of "JIM-ME, JIM-ME, JIM-ME" hailed from the dingers. They howled like wild dogs in a manic lather. Paddy, Big Mike, and mild-mannered Charles Finick also cheered with their brethren, abandoning their umbrellas to join the Faugh a Ballagh war cry of the mighty Irish.

"Turning for home it's still Jobs. On his shoulder is Hand. Thyme is running fast, and so is Flynn! And now Hand makes his move. Jimmy Flynn continues to push. It's a battle of four. It's Hand! It's Thyme! It's Jobs! A surge by Flynn! Now it's Hand, Thyme, and Flynn. Here they come!

"Jobs is there. So is Jimmy Flynn. But Thyme has expired.

"Jobs, Hand, and Jimmy Flynn BATTLING IN THE FINAL YARDS!

"And as they cross the line it's…"

The grandstands fell silent, collectively holding their breath.

"It's—it's—

"JIMMY—HAND—JOBS!"

The announcer fell back in his seat, wiping sweat from his brow, and exhaled. "Now that's a great finish, folks."

Paddy, exalted and celebratory, raised his arms in victory, high-fiving Big Mike, as Charles Finick, the business executive, reeled with the loss of Jobs.

Paddy held up a winning ticket. "I'll be damned, fellas," he shouted. "I called it. I won the trifecta!"

"How'd you know, Paddy? How'd you do it?" asked Mike.

Paddy, a true visionary, boasted, "That's just the way I saw it, fellas." He took a deep breath, sighing in relief, wiping sweat from his brow. "Jimmy Hand Jobs."

7

Oh, Jesus
~ Arizona, 1993 ~

In his youth, Coach Jeremy Jones had thought of nothing but football. He played quarterback, fullback, and middle linebacker and sometimes returned punts. He was not afraid to hit, or be hit. He would do anything to help his team win and despised watching the action from the sidelines. His toughness on the field labeled him a player's player and so he was voted team captain.

As a senior at Oracle High School, he had dreams of scholarships and playing Division 1 football. He had a shot of winning the state championship his senior year, but a last-second throw into the endzone went through the hands of his receiver. He blamed that game, and the receiver, for never getting his shot at a Division I school. Others would tell you his grit was simply greater than his athleticism. *Too short. Too slow. Too average.* When he walked on at the University of Arizona, they cut him within two weeks. But he loved the game and pursued coaching after graduating with a degree in sports management. He eventually landed an assistant coach job at a respectable

Division II college that had a winning program, until, as luck would have it, he arrived. Then they began a record losing streak of nine in a row. So, he moved on, and then moved on again, and yet again. Wherever he went, his teams lost. He realized it was much easier to find a job than to keep one.

After a dozen years of failed college coaching stints, he returned to Oracle High School to accept the position as head football coach. His distinguishing mark at Oracle High School was losing every game he ever coached. His teams went 0-29 over a span of three years, and those that still cared wanted him removed. Coach Jeremy Jones might have been the worst football coach to have ever walked the sidelines in the state of Arizona, and possibly the country. But, surprisingly, he was liked by Stephen Strawbag, the aging athletic director, who remembered him as a headstrong and athletic kid, taking the team to the title game in his senior year. For that reason, he was not fired from coaching altogether, but politely asked to coach another sport.

"Cross-country?" Coach repeated, scratching his head.

"I don't think you can fuck that up. I think it's impossible," said Stephen.

"Anything is possible."

"Look, Jeremy. I'm on my way out in a few years. I want one winning football season and a shot at the playoffs. I don't see that happening with you running the show."

"I don't know a thing about cross-country, except all those skinny kids get stuffed into lockers by my football team."

"Your ex-football team," Stephen corrected him. "Don't feel sorry for yourself. I hear there's a great group of freshmen joining cross-country this year. Have you ever heard of Billy Ball?"

"Richard Ball's son? I'm not coaching ol' butterfingers' son. That son-of-a-bitch cost us the state championship my senior year. Remember? I threw that perfect spiral into the endzone and when that big ape jumped to catch it, it went right through his damned fingers."

That was true. My dad had blown it. And Coach Jones remembered it well, telling me on the first day of practice. "Your daddy is the reason why I'm standing here," he said. He held his fingers an inch apart. "I was this close to landing a scholarship."

I couldn't care less, but thanks to his story, things began to add up around the house. Like when I slipped through Dad's hands on the day I was born and he dropped me on my head. Or, when he'd dropped a watermelon, a casserole, a wrench, or a beer, or any one of many things in my youth. I'm happy I didn't inherit that trait from him. But one thing we did have in common: we were responsible for losing the only two state championships in the history of Oracle High School. Us Balls were now famous at Oracle High School for all the wrong reasons.

Strawbag pressed on. "This is running, Coach Jones. You won't have to teach Billy how to catch a ball."

Well, that was four years ago, and he still didn't know much about cross-country, but he didn't have to, because when Jackson Ashworth, Piper Cox, Tuba, and I walked onto the track our freshman year, all he had to do was sit back and watch the show. Strawbag was not kidding. We'd make any coach look good.

The four of us made the varsity team that first year. All we needed was one more star. We found him our sophomore year. Henry Fly transferred from California and suddenly we were the Fly Five, capable of beating any other top five in the state. Sometimes the stars just align that way.

Now, Coach was an odd choice to lead our team. He was built thick and as solid as a cement block, with a square face that reminded me of a pit bull, the ones that had seen a fighting ring, with battle scars on his head, and tiny, cropped ears. And at only forty years old, his hair was stubbled and graying. His eyes were set far apart and framed a stout nose, flattened one too many times from his days on the football field.

He didn't understand us runners. Because we were not a tough-looking bunch, he assumed we were not tough at all. He couldn't let go of his football psyche in this way. So, he trained us as such. Instead of running, we lifted weights. Instead of stretching, we lifted weights. Instead of doing drills, hill repeats, fartleks, or giving us advice on proper nutrition, we lifted weights. It seemed Coach was determined to turn us into something we were not. And he never gave up, even when we had. Collectively, we would lay under barbells of hell, trying to bench press whatever weight Coach thought was acceptable, usually dropping the bar on our meatless chests, bug-eyed and crying for help.

Once, in the middle of such a workout he told everyone to stop what they were doing and to gather around for a talk. Coach was in a sour mood, and who could blame him? He'd been removed from the one thing he loved— football. His entire paradigm had shifted. And I considered how we looked through his eyes; our thin arms, thin legs, and overall feebleness. His only association with us runners prior to this gig was pulling us out of lockers. He'd hear a shout, a pout, and then investigate, finding a scared runner folded in a contortionist way, all teary-eyed and swollen. And he'd rip him from the locker and tell him not to do it again. As if the runner had crawled in there on purpose! And girls—forget the girls—he didn't know what planet they were from.

He began an impassioned sermon about toughness, having faith in God, and what that meant. He launched into an anecdote about when he'd been cut down in a football game, fielding a punt.

"It was like this," he started, animated, reliving the moment with his arms held straight out, showing us what it's like to catch a ball falling from the sky. "I was underneath the ball, waiting and waiting for that damn thing to drop, praying to almighty Jesus, Himself." Coach crossed himself. "You get religious real fast when you're a sitting duck waiting to get whacked like that. But it just hung up there on a breeze and wouldn't fall fast enough. We were losing the game, so I already had it in my mind that I was going to catch it and run it back instead of calling for a fair catch, despite the defenders bearing down on me. You know why?"

Because you're stupid.

"Because I'm tough. My team needed me to be tough."

89

"So, then what happened?" asked one-hundred-pound Piper Cox, genuinely baited and wanting to be tough.

"What happened? I'll tell you what happened. As I'm still waiting for that ball to drop, a defender barreled into me like a goddamn torpedo. Hit me square in the gut. I laid unconscious for a second, farted like a cow giving birth, and when I finally stood up, I knew something wasn't quite right down below." He pointed to his backside. Coach paused to make sure he had everyone's attention. "I'll be damned if that guy didn't knock the shit right out of me, he hit me so hard."

"You shit your pants?" asked Piper, taken aback now.

"Well, yeah, I shit my pants," said Coach. "That's the point!"

I didn't understand how shitting one's pants equated to toughness, but I wasn't going to interrupt. Coach was in the thralls of his story.

"What'd you do then?" Piper asked.

"You know what I did? I stayed in the game, which I guess, is actually the point."

Oh, I got it now.

"You pooped your pants and stayed in the game?" Jenny Ledge shouted, alarmed.

"That's what I'm telling you, Jenny. You've got to toughen up out there and start shitting your pants, so to speak."

"You weren't humiliated?"

"Why would I be humiliated? The team rallied behind me."

I bet not.

"And, I threw a beautiful spiral as time ran out and we won the game." Coach stopped, momentarily lost in thought, reliving the moment. "It was the best day of my life."

"The day you shit your pants?"

"The day I shit my pants."

* * *

I didn't expect Rigby to embrace the idea of dating someone recently disgraced, and an accused felon, but I didn't expect her to avoid me either. Or worse, to pretend she wasn't avoiding me. But that's exactly what she was doing after five months of dating, which in high school gets your photo in the yearbook as Best Couple. During that time, she'd professed her absolute, sometimes, almost, and rare like for me. It was a relationship that renewed daily.

I found her sitting in the cafeteria with her friends from band. When I approached, an uncomfortable silence fell about the table. A few band geeks looked away, which I found disturbing. In high school, there is a social order. Among the guys, the jocks—with the exception of cross-country runners—sat at the top. Below them, in order, are funny guys, smart guys, guys that could drive, guys who'd supposedly had sex, guys who could dance, guys who followed Jesus, rebels, goths, Glee Club guys, then cross-country runners, and finally band geeks, who sat one rung above stoners and dropouts. So here I was getting shunned by a group of kids beneath me on the ladder of hell. And that just wasn't right.

"What's wrong?" I asked a nameless, pimple-faced, pasty freshman. "Split a reed? Blew too hard?" Rigby ushered me to another table. She was pissed off and poked a finger in my chest.

"You're embarrassing me!"

"It's like I've got the plague," I said, trying to make light of it. "Where have you been?"

"Busy," she said.

"I've called you twenty times. You're never home."

Rigby looked away. "My parents—"

But she was interrupted by the intercom.

William Ball. William Ball. Please report to Coach Jones' office.

"Never mind," she said.

"I'll call you later." I mimed dialing a rotary phone, because she hated it when I did that.

I walked out of the cafeteria with a sense of urgency. I was excited, thinking Coach might have gotten the disqualification overturned. But as I approached his office, I was overcome with a feeling of dread. I thought about the story he'd shared about toughness.

Coach sat behind a metal desk, hands intertwined, wrestling his thumbs. Above him hung a banner that read "WINNERS WELCOMED HERE." To his right, Athletic Director Stephen Strawbag leaned against a bookcase. He also looked disconcerted.

Before I could ask why I'd been summoned, Coach motioned to a very thin lady sitting to his left who looked mummified and in her sixties. She had a pinched face, and gray, brittle hair that was cinched tightly with a braid, the way a plastic garbage bag might look, stretched and tied. She wore a drab, gray pants suit and sat with perfect posture. She did not say hello, as say a human might.

"Whoa! I'm not ready to commit to a college," I said, holding my hands up in defense. "Early signing period isn't for another three weeks." But nobody laughed. Coach gestured for me to take a seat.

"Son, this is Clarise Dunkinschits," Coach said.

"That's Dragenschits," the woman corrected.

"Yes. Sorry. This is Mrs.—"

"Ms."

"Ms. Drag-en-schits," Coach said, pronouncing each syllable in slow cadence. "She is the deputy director of the Arizona High School Activities Association, which governs all high school sports in the state of Arizona."

Ms. Dragenschits nodded her approval.

"She drove down from Phoenix today to deliver some difficult news."

I turned to her. But she motioned for me to direct my attention back to Coach.

"Mrs.—I mean, Ms. Dragenschits is unable to speak."

She pursed her lips, disapprovingly.

Coach held an AHSAA rule book in his hand. "According to policy, all disciplinary action must come from the head coach." Begrudgingly, he added, "So, I guess that's me."

The bottom of my stomach dropped out, anticipating his next words. Was this the moment Coach prepared me for when he preached about toughness? Was this the gut punch that was going to make me shit my pants? I looked up at Mr. Strawbag for assurance, but he avoided my eyes and looked down at his shoes. Then, I eyed Ms. Dragenschits.

"Let me get this straight. You came here to deliver news, but you can't actually *deliver* the news?" I could feel where this was going, and I couldn't contain my brassy cynicism.

She did not acknowledge me. "Mr. Jones, please continue."

"That is correct, Billy. Son, this isn't easy. Since you've been charged with a felony, AHSAA rules require me to formally suspend you from the team until this is cleared up."

I sat high in my chair, ready to unleash, but Coach immediately motioned for me to sit back, putting his hand in my face.

Ms. Dragenschits nodded again, and motioned for Coach to continue, acting as a medium for her delivery.

"We don't have a choice, Billy. If we don't suspend you, we'll forfeit our previous meets, and also risk the team's eligibility for track and field in the spring. You wouldn't want that to happen, would you? Think of your teammates."

"I think my teammates will find this ridiculous. As should you. That's what I think." I was hot.

"I'm on your side, Billy. We can appeal. But that will just delay things and we want you back for track and field. This is just temporary until it gets worked out."

Ms. Dragenschits looked on from her corner chair. Her face was cold and indifferent. She held the rule book in her wrinkled hands as if it were the Bible, as if she were a good Christian protecting the sanctity of the written word. She spoke in a nasally, monotone voice. "To protect the student athletes, a person charged with a felony will be removed from a team until charges are either dropped or said party is found innocent. It is written here in section eight, paragraph six of the AHSAA rule book. The rules will be upheld, Mr. Ball."

"The stone speaks?" I asked.

"That's enough, Billy!" Coach interjected. "Please show Ms. Dragenschits some respect. "It's just a formality."

"Just a formality," Mr. Strawbag repeated.

But I knew otherwise. I knew it wouldn't be cleared up soon at all. Not when adults are involved. Not when lawyers are involved. Not when bureaucrats wielding rule books and preaching the safety of students are involved. This would take time.

It had been a week since I'd entered my plea at the courthouse, yet I hadn't even heard from my court-appointed attorney.

* * *

I didn't go back to square things up with Rigby that day. I didn't tell Charlie, or any of my teammates. I walked off school grounds and across the parking lot to my car. I passed a white sedan with government plates that surely belonged to Ms. Dragenschits, holding back the urge to kick it. I proceeded to my Malibu, gunned the engine, and sped home, thinking how things were spiraling out of control and how I would have to deliver more bad news to my parents when they returned home from work.

When I unlocked and opened the door, Jet rushed past me, bursting outside and peeing dangerously close to a jumping cholla.

"Easy boy. You really need to be careful of those things."

After a long minute, he came to me, still cross-eyed after all these years, wagging his tail and looking for a kind hand.

"I'm a wanton criminal and ex-high school runner," I told him. "And how is life treating you these days?"

He jumped up and licked my face. In return, I petted his block head and scratched behind his ears while he wiggled and squirmed. To be a dog must be blissful. They're incapable of second emotions, like feeling shame or humiliation. I picked up a ball and threw it for him to chase.

"Go on. Go get it, Jet."

But he just stared at me with those crossed eyes, looked at the ball, then back at me, before turning and walking inside the house. *I'm not getting it. You get it.*

"You're the only retriever on the planet who doesn't retrieve the ball." But Jet didn't care. He was his own happy self.

Instead of following him inside, I went to the mailbox and opened a letter from a school that had offered me a scholarship. These letters always lifted my spirits, reminding me that life after high school existed.

Dear Mr. Ball,

Through our continued evaluation of your qualifications, your recent disqualification from the state finals meet, for violations not becoming of good character, has been brought to our attention. Furthermore, upon inquiry, we were also notified of a felony criminal charge that was served to you and remains open.

At this time, and in accordance with the NCAA Bylaw 15.1.6., our scholarship offer, which is subject to our discretion, has been withdrawn.

We reserve the right to pursue your interests in the future, should conditions permit. Until then, we wish you the best in your college search and in your future.

Gene Simonson
Head Coach

There were two other letters addressed to me from other colleges.

Oh, Jesus. No No No!

My brain fired, triggering a rush of nerves and a flush of water that flooded my bowels and breached my sphincter. And just like that, I shit my pants.

Oh, Jesus.

8

Flight School

Personally, I like living. During a fight or flight response I always choose the latter, or perhaps the latter chooses me. It's possible, in my youth, the cruelness of the desert had worn me down over time and so I cower easily now, but I think that's just how I'm hardwired, like a desert rabbit, trepid and afraid of stepping from the brush and into the wide open. When I sense the slightest danger, I run as fast and far as my legs will take me.

This has always upset my dad. When I was a kid, a real kid, not my eighteen-year-old version, he would tell me to stand my ground, to fight and be a man. This is why he chose not to accompany me to the courthouse the day of my arraignment. He wanted me to stand up and be a man. He wanted me to take responsibility and deal with it like the adult the courts said I'd become. Since my birth as a preemie this had been Dad's agenda for fear that I would never grow into myself, or the self he envisioned. *Stand up and be a man.* I'd heard him say it a thousand times.

One such time was after an altercation during my first month of high school.

In my adolescence, I'd become girl crazy. But like most kids I entered high school as an awkward teenager with disproportionate limbs, boney, pimpled, and insecure. I stood five-foot-six and weighed 110 pounds, and most often I had a finger up my nose and a boner in my shorts. I smelled of body odor. I was a real catch, a real brute.

Dana was a year older, a sophomore, and I'd noticed her at lunch like every other boy. She had black, opaque eyes that tugged on me the way black holes swallow stars. Her stringy, matching hair fell to the small of her back and sashayed in rhythm with her cadence when she entered the cafeteria. Boys craned their necks to get a better look at this igniting spark coming of age. Girls noticed too, jealous. She walked with the confidence of the popular crowd. And she became the epicenter of baffling, newfound desires that consumed my heart with want and lust and things that were unfolding in my changing body, but I did not yet understand. Girls do that to adolescent boys, especially girls like dreamy Dana. I wanted to talk with her, but I didn't have it in me to approach her. So, I did nothing.

One day I was eating lunch with Charlie. When Dana entered the cafeteria and sat down two tables behind us, Charlie noticed my flushed face.

"Give it up. She's way out of your league."

"What?"

Charlie motioned for me to wipe off a glob of peanut butter that had fastened to my chin like another pimple.

"I see you looking at her."

"Not true."

"True."

I couldn't lie to Charlie. "Sure, she's…okay."

"What do you like about her?"

"She's…" I stuttered to find the right words. Words that adolescent boys choke on, like *beautiful* and *pretty*.

"What?"

"Come on, Charlie," I said. "Look at her."

Charlie glanced at Dana again, who was just out of earshot.

"Don't!" I said, under my breath. "Don't draw attention to me."

"She's pretty," Charlie acknowledged. "Do you want to meet her?"

"No," I said. "I mean, yes."

"It's simple. Go drop a fork or step on her toe, or accidently bump into her. That's how boys usually do it."

"That works?"

"No, but that's how boys usually do it."

"Not going to happen. Besides, she's dating Danny Morales." Danny was a senior, with patchy, black facial hair. His hulking biceps were always on display, extending from a tattered, sleeveless muscle shirt. His nose flared like the nostrils of an agitated bull.

"I have a plan," Charlie said.

I don't know why I agreed to it, given the likely outcome, but when Dana entered the cafeteria the next day, we took a seat next to her. Danny Morales was nowhere in sight.

Charlie kicked me under the table, and I winced. I was tongue-tied, unable to speak.

So, Charlie took the initiative. "These mashed potatoes suck," she said, piledriving her spoon into them. For effect, she pulled the spoon out, turned it upside down, and laughed when the potatoes clung to it like cement. She queued me, but I was still speechless.

Then she said, even louder, "These potatoes are fucking awful!"

Words stuck in my throat like the potatoes on her spoon, but this very silence was enough to catch the attention of Dana, who turned to us now, judging me.

"Aren't you going to respond to her?" Dana asked me.

My mouth was dry, but at that moment, I found the courage to speak. "They taste like a javelina's ass."

Dana laughed. "Have you eaten any?"

"A javelina's ass?"

"The potatoes," she said.

"No," I said. "I mean, yes. I've eaten potatoes, but not *these* potatoes. I've eaten a pig, but not its ass. At least I don't think so."

"You're a funny little freshman," she said. "And cute," holding my eyes a second too long. "What's your name?"

But the next thing I knew, her boyfriend, Danny Morales, was there, standing over me with a menacing growl. He yanked me from my seat by my shirt collar with those burly biceps, while Charlie, Dana, and others looked on anticipating my death. He held me close to his face and told me to look him in the eye, that he was going to tell me about life, and how he was about to end mine, but my focus gravitated toward his mouth, and then his patchy mustache, which like everything in Arizona was slow to take root. Spittle and small bits of chewed food were lodged in it and shot onto my face with his every word. I squinted. I gagged. Only the tips of my toes were in contact with the floor now as he held me high and tight, face to face. Then, my eyes grew wide as I anticipated the inevitable.

My heart raced like that scared little rabbit I'd conjured up in my mind. And just like a rabbit, I somehow squirmed out of his grasp. My feet found purchase and I took flight. I pivoted and escaped his clutch, darting away, knocking over a chair, nearly falling, righting myself and running into a classmate holding a tray of food, knocking it to the floor, nearly falling again, looking for traction but slipping on spilled milk and mashed potatoes, not bothering to say sorry, or helping to pick it up, because self-preservation had taken over, fear had engulfed me, and I was running to escape a monster, a real-life senior in high school, who wanted me and everyone else to know he had real biceps, a mustache in the making, and a pretty girlfriend.

I continued to bounce off people, tables, and chairs, like a pinball looking for an exit. Finally, through the doors I went, while Danny shouted at me to come back and fight, to stand up and be a man, while others laughed at my cowardliness, their voices fading with every step taken, until I was finally free.

I never bothered to ask how, but this story had made its way back to my parents before I'd returned home from school.

At dinner, Dad sat hunched over his plate like an ogre, pensive. And despite disapproving looks from Mom, he launched…

"Son, really?"

"What?"

"You know what. We heard all about the incident at school today."

"Oh yeah, the fight," I said, nonchalantly.

"I heard there was no fight. I heard you ran away."

"Richard," Mom said. "Not at the dinner table."

"I—"

"You ran away."

"He had a mustache!"

He turned to Mom, who still answered to Jesus Christ in our house. "Jesus Christ, did you teach him that? Did you teach him to run away?" Dad had seeded the nature versus nurture talk again, a favorite subject when it came to me.

"There's no need for that kind of talk." Mom was having none of it.

Dad turned his attention back to me. "Stand your ground. Fight and be a man!"

There, he'd said it. Danny Morales had said it too when I was running away. It seemed that everyone wanted me to stand up and be a man, except for me. I wanted to be the rabbit.

"Have I taught you nothing?"

"He had a mustache, Dad!"

"Punch me," he said, holding out an open palm to catch the blow.

"Richard!" Mom was hot. "This is a family dinner!"

I didn't take his bait.

"That's what I thought," he said. "You're soft."

The truth is, I didn't understand why I had run away. Inevitably, problems unresolved find you. Proof? Danny cornered me at the tetherball court three days later. I was so scared I took the first swing; a roundhouse that caught nothing but air. I spun full circle and I fell on my ass. Danny laughed and kicked me in the face, while dreamy Dana looked on with indifference.

But for now, as I sat in front of Dad defending myself, I knew that my flight response was primal, that I was hardwired through my genetic code to do what was best for my very survival. Fighting Danny Morales that day in the cafeteria would have been suicidal. Something deep inside me had said so. And because of that, I'd fled.

Finally, I spoke up. "I can fight," I told Dad, defiantly.

"But you didn't."

"But I can."

"Even if you'd gotten beat up, you'd have learned from it."

"Learned what?"

But Dad didn't answer. He shook his head.

"I would have learned to run away and to live another day."

Dad's eyes bore into mine, surprised by my backtalk. With this, he cut into his steak, dipped it in sauce, chewed on it for a while, and said, "You have more fight in your tongue than your fists."

"Yes, he does," Mom said, proudly. "That's a special kind of fight."

"Must have gotten it from you," Dad said to her.

* * *

That was three years ago, and as I grew older, I recognized that my flight response wasn't only triggered by the threat of immediate harm. It also stemmed from other threats, pressures slow to boil, like the very unfamiliar ground that I found myself in now.

I'd just read the letters, all expressing concern about my character and rescinding my scholarship offers. After I'd cleaned myself up, I felt the need to escape. I was going to run. It was that simple.

I rushed out the door as Jet barked at me to take him. But I didn't look back. I took off in a full sprint toward the Arizona Trail. It was there that a large group of day hikers had gathered at the trailhead, impeding my access. I did not slow down. I skirted them like a missile gone awry. Someone yelled at me to be careful and respectful. I didn't acknowledge. Instead, I ran harder. I tilled the earth beneath me with the force of my feet, pushing the physical limits of my sinewy muscles and thin bones, running faster than I thought possible.

I ran hard, blood capsulized in my lungs, filling my mouth with the taste of iron.

Blood.
Escape.
Survival.

I ran so hard my mind took me to another place, another realm, where I chased fantasy.

I was the rabbit in a dead sprint, outrunning the coyote. I was the rabbit outrunning the so-called justice system and Judge Carol Bell. I was the rabbit outrunning Clarise Dragenschits and the bureaucrats who would not budge from policy, the biased journalists who only had one story to tell, the high school administrators, and Coach Jeremy Jones, a pawn to authority. I ran from the disappointment of my dad, and oddly, the understanding and compassion of my mom. I was the rabbit, running from Danny Morales, the bullies of my youth, and my longtime running nemesis, Christmas Day, the said winner of the state meet, though he did not beat me that day. I ran from my classmate's heckles and orchestrated chants of "Balls" in the hallways of our school.

And yet still I ran faster, and faster, scaring two chubby tourists yak-yaketing in their safari hats, carrying walking sticks, unaware of my approach until I split them, looking beyond me for something giving chase, something monstrous, something awful, harmful, wondering if they too were in danger, wondering what could possess this reckless abandon to tear through the desert faster than any human should be capable. But they could not see what I very much knew to be after me—a monster without arms and legs, a monster without physical definition, hell-bent on annihilating me with a baseless, irrational agenda. But the tourists didn't know. How could they? They thought I was loco, bent, and warped from too much time in the Arizona sun.

Still, I chased the fantasy. Deeper I went. I was no longer the rabbit trying to escape. I was the coyote giving chase now with keen senses. Every living thing baited my instinct. I overtook a jogger without announcing myself. She shuddered, her shoulders rounded and caved in defense of an unknown predator as I sped by her. I did not turn and tell her I was sorry. I did not say anything at all. Instead, I laughed. I enjoyed the evils of my avaricious intention and the hierarchy of the natural food chain, where the inferior is simply overwhelmed and then eaten. I looked for more, weaker foes, but I saw no one else as I ran farther into the desert. And yet, I ran faster—and faster still—until I was well beyond any recognizable point of the trail, too far out for animals lesser than me to come back from.

And then my mind sank into the impossible. My fantasy morphed into something deeper, something faster. I was pure. I was energy chasing the speed of light. I was $E = MC^2$. My thoughts took me to Albert Einstein and his theory that time is not absolute, that time slows down, the faster an object travels in relation to another. And if I approached the speed of light my body would appear to shorten in length until, *poof*, I'm gone like the Starship Enterprise, absorbed into the infinity of everything and nothingness—a mass consumed, eaten whole by the cosmos. Blink, and you'll miss me. Blink, and I'm gone forever. That's what I wanted. That was my fantasy—to disappear.

But no matter how hard I ran I could not shed time. I could not catch the light. I could not push it off me. It clung to my shoulders with the weight of dread, crushing my cause. I fought to disappear. I fought so hard that my lungs burned with every breath. I fought so hard that my temples throbbed, and my head ached with pressures I knew nothing about. And still, I went faster. I leapt over fat rattlesnakes stretched out on the trail, warming themselves. I ran past a decomposed cow, its bones scattered by the scavengers of the desert. And I laughed at its fate, wishing it better luck next time. I was evil, and I did not care. Rage welled inside me. Rage released me.

I ran through dry, sandy washes that would slow mortals. But I was anything but mortal now. I flattened rises and bluffs with my aggression. I zigzagged through patches of saguaro cacti, skirting them by inches, avoiding their long needles that would surely impale me with one false step. But like a destructive force, a juggernaut, I ran for miles and miles straight into the desert as if swimming too far out to sea, not caring, but only wanting to suffer and drown in pity. Three miles behind me, then five, then ten, and I kept going and going as fast as I could, clinging to the fantasy of running the speed of light and vanishing. *Poof! I'm gone!*

But I was not gone, and time did not slow down, and my heart, my lungs, and my legs betrayed my wish. While time was not absolute, I surely was. I'd reached my limit. I slowed, and slowed, until I could only muster a jog, and then a shuffle, and then I could no longer even manage that. I walked in defeat and took refuge on a large granite rock beneath a giant saguaro cactus with arms that stretched out before itself, as if to embrace my failure.

Where was I? How long had I run? I'd run beyond the tourists, beyond the joggers, beyond any sign of humanity or recognition of my whereabouts, deep into the lair of the desert where time stood still, and silence engulfed me. Even the sky, usually lively, was blanketed by clouds hiding the sun's western migration. There was no movement of any kind, and so the measure of time was lost.

The desert drew me in like kin, heightening my senses. My eyes absorbing all it surrendered. A mosaic of desert flowers appeared to my right. Yellow cactus apples budding from prickly pear to my left. Red flowers capped the spindly branches of an ocotillo tree, raking twenty feet into the air like little torches aimed to set the sky ablaze. Undistinguished creosote bushes pattered around me, lairs for rattlers and other poisons. Directly in front stood a palo verde tree, its smooth, green bark spooked with such vivid color that I shook my head in realization that I had never noticed until now. The ultra-keen awareness of my surroundings overpowered me. And I simply lost it and began to cry.

I cried for want and need and the anguish of being a powerless teenager, and worse, an incapable young adult. I cried for loss and failure. But mostly, I cried because my tears were all that I had left. They were something. They were real. And they were mine.

The crush of teenage angst overwhelmed me. A wish overcame me that I should die out here. *Poof! I'm gone!*

That's what I wanted, and when I came to my senses and recognized my state of being—depleted and dehydrated—I considered that I might get my wish, miles and miles from nowhere.

But the desert had other plans for me, and so I would fail at that too.

A thunderous cloud burst directly overhead, as if the sky was laughing at my anguished, ridiculous thoughts. A hard wind blew at my back, followed quickly by sheets of rain. I was instantly drenched and cooled. I lifted my head toward the sky, blinking in its spit, the rain cleansing me, steadying my heart rate, soaking my shirt and shorts. I opened my mouth, my tongue held out to catch the gift.

And when it slowed, and when it finally stopped, I felt overwhelmed by sense. The desert sparked and came to life. A long-legged roadrunner, with a worm hanging halfway out its beak, ran across a newly formed stream alongside the trail. The rain had also released the petrichor scent from the surrounding creosote bushes; the fragrance earthy and fresh. I started to cry again, but this time out of longing—the scent reminiscent of Charlie's hair when she'd brushed up against me.

Charlie—the one constant in my life who always had my back. She was moving on. I was not. Was it too much to wish for that she was with me right now? Of course it was. She would tell me I was as crazy as a desert bat.

I pushed myself from the rock and began to contemplate my long run home. I had no idea how long I'd been out, or how many miles I'd put behind me. I'd lost track of time by trying to outrun it. But I felt refreshed now and knew there was no time or distance that would hamper my ability to return home. The run, the rain, the rage had all cleansed me and I felt anew, as if I'd exorcised my sins. As if the rain had somehow baptized me. And as if on cue, the sun released from behind the clouds with a certain brilliance, gifting a spectacular rainbow as wide as that could fit in the western sky. I stood for minutes admiring it. And when I gathered myself and began to run, retracing my footprints at a pedestrian pace, shapes bent and warped underneath it in iridescent light. It was then that I spotted something shimmering, flashing, just beyond the trail. It appeared metal, something man-made. I studied it from afar, but I could not make it out from the trail. I walked through the wet brush and picked it up.

In my hand was an open pocketknife. It was heavy and I sensed that it was decades old, its blade corroded from exposure and time. Then I noticed something that I could barely make out, an etching on its wooden handle. I rubbed it as clean as possible, trying to make sense of it. And one letter at a time, it revealed itself. F – L – Y – N – N.

The name, Flynn. My mother's maiden name.

9

Hometown Hero
~ Pennsylvania, 1933 ~

The morning that Jimmy Flynn ran pantless at a breakneck pace for thirteen miles from Pittsburgh to Wilmerding, Father McClary's congregation at St. Aloysius Church was just letting out, clogging the sidewalk and spilling onto the street. The congregation was dressed in their finest clothing, though despair was in their eyes and everyone and everything looked worn and ill-fitting.

It was another typical Sunday in the midst of the Great Depression, where the God-fearing Catholics of Wilmerding prayed for spiritual salvation and economic recovery. And jobs. Always jobs. But after four years of economic ruin, they had grown tired of their idle prayers falling deaf on God's ears. So, they tried another route, and through intercession they prayed to Jesus, Mary, and all the saints. Still, no word from God. Then, they turned to an even higher power, the Westinghouse Air Brake Company, which built the town during the Industrial Revolution and employed eighty-five percent of Wilmerding's workforce when times were good. However, this communal deity offered no salvation either, and worse, had cut fifteen hundred of its employees in recent years. For those whom they still employed, they rescinded many of their benefits, such as medical, disability, and group life insurance, essentially slamming the gates of St. Peter in their faces. The good people of Wilmerding couldn't afford to live, and neither could they afford to die.

Father McClary had no answers. His sermons of hope had grown cold, and his congregation's faith waned. He consoled his followers by acknowledging the difficult times, and reminded them that the Israelites wandered the Sinai desert for forty years, ten times longer than the current economic collapse, surviving on quail and manna, and how they were eventually led to the Promised Land by Joshua. "Have faith. Salvation will come unexpectedly when things look most bleak," he said in parting, shaking hands with his flock outside the church.

And this time, it seemed that God did answer his call, intervening in the oddest way: Jimmy ran into and fell on top of Father McClary, butt-naked. The incident initially drew gasps from the churchgoers, who crossed themselves and prayed for Father McClary and the boy's salvation, but later, around family dinners, at work, and at Joe's Bar and Grill, the incident drew laughs. Father McClary's words had stirred the pot. He'd shouted at Jimmy, "Holy Mother of Shit! Where are your pants, son?" Then, when Jimmy's full story came to light—the botched robbery of Paddy O'Donnell's coffee shop, the weapon of choice (a pocketknife), the ensuing brawl that dispatched his pants, and the police chase that ended in their hometown—the excitement it caused in their quotidian days lifted the town's spirits, and launched Jimmy to celebrity status overnight. Whether or not he was Wilmerding's savior was debatable, but if nothing else his actions endeared him to the dingers. That could have been the end of Jimmy's tale, but...

Three weeks later, the run at Schenley Oval launched him from celebrity status to bonafide hometown hero status, something the five thousand citizens of Wilmerding desperately sought from one of their own.

Paddy O'Donnell once held that title, but his business dealings in Pittsburgh had pulled him away from Wilmerding over the years, and Paddy, while revered, was someone unrelatable these days. As economic conditions had deteriorated in Wilmerding, Paddy's own success had rocketed to incomprehensible heights, conjuring feelings of resentment. Paddy had become too big, too successful, too lofty for the average dinger. Hope was a carrot at the end of a stick, but Paddy's rise to wealth was out of reach. Even Paddy knew this to be true, and in an odd way, he too was looking for a hero who could inspire the community in the same way he once had. His time as a grocery store clerk, supplying the hard-working dingers, had long since been forgotten. Heroes were everyday people who rose above adversity. While that bill fit Paddy years ago, his story was no longer relevant.

Jimmy Flynn was the Chosen One now. The dingers saw themselves in Jimmy, the scrappy kid down on his luck, struggling to survive in the midst of economic collapse. Someone who had risked everything to help his family. Someone who's dad had lost his blue-collar job at the Westinghouse Air Brake Company years ago, like so many others. In him, they saw a kid with fight and vigor, willing to lay it all on the line and stop at nothing. In him they saw hope.

It was a strange feeling for Jimmy, knowing that just weeks ago he was practically invisible, a virtual nobody in his hometown. His family had been so poor that he ran thirteen miles into Pittsburgh to beg for food and money in anonymity. Then he ran back, after filling his pockets with what meager handouts he could scrounge.

Now, the morning after the race at Schenley Oval, he woke as a hero, on his way to meet Paddy and Mike for breakfast at a local coffee shop across from the Westinghouse Air Brake Company to collect his winnings.

He nursed a hangover from a celebration that went well into the wee hours of the morning. After the race, the dingers had returned home with a few extra dollars in their pockets, mud caked in their hair from storming the sloppy track, and a thirst for more alcohol. A tattered group of party-goers had banged on the Flynns' front door and pulled Jimmy and his dad, Daniel, out of their home, and then into Joe's Bar and Grill, to applause and offers of free drinks.

He felt nauseous, and his steps were choppy and crooked. His foot caught an upheaval in a sidewalk that had cracked and gone unrepaired, like everything in town, and he stumbled to right himself. Years ago, there were no cracks. What happened?

His dad, Daniel, had a waxing nostalgia, haunted by the past, which he said was a far better place than the present. He told stories of a model community, built by the Westinghouse Air Brake Company, or WABCO as he referred to it. Years ago, Wilmerding was rich with culture and offered hope to thousands of unskilled laborers, many immigrants, looking for a steady foothold. "When I landed a job at WABCO, I thought I was set for life," Daniel said, bitterly.

He said Wilmerding was America's first company town, a planned community of nearly five thousand residents where all streets led to the center of town, the great hub of industry, WABCO. Air Brake Avenue was lined with perfectly spaced trees and arc lampposts that illuminated artistic charm and the rippled waters of Turtle Creek, making for strolls along this path a wanting pleasure that represented a good life. On a hill, a few blocks from the factory, stood a prominent, turreted castle, which officed the company's management and administrators. Beyond, WABCO housed many of its employees and their families in *Westing* homes, which had running water and sewer lines, a novelty for many of its unskilled, immigrant labor force. Daniel passionately remarked that he had bought into the vision of the company, and pointed out that George Westinghouse had invented weekends, and was ahead of his time by providing employee benefits to promote loyalty to the company. He said Mr. Westinghouse spoke of mutual interests and friendly fellowship, and his careful assiduity ensured that every employee was a company man, like it or not. Daniel liked it. "Of course, all of this created

117

welfare capitalism," Daniel said, "We were, still are, solely dependent on the company to feed us, house us, wipe our noses. Understand, Jimmy? WABCO rules the town and the well-being of its people."

When things were good, it felt like living in a bubble of prosperity, but when the Great Depression hit, and orders for air brakes came to a grinding halt like the trains they were built to stop, the bubble turned into a prison that no one could escape. With no other employers in town, Daniel rode the trains to find work at nearby steel mills and coal factories, but they too were collapsing under economic hardship, and after a year he gave up.

Jimmy recalled his father's tale that WABCO held beautification contests for best lawns and gardens to promote the upkeep of the company-owned homes, and that his mother, Shannon, had never been so proud the day she won. Now, with his dad out of work—laid off—the company was sending him eviction notices, even though Westing homes far exceeded the number needed to house its current workforce.

Like many on their street of row housing, theirs was in ill-repair. There was no interest and no money to fix things like missing shingles and peeled paint, and the once manicured, winning lawn now succumbed to foot-high weeds and was littered with shredded eviction notices, other discarded trash, and a washboard kitchen sink, which Jimmy threw up in on his way home from Joe's Bar and Grill last night. After only a few hours of sleep he was late meeting Paddy and Mike, tripping over himself and the uneven sidewalk in a pulsating rush to get to the coffee shop.

Paddy and Mike were already there, sitting across from each other at a small table with four seats. Paddy was reading the Sunday paper, troubled. Mike sat sideways; his body large behind the dinette table. He sipped his coffee, glancing up at a wall clock.

"He's late," Mike said.

"You gotta be somewhere else?"

"As a matter of fact, I do," Mike said. "I'm taking my niece to see *King Kong* this afternoon."

"*King Kong?*"

"Just got released. It's about a big ape that gets loose in the Big Apple."

"They finally made a movie about you."

"Very funny, boss."

"Maybe you should pay more attention to the business," Paddy said. He waved his right arm in an exaggerated, circular motion above his head. "All of this is coming to an end."

"This coffee shop is going out of business?"

"No, genius," Paddy said. "I mean…" He considered the right words. "Yes, the coffee shop. Not *this* coffee shop. *My* coffee shop, in Pittsburgh. All of our businesses—the insurances, the booze. Everything!"

Mike, jittery from the coffee, tapped his fingers in a fast rhythm on the wooden table. He was missing a pinky on his right hand; a casualty of the job. His four-fingered tap sounded like a galloping horse. "Not following, boss."

"Follow this." Paddy pointed to an article in the newspaper. "That wet Democrat, Roosevelt, is pushing to end Prohibition. He wants to ruin us all."

"Ruin us?"

"Don't you read the papers? Pro-hi-bi-tion!" Paddy said, hanging on each syllable. "Roosevelt wants to repeal the 18th Amendment. He just legalized low-alcohol beer and wine sales, as if anyone would ever drink that piss. Says sixteen states will jump on board this month and by the end of the year, enough states will be on board to get rid of Prohibition altogether. Says the tax revenue from liquor sales is needed to pull the country out of this mess."

"What mess?"

"The Depression, genius." Paddy reached over and smacked Big Mike on his big forehead, leaving a big, red mark. "Are you retarded?"

Mike shrugged, not denying it.

"The government is desperate for revenue and wants in on the action. Roosevelt says he needs it for his New Deal."

"Our action? That ain't fair!"

Paddy set the paper down, surveying his thoughts. "Maybe it's all right," he said. "Between you and me, I'm getting a little tired of this racket. I've made enough money to live a good life – forever. And I'm tired of looking over my shoulder for one of those Italians to whack me off."

"Ain't nobody going to whack you off, boss. Not on my watch."

Seconds of awkward silence followed.

"Admirable." Paddy rolled his eyes. "All I'm saying is maybe I should pivot and explore new opportunities." Paddy paused. "Like gambling! I got chills yesterday watching Jimmy win that race. Surely, there's plenty of chisel in gambling."

"We don't know anything about that racket."

Paddy ignored his comment. "I won a mint off that kid! You too?"

Mike said nothing.

"Tell me you bet on the kid. Tell me you bet on Jimmy."

Mike tapped on the table again with his four-fingered hand.

"You really are retarded," Paddy said.

"I won." Mike took exception. "Not big. I played the field and did all right."

"My only problem is what to do with him next? Nobody around here is going to race against him now."

"True. But the dingers love him."

"Sure, they love him. Nobody in this town has had anybody to root for in a long time."

The coffee shop door creaked open, letting in the morning chill, and a tiny bell hanging from it rang, announcing Jimmy Flynn's entrance. Paddy and Mike, dressed in Sunday suits, waved him over. Jimmy stopped short, not sure where to sit. It would be awkward to sit next to Paddy, and Mike's three-hundred-pound frame left little room.

"You look like a bum," Paddy said.

"I am a bum," Jimmy replied, hoarsely. Despite the cold, he'd left his jacket behind and wore only a dingy white undershirt and tattered khakis.

"You don't smell so good, neither." Paddy's mouth was stuffed with eggs and sausage. "You're ruining my breakfast."

Two tables across, a nicely dressed, distinguished man in his forties and a much younger woman intertwined feet and stared into each other's eyes the way unscrupulous lovers do, oblivious to anyone else. They flipped through the pages of a magazine, oohing and aahing. She wore a red polka-dot dress, and her dyed-blonde hair exposed black roots. She smelled of cheap perfume, which compounded Jimmy's nausea.

"Sit down, Jimmy. You don't look like no champion today," Paddy said, seeing the sting of a rough night on his face.

"What is that couple oohing and aahing over?" Jimmy asked.

Paddy glanced the couple's way. "A travel magazine. I think they're planning to run away together based on their footwork."

Mike laughed. And Jimmy reluctantly took the seat next to him.

"Here, you want my eggs? I'm full," Paddy said.

Jimmy's eyes followed the runny yolk as it spilled and coagulated along the contours of Paddy's plate.

"Look, I've got something that's going to make you feel a lot better. After our local animals carried you from the Oval yesterday, I never got a chance to give you your cut."

Paddy removed an envelope from his chest pocket and placed it on the table, sliding it over to Jimmy. "Your winnings," he repeated. "You ain't no bum no more."

"Trust me," Mike said to Jimmy. "It's a lot of cabbage. You'll be buying breakfast."

Jimmy picked up the envelope. It felt surprisingly heavy.

"It's 375 dollars," Paddy said.

Jimmy swallowed hard.

"Don't open it here. Some punk-ass kid might bust through that door wielding a pocketknife and rob us," Mike said.

Paddy and Mike exchanged a hard, rolling laugh. But Jimmy sat motionless, imagining the money inside. Imagining how it was going to help his family survive. Imagining his mother in new shoes, his sister in a new dress, and his dad able to smile once again. The eviction notices would finally stop. He opened his mouth to speak, but the only thing that came out was an incoherent string of gibberish.

"Jesus, kid. Are you retarded or something?" Paddy said. "You and Mike related? You gonna thank me, or what?"

"I ja-ja-just never seen this mu-mu-much..." And suddenly, his head swiveled. The next thing that came out of Jimmy's mouth wasn't a word at all, but a gush of vomit that exploded onto the black and white, linoleum checkered floor.

"Christ!" Paddy shouted.

The couple seated next to them shrieked and gagged, and together they quickly exited the restaurant, disgusted, leaving a few dollars on the table.

Mike chaffed them in passing as they exited. "Hey, you forgot your magazine."

"Well, there goes a perfectly good breakfast," Paddy said. "I agree with you, Mike. The kid is definitely picking up the tab today."

Had it been anyone other than the revered Paddy O'Donnell, the restaurant's proprietor, a staunch man with scornful, dark eyes, the three would have been made to clean up the mess and then kicked out. But minutes, and several respectful apologies, later, the mess had been mopped up by the cook, who also held the title of janitor, and commented in broken English that the smell was not so good. The proprietor moved them to another table, away from the incident. "More eggs," he yelled back at the cook. "Bring them more eggs."

"No more eggs," Paddy said. "We're done eating eggs."

"Yes, sir, Mr. Paddy."

Paddy turned back to Jimmy. "You're done throwing up."

"I feel much better. Thanks for asking."

"Look at me, kid," Paddy said. "I wasn't asking. I was telling."

Jimmy nodded.

"Mike and me—we've been talking. We don't know what to do with you. Nobody is going to race you. You beat Pittsburgh's finest and you're dead to me now."

"You're going to ka-ka-kill me?"

"I ain't going to ka-ka-kill you," he mimicked. "How many times have we had this conversation? And why are you suddenly stuttering like an invalid? Between the two of you morons, you're driving me fucking nuts. Mike suggested that we put you on our payroll, employ you as a runner. You'd make the rounds collecting insurance payments. But with your boyish looks, nobody would take you seriously. You'd come back with a black eye, and then Big Mike would have to blacken the other one for not collecting. Nobody wants that. Not even Mike."

"I wouldn't mind," Mike said, evenly.

"So, what am I going to do with you?" Paddy contemplated, twiddling his thumbs.

"I've got an idea, boss. Run him out of town."

"Out of town? Where?"

"Boston."

"What's in Boston?"

"The Boston fucking Marathon. Twenty-six miles, boss. It's in three weeks. Half a million people show up to watch these idiots run on Patriots Day, a holiday in Boston where everyone gets the day off work. My cousin Sammy lives up there. Says wagering is big." He turned to look at Jimmy, who was as white as a ghost, not liking where this was going. "Run the kid up there, boss. Nobody knows him. We'll get great odds and make a killing."

"Or we'll get terrible odds," Paddy said, weighing the possibility. "Nobody knows him. Nobody likes risk." Paddy paused. "What about the purse? What's the purse?"

"No purse, boss. It's an amateur race. There ain't no money on the line, officially."

125

"No purse?" Paddy considered. "Then why do they run?"

"I don't know, boss. Glory, I suppose."

"And you're sure we can bet on it?"

"Yeah, Sammy can hook us up with the right people. He bets on it every year."

Paddy scratched his head. "I don't know. Betting aside, are you telling me these idiots run twenty-six miles?" Looking at Jimmy. "No offense, kid."

"Yeah, twenty-six, if you can believe it, boss."

"Morons." Paddy turned his attention to Jimmy, who was listening intensely, anticipating the path of the ask. "Jimmy. That day you fucked up the robbery. One thing that's been bothering me. How'd you get there?"

"I-I..." he stuttered again, nervously. "I ran there. The—that morning."

"You ran thirteen miles there, robbed my coffee shop, and ran like the devil thirteen miles home?"

Mike weighed in. "I ain't that good with math, but that's twenty-four miles, boss."

"Shut up, Mike. You only got nine fingers. I got ten. And that's—damn. That's twenty-six miles."

Paddy turned his attention back to Jimmy. "So, Jimmy..."

"Well, yeah. I do it all the time, four or five days a week. I ain't got money for the train and I ain't got nothing else to do. And I ain't wantin' nobody 'round here to see me begging. Especially my pops."

"You run over a hundred miles a week?" Paddy said, comprehending the toll.

Paddy and Mike exchanged looks, shaking their heads in sublime astonishment.

"That's not human," Mike said.

"Jimmy, look me in the eyes and tell me you can run the twenty-six," Paddy said. "I've never met anyone that can run that far. I've never known anyone that *could* run that far. And I've never met anyone who runs as fast as you. Look at me and tell me the truth."

Jimmy met his eyes, and for the first time that morning, his focus was clear. With both hands he clutched the envelope that held the 375 dollars. "I can do it, Mr. O'Donnell," he said. "I can run the twenty-six." And this time, he did not stutter.

"You better not be lying," Paddy said. "And you better be able to run the twenty-six fast."

"Faster than the train we'll throw you under if you don't," Big Mike added.

10

Sharks, Uncharted Waters, and Lifejackets

B ootlegging was a tough business with long hours. Between operations, delegating authorities, extortions, bribery and coercion of public officials, money laundering and tax fraud, manipulation of the press and public opinion, the never-ending strong-arming mixed with occasional bloodshed, Paddy O'Donnell was left with little time to enjoy the fruits of his labor and appreciate his saintly contributions to society. After a decade of shenanigans, he was burning out quickly.

But walking away from the organization—the organization he'd created—was a death wish. He'd made too many enemies, and if found in a weakened and isolated position, they'd begrudgingly hunt him down. There was no way out. That is, until he saw the newspaper article that mentioned Roosevelt's promise to end Prohibition, which would essentially collapse his business.

A whimsical promise to his organization to re-align would never happen and he'd fold up shop. His enemies would be busy adjusting, scurrying for their own survival, and Paddy would slip into the shadows, disappearing over time.

Outwardly, he expressed indignation over Roosevelt's plan, but inwardly, he welcomed the thought of starting over and leading a quieter life. Since he'd acquired more money than he could ever spend in a lifetime, the possibilities were endless, even tantalizing when he lay awake at night, losing himself in a fantasy that had grown stronger since meeting with Mike and Jimmy in the Wilmerding coffee shop, when on his way out he picked up the *Arizona Highways* magazine that had been left behind by the flirtatious couple.

On its cover was a photograph of a huge saguaro cactus with more arms than he could count. It was silhouetted against a sunset that bled reds and oranges and pinks and purples. The image warmed him, and he tucked it away as he stepped into the damp chill of a spring morning in Allegheny County and the sight of a massive smokestack, silhouetted against a dirty, gray sky—an image that chilled him.

He'd leave Pennsylvania and disappear to another state, perhaps another country or continent. In his fantasy he'd carry a suitcase full of cash and travel undercover. He'd head west and buy a ranch and spend his days riding horses into brilliantly colored sunsets, painting himself onto the cover of the magazine. He'd discard his suits and fedoras in favor of chaps and cowboy hats.

Or maybe he'd head south, sail the Caribbean under starlit skies, and eventually settle in Key West, spending his days deep water fishing for blue marlin with someone who enjoyed great literature and the culinary arts. He'd change his name, grow a beard, lose weight on a diet of seafood, discard his suits and fedoras in favor of shorts and straw hats, drop the Pittsburghese and learn Spanish, read Ernest Hemingway, and take on a new identity, morphing into someone…happy.

Happy Paddy, he mused.

For now, he wasn't going anywhere. And not going anywhere was okay, for now.

Jimmy Flynn had been a welcomed distraction. Just as Wilmerding had adopted him as their collective son, Paddy felt the same—though somewhat subjugated, he'd admit. Watching the race at Schenley Oval was the happiest moment he'd had in years, and now that he'd made the decision to run Jimmy in the Boston Marathon, the mere distraction had become an obsession.

There were so many plans to be made. Boston was only three weeks away. He'd delegate responsibilities to his captains to keep the business running while he was gone. He put Big Mike in charge of travel arrangements. Bettors needed to be lined up.

But this took a backseat to the all-out promotional puffery he had in mind for Jimmy Flynn.

With good reason, of course.

Paddy understood winning. He understood people. And he understood that raw talent would not be enough to get Jimmy across the finish line first in such a prestigious race. It would take his own creative genius to help Jimmy rise to the occasion. And he had the perfect plan to get it done. He would play on the character of a hard-nosed, guilt-ridden, and guilt-driven kid with a chip on his shoulder whose lone driving force was to do right by his family. So, Paddy would charter a bus and fill it with dingers. Nothing would motivate Jimmy more than his people waiting for him at the finish line with their hopes and dreams in hand. And if that wasn't enough, he had some other magic up his sleeve.

It all started with building the hype of Jimmy Flynn.

He paraded Jimmy in and out of Joe's Bar and Grill, and along Air Brake Avenue, encouraging him to engage with locals, thanking them for their support. Jimmy's training runs were kept in town so the dingers would see him, cheer him on, and buy in. He was on display every waking moment.

Paddy's intention was to put the entire weight of the community on Jimmy's shoulders, knowing the only way for him to shed it was to deliver a victory in Boston.

And it went as planned. Each day, Jimmy's star shined brighter. His confidence grew. A stranger's wishful thought turned into a pat on the back, a mention of good luck turned into a handshake, and the mention of him running Boston turned into a shout of victory. With Paddy's influence, the *Pittsburgh Gazette* touted him as "The Hope of Wilmerding." Even Jimmy himself bought in.

Paddy staged a sendoff party with the look and feel of a presidential campaign stop, complete with red, white, and blue balloons, a ragtag high school band, free lunches, and banners that read "Jimmy the Rabbit" and "Next Winner of the Boston Marathon." He invited the press, with special accommodations for the executives at

Westinghouse Air Brake Company, who offered the lawn of the WABCO castle as the venue. He asked Father McClary to attend and say a little prayer for Jimmy, to send him off with God's blessing. At first, he declined. But Father McClary, a master of coercion himself, negotiated several bottles of whisky before agreeing and delivering a heartfelt, alcohol-influenced prayer. "I've always believed in you, son. God believes in you. God wants you to win Boston. Glory be to the Father, the Son, and to Jimmy Flynn. Amen." A raucous applause erupted as Father McClary considered his own fate to wind up in Hell.

Jimmy Flynn's run in Boston was going to be the biggest event ever for the citizens of Wilmerding. But there was more to the story than the *feel good*, especially for this community, which was financially tattered.

Rumors spread quickly that Paddy had somehow fixed the race. There had to be a rub if he was involved. And they all wanted in on the action.

The dingers who made the trip filled their pockets with whatever money they could rummage. Many carried the favored cash of others. Thanks to Paddy, they were crazed with the collective brilliance of sheep.

And together, when the caravan departed Wilmerding, they paddled out to sea in deep, uncharted waters where the sharks swim.

***

In 1933, the Boston Marathon was already thirty-seven years old and a tradition in New England, the epicenter of America's distance running. Though, some things still needed working out. Performance-enhancing substances were neither frowned upon or illegal. Nobody called foul. Wagering was legal, bookies were easy to find, and the marathon cost a dollar to enter, which was not insignificant for the mostly blue-collar runners of the time. But despite the tough economic times, cash bloomed like newly budded, spring leaves when it came to betting on the marathon.

For gamblers of wealth and means, wagering was serious business and they sought each other out in the lobbies of luxurious hotels and expensive restaurants. Sammy O'Sullivan, Mike's cousin, arranged a betting party in the lobby of the opulent Lenox Hotel; the same hotel where Paddy, Mike, and Jimmy were staying.

Paddy was dressed impeccably in a tan pinstripe suit, with a white fedora and a wool paisley scarf tied around his neck to calm April's Back Bay chill. He stood confidently, posed next to a colorful floral arrangement set in an ornate, red vase, sitting atop a mahogany pedestal. His white, wingtip Oxfords shone in the glow of the polished marble floor.

"This is my cousin, Sammy the Shark," Big Mike said, making the introduction.

"Sammy—the Shark?" Paddy asked, holding back a laugh. "Isn't that a little overdoing it? We might be gangsters, but come on."

"He's a loan shark, boss. My comment was meant in jest."

"I'm a lender," Sammy O'Sullivan politely corrected, amused. "I make loans to people down on their luck. I provide a public service, just like you do."

"If you see people walking around with broken fingers, it's likely the work of Sammy," Mike said, holding up his four-fingered hand to make a point.

"Do I need to remind you, Mike, that collections are a very different business than lending," Sammy said with a thin, villainous smile. "And I had nothing to do with your lost finger, cousin. Although, I'm sure you owe me money long forgotten."

Paddy was enjoying the banter between the two cousins. But watching them was awkward. Big Mike was a huge man, with a menacing, brooding disposition. Sammy had a slight build, lively blue eyes, a weak chin, and a wispy tuft of blond hair that sprung from his head like a spring dandelion that had barely taken root.

"How are you two related?" Paddy asked, incredulously, unable to hold back a laugh.

"It is odd," Sammy answered. "Obviously, I got all the looks and a much larger…brain. No offense, Mike."

Sammy the Shark had all the confidence that his physicality didn't suggest. With astute mannerisms, he stood tall for his size, and spoke with poise and certainty. Paddy took an instant liking to him.

"I appreciate the hospitality, Sammy. It was nice of you to invite me to this impressive gathering."

"It's my pleasure, Mr. O'Donnell. I enjoy betting on the marathon. I assure you, I'm here for my own personal interests as much as yours. Mike tells me you've brought a contender. Mr. Jimmy Flynn—the Rabbit? Tell me, Mr. O'Donnell—"

"Paddy—please call me Paddy."

"Tell me, Paddy," Sammy corrected. "Do you know much about the marathon? You'll attract a lot of bettors if you do. But you'll attract even more if you don't."

"I didn't know anything about it three weeks ago," he admitted. "But I've done my homework. Plus, I know Jimmy and what he's capable of. I ain't never seen a kid who can run like him. And I also know how to make him run his best."

"How will you do that?" Sammy asked. "Did you threaten to kill him?"

Given Paddy's profession, the mention carried weight, and the three laughed heartily.

"My apologies, Paddy. Mike told me you brought his family along with a busload of people from Wilmerding. How very smart of you."

"Part of the magic," Paddy said. "I suppose you're familiar with the race?"

Sammy politely laughed. "Mike didn't tell you?"

"Tell me what?"

"I ran the marathon three years ago. I toed the line with some of tomorrow's favorites."

"You're a runner?"

"Indeed, I am. I bet on the race every year because I have a good sense of who's in form and who's not. I'm an actuary by trade, so I make it my business to know each runner's abilities to cover my bets. I know the course and understand the strategies in play. I know the rookies will start out too fast and suffer later on. I know how the weather will play into the race. If it's hot, the Canadians will suffer. The race isn't too difficult to predict, barring a virtual unknown like your runner, Jimmy Flynn. I admit, unknown talent is a variable I do not like."

"I told you so," Paddy said to Mike.

"But I'm not concerned. Out of the 250 runners tomorrow, there's only a handful that have a shot at winning. The public doesn't understand this. But I do."

Paddy listened attentively.

"I assess everything, Paddy. I'm assessing your runner right now. I see him talking to that pretty girl working the front desk. He's not thinking about the race. He's thinking about her; about *being* with her. He sees her softness, which in turn, makes him soft."

Paddy raised an eyebrow. He understood Sammy's point. Jimmy did look soft. He was charming the front desk clerk, pointing to his canvas, rubber-soled running shoes, which peaked out from beneath the folds of his ill-fitting trousers. He was clearly engaged in light, flirtatious conversation.

"Your boy isn't going to win. But I'll do you a favor and give you three-to-one odds he won't place in the top five. I'll do this because I like you, Mr. O'Donnell. And I like my cousin, Mike. He's good people, which makes you good people. Your one hundred dollars against my three hundred. You won't find better odds."

"With all due respect, Mr. O'Sullivan, I expect Jimmy to win. Top five certainly won't be a problem." Paddy pulled a hundred-dollar bill from his pocket. "Who holds the cabbage?"

"It's a gentleman's bet, Paddy. We'll make the exchange back here tomorrow."

Paddy shook Sammy's hand with great enthusiasm as they parted ways. As other connections were made, Paddy's misguided, misjudged confidence stood out brazenly in the affluent and knowledgeable gathering. He percolated energy, eager to bet, despite himself.

Later that afternoon, Paddy tallied up his wagers: twelve hundred dollars. It was the most he'd ever bet, leaving a little knot in his stomach, but laced with excitement. His bets were across the board, sometimes wagering Jimmy to win against the field, other times Jimmy against specific runners. He combined those with hedge bets that had him placing in the top five or top ten. He calculated that if he won all his bets, he would take home nearly six thousand dollars. *Real money.*

"Time to go, Jimmy. We're having dinner with your family and all the dingers."

"My family doesn't have money to eat at restaurants, Mr. O'Donnell."

"Relax, kid. I'm paying for everything." While the three had rooms at the Lenox, Mike had arranged cheaper lodging and dinner at an Irish-owned restaurant in South Cove for the dingers. "Your parents told me they haven't traveled in four years. Let's not keep them waiting."

"I can't tell you what this means to me."

"You can tell me what it means to you by winning tomorrow, Jimmy. The dingers came here to watch you run. Don't disappoint them. Most certainly not your family."

And that was the rub. That's the way it would go down, as Paddy saw it.

At the restaurant, they were seated in a large private room. Paddy, Mike, Jimmy, and his family members sat shoulder to shoulder at the head table, facing the other guests.

Newly legalized low-alcohol beer was served, but the dingers snubbed it in favor of whisky that appeared suddenly and plentiful, despite the Prohibition laws.

Paddy stood. "Ladies and gentlemen. Dingers. I'd like to propose a toast to Jimmy."

When Paddy spoke, the room fell respectfully silent.

"Once in a lifetime someone like Jimmy Flynn comes along. A beacon of light that lifts the spirits of an entire community. A community that is in need of a lift."

Someone yelled, "Amen!"

Paddy looked down in admiration at Jimmy, who sat next him, abashed. "Tomorrow, when you're running, you remember the good people of Wilmerding who are proud to call you their own. You remember your parents, Daniel and Shannon, and your sister—what's her name."

"Maggie," Jimmy helped.

"Yes, Maggie." Paddy acknowledged the family with a nod. "Be an inspiration to Maggie. Remember your Irish ancestry and the fight that has been passed down to you

139

through generations. Give 'em hell, Jimmy, and may the luck of the Irish be with you."

Shouts of "To the Irish!" rang throughout the room.

"Sláinte!" Paddy shouted.

"Sláinte!" echoed the dingers.

Drinks were thrown back with haste, and a robust applause ensued. Paddy added, "And for crying out loud, keep your pants on tomorrow!" The room burst into heavy laughter and applause. Paddy, reveling in the attention, shouted joyously above it all. "This kid is going to do great things tomorrow! YOU CAN BET ON HIM!"

After an impressively large dinner of corned beef and cabbage, Daniel, a mere skeleton in clothing, pulled his son aside and handed him a pouch. "Jimmy, I haven't been able to give you much these past few years. But I want to make up for it now. In this bag is something that will help you tomorrow."

"What is it?"

"Amphetamines."

"What's an an—fetameen?"

"It's speed, Son. These pills are magic. You'll run faster. I used to take them at work when I was low on energy. You can thank me after you win."

"I'm thanking you now, Dad. You're the best dad in the world."

"You're welcome, Son. We'll be waiting for you at the finish."

For the dingers, it would be a late night. They took Paddy's remark to bet on Jimmy quite literally.

They found bookies in this Irish part of town who were all too happy to take their money. "Who is your runner?" they asked, amused. "Jimmy who?"

But the dingers turned up their noses and bet heavily.

***

Later that night, Jimmy was unable to sleep. The room at the Lenox was elegant, a richness he'd never known. He lay between a fine, down-filled duvet and crisp white sheets. An ornate fireplace decorated the far wall, the crackle and pop of burning wood, flames sparking and dancing and eventually abating, until only embers remained. But not before one last flicker, a final breath, caught and reflected off a crystal ceiling lamp. Then, darkness. He turned on his side and then flipped to the other. The excitement, the weight of expectation. It was all too much.

He got up, got dressed, and considered a stroll to calm his nerves.

When he made his way to the hotel lobby, he encountered the front desk clerk.

"You're still here," he said, surprising her.

"Double shift," she said indignantly, trying to place him. "I need the money."

She was older, perhaps twenty-five, and exhibited a certain refinement, a rub of working at the luxury hotel, but also a certain tiredness, also a rub of working at the

141

luxury hotel. Her black hair brimmed under a red felt, cloqué hat, the color matching her lipstick. She was even prettier than he remembered her eight hours earlier.

"You're lucky," Jimmy said. "Where I live, nobody has a job."

"Is that so? Well then, I suppose I am lucky."

Her eyes gravitated to his shoes. "Hey, I know those shoes. You're the boy from the reception today." She softened. "Shouldn't you be in bed by now? Long day for you tomorrow."

"I can't sleep. The room is too nice," Jimmy said. "I just lie there with my eyes wide open, appreciating it."

"All I want to do *is* sleep," she said, lips pursed. "Short walk home, thankfully."

"Walking this late?"

"I do it every night."

"Ca-ca-can I walk with you?"

"I don't think so."

"Just to keep your ca-ca-company." He paused to catch his words. "Sorry, I get nervous sometimes. Honestly, I could use the company too, if you don't mind."

She studied him for a long second. *Harmless.* "I don't even know your name."

"Jimmy," he said, looking up now. "My name is Jimmy Flynn, tomorrow's winner of the Boston Marathon, at your service." He curtsied and she smiled. "But I didn't catch *your* name."

She pointed to her nametag: CATHERINE BECHARD. She was intrigued by this enigmatic young man, whose confidence rose suddenly when he'd mentioned the marathon.

"You know," she said, fetching a cigarette from her purse. "I watch the marathon every year. I envy you. Maybe one day I'll run it."

"Dames don't run."

Ignoring his reply, she lit the cigarette, blowing smoke in his face.

She couldn't deny a certain charm about him, and given the circumstances, what was the harm? "Fine. You can walk me home. I'll even share my cigarette with you. But if you try to hold my hand, or kiss me, or anything creepy like that you won't be able to run away fast enough. Got it?" She said this with such softness in her voice the words didn't match her conviction.

"Got it." He crossed his heart. "I promise."

"Say, you have any idea what you're getting yourself into? You're pretty confident for a kid. I'm assuming this is your first go at it."

"Well, first of all, I ain't no kid. I'm nineteen. But I'll listen if you've got any advice."

"I've got lots of advice. Come on, now."

She said good night to the doorman, and they exited the hotel and walked north toward the Charles River under a crisp sky and a canopy of stars. They shared the cigarette, but Jimmy coughed several times, unaccustomed to it.

"You should take up smoking," Catherine told him. "They say it's good exercise for the lungs. You'll run faster."

"Yeah, I think I've heard that."

When they got to the river, a fat moon hung low, casting an iridescent glow over its roiled waters. A cool breeze swept across, and a lone dory, moored to a tree, rocked back and forth in a small wake, the river gently lapping at its sides. Geese squawked and parted as they approached.

Jimmy stopped to admire and take in the tranquility of it all, looking beyond the river now to an impressive stone cathedral; its spires clearly outlined against the backdrop of the lit night sky. He looked back at Catherine, whose features were caressed in the dim light, her eyes soft and drawing. "I've never seen anything so beautiful," he said. "It is quite beautiful," she agreed, mistaking the target of his comment. Jimmy was quiet now, absorbing every soft contour of her unblemished face, pouty lips, a high neckline, and the refined way she held the cigarette in one hand, occasionally blowing smoke out the side of her mouth like someone worldly and experienced.

But when he finally spoke, his words flowed freely without stutter. He told her about his hometown, his family, and the busload of dingers that followed him here to cheer him on. He told her about his excitement to run the marathon, his expectations to win it, and she, in turn, said he was swimming in uncharted waters.

He told her about Paddy, his financial support, and his unyielding belief in him. And she, in turn, said that Paddy was swimming with the sharks.

"I thought you were sweet," Jimmy said, frustrated with her counters.

"I'm honest. Ain't that sweet enough?" She pointed to his shoes. "Unless there's magic in those shoes, you can't win. And unless Paddy is working a huge angle, he can't win neither. You can't just show up to this race and take the city by storm. It doesn't work that way."

Jimmy picked up a stone and skipped it in the river. "What do dames know, anyway?"

"I've been working at the Lenox for four years. I've seen them guys before. They're sharks. You and Paddy were being served up on a platter today. You show up with big dreams and big money, but you always leave like a beaten dog, and sometimes, so broke, you can't even settle your bill."

Jimmy felt the punch of her words. *She doesn't know me.* He believed he would win, because Paddy, his family, and the dingers told him so.

Sensing his frustration, "Look, here's some advice. Sprint from the start and don't never look back. Send them other boys a message that you ain't messing around."

"And that'll work?"

"Of course it will work."

"But—"

"You asked me for advice. And that's what I'm giving you."

They came to a stop in front of a four-story brownstone. "This is where we say good night and goodbye. And be quiet. Everyone's sleeping."

"It's been a pleasure to meet you, Catherine Bechard." He held out his hand to shake hers. "Will I see you tomorrow?"

"Maybe. I'll be at Kenmore Square with my younger sisters. That's our favorite spot to watch." Then, she softened. "Look, you and me. We're a lot alike. Both of us are looking for a break, right? I don't know your future, Jimmy Flynn, but you've got courage. I can see that in you. Me? I've got big dreams too. I'm heading west to Los Angeles as soon as I can save up enough money to get out of here. I want to be a movie star like Jean Harlow, lie in the sun every day, drink fancy cocktails at night, and dye my hair blonde. I want to own a pretty house with a big yard and a small dog, and host dinners for important, intellectual peoples."

She leaned in and kissed him on the cheek, leaving a residue of her red lipstick.

"You said…"

"I said *you* couldn't kiss *me*." She smiled coyly. "I said nothing about me kissing you. Other than those big blue eyes, you ain't much to look at, Jimmy Flynn, but you sure are sweet. Besides, it's just for good luck. Don't get all sentimental about it." She pulled a key from her purse and opened the lock, letting herself in.

"Wait," Jimmy said. "Do you have any more advice? You said you had a lot of advice."

She paused and then rummaged through her purse, pulling out a small pouch.

"What's in it?"

"Cocaine."

"What's ca-ca-cocaine?"

"It's magic. Snort it before the race. You'll jump off the line so fast nobody will ever catch you. Poof, you're gone! It's the only chance you have at winning."

"This *is* my lucky day," Jimmy said. "You're an angel. Heaven sent!"

"You can thank me after you win," she said, turning now. "And I ain't no angel."

The door swung back on Jimmy's face and locked behind her. "Good night, Catherine," he said to a closed door.

Under a shifting sky he ran back to the hotel at full speed in his magic shoes, holding the pouch of cocaine, enamored. When he got to his room, he took out his pocketknife and carved his initials on the side of the fireplace.

J F

Folks are going to remember me. I'm gonna be someone. And this time, when his head hit the pillow, it was full of dreams so big, he slept like a giant.

***

Meanwhile, Paddy and Mike met Sammy O'Sullivan at an Irish pub for a nightcap. Sammy was waiting for them outside when they arrived. Sammy pushed open the pub door to find the bar packed and celebratory on the eve of Patriots Day. A row of working-class men sat shoulder to shoulder, pints in hand and engaged in exaggerated exchange. Sammy headed straight for the bar. Upon seeing a familiar face, the bartender asked, "Is it yourself, then?"

"And my two suits," Sammy responded.

The bartender motioned for three drunken dockworkers to clear out so that Sammy and his guests could take a seat. Sammy was clearly VIP here. But Sammy told the dockworkers to stay put and bought them three pours.

"We'll sit in the snug tonight," he told the bartender.

The adjacent small room offered a bit of privacy in the clamor of the crowd. Paddy sat, sipped his pint, and felt the release of a long day escape him. He ordered a second pint, and then started on the whisky.

"What gives?" Paddy asked. "The bartender was about to throw those guys out to offer us a seat at the bar."

"I'm a face in here. Half of these chumps owe me money."

Mike and Sammy continued to throw barbs at each other, as relatives do. Paddy continued to enjoy the exchange between the cousins, but tonight he found himself in a tired, melancholy mood, and drunk on confession.

"We're all rich beyond our means," he started. "I don't care if Prohibition comes to an end. I'm ready to move on to better things."

Sammy, taken by surprise by Paddy's openness, agreed. "Things are definitely changing in this country. Personally, I don't care to be a loan shark for the rest of my life."

Mike couldn't believe his ears. "You two are fucking nuts. We're making a killing." Then he turned and disappeared to find the john, leaving his boss and cousin to continue the conversation.

"Have you ever thought about what you want to do in your next life?" Paddy asked, poignantly.

Sammy paused, and his demeanor turned inward. "I don't know, Paddy, but I think about the possibilities all the time," he said with a sense of longing. "Perhaps I'll head south, sail the Caribbean under starlit skies, and eventually settle in Key West and spend my days deepwater fishing for blue marlin with someone who enjoys great literature and the culinary arts. Maybe I'll change my name, grow a beard, gain weight on a diet of conch chowder and key lime pie, discard my suits and fedoras in favor of shorts and straw hats, drop the Boston accent, and learn Spanish, read Ernest Hemingway, and take on a new identity, morphing into someone—happy."

Paddy sat slack jawed. "Did you just…" But his words fell away and he fought to catch his breath. As if the Blarney Stone had fallen on his chest, Sammy's words had rendered Paddy unable to breathe or speak.

11

Thank You No Thank You

Jimmy woke abruptly. The ringing startled him, and when he reached to answer the phone, he knocked it to the floor. There lay Big Mike's gravelly voice, shouting at him to wake up. As he tried to retrieve the phone, his foot caught in the sheets and he fell out of bed, crashing down on it.

"You're late. Get down here now!" The phone clicked dead.

Marathon day had arrived. Jimmy placed the phone back on the nightstand and gathered himself. Sunbeams shot in through an east-facing window, illuminating him in a vivid light. He stood in his cotton underwear and caught his thin frame in a full-length mirror. There was no separation between his undefined chest and flat stomach. They locked together like dovetailed boards. His pale skin was taut with the elasticity of youth, stretched over sinewy muscles and snappy ligaments that held the strength of galvanized cables, capable of propelling him forward at unnatural speeds. His wasn't a man's body. His wasn't a boy's body. His was something in between—a body nimble and performing.

He felt good and ready, and dressed quickly in his black and white checkered running outfit. He tried to relieve himself, but soon gave up knowing that Paddy and Mike were impatiently waiting for him. He hurried out the door, but not before tucking the two pouches containing amphetamines and cocaine in his shorts. He glanced back at the bed and the feather duvet, and in a moment of peace he inhaled deeply, imagining himself slipping back in it later that night when his muscles ached and his feet were sore and blistered. It was going to be a glorious day, he decided. He shut the door and rode the elevator down to the hotel restaurant.

"You're late," Mike repeated, annoyed. "You're always late. For such a speedy guy you move like a fucking snail. Now sit down. This is serious business. We gotta have a little talk."

Paddy nodded his agreement.

"I ordered you a steak, medium rare, and three eggs," Mike said. "You're going to need the energy. And one more thing—you're welcome, Shit for Brains."

"Woke up on the usual side of the bed, I see." Jimmy, with his newfound confidence, was having none of it this morning, not even from Mike.

Paddy was nose-deep in the newspaper, reading an article about today's marathon. He scrolled the pre-race favorites, reading the names with growing agitation. "Not one word about you, Jimmy."

"It's okay, Mr. O'Donnell. They'll write about me tonight. They just don't know me yet."

"That's what I want to hear," Paddy said. "How do you feel?"

"I feel great. But I can't crap," he said, dryly.

"That ain't good." Paddy called to the waiter, "Bring this kid a cup of coffee. And make it strong. He can't crap." There was no jest in his voice. He was dead serious.

"But I don't drink coffee," Jimmy objected.

"You do now. Caffeine is a stimulant. It'll get your system working. You've gotta crap if you want to run fast, Jimmy."

"Yes, sir," he said. "So, what is it that you wanted to talk about?"

Paddy motioned to Mike, who smiled, but awkwardly so, as if it pained him. "We got a little surprise for you," he said. "Paddy and me, we've been thinking. You're a good kid, and we're doing everything we can to help you out. So, we bought you a little something for good luck."

"You've already done so much."

"Yeah, but this is special," Paddy said. "You know those horses at Schenley Oval? Those thoroughbreds run forty-miles per hour. You know how they can do that?"

"Training?"

"Yeah, that's right, Jimmy. Training. But sometimes training ain't enough, so they give them some magic powder called strychnine. Makes them run faster."

"What's strick-nine?" Jimmy asked.

"It's magic," Mike answered. "Didn't you hear a thing Paddy said? One of the horse trainers at the Oval swears by it. It makes your muscles contract and fire faster. Consider it a gift, shithead."

Paddy felt high on knowledge. "Get this, Jimmy, the winner of the 1904 Olympic marathon used it. Won him a gold medal. Mixed it with a little brandy and called it a cocktail. So, we're going to give you a little cocktail here and there along the course and you're going to drink it and run like a fucking thoroughbred horse today."

Running like a thoroughbred horse excited Jimmy. He was clearly in the throes of tremendous luck since arriving in Boston. He didn't mention the other magic he'd been given. The more magic the better, he thought.

"That sounds great, Mr. O'Donnell. I don't know what to say. I can't thank you enough."

"You can thank us after the race," Paddy said.

From behind, the waiter approached. "Sir, your coffee."

"Drink up," Paddy said. "That ain't no request." Within earshot of other diners, he hollered back at the waiter to bring a second cup. "Can't take any chances. He's got to crap!"

They drove the marathon route backwards to the start in Hopkinton. For Paddy and Mike, it seemed like an impossible distance to cover on foot. Paddy shifted his weight behind the wheel, uncomfortable. "Christ, we've been driving for forty-five minutes."

"I can't believe anyone would want to run this thing, much less watch it," Mike said, disgusted, seeing a few lawn chairs lined up, blankets spread out, and tables already set up.

Jimmy sat in the back, wired from the caffeine. He was intrigued by his hands and feet which seemed to have a life of their own, tapping the armrest and the floorboard. But the coffee also squeezed his insides terribly. The steak and eggs moved through him, rumbling louder than the growl of the Cadillac's engine.

"Christ, this is a long race," Paddy said. "Say, I've been reading up on strategy, things like that. Don't do anything stupid out there, okay? There's going to be a headwind. Tuck in behind the leaders. Let someone else do the work. Maybe take them in the Newton hills we just passed. You told me yourself you love running up hills. I read that's where the race is won."

Despite Catherine's advice to start out fast, Jimmy considered Paddy now.

Jimmy rapped the seat next him like a drum. "Newton hills. Tuck in. Don't go out too fast. Drink the cocktails. Okay, Mr. O'Donnell. I've got it. Good plan," he said with an elevated voice and a fast cadence. He was ready to launch, bouncing in his seat.

"You all right, kid? Maybe you didn't need that second cup."

The white steeple of the First Congregational Church in Hopkinton came into view. "We're here," Paddy said. "Look at all these runners milling about, bumping into each other like a bunch of headless chickens."

"Good God, they're hard to look at," Mike said.

"Say, I've gotta crap really bad," Jimmy shouted. "Let me out!"

155

The caffeine had done the trick, just as Paddy had told him it would. He hurried from the car and found a toilet inside the church and relieved himself. As he exited the stall, he considered how lucky he was. It seemed that everyone had his back, coming to his aid at the last minute with magic pills, white powder, and now the promise of cocktails along the course. He crossed himself in the name of the Father, the Son, and the Holy Spirit, and thanked God for all His magic.

Now he stood in a long line of runners, waiting his turn to register for the marathon. He felt rich and prideful to be here, appreciative that Paddy had given him a one-dollar bill, the entry fee for the marathon. He clenched it in a fist. In his pants were the two pouches. As instructed by his dad, he opened the first pouch and lifted an amphetamine from it, swallowing it with a cup of water. Then he opened the pouch with the cocaine, the gift from Catherine. She'd said to snort it. He rolled the one-dollar bill, sticking one end inside the pouch, and other up his nostril.

He felt a burning sensation and he teared up. But he also felt elated and empowered, and he twitched in line until his turn came to register. He unrolled the dollar bill and handed it to a nice lady in charge of registration. "My entry fee," he said, all smiles. "Jimmy Flynn, from Wilmerding, Pennsylvania. I'm nineteen years old and I'm so happy to be here."

"Good luck to you," she said, blowing residue off the dollar bill and then handing him race number 254.

Then, an official asked him to step on a scale so that they could record his weight. Jimmy happily asked the official if he'd hold the pouches, which he obliged. The scale registered 134 pounds.

"Good luck out there," the official said, handing him back his pouches. "Out of curiosity, what's in these?"

"Cocaine and amphetamines," Jimmy said without blinking. "My magic."

"I don't know what that is, but if it's magic then it must be good."

Thirty minutes later, Jimmy found himself on the starting line of the thirty-seventh annual Boston Marathon. Runners self-seeded, simply and innately understanding the hierarchy of the animal kingdom. Jimmy's cocaine and amphetamine-influenced confidence put him in the front row with the favorites, who eyed him with wary and cautious skepticism. He felt amazingly light and spry, jumping in place without knowing or caring why. A runner to his left advised him to save his energy, and Jimmy looked at him with dilated, crazed eyes and said yes, but continued jumping in place. From the east, clouds sauntered in like fluffy balls of cotton, their edges brimmed in silver against a brilliant blue sky. And Jimmy rabbit-holed into a trance watching coronas form behind them, his fixation so strong that he sensed his entire body rise up to meet the sun. Time had somehow stopped in his blind euphoria.

So, this is what it's like to be on the starting line of the Boston Marathon.

Then he felt the hand of someone pushing him in the back as the field surged forward anticipating the start, bringing him back to the *now*.

And the *now* was thick with runners' sweat and odor and angst. They vied for position on the starting line as time counted down. Five hundred spectators pushed in from either side with a suffocating presence. Atop a large, black sedan that would lead the runners out, the race director shouted a few final instructions, interrupted by ear-piercing feedback from the hand-held capacitor microphone. Jimmy looked to his left at the turret clock mounted on the white steeple of the First Congregational Church, its mechanical arm seemingly stuck before—*click*—striking twelve. And as it did, a puff of smoke rose from the starter's pistol, and the runners plunged forward with poetic symmetry and speed.

Jimmy, in his euphoric state, shot to the front, immediately gapping the field of 250 runners. Within a half mile, a small pack of favorites formed behind him. None gave chase to the unknown runner. None took him seriously. The seasoned runners had seen this stunt many times from rubes.

The early miles felt easy and he stretched his lead to several hundred yards to the dismay of the race director, who sat atop the lead-out vehicle, announcing Jimmy's unfamiliar name over the hand-held microphone to the cheering crowds.

But as they entered Ashland at mile five, the chase pack caught him. His legs felt heavy now, his breathing labored, and the euphoric feeling he'd had at the start was gone. He hadn't taken an amphetamine or snorted cocaine in nearly an hour. He reached in a pouch and took out a pill and choked it down without water. He waited. But the burst of speed did not come this time. He cursed his dad for not giving him better magic. He still clung to the lead pack for several miles until it became impossible, falling away by the time they reached Natick. Here, he pulled the other pouch from his shorts, but with nothing to snort the cocaine with, he shook its contents into his mouth until there was nothing left but white residue on his nose and cheeks. He cursed Catherine for not giving him enough magic.

Everyone had shorted him.

And where was Paddy? Where was the cocktail he was promised? He cursed Paddy too.

By the time he got to Wellesley College at mile twelve, he had lost over a minute on the lead group, which had thinned now. Two leaders were clear, dropping a half dozen others who spread out in front of Jimmy. He choked down another amphetamine, just as Paddy's green Cadillac rolled alongside of him. It had been impossible to weave through the runners early on in the race, but Paddy had finally caught up.

"Take this, Jimmy!" Mike yelled from the passenger's seat, handing him a small cup. "I just mixed it. A little brandy and strychnine. Take a good swallow, kid."

"I'm dying," Jimmy shouted, panicked and crazed. "I can't feel my legs!"

"You went out too fast!" Paddy yelled from the driver's seat. He was hot. "You idiot!"

Jimmy took the cup, drank the cocktail, and pushed on. A mile later, he could feel his muscles fire and contract, and the magic renewed. With Paddy and Mike closely following, he stopped in his tracks to tell them how happy he was and that he felt better.

"I feel better!" he shouted, a sardonic smile creasing his face, a portent of things to come.

"Don't stop to tell us!" Paddy shouted. "Are you nuts?"

And Jimmy was.

Mike added, "Why are you smiling?"

"I'm smiling?"

"Just keep moving, Jimmy! The hills are coming. You love hills. Your family and the dingers are waiting for you at the finish. Go!"

High on cocaine, speed, brandy, and strychnine, Jimmy picked off runner after runner when he got to the Newton hills, and not until he crested the last of the hills did he spot the two leaders.

Only six miles left. But the magic was working now in mysterious, vicissitudinous ways, and the two runners ahead appeared to suddenly split into four, and then the four split into eight, and he shook his head to set it straight, but the eight fractioned and he grew confused.

A mile later the sardonic smile returned, contorting his face. The crowd cheered him on; the runner with the dilated, ghostly eyes and the fixed stare.

He stopped again, and this time opened a residential mailbox for no apparent reason. He took out a letter, tore it open, and stared blankly at it.

Paddy stopped his car. "What in the hell are you doing, Jimmy?"

"This letter. Makes no sense," Jimmy said, delusional.

"Jimmy, you're in the Boston Marathon! Snap out of it!"

Mike handed him another cocktail; an extra special one. He'd slipped a pinch of heroin in the already flammable concoction without Paddy's knowledge. "Drink it!"

Jimmy did, and handed the letter to Mike.

"Get going, Jimmy! You're not far off the lead!"

And he turned and began to run at a fast clip as if nothing was wrong. But a mile later his gait shortened again. His legs began to seize up, reducing him to a mere hobble.

At Kenmore Square, with a little more than a mile left, he stopped again; this time in front of a traffic stop sign that, in his delusional state, he mistook for Paddy.

"I don't want to stop, Paddy! Don't make me stop!" But the object would not respond. And he became enraged, and kicked it. "Can I go now? I can win if you let me go."

Perplexed bystanders cheered him on, shouting for him to give it hell, and then, out of the crowd, a woman stepped forward and put a finger in his face. She yelled things unbecoming, and he thought it was Catherine, and it might have been Catherine, but his mind was gone and his vision blurred, and the blur screamed again and slapped his face, and this time he heard the plea to get moving, but he could not because the object he thought was Paddy clearly said STOP. And the green Cadillac once again pulled up from behind and strange noises came from it that Jimmy could not understand, and someone got out and turned him away from the sign and back onto the course and pushed him a second time and a third time while he stumbled until his feet found purchase, and he was running again, while the bewildered spectators screamed at him in a nonsensical roar, and he covered his ears in fear and consternation, viewing them in nebulous ways of color and mass, shouting and pointing, and cheering and jeering, and he ran and he ran and he ran until he made the last turn onto Boylston Street where the finish lay somewhere distant, kaleidoscopic in vision, as the masses of people framed and blurred the edges of his approach, his legs cramping, his back arched in spasm, his face inhuman, unrecognizable, and he ran and he ran and he ran through the tunnel of noise, until he knew no longer if he was running at all, and until everything went black and he went down and could hear no more.

And then peace…

Lovely peace.

In a dream, someone had him by the arms, pulling him forward. *But to where?* His legs stretched out rigidly behind him, unbending like two boards, his feet and toes plantarflexed, dragging, digging, and scratching the asphalt beneath him.

In a dream, someone dropped him, and he lay crumpled beneath muffled shouts and muffled screams, and then someone once again had his arms, pulling him forward. But this time, his chest abraded the asphalt. Though he felt no pain.

In a dream, cameras flashed and policemen shouted to steer clear and give him space.

In a dream, someone was prying his eyes open, but he couldn't see. Someone was yelling in his ears, but he couldn't hear. Someone was punching him in the face, but he couldn't feel. This was his catatonic reality.

In a dream, he looked down on his prostrated, hunchbacked body from ten feet above, then twenty, then fifty, his spirit taking flight now, above a melee where his parents turned him supine and knelt over his body; his dad pounding away at a stopped heart, shouting for help, while Paddy argued and Big Mike exchanged blows with race officials, and the dingers broke out onto the streets, running this way and that way and not knowing what to do or where to go or who to punch or who to console because in a dream their savior was dying.

And the savior succumbed to darkness, seeing nothing below him now even as his spirit took to the winds and into the ether.

But not before one final thought: *So, this is what it feels like to be at the finish line of the Boston Marathon.*

12

Chemistry Lessons
~ Arizona, 1993 ~

The first time I had sex was with Diana Prince, my court-appointed attorney, who identified as Wonder Woman. She was a real go-getter and her zest for physical want matched mine. She called herself an athlete. Certainly, her small frame suggested that. But after we woke the following morning, and had sex again, she lit a cigarette and smoked it in bed.

I was in over my head, but I liked being there in her presence. She placed the still-smoldering cigarette on the nightstand. She curled next to me, her sodden skin sticky on mine, a dark, pigmented areola with an anxious nipple poking out from under a fine, white sheet. Her charcoal-colored hair lay flat, its ends clumped with the sweat of our romp.

She reached for the cigarette and offered it to me. I took a drag and coughed. It made me dizzy and I told her so. She laughed at the novelty of my innocence.

She said, "Again, let's do it again." And I said, "Okay."

She took the top position, grinding me like stone to corn. Her hands clasped my shoulders, digging in, all nails, pinning me like her prisoner.

Welcome to manhood, Billy.

Now, I don't know where sound originates in the human body, but somewhere deep within her something began to percolate, a soft, low hum, so faint I could barely make it out. "Oh God," she whispered, biting her lip. She ground faster now, and that sound, that beautiful sound like a purr of a finely tuned motor, grew louder, welling inside. I was taken aback, her face grimacing like she was in pain. But she just kept on keeping on. The engine louder now. "Oh God, Oh God!" she said. By the time she reached three *Oh Gods*, she was whistling like a tea kettle, her eyes rolling back in their sockets like two white stones, demon-like.

"Did you...did you..." But she didn't respond. Instead, she collapsed, falling off the bed.

She'd blacked out!

She was up before I could offer my hand, crawling back next to me, pressing into me again, her hand flat on my boyish chest.

Damn, she whispered.

She turned on her stomach, sighed and stretched, and I walked my fingers the length of her backside now, admiring the sheen of her skin, and the tan line that wrapped her waist like a belt—the demarcation of public and private. I crossed over into the private. At this, she shuddered and purred.

I liked playing adult.

I was eighteen years old, a man in the eyes of the law, but still a child in other, theatrical ways, subjugated to influences beyond my control. As Alice Cooper once sang about being eighteen: "I'm in the middle, without any plans. I'm a boy, and I'm a man."

Basically, I was just overpowered by a libido driven by hormonal chemical reactions. It was simply my time. So, despite the charges brought against me by the State of Arizona, things were definitely looking up from a week ago when I had thrown myself a pity party, running at top speed for hours, trying to disappear and outrun my troubles.

The day of that run, when I'd returned home, I'd worn the fatigue on my face and body, my eyes distant and lost. I'd stood crooked in the kitchen, as my parents viewed me with disdain. A zombie, a blank canvas.

Dad had pointed out that I was fifteen minutes late for dinner.

"You're fifteen minutes late for dinner," he'd said. When Dad was hungry it was a national emergency.

I'd found my voice. "I'm fine, Dad. Thanks for asking." I was not in a civil mood. I was in a civil war.

His expression: angry.

Mom stepped in to defuse the exchange.

I weighed the decision to tell them that I'd been kicked off the cross-country team and received three letters rescinding scholarship offers based on my questionable character.

167

Then, for some unknown reason, deep-rooted in teenage angst I suppose, I said. "I'm eighteen, and I don't know what I want."

"What?" Dad asked.

"I said, I'm eighteen, and I just don't know what I want."

"Are you quoting Alice Cooper?"

"Of course I'm quoting Alice Cooper. I'm in the middle, without any plans. I'm a boy, and I'm a man."

"Goddammit, have you lost your mind, Billy? How about you get out of this kitchen and take a shower. Your Mom made enchiladas and they're getting cold. You may be eighteen but you act eight."

I turned to leave.

"And what's that in your hand?"

"A knife." I walked away without offering an explanation.

The hot shower left me in better spirits. I was out in five minutes and joined them for dinner. The aroma of enchiladas took away the sting of another worst day of my life, if only for a moment. I quickly assessed their mood. With cheese hanging from the corners of Dad's mouth, he was in a happier place.

I placed the pocketknife on the table.

"Your maiden name is etched into its handle," I said to Mom. "Read it."

She did, looking up now, stupefied.

"FLYNN," I said.

"I can read. I just don't know what to say."

I told her I'd found it during my run on the Arizona Trail. How its blade had flashed in the sun, like a beacon. "Do you think it belongs to you?"

"Likely your great-grandfather, James. There are no other Flynns in the area."

If only knives could talk. This one would tell the story of Jimmy Flynn and his attempted robbery of Paddy O'Donnell, the demise of Wilmerding, the 1933 Boston Marathon, and its cross-country journey to Oracle, Arizona.

I placed the knife back in my pocket and swallowed hard. My life was blowing up before my eyes. I wanted to use the analogy of a snowball, but in Tucson we talk about tumbleweeds—the dead creosote bushes uprooted and blown across the desert floor, gathering debris, and sometimes each other, joining forces like wayward ghosts, haunting everything in their path with skeletal frames and teething thorns. The incident at the state cross-country finals was so ridiculous that it reminded me of such a burgeoning tumbleweed, uprooted and pushed along by a hot wind spewed by bureaucrats, attorneys, and plain circumstance that made no logical sense, and only followed the wayward path of its own ghostly agenda.

I spilled it all. I told them that an awful woman named Ms. Dragenschits had driven down from Phoenix and suspended me from the cross-country team as a safety precaution for the welfare of my teammates. That it was out of the hands of Coach, the athletic director, and even Principal Stevens.

Then, from my other pocket, I produced the letters that I'd torn into pieces. I let them fall onto the table. "These are my scholarship offers. They've been rescinded. Each one questioned my character and wished me good luck in my future endeavors. I don't know how they heard about the incident, but I'm certain they don't know the truth. If they did, they wouldn't send me these letters, right?"

Mom reached across the table and put her hand on mine.

Despite a sometimes-awkward relationship I had with my parents, they always had my back. They recognized the gravity of my situation and that the tumbleweed was indeed at the door.

"We need to stop the bleeding," Dad said. "Your lawyer finally called. Go see her. In the meantime, I'll call Principal Stevens and give him a piece of my mind."

The next day I drove down to the courthouse to meet with my court-appointed attorney for the first time. She had a lovely, promising name—Diana Prince.

* * *

Diana Prince was the only daughter of a widowered, evangelist preacher who fancied himself after Billy Graham. As a child, she'd sit on the edge of her seat in the first pew, eyes wide, absorbing every God-channeled word that her father spoke. He'd passionately shout to his congregation about the evils of everything secular, that

America had lost its moral compass, slamming his fist into the podium to decry such horrific evils as racial integration, homosexuality, feminism, the erosion of the nuclear family, and of all things, evolution. He would do this while scratching his armpit, swaying back and forth, and jutting his chin out like an ape, gibbering that God had created man after Himself. Toward the end of each sermon, he'd ask Diana to join him on the altar. He'd remind his congregation that children are proof of God's love, and it was their inherent duty to protect them from these prevalent evils that threatened their very existence.

He lived by his word, homeschooling her, shielding her from a corroding public school system that tolerated immorality and blasphemed God.

She studied diligently, and at the end of each day he'd reward her with an hour of television. She'd excuse herself to watch *Wonder Woman* for all the reasons a child might. Except, Diana was no ordinary child.

She recognized that Wonder Woman was a unique character, one without peer. Wonder Woman was fierce, feministic, and independent.

Diana's father would not approve of such a character, so she kept these observations close to her heart. Until one day, she discovered that she and Wonder Woman shared the same name: Diana Prince.

Her fate was sealed. Diana Prince, the child, would become Diana Prince, the superhero. She ran to her father and told him of the coincidence.

He dismissed her. "How cute."

"It's fate!" she said. "I'm meant to save the world."

171

But her father shrugged. "She's not real, Diana. She's a cartoon character. And besides, what do little girls know about saving the world?"

The question troubled Diana. Her dad tried to save the world every Sunday, and failed miserably with his inept words. Wonder Woman, on the other hand, succeeded in every episode. She stomped her feet, as children do, and shouted, "I want to save the world!"

"You, sweetheart, should be a lawyer."

"Lawyers save the world, Daddy?"

This made him laugh, but the thought of his daughter fighting crime and sending criminals to jail also made him happy.

For many years after, Diana would lay sleepless in bed, rehearsing closing arguments with juggernaut intelligence, for when she would save the world from injustice.

This drive would culminate at age twenty-five, when she was the youngest in her class to graduate from law school, take the bar examination, and be hired by the Tucson Municipal Court System as a public defender, making forty-five thousand dollars a year, nearly twice as much as her father had ever made. She purchased a top floor condo in the affluent Tucson foothills, and in the evenings, she'd sip margaritas on her patio, looking out at the twinkling city lights, imagining all the criminal activity that was surely being committed, excited to wake to a new day and save the wrongly accused.

Early on, she was very motivated. Then she began working her caseload, her fat files, and realized that the thugs she was defending *were* indeed criminals. Her closing arguments always fell short, her clients were always found guilty, and ultimately, she felt the chief role of her position as a public defender was to simply plea bargain and negotiate a lesser sentence. Soon, she became disenfranchised with her mission to save the world.

That is, until William Ball walked through the door of her courthouse office.

Diana looked up from a stack of files so thick she could barely see over them. She quickly put on her best face, smiled, stood up, and extended her hand. She wasn't sure what she saw in him, perhaps the handsomeness of youth, or the mercy of an athlete wrongly accused. But she took one look at him, and said, "I can save you, William Ball."

* * *

I was not a good student. I got a D in chemistry and often slept through class because it was right after lunch when the tryptophan coma kicked in. I'd unsuccessfully fight the weight of my eyelids while drooling on my desk, waking up moments later with a sudden burst of motion that scattered my books, much to the amusement of my classmates. But despite this, I did learn a few things. I learned that when one element is introduced to another element it forms a compound, and strange, or wonderful, or horrible things can happen. Sometimes, nothing happens. Sometimes, things bubble over or blow up. And sometimes fire ignites.

What I didn't understand was the mechanics of attraction, how elements conspire to spark raw, physical impulses, the way a cold wind slaps one's face, flushing cheeks and dilating eyes. I didn't understand how a spark in a woman's eyes, a handshake held longer than it should, and the fragrance of her morning bath could linger and cause such an intense reaction.

But all of this happened the first time I met Diana Prince. And it didn't make sense. We had nothing in common, other than my freedom—which I guess is saying a lot.

I was eighteen. She was twenty-five. I was still in high school. She had graduated law school. She was in a position of power, and I was at her mercy. She was a real adult, and I was just playing one like in the lyrics of that Alice Cooper song.

We were anything but equals, but perhaps that was the attraction. Perhaps our opposite, yet complementary qualities, were the AC/DC in this strange reaction that disregarded sensibility and all things ethical.

At my age, I rarely interacted with anyone professional, other than my teachers, who were all much older and tired looking. But Diana was lively, even as she sat behind her desk in a well-fitting blue blazer and a white silk top that covered a thin, athletic build. Her hair was cinched, with two wispy strands that hung and curled on either side like gift wrapping.

I can save you, William Ball.

She motioned for me to sit down. I did so with my hands in my lap, looking for signals in her expressions as she perused my file. She smirked and then chortled.

"Amused?" I asked.

"I'm dumbfounded. It's the weakest case I've ever defended."

"It is?"

"Just when you think you've seen everything." She looked at me with lively eyes. "You are truly a danger to society, Mr. Ball. How did you do it?" she asked, laughing.

"It was easy. The perfect crime," I said, playing along. "I removed my shorts because I'm sick in the head and I sought to expose myself to my family, my girlfriend…" I paused. "Ex-girlfriend, and complete strangers, for no other reason than my personal gratification. Apparently, that's against the law. Who knew?"

"Who knew?" she echoed. "Unfortunately, that's not the real issue." Her tone changed. "The misdemeanor charge will be easy to get dismissed. You have no record. But what happened at the finish line?"

"I stumbled and fell. That's all I remember."

"The report says you grabbed and held on to a ten-year-old girl to shield yourself. That she screamed for you to let go, but you wouldn't. That you kept her against her will."

"That isn't true," I said, indignantly.

"The prosecution has a witness who says otherwise."

"I reached for something, for someone, to stop my fall. It happened so quickly. If I did touch her, I certainly didn't mean to."

"What we have here is a very upset father who pursued charges against you. And since it happened on the grounds of an elementary school it complicates the issue in the eyes of the State."

"Who's the witness?"

"Can't say. The witness is protected during this pre-trial phase. Do you know if there's a videotape of the incident? That would trump any heresy from a witness."

"There was a television reporter there," I offered.

"I already checked, but he didn't have you on camera once you crossed the line. All he had was shaky footage of you approaching with your…well…your penis flipping around, and a huge…smile on your face, with your arms in the air like a real champion, and people gasping and hollering and laughing. He said he could hear the girls working the finish line screaming for their lives as you approached them. Jesus, Billy. You really did it, didn't you? You're famous."

"For all the wrong reasons."

"I read about it in the Sunday newspaper. It was a big deal, the state championship and a local runner competing for the title against that other young man, the good-looking one. What's his name—Christmas Day?"

"Yeah, Christmas Day. Memorable name and chiseled face. Total dick."

She laughed. "For what it's worth, I felt sorry for you. And when your case appeared on my desk, I felt twice as sorry because it shouldn't have ever come to this."

"But you're going to save me, right? That's what you said."

"Of course. Us runners, we have to stick together." She stood and hiked up her skirt several inches to showcase her legs. "Wonder Woman legs. Don't you think?"

She was coyly playing me, and I was confused by this game, by this adult, who took no shame in showing me her legs. And I shook my head with unsavory thoughts.

"So, can you get the charges dismissed?" I asked, focused and back on point.

"That's what I do."

"Is that something you do often?" I pressed.

"William—"

"Billy."

She looked at me squarely, clearly in charge. "You were late. I'm hungry, and I'm buying. Follow me and we'll talk."

We climbed into her car, a black BMW. "Have you ever ridden in one of these?"

"I prefer something that regularly breaks down. I drive a '76 Malibu."

She pulled out of the parking lot and turned onto Oracle Avenue, punching the gas pedal as my head snapped back in response. "I love power, don't you?" she shouted.

At lunch, we sat on a red Saltillo-tiled patio of a Mexican food restaurant, shaded with pink bougainvilleas. Our table overlooked the city, and I confessed my fear and lack of faith in the legal process, telling her I had already felt the fallout of the charges, using the tumbleweed example, and how everything in my life had been turned upside down because of the incident.

She reassured me that things would be fine. "You're a man with a clean record. You're a man with a bright

177

future." While Dad often *told* me to be a man, Diana actually *called* me a man, and every time she used that word, my chest grew large and eclipsed my high school self, the kid who struggled with insecurities, tormented by an unknown future. And perhaps I was a man, finally.

I'd grown up quickly since the felony charge, especially as I considered my younger teammates, the Fly Five. They weren't men in the eyes of the law yet, nor public opinion.

Jack Ash claimed to have lost his virginity on multiple occasions, which didn't make any sense at all. I wanted to call him out, but I never did because his stories were so entertaining. The splendid affair would always take place with a complete stranger with whom he shared an acute magnetic attraction in a semi-public setting, like the back of a bus, a park bench, or a holiday party. The ambiguities always made it impossible to confirm such acts. Jack was handsom and gregarious, and girls would steal looks when he wasn't paying attention. So, I had no doubt it would happen sooner than not, but when it did, I doubted anybody would ever believe it.

Tuba enjoyed shoving quarters up his nose to win bets. Basically, he'd ask for a quarter and say, "If I can stick this up my nose, I get to keep it." Few doubted that he couldn't, but took the bet to witness the absurdness of a fool. Often, he'd stick a quarter up each nostril and make fifty cents. And occasionally he'd stick two quarters up each nostril, which he considered lunch money. That was a stretch for him, and it stung so badly that he'd tear up during the act. But a dollar was a dollar and worth every eye-stinging teardrop. He had his sights on eight quarters if he could ever find a person who'd take the bet. Once, when Kathy Zanath, his history teacher, caught him in the act of ramming quarter number four up his nose, she pleaded with him to stop before he damaged his septum. "Your head is not a piggy bank, Tuba. Do you understand? Now please put down that quarter and wash your hands." She then called his mother to ask if she could see his Individualized Education Plan because she couldn't find it in his school file. Tuba's mother replied, indignantly, "My son is not retarded." To which Mrs. Zanath responded, "Are you sure?"

Piper Cox weighed 110 pounds. He rarely said anything, and if he did, he usually mimicked Loony Toons characters like Bugs Bunny, Daffy Duck, and Bullwinkle, which made him so irritating that he was impossible to be around. Once, warming up for a meet, he ran behind me and Charlie, saying "beep beep" like the fucking Road Runner. I wanted to punch him in his fucking beak, and when I told him so, he replied like Foghorn Leghorn: "That's a joke, I say, that's a joke, son." And so, I did punch him, and then he mimicked Porky Pig: "Th-th-that's all, folks!" Looney Tunes was the only language that got through to him. There was something seriously wrong with that kid.

And Henry Fly, the transfer from California, thought he could buck the social status of a lowly cross-country runner. He wore a bright orange Polo shirt nearly every day, and rarely removed his aviator sunglasses. He gelled his hair and stood with brimming, wanton confidence that was never matched by his actions, especially when it came to girls. He tried really hard to look like he wasn't trying

179

really hard, causing him incredible anxiety and ill-timed gas. Henry Fly was a sad example of hope, who despite trying harder than anyone, he had no friends other than us, his teammates. And, sadly, we were ordered by Coach to like each other.

So, yes, I truly liked it when Diana referred to me as a man, because when I compared the label to my teammates it certainly fit.

After lunch, Diana drove me back to the courthouse, and asked why I drove a pink muscle car. "It's red," I said in my deepest voice.

***

The following day I ran with Jack Ash before school. I told him that the prosecuting attorney had a witness and that the one thing that could trump that witness was a video of the incident. And that's when Jack stopped cold in his tracks and shouted, "Dude! There *is* a video! The race director said so. He said Jeremy Sommers' mom had recorded it with her camcorder." Jeremy Sommers was a runner from a rival school in Tucson. "Said they were going to look at the tape to see if you'd pushed Christmas into the cactus patch, but I guess when you admitted it—"

"I never admitted it!"

"Well, they *said* you admitted it. I guess they never asked to see the tape, given that."

"And you're just telling me about this now?" I said, incredulously. I didn't know whether to strangle Jack or hug him.

"Sorry, man. I've been sort of busy," he said. "Jenny Ledge has been taking up all my time. I think she wants to do it, if you know what I mean."

"Not really," I said. "Say, do you know if Ms. Sommers taped the finish line, too?"

"Dude, I have no idea. I just remember the officials telling Coach they had tape of the incident. Coach never asked for it. I guess he forgot, since you admitted it and all."

"I didn't—"

"Yeah, yeah, admit it!" he corrected.

Ms. Sommers' address was listed in the phone book. And Jack, being a great friend, and now guilt-ridden with obligation, offered to obtain the videotape from her. He didn't call. He simply drove to her house and knocked on the door.

Hours later, Jack hand-delivered the tape to me. "I didn't even have to ask for it," he said, boastfully.

The next morning, I blew off school again and drove down to the courthouse to see Diana. Going through security always caused me anxiety. More so today. When I sent the tape through the metal detector, I asked the Samoan guard if the x-ray would harm it, but he merely grunted at me. A minute later I stood in Diana's office with the tape in hand that would exonerate me.

"Okay, Billy. Let's see what we've got here." She pushed the tape into a VCR and hit PLAY on the remote.

The quality of the tape was poor, and Ms. Sommers had a shaky hand, but she had captured the collision between me and Christmas going down in the cactus patch. I made my case that I hadn't interfered or tripped him. "This is going to vindicate me," I said, excitedly.

But Diana reminded me of the real issue—the finish line. We watched and winced with every step of my naked ass running away from Ms. Sommers' camera. A few frames later Ms. Sommers zoomed in on my butt and could be heard saying, "Oh my! What a nice bottom that boy has." Diana glanced at me and winked, and we both laughed. But Ms. Sommers had indeed captured me stumbling into the chute.

After that, things were less clear. Blocked by scattering volunteers, we could only see my head moving through the chute. The young girl that I had allegedly grabbed and hid behind was never in frame. Diana rewound the tape over and over, studying it. Then her face lit up. It was clear to her that after I'd fallen and gotten back up, that I'd moved through without stopping.

That Friday, she asked to meet with me again. A celebration was in order. After showing the prosecuting attorney the tape, he agreed his case was weak, and that at his earliest convenience—meaning the following week because of the Thanksgiving holiday—he would drop the case. Diana took this as an absolute victory, and wanted to meet over dinner to deliver the good news. We met at the Mexican food restaurant again, and this time the view was like no other. My eyes were no longer clouded with worry. Instead, I took in the city lights that sprinkled to life against the backdrop of blunted color as the sun lost its grip on the day. "I'd like to buy you a margarita," Diana said. "But the legal drinking age is twenty-one."

"I can do time as an adult, but I can't drink," I said sarcastically.

"There's a lot of hypocrisy in the world, Billy."

"I won't tell anyone," I assured her. "You saved me."

"I did." As she said this, her face lit up, her eyes capturing the pinpoints of the city lights. The sweet-smelling fragrance of the bougainvillea hung in the air.

She ordered the margaritas.

It takes three things to make fire: oxygen, heat, and fuel. For us, the oxygen was the relief we felt now that the case was over. We could finally breathe. The heat was our spirited, eager youth—lustful, craving, intoxicating. And the fuel was the margaritas. Potent devils!

One margarita led to a pat on the leg that turned into an exploratory stay.

Two, and the stay turned into a rub.

Three, the rub turned into a match-strike, igniting our sensualities and indiscretions.

I finally understood chemistry, the rush of adrenaline that made my heart pound, and the flood of dopamine that rewarded my brain with feelings too easily mistaken for love.

And that's how I lost my virginity to my attorney, Diana Prince. Wonder Woman.

13

No es mi culpa; solo soy un adolescente estúpido

My parents say that all teenagers are stupid. They say it's not our fault because the adolescent brain is still growing, adding connectors, and while it understands the difference between right and wrong, it's overly influenced by raw emotions. Until it prunes itself of unnecessary neurons and becomes more efficient in adulthood, we practice risky behavior and do stupid things.

So, while my parents boasted and sometimes fought over whom I most resembled, which characteristics and traits each had passed down to me, neither was willing to claim my brain until they saw the adult version of it.

I drove home from Diana's with that thought in mind. It wasn't completely uncommon for me to stay out overnight, but I'd never lied to my parents about my whereabouts. With Diana hanging on my shoulder at the restaurant, I'd called them from a payphone and done exactly that.

I felt invigorated and renewed, and craned my neck out the window to feel the cool morning air sweep through my hair. The desert sparked and came to life. A passing shower had left patches of low-hanging clouds butted against the craggy base of Mount Lemmon. They appeared lively, like fields of cotton. I pulled my head back in the car wishing I had a convertible, something I had been dreaming about for years.

Maybe today's the day I take your top off.

I continued the drive north on Highway 77, passing a roadside stand of pumpkins.

Charlie.

Pumpkins always reminded me of her. She'd tried to grow them in her backyard since she was six years old, and not once did she succeed. It might sound like a small thing, but to Charlie, it was not.

I turned the car around and purchased a pumpkin, placing it in the passenger seat, securing it with the seatbelt, and talking to it occasionally for good measure. And damn if it didn't talk back, asking me if I was going to tell Charlie that I'd slept with my attorney.

Is that bad? Will Charlie be angry?

When I arrived home, I called Jack Ash. "Bring your blowtorch. We're going to cut the top off of my Malibu and road trip to Mexico. I'm free. The charges are being dropped."

"We need to invite the Fly Five," he said. "State champions or not, this is a cause for celebration."

"One more thing," I said. "If my parents ask, tell them I stayed with you last night. I'll explain later."

Jack contemplated the ask. "Tell me you did it," he said. "With Rigby?"

"No, not with Rigby," I said. "We're done. Just come over."

Before I hung up, Jack asked me if I'd heard about Tuba.

"What's up with Tuba?"

"He was running in the desert this morning..."

***

For all its beauty, Southern Arizona is still a wild, lawless wasteland; so sparse, it attracts unsavory characters and drug smugglers. So, when Tuba was out for a run, and saw a twin-engine plane flying low, circle, and drop a dozen black bags out its side, he backed off, as instinctively as if he'd heard the rattle of a western diamondback. Such is the risk of running in the remote desert.

Camouflaged under a palo verde tree, he considered high-tailing it out as fast as his legs would take him. But Tuba, the kid who would shove a quarter up his nose to win a bet and risk a deviated septum, was an opportunist and couldn't help but see the business opportunity. One bag had stuck on the plane's door. It dislodged a full fifteen seconds later than the other bags, landing just fifty yards from where he stood. He cautiously moved in its direction. On impact, the bag had split its side on a cholla cactus.

Marijuana plants spilled out like entrails. Their sugary, crystallized buds shimmered like diamonds in the low scrape of the morning sun. He'd already be dead if anyone saw, but the plane was long gone and there were no immediate perceived threats. He tucked his shirt and stuffed handfuls of the plant into it, and then ran as fast as his legs would take him back to his car.

Tuba could run a five-minute mile, and he was exactly that far away by the time three groundcrew members came for the bag. Seeing it hung up on the cactus and torn open, they had no reason to suspect any of the plants had been removed by a passerby. Until they saw the swish of a Nike footprint in the dirt. They would not give chase. They too were looking to make a quick escape.

* * *

I showered and took a seat at the dinette table. Mom had made me a tuna sandwich, but I didn't want to stick around. I held the pumpkin in one hand, steadied it against my belly, and snatched the sandwich with a quick thank you.

"You're not going to stay?" she asked, incredulously.

"I've got to see Charlie."

Her eyes expressed the sadness of any parent relegated to the back of their kid's priorities. She was really going to miss me when I went to college next year, and it showed in these acts of kindness that followed me around the house. She still insisted on doing my laundry, feeding me, and vacuuming and cleaning my room. And, sadly, I allowed it.

Guilt is gravity, but its pull didn't match my need to find Charlie, and so I rushed out the door.

I carried the pumpkin with the importance that some boys might carry a bouquet of flowers. I wanted to share the good news of my legal case, but I needed to give her the pumpkin, which might seem silly, but it meant something to me and I hoped it would mean something to her.

I rang the doorbell, but nobody answered. I searched the backyard, but she wasn't there either. I spotted the failed pumpkin patch. The vines had grown, but only prenatal babies hung from them, having given up before their time. I understood why they made her feel so sad. They *were* sad! I returned a few minutes later with Scotch tape and fastened the pumpkin to a vine.

Jack Ash arrived an hour later with a blowtorch in one hand and a grinding wheel in the other. "Let's get busy!" he said.

"Let's do this!"

"Don't you have something to tell me?" he asked.

But I cut him off, pointing at Mom, who stood behind me, arms crossed.

Jack rolled his eyes. He'd have to wait.

Shortly thereafter, the rest of the Fly Five arrived.

Jack flipped a clear-plastic welder's mask down over his face, then approached the Malibu with the fiery blowtorch like a warrior going into battle wielding a sword.

It was the end of an era for that car. In its glory days, it was a hungry, mean-looking animal whose engine roared thunderously under the weight of my foot. But now it looked like a defeated beast, readied for execution.

Dad came out to watch, and to witness. He shook his head disapprovingly, as if confirming his thoughts that all teenagers are indeed stupid.

Jack cut into the frame with abandon, and all went swell until the roof sparked and caught fire, but Piper Cox quickly extinguished it with a garden hose. When we were ready to pop the top, each of us grabbed a hold and lifted it off. Then we sat back and admired our work, as if we'd accomplished something worthwhile.

"What if it rains?" Piper asked.

"I hadn't thought of that," I said. "Does it rain in Mexico?"

"And it's still pink," Henry Fly pointed out. "That's going to be a problem."

"It's not pink," I said. "It's red."

"He's right," Jack said. "It may have been red. But it's pink now."

"Five guys in a pink convertible." Tuba shook his head. "We've got to paint it."

Piper wasn't following, but Jack whispered a foreign word in his ear. "Girls."

An hour later, while Jack smoothed out the metal edges, the four of us returned from the hardware store with a case of green spray paint.

There was no turning back now. When we finished, Tuba was the first to speak up.

"It's perfect," he said.

To me, it looked like a can of worms.

"¡Aquí vamos, México!" Jack shouted.

"Pronto."

After the Fly Five left, Charlie showed up with the pumpkin I'd placed in her patch. She wore an orange, fuzzy sweater that her hair clung electrically to. She looked fully charged. "Did you have anything to do with this?" she laughed.

"Must have been the Great Pumpkin, Charlie."

"This made my day," she said. "I thought I'd grown it. Then I saw the Scotch tape."

"Anything for you, Charlie."

She punched my arm.

"Is that your car?"

"What do you think?"

"I think…I love it!"

Charlie and her zest for life. There was no equal.

"Let's take a ride and catch the sunset," she suggested. "I love convertibles."

We drove through town, past Biosphere 2, and into the desert as the sun bled red. Charlie made a comment about that *new car smell.* I loved her perspective.

I told her about the case. "I'll be free next week," I said.

The Malibu chugged up a hill, spewing white smoke behind it, and we stopped at an overlook with sweeping views of the desert.

It was time to celebrate. She carried the pumpkin to a high ledge with a hundred-foot drop. I followed. She handed it to me, and I knew exactly what to do. I reared back and heaved it with all my might into the void,

191

watching gravity take hold, falling, falling, falling until it hit and exploded onto the rocks.

"And that ends the life of another pumpkin." I crossed myself.

Charlie mimicked me. "Humiliating."

"Pumpkins are the most humiliated fruit in the kingdom."

"Worse than a banana?"

"Well, sure. You can peel a banana, which I'm sure is embarrassing if you're the banana. Laying there all naked and cold on the kitchen counter for the rest of the bunch to see with no hands to cover yourself. If you're lucky someone smears you with chocolate to cover your shame. But imagine being a pumpkin. Growing up all cozy in a pumpkin patch alongside your pumpkin patch friends, just minding your own business, growing bigger and rounder each day, getting lots of nutrients, basking in the sun, maybe feeling good about yourself because you're clearly the best-looking one in the patch. Life is good, right?

Then, some overzealous kid with snot running down his nose rips you from your vine for that very reason. Next thing you know you're rolling around in a dark car trunk, scared and alone. Later that day, that same snot-nosed kid pulls out a knife and freaking scalps you. Ouch! What the fuck? He reaches inside and pulls your brains out. He laughs. But that's only the beginning. Then he carves googly eyes and a one-toothed smile on your face, and puts you outside for all to see.

But it gets worse. He lights a candle, places it in your head to accentuate your new, stupid face. Trick-or-treaters drop by, point, and laugh—at you! Days go by. Cold nights pass, and you start rotting. You stink. Your face sags and your eyes droop until one day you hear someone say, "It's time." *It's time for what?* What could they possibly do to you that hasn't already been done? But ol' Snot Nose picks you up, carries your soft, emaciated body down the driveway, and smashes you to smithereens on the street. Now, that's humiliation."

Charlie nodded. "This one certainly went out with a bang. Great toss. Orange fireworks against a blood red sky. How about that?" Charlie beamed.

"I liked it," I said with enthusiasm.

Charlie knew how to celebrate.

Though perhaps a bit too soon.

* * *

On Monday, I received a call from Diana who needed a signed affidavit from Ms. Sommers, stating the videotape was hers in order to file a motion to dismiss. Just a formality, she assured me.

I called Jack Ash to give him an update. "My attorney is visiting Ms. Sommers today to get her to sign an affidavit."

Silence.

"Jack?"

"She can't do that," he finally said.

"Why not?"

"I…"

"You what? You said she gave it to you. That you didn't even have to ask her. What's the problem?"

"I never said she gave it to me. I *said* I didn't have to ask her for it—because I didn't ask her for it." He cleared his throat. "I, uh, stole it."

"You what?"

"I stole it," he repeated. "Nobody was home and I knew how badly you needed the tape. I walked in and removed it from the camcorder."

I was hot now, comprehending the gravity of his actions.

"I was doing you a favor, Billy. I don't even know what an affidavit is. How would I know that? I'm just a stupid teenager."

I hung up and immediately called Diana.

"William! Are you crazy? We can't introduce stolen evidence. This changes everything. Not to mention, your friend is going to jail."

"Not if you don't say anything. The prosecuting attorney is out until next week. We can put it back. Then we can ask for it legitimately."

Diana thought about this. "Fine. But this is crazy, William. If Ms. Sommers finds it missing, you're screwed."

* * *

It's not every day one's attorney agrees to a crime, but that's exactly what Diana did. That she had slept with me weighed into the decision. She kept talking about violating ethics laws, and the possibility of getting disbarred. So, now she was hedging her bets and doubling down.

The next morning, Jack Ash and I drove back to Ms. Sommers' house, snuck in, and placed the tape back into the camcorder.

That afternoon, Diana drove to Ms. Sommers' house, relieved.

Ms. Sommers greeted Diana at the door, but didn't invite her in. She was a God-fearing woman with pursed lips and a bun-topped head. She wore a purple Mumu and stood cross-armed in a defensive posture, remembering her last interaction with an attorney ten years earlier that ended with a divorce. With a husky voice, she said, "I'm not feeling well. What can I do for you?"

"I understand you recorded the finish of the state championship race. I was hoping it might show something that would help Mr. Ball."

"Yes, I taped it. I told the race officials I taped it," she said, defensively. "But they never asked to see it."

"Well, the officials were interested in the crash that ended in Mr. Ball's disqualification. This is a very different matter, Ms. Sommers. This is about a criminal case of an incident that allegedly took place at the finish line."

"Ms. Prince—"

"Diana, please call me Diana."

"I was standing far away, watching for my son to finish. I don't think I can help you. Besides, there's personal stuff on that tape."

Diana had thought this was going to be an easy ask, and now Ms. Sommers was balking. "I understand, Ms. Sommers. I promise to personally return it when this is over. It's for Billy, after all." She pulled out the affidavit from her briefcase. "I just need the tape, and for you to sign this."

"That looks really…official."

"It's just a formality, Ms. Sommers. I know you want to do the right thing."

"Look, I'm running a fever. I'll call you tomorrow." She shut the door, leaving Diana without the tape, and without a signed affidavit.

* * *

One of God's little mysteries is how anyone communicated in 1993. It was usually done with voice messages left on answering machines that no one knew how to operate. I hadn't heard back from Diana yet, so I assumed the meeting with Ms. Sommers went well. But I called anyway, and left a message. "Just checking in," I said. "Heading to Mexico with my teammates."

My parents left for work, and one by one my teammates arrived. They tossed their backpacks into the trunk of the Malibu. Tuba threw two bags in.

"My mom made us left-over turkey sandwiches," I said.

Tuba pulled out a joint, and said turkey sandwiches are better high. He held it out for all of us to see.

Piper Cox, dressed in a Tweety Bird T-shirt, reached for it, curiously so, as if he was seeing one for the first time. He took hold, and held it to the sun. Expecting what, knowledge?

"You ever seen one of these before, Piper?"

"No."

"Well then, let's get this party started," Tuba said.

"Where'd you get it?" Piper asked.

"Little run in the desert this weekend. Like Tweety Bird, it fell out of the sky. I have more where this came from."

That was an understatement. One of his backpacks was stuffed with weed. He'd schemed a wonderful scheme. He'd sell it to the college students on Thanksgiving break in Puerto Peñasco. In a twist, his plan was to smuggle marijuana *into* Mexico.

Tuba lit the joint, took a hit, and passed it to Jack. Jack took a hit, long and deep, and when he exhaled, he coughed, and disappeared behind a cloud of smoke.

"Easy, Jack," I said. "It's not a competition."

Jack was still coughing when he passed the joint to Henry.

Henry pinched it between his pointer and thumb, and also took a long drag before launching into a drumming cough.

"It's hard to look cool when you're bent at the waist, coughing," I said to him.

I took my turn, and passed it to Piper. Once again, he held it up to the sunlight so that it silhouetted, and he twisted it in his fingers to catch all angles. He sniffed it before pursing it to his lips. The four of us pumped our fists, encouraging him, telling him to go for it.

Mind you, all of this was taking place in my driveway, and in clear sight of neighbors and anyone who happened to be passing by.

Piper took a hit. He didn't so much as cough.

"Piper, you didn't do it right," Tuba said. "You've got to really inhale and hold it down. Try again."

This time, Piper sucked hard. He held his breath, and looked at each of us for approval. And when he couldn't keep it in any longer, he exhaled exhaustively.

"Yes!" Tuba shouted. "That's more like it!"

"I don't think it worked," Piper said. "I don't feel anything." So, he took another hit.

"Dude, don't bogart the joint!" Tuba said.

We passed it back and forth until it grew so small it burned Jack's fingers. He tossed it out onto the street.

We were exaltedly stoned, and our stupid words became insanely funny because, in this realm of detached perspective, words took on new meanings that we couldn't make sense of. "It's like I've got a little standup comedian in my pants," Tuba said.

I couldn't remember the last time we'd laughed so hard—reflexively, to the point that my gut hurt even as I tried to stop.

"That is one ugly-ass car," Tuba said.

"You said you liked it," I reminded him.

"I was lying! This weed is like truth serum."

"You know what this car needs?" Jack said. "Personality!"

Piper grabbed a can of black spray paint and went to work on the driver's side door. When he finished, he stepped away, revealing an image of Speedy Gonzales. *"¡Arriba! ¡Arriba! ¡El ratón más rápido de México!"* he shouted. Proof that even a misfit like Piper, who had an unhealthy affinity for Looney Tunes characters, had a place in this world. We all lost it, and fell to the ground holding our guts as if bowled over.

From across the street, Old Man Baldwin appeared in his front yard, wielding a straight cane out in front of his crooked body, shaking it with his shaky hand, and weakly shouted, "You're a disgrace to your generation. You're all drug-smoking thugs!"

I straightened up quickly. The last thing I needed was him in my business and telling my parents. But, given my mental state, I answered, "We're not thugs. We don't do drugs. We're athletes, Mr. Baldwin."

Jet was at my side, and he started barking. He was fixated on the cane Old Man Baldwin was shaking. He darted across the street and grabbed hold of it. "The struggle is real," I said, watching them fight for it. But Jet lost interest and came back, happy to have played for a good minute. Old Man Baldwin shook the cane extra hard this time, calling him a bad dog, and threatened to have him locked up. But threats from an old man shaking a chewed cane only made us laugh harder.

"Stupid teenagers!" he shouted as he shuffled back into his house.

"I may be in deep shit," I said. "Good boy, Jet. You almost got that stick." I patted him on his head and he proudly looked up at me.

When the laughter subsided, Henry said, "Aren't we supposed to be in Mexico by now?"

"I'm in no condition to drive," I said. "I am so high!"

"Me neither," Jack said. "Let's just eat these turkey sandwiches and stay put."

Piper piped in. "I feel fine. I don't think it took." He said this so confidently that we had no reason to believe otherwise, even if we knew better.

So, it was settled. Piper Cox would take the first turn behind the wheel. We took our seats, with Piper adjusting the driver's seat so that he could see over the steering wheel. I took the passenger seat, and Jack, Tuba, and Henry sat in the back.

"*¡Vamonos!*" shouted Jack.

And Piper, at a speed so slow it didn't register on the speedometer, rolled into the street. He never saw the missile honing in.

Diana slammed on the brakes, avoiding a direct hit, avoiding Speedy Gonzales, but clipping the rear end. The impact spun the Malibu sideways, rocking it back and forth, wounded and creaking under its own weight. Then it settled.

The Malibu's frame had bent, and my door stuck as I fought to push it open. I crawled over the top, stepping down into a puddle of fluids that were leaking out. One by one, we managed to walk away, Piper holding his head where a nasty cut had opened.

Diana was out of her car now too. She had her back to us, assessing the damage. Her arms flailed, and she shouted God-laced obscenities with the fervor only her evangelical father could have matched. She sought out Piper.

"Look what you've done!"

But Piper was tending to his bloody head and didn't respond.

Old Man Baldwin had come out again, shouting something inaudible. Other neighbors filed out of their homes too, some running to offer help.

Diana looked for other prey. I was up next. "You're facing a felony charge. You can't just pick up and go to Mexico! I drove here as fast as I could to stop you."

I met her eyes, but I couldn't shake a ringing in my ears. Her words shot like spittle, and I shielded my face. Somewhere distant I heard sirens.

"I need a goddamn cigarette!" she said, rummaging through her purse. When she struck the match, it slipped from her fingers and landed in the mix of leaked fluids—and ignited.

I found my voice. "Run!" I screamed. "Run!"

We scattered in every direction as the flame grew legs and targeted the Malibu, igniting and engulfing it.

Charlie suddenly appeared. "What's happening?"

"That woman ran into us and blew up my car," I said, pointing at Diana.

The flames eventually subsided, and the chemical smell of burning tires and upholstery gave way to the smell of burning marijuana. Anyone with a nose smelled trouble, and Charlie raised an eyebrow. "I have no idea," I said.

Truly, I didn't. Then it hit me—Tuba!

Old Man Baldwin stammered over to the cops now, who were securing the area. He pointed a shaky finger in my direction. After that, it didn't take long for the interrogations to begin.

Piper sat on the sidewalk holding his head. His forehead ceased bleeding, but other wounds were about to open. Since he'd been the driver, the police kneeled in front of him now, and began questioning.

I'm not sure what was sadder: watching the police cuff and stuff little Piper into the back seat of the squad car, or watching the tow truck load the carcass of my Malibu on a flatbed. Neither left with fanfare.

An hour after the crash, Diana was still fuming. With purpose, she approached me and Charlie, and I lowered my head like a dog readying itself for a beating. Charlie rubbed my back.

She postured, arms crossed, studying Charlie.

"Diana, this is my best friend, Charlie," I said. "Charlie, meet my attorney, Diana Prince."

They surveyed each other.

"Diana promised to save me."

Charlie once told me that women share an innate language that men don't understand. It can be delivered in many ways: direct eye contact; a flat, cold voice; an imposing posture; and even subliminally. Charlie sensed a strong dislike for Diana, and not one to back down, she stepped forward to greet her, initiating a handshake, meeting her eyes. "Looks like she's doing a real bang-up job of that."

But Charlie was wrong about men not understanding. I understood their language perfectly.

I'm not stupid.

14

What the Hell?
~ Boston, 1933 ~

Death came easily for Jimmy Flynn. It was the living part that was hard. He was free now, weightless, as if holding onto a bouquet of helium balloons that raced skyward, taking him to beckoning light somewhere distant where the pale face of New England grew warm and blushed red, soft, and inviting like the Arizona sunset he'd seen on the magazine cover. It was the first time in his existence he'd known peace.

A final glance back revealed the chaotic scene of the hapless survivors; his father and mother kneeling beside the vacated body, his father pounding on its chest with all his might, his mother shouting at it to wake up.

Don't they understand that I'm no longer in there? Don't they get it?

But his father pounded away and his mother cried out, pleading for him to return to a place he was all too happy to leave; a place rife with daily struggle and despair and pain and pity, a place where the humans scurried from one meaningless task to another looking for purpose.

Maggie stepped forward and dropped a yellow daffodil on the body's chest.

None of this mattered to Jimmy-in-flight.

And still, his dad pounded away, and his mother cried out.

And damn it all to hell if it didn't work.

Weighted by the breath of life, he began falling back to Earth, as though each balloon in the bouquet was popping one by one. The restful, warm colors dulled, and the gray sky returned, and he fell and fell and fell, right back into that pale, cold body that he no longer needed or wanted, that lay supine on the grated, black asphalt just beyond the finish line of the Boston Marathon.

"Step aside! Give him air!" shouted a crazed doctor at the scene. "I've got a pulse. A pulse, I've got."

Mother fucker, I'm back.

Overdosed, he labored in a catatonic state, unable to open his eyes or speak. But he sensed, and heard intermittently, the chaos that surrounded him, and worse, he felt the pain return in waves, coming back compartmentally as blood galvanized his veins. Someone held his wrist, slapped his face. Then a sharp, stabbing pain announced itself in his ribcage as he choked and labored to breathe. And he cursed again and again, if only subliminally in his head.

Had Jimmy Flynn been able to open his eyes he would have seen his father kneeling over him, his face lined deeply with anguish. He would have seen his mother gripping his arm, struggling and refusing to let go, before eventually being pulled away, then crossing herself as he was loaded into an ambulance. He would have seen his sister, Maggie, standing off to the side with scared, unknowing eyes that reflected her yellow dress and a bouquet of yellow daffodils that she had planned to give him after the race.

He would have seen Big Mike and Paddy arguing with a race official who insisted that dragging a runner twenty feet to the finish line was against the rules, leading to disqualification and nullification of a fifth-place finish. He would have seen Paddy give up and walk away, before Big Mike, too angry to control himself, threw a right hook that connected squarely on the chin of a race official, buckling his knees and dropping him like a sack of Irish potatoes.

He would have seen the melee that ensued and the five cops that jumped Big Mike, as he stood his ground, then chased to higher ground, stepping up onto the base of a lamppost where he clung with one arm, swinging with the other one with savage abandon like King Kong swatting down planes. But they overwhelmed and brought him down, subduing him with a billy club chokehold, and eventually cuffing him and forcing him into a police car while he kicked and spat.

And he would have seen the dingers scatter like rats, unsure of what to do, guilty of nothing but hope, ignorance, and association.

* * *

There was a lot of sorting out to do after the race. Eventually, Paddy made his way back to the Lenox Hotel to settle his bets, a painful act under the circumstances. He considered welching because, despite the ruling from the race official, he vehemently disagreed with the outcome.

Sammy O'Sullivan was first to greet him.

"Tough luck about Jimmy," he said.

"He got robbed," Paddy said. "And now everyone wants to rob me."

"With all due respect, Big Mike dragged Jimmy across the finish line."

"Jimmy would have gotten up and finished. He's a gutsy kid," Paddy argued. "A fifth-place finish would have hedged."

"He was unconscious, Paddy. They took him away in an ambulance. He wasn't getting up to finish. Look, Mike meant well."

"Mike is as dumb as an ape. Punched the race official. Then he climbed up that lamppost, swinging at the cops. Did you see him?"

"It was a scene right out of *King Kong*," Sammy said. "Have you seen it?"

"No, but your big-ape cousin cost me money." Paddy spied the bettors who were arriving now. "Look at them. They're like vultures." He removed a cigar from his suit pocket, lit it, and blew a ring of smoke in Sammy's face. "Nobody has asked about Jimmy."

Sammy fanned the smoke away. "How rude…of me," he coughed. "How is the boy?"

"He's at the hospital. His old man nearly beat him to death. Broke his ribs."

"I think he was just trying to—"

"Kill him?"

"Revive him, actually."

"Well, he can't run with broken ribs. What good is he to me now?"

"The ribs will heal, Paddy." Sammy took out his notepad. "There will be other opportunities. In any event, let's get back to business. You owe me one hundred dollars."

Paddy paid him. "This means you have the honor of bailing Mike out of jail."

"Yes, of course, Paddy. I'll add it to the debt Mike owes me this lifetime."

"And as soon as you do that, we're hightailing it back to Pittsburgh in the morning. I've had enough of this town."

"What about Jimmy?"

"Jimmy's parents will stick around until he's released from the hospital. They'll take the train home. I'm moving them here to the Lenox later this afternoon."

"That's kind of you, Paddy. You are truly a gentleman of wealth and means."

Paddy brushed aside the compliment. "I don't feel like no gentleman today. I've got thirty dingers running around town that want to kill me. They're out for blood because they lost a few bucks." He shook his head. "I'm telling you, Sammy, this isn't the way I figured things would go down."

"Betting on the marathon rarely goes one's way," Sammy offered. "And mixing it with a cause is never a good idea. It's a combustible formula."

"Just tried to bring a little joy into the dingers' lives." Paddy turned to greet the wide-grinning vultures who were at his side now, looking for payment.

He exhaled another ring of smoke, and called to a waiter to bring him whisky.

"Sir, it's still against the law."

"Bring me some damn whisky," he shouted. "I'm Paddy O'Donnell!"

* * *

The following morning, Paddy warmed himself next to the lobby fireplace. A hangover was palpable on his swollen and flushed face. His suitcase lay next to him.

Sammy O'Sullivan walked in with Big Mike in tow. "I knew the race official. Nice man with a big headache. I gave him ten dollars and he dropped the charges."

A minute later, Jimmy's family arrived. They gathered around Paddy, looking for direction, looking for him to make sense of what had happened. But Paddy was 1,200 dollars poorer today, and was feeling unusually down. He sat quietly, leaving everyone uncomfortable in his presence.

Daniel was the first to speak. "Thanks for moving us here to the Lenox, Mr. O'Donnell. This is a fine hotel."

"Sorry about your boy, Mr. and Mrs. Flynn," Paddy said. "I understand he's in a lot of pain. But he'll be able to travel in a few days."

"Yes, he'll be fine."

"He nearly pulled it off."

"Almost, Mr. O'Donnell. Just twenty feet short."

"I don't know what else I could have done to get him to the finish line," Paddy said. "Twenty feet short."

"Twenty feet short," Big Mike echoed, nursing a swollen, purple eye.

Sammy reminded them that it's a long race and finishing is never guaranteed.

"I should have mixed a stronger cocktail," Paddy said, dismissing Sammy's comment. "It's my fault. He needed more strychnine."

"It's not your fault, boss," Mike said. "I did the mixing. I even mixed in a spot of heroin on that second cocktail. But not even that got him to the line. It's my fault, boss. Twenty feet short."

Paddy was copacetic. "It's okay, Mike. You did your best."

Catherine, working the front desk, overheard the conversation. She took a seat next to Daniel. "I hope you don't mind me interrupting. Look, me and Jimmy, we went for a walk the night before and I gave him a little bit of my own magic—cocaine. That stuff does wonders for me when I'm dragging at the end of the day."

"That was kind of you," Daniel said.

211

"But I shorted him," she continued. "A little extra would have gotten him to the finish line. It's my fault." She hung her head. "Twenty feet short."

"It's not your fault," Daniel said. "It's mine. I gave him some amphetamines at the pre-race dinner. Those pills gave me stamina when I worked at the factory. But they're probably expired by now." He too hung his head. "Twenty feet short."

"Plus, you broke his ribs," Mike said bluntly.

"Well, yes, I did that too," Daniel said. "I was…" He cleared his throat. "Trying to save his life. No man is made to run twenty-six miles. The distance must have stopped his heart."

"You nearly killed him," Mike said.

Behind Paddy, a waiter making the rounds asked if anyone needed more coffee. "I couldn't help but overhear," he said. "It's my fault. I should have given that boy a third cup." He lowered his head and walked away.

Paddy was moved, processing each of their accounts. "Don't you see what you've done?"

No one answered.

"I'm sitting here listening to each of you take blame. But you did your best to get Jimmy across the finish line, and I've got to say, I'm proud of you. I really am." The tough bootlegger from Pittsburgh found himself speaking earnestly. A tear rolled down his cheek. "I have to say, I love that kid, I really do. But clearly, he's just not good enough. Jimmy is the one to blame."

Sammy, the loan shark and Boston Marathon veteran, sat slack-jawed, hearing, processing the dysfunction of the conversation. He bit his lip. It was a gathering of well-intentioned, well-meaning idiots, the likes he'd never seen.

And in unison, as if conducted by a baton-wielding maestro, everyone chorused, "Twenty feet short."

* * *

The following day, Jimmy opened his eyes. A tall, lanky man stood at the foot of his bed with unkempt, bristled white hair and weighted jowls and wearing a white coat. With rapid, exaggerated movements, he was writing something on a clipboard. Jimmy examined him in a surreal manner, the way one might wake from a dream, before turning his observations inward.

He was dressed in a white gown, and most of his body was covered in white linens. The room itself was stale and undistinguished with nothing on the walls but white paint. Blinding lights shone down on him from a low ceiling. Jimmy squinted.

"Did I…make it? Are you…God?" His throat was dry and his voice was hoarse and he wasn't sure if God heard him. So, he tried again.

"Is this…Heaven?"

"You're awake. You woke up," the man said, delighted. "That's good. We need the bed."

Jimmy's vision blurred, and he suddenly felt too nauseous to reply.

"No, this isn't Heaven. I'm not God. And I'm not Saint Peter here to let you into Heaven. I'm your doctor." He talked fast and without direction, all the while scribbling something on the clipboard. "Welcome back to Earth, Mr. Flynn."

Jimmy tried to say something, but coughed and winced in pain.

"Don't talk, Mr. Flynn. You've got broken ribs. Talking and broken ribs don't mix. Breathing and broken ribs don't mix. You got broken ribs because you died. Your father beat on your chest like he was going to kill you, but you were already dead. So, I let him."

"Dead?"

"You were dead for two minutes, Mr. Flynn. You didn't have a pulse. Can you hear me all right? Are you deaf?" He scribbled *deaf* in his chart.

"I didn't…feel dead," Jimmy said with a weak voice. "But I feel…like I might die…now. My head…is killing me, and it hurts…when I…breathe."

"The ribs, Mr. Flynn. Don't talk. And trust me. You were dead. But your father saved you."

"My pops?"

"Yeah, he saved your life."

"But…you said…I died."

"You did. Your heart stopped. Are you stupid, too? I just told you that." He scribbled *stupid* in his chart.

"I don't think…I died. I could…sense…things. I could…see things."

"The brain can survive for minutes after the heart stops, Mr. Flynn. Neurons keep firing. That is, until the brain runs out of oxygen. Not fair, is it? You can still hear things. You can still feel things. So, let's say you die, Mr. Flynn—well, you did die, Mr. Flynn, and someone calls you an asshole after you've passed. You hear them loud and clear but you can't reply. You can't get the last word in. You can't tell them to go fuck themselves. Can't even stick up for yourself. So, you die, pissed off and humiliated, because everyone around you is calling you an asshole and you can't defend yourself."

Jimmy started to say something, but Dr. Sheets stopped him with a raised finger.

"Don't talk. You're lucky to be alive, Mr. Flynn."

"Someone...called me...an asshole? When I was dead?"

"Well, no, Mr. Flynn. I'm not saying anyone called you an asshole when you were dead. But I'm not saying anyone *didn't* call you an asshole when you were dead. Those fans of yours were pissed off that you had lost their money. My point is, Mr. Flynn, you couldn't tell them to go fuck themselves, despite yourself, because you were dead. You're lucky to be alive."

"Am I?"

"I guess that depends on the life you had before you died."

Jimmy pondered that. "Hey...did I...win?"

"The marathon?"

Jimmy nodded. It was the last thing he remembered before dying.

"No. You didn't even finish. The finish line, you didn't even get there. How could you win without finishing? Are

215

you *that* stupid?" He scribbled the words hastily in his chart, *that stupid*, and underlined them. "You didn't finish."

"Yes. I did."

"No. You didn't. I was there. You didn't finish, Mr. Flynn."

"But I saw myself…lying just beyond…the finish line." He fought for breath. "I finished."

"You what?"

"I saw myself…from up above."

"What do you mean, you saw yourself from up above? You were lying on the ground with your eyes shut. Dead. Dead. Dead! Maybe you're delusional too. Maybe I should add that to your chart." He scribbled *delusional* in his chart.

"I saw you…your white hair… and my dad…and my mom…all trying to bring…me back."

"You're nuts, Mr. Flynn. Maybe that's your problem. Maybe you're in the wrong wing of the hospital. You should be in the nut ward. Don't ever tell your doctor that sort of thing. You know why? Because I can certify you as a nut job. Then you know what happens? They take you away, put you in a straitjacket and lock you up. You get to spend the rest of your life in some nut house in upstate New York eating green beans, applesauce, and soup from a straw and drinking milk from plastic cups, talking about seeing things from up above and just confirming to everyone that you're a nut job. They'll never let you out, Mr. Flynn. Don't say those things. Not to me. Not to anyone." He scribbled *nut job* in his chart. He underlined it twice. Then he wrote *green beans*.

Jimmy nodded, understanding. It hurt too much to talk. It hurt too much to breathe.

"You were out cold, Mr. Flynn, and that big ape dragged you across the line. Got you disqualified. You fell short."

"Big...Mike?"

"Yeah, Mike O'Sullivan, the big ape. I had to give a police report. I never forget a name. When you collapsed, he ran from his car and dragged you across the finish line. Then, after we brought you back to life, he punched the race official who disqualified you. He made a run for it after he got jumped by the cops. Laughable really. I mean, you died and came back to life, and that was kind of funny on account I've never seen anyone come back from the dead like you, but that Mike guy made my day—under the circumstances, that is. He stole the show. I mean, after you stole the show by dying, that is. It was quite a scene."

A bouquet of yellow daffodils lay next to him. Jimmy motioned with his head, inquiring.

"From your sister. Maggie, right? She was in tears when they brought you in, but I told her you were going to be all right. She cheered right up. She left you those flowers."

"Yes...I recognize..." But Jimmy stopped short of finishing his sentence. He had a fleeting memory of seeing Maggie lay a daffodil on his chest when he lay dead in the street, but he didn't dare tell Dr. Sheets this now. He didn't want Dr. Sheets to send him away to the nut house. He didn't want Dr. Sheets to think he was a bigger nut job than—Dr. Sheets himself.

"Great kid, that Maggie," Dr. Sheets repeated.

Jimmy had had enough. This man was not God, he was not Saint Peter, and he was not an angel, though he might have been a liar, because even in his confused state he questioned if Dr. Sheets was a real doctor.

"Is this...Hell?" he asked. "I'm in...Hell, aren't I?"

"I guess that depends on the life you had before you died. Was it good?"

"I'm...feeling kind of...tired," Jimmy said, wishing, once again, that he was dead.

"Yes, of course you are, Mr. Flynn. You should be tired. You ran a long way, and you died for two minutes. That would make anyone tired. Get some rest, Mr. Flynn. And don't tell anyone you flew off to Cuckoo Land." He scribbled in the chart *Cuckoo Land*. He underlined it three times.

"Wait, Dr. Sheets," Jimmy said, before the doctor turned to leave. "Do you...have any idea...why I...died?"

"Yes, I do, Mr. Flynn," he said, looking down, reading his chart. "You were admitted unconscious, with severe hypertension, a high fever, sweating and convulsing. Your pupils were dilated. I have no idea what could have caused all that. It's not important. But I know why you died. You had a heart attack, Mr. Flynn." Dr. Sheets paused, holding his chin in his hand, being *doctor-like*. "Twenty-six miles is a long way to run, Mr. Flynn. Run twenty-six miles and you can die. You did die. I've been telling the race organizers that for years. It's why I show up at the finish line every year. You ran too far and your heart stopped. It's that simple, Mr. Flynn."

"I drank…a lot of coffee…that morning," Jimmy said, offering a cause.

"That wouldn't stop your heart, Mr. Flynn. Trust me, I'm a doctor. It was the distance that killed you. Now, here, I'll write you an opioid prescription for the pain. Opioids are good for you, Mr. Flynn. Those ribs are going to hurt for weeks."

"Thank you…Dr. Sheets. Anything else…I should know?"

"Yes," he said. "Stay away from coffee."

* * *

Jimmy's return to Wilmerding was to have been a joyous celebration, a party bigger than his sendoff. It was to have been a hero's welcome, a community cake baked and served up by the great Paddy himself. But when the Flynns stepped off the train four days after the marathon, nobody was there to greet them. Not even Paddy showed.

And while Paddy had gotten some of the ingredients right—hope, pride, and passion—things went awry when he'd baked in too much confidence while encouraging the hard-working people of Wilmerding to bet their meager savings on Jimmy. So, when Jimmy lost, the town lost; the cake collapsed.

The Flynns exited the train station and began their short walk to their WABCO-owned home. It was a pleasant spring afternoon with budding leaves, plenty of sunshine, and chirping birds that competed only with the din of the Westinghouse Air Brake Company. Which, despite the noise, was a welcoming sound of the still-employed. Jimmy moved gingerly, still stiff from the marathon, still nursing broken ribs. He stopped often to catch his breath. Dr. Sheets had been right though; he did love the opioids.

Daniel and Shannon walked ten feet ahead, carrying the family's suitcases. Maggie, eager to get home, was out in front, skipping along, as kids do.

"Look," she said. "Someone is moving! I bet they're going somewhere nice." She pointed to a sign that read "MOVE." Daniel paid no attention. Things more pressing were on his mind.

"This person is moving too," she said, pointing to a similar, handwritten sign placed on the lawn of the next house. She skipped down the street. "And that one, too."

All the signs read "MOVE."

Daniel had a sinking feeling by the time they'd walked three short blocks. Shannon sensed it as well, and the two of them eyed each other with consternation. Five minutes later, when they arrived home, their worst fears were realized.

A cardboard sign, crooked in their lawn, read "GO TO HELL!"

Daniel tore the sign in half, tossing it aside on the weedy lawn.

The front door was padlocked, and an envelope was taped to the adjacent window. Daniel didn't need to open the envelope to know what was in it. But, apprehensively, he did.

"They've finally done it," he said, his head hung. "It's a final eviction notice from WABCO. It says I'm to go down to the office. An officer of the company will accompany me back up here. He'll let us in. We can take whatever we can carry."

"Whatever we can carry?" Shannon said, incredulously. "What about our furniture, our silver and china, and our paintings? What about Maggie's dolls and dresses?"

"Says they'll sell whatever's left to offset our debt. Says it's their legal right."

"What the hell!" Shannon spat. "I thought we'd settled the debt after Jimmy's win at Schenley." She pointed a finger in Daniel's face. "You told me you settled with them!"

"I paid them two hundred dollars. We needed the rest to eat." He read on. "The notice says we still owe four hundred dollars in back rent. But they've closed the books on us. They've given us up for dead."

"We *are* dead," Shannon said.

"Dead ain't so bad," Jimmy said. "I've been there. Beats *this* life."

Daniel got in his son's face. "Shut up, Jimmy! You're scaring your sister!"

"Do we have any money left?" Shannon asked, indifferent to their quarrel.

Daniel backed off, still glaring at his son. He reached in his pocket. "Twenty-five dollars. Plus, sixty in the bank. We're fine, for now."

"Where are we going to go, Daniel?"

"I don't know. Apparently, the town thinks we should go to hell."

"Pittsburgh? Oh no, I'm not moving to Pittsburgh!"

Daniel settled her. "We'll get a hotel room tonight and figure it out tomorrow. We're fine tonight. We're fine tomorrow. We're fine."

"I'll call Paddy," Jimmy offered. "He'll give me a job when my ribs heal." He followed his comment with a snarky question, still upset that his dad got in his face. "Why'd you have to go and break my ribs, Dad? Why'd you have to bring me back to this—*life?* We don't even have a roof over our heads."

"Why you…" Daniel came at him again with clenched fists. "I'll break them again if you don't shut up!" He held a fist to Jimmy's face.

Maggie began to cry and tucked in behind Shannon.

"Stop!" Shannon shouted. "Act like grown-ups, for God's sake."

The two stood chest-to-chest, sticks and fists, fists and sticks, glaring at each other, gauging each other, ready to unleash their pent-up fury. But neither looked capable, so thin and broken in their dingy suits that hung from them like bum's clothes.

"I'm sorry," Jimmy said, backing down. "I'll call Paddy. He'll find us a place to stay."

"This isn't the end of us," Daniel said, assuredly. "This family is going to be all right."

"It's certainly the end of us in Wilmerding," Shannon said. "We've been ostracized."

"Kicked out of this shit hole," Jimmy mocked.

But his mom was right. Since he'd lost the race, the town had no use for any of them. Jimmy had gone from hero to zero overnight. And it was no coincidence that WABCO finally evicted them in their absence. They had a lifeline in Paddy, but didn't know where they'd sleep that night, or any night thereafter. That much was clear. Their lives in Wilmerding were over, and it was time for them to move on, somehow, somewhere.

15

Sky Daddy
~ Arizona, 1993 ~

Once, when Charlie and I were kids, not the kids we'd become, but real kids—freckled, gap-toothed, and wearing the dirt from a well-played day—I swung on the tire that hung from the big palo verde tree in my front yard, while Charlie ran up and down the street for what seemed like an impossibly long time. Her legs pumped with abandon like she was meaning to get somewhere in a hurry. She waved hello with each pass, and I waved back, but without the same enthusiasm. I thought it was peculiar that anyone would run with such determination for no good reason. She wasn't playing Tag, or Red Light, Green Light, or anything important. She was just running.

When she tired and stopped I asked her why she was running like that, and she replied that she didn't want to go home. Her face was flush, and her blonde hair fell straight, weighted by sweat. Then she told me she was going to run across the Grand Canyon and asked me which way it was. I pointed north.

"Wanna run it with me?"

"I don't run, Charlie. I swing."

Just then, her mom's pitched, angry voice called her home.

I rarely saw her mom. When I did, she was either yelling at Charlie or swearing about things I didn't understand. Her voice knew no boundaries.

I saw her dad even less. He'd always drive away from the house looking troubled. Then, one day he simply disappeared. I never saw him again. Charlie's mom told her that he'd run off like a worthless son-of-a-bitch that she knew he'd always turn out to be. She said he had all his shit piled in his car and wasn't coming back.

"He isn't coming back for dinner?" I asked.

"He isn't coming back for breakfast or lunch, either."

"Oh."

Years later Charlie started talking to someone she called Sky Daddy. She'd have these lengthy conversations asking Sky Daddy to explain the mysterious ways of adults—why they drank, why they fought, why they left, why they didn't come back, why they ignored their kids, and why they bothered to have kids in the first place. We might be in the middle of shooting marbles, or swinging from a tree, or catching lizards, when all of a sudden, she'd stop and ask Him for guidance. I didn't understand why she needed Sky Daddy's permission to pull the tail off a lizard. But she asked, just the same.

Once she asked Him why He lit the Arizona sky on fire at sunset, and He replied that the sky was a reflection of Himself, and that He often blushed at the end of the day, so embarrassed by those He'd created in His own image.

I'll be honest. I didn't necessarily believe in Sky Daddy, but if Charlie thought He was real then I was onboard.

But even with her belief in Sky Daddy, I didn't think she was enjoying her childhood. I mentioned this to my parents, and they told me that girls grow up faster than boys, especially girls like Charlie, and I said I didn't much care for that because I just wanted for us to stay twelve years old forever and pull tails off lizards.

Unfortunately, that wasn't going to happen. Charlie was growing up fast.

Her mom was a real estate agent and worked long hours. She went to social hours, networking for new business. She went to dinners with important people, always leaving Charlie to fend for herself. Often, she stayed out late, imbibing too much, and sometimes not coming home until the next morning, leaving Charlie all by herself to get ready for school.

Charlie would wake herself, dress herself, feed herself, gather herself, and be at the bus stop with time to spare. And when the bus driver said I hope you have a good day, she'd say okay. Because she *was* okay.

Independent Charlie.

Charlie with a mouth.

Capable Charlie.

Charlie the problem solver.

Charlie with a plan.

Because she believed Sky Daddy had her back.

A few years later, she asked me again about running the Grand Canyon with her.

"You want to run it with me, BB?"

227

"I'm no runner," I said.

"Your great-granddaddy was a runner," she reminded me.

"That may be so, but I don't run," I told her. "What are you going to do with all that running, anyhow?"

"I'm joining the cross-country team next year in high school," she told me. "Then I'm going to run in college and they're going to pay me because I'll be a star."

"They'll pay you to run?"

"It's called a scholarship. It's like getting paid. You get a uniform and get your picture in the newspaper. Sometimes they feed you. You get to go places and take a bus—not a school bus—but a fancy bus like those Greyhounds with those big cushy seats. They got toilets on board. You get to stay in fancy hotels like Holiday Inns and Howard Johnsons with maids that make your bed, and air conditioning that usually works, and take showers and dry off with clean towels. Imagine that! You don't have to go to classes or nothing like that. All you gotta do is run."

"You sure about that?"

"What?"

"Not going to class."

"Not when you travel to meets, you don't. But…" She leaned closer, and spoke in a whisper, "Sometimes they get people to take your tests if you're stupid or lazy. I read all about that. But I'm neither."

Years later, these were the things I reflected upon as I sat with Charlie in my driveway, hours after the accident. Charlie, despite her upbringing, was on the right path, headstrong and purposeful. I envied her strength. I, on the other hand, didn't know what my future held, the next day or a year from now. *Just like that Alice Cooper song.*

There was nothing left to look at but the charred remains of my car that still bled out onto the street. Diana stuck around just long enough to see her BMW and my Malibu loaded onto two flatbeds and towed away. Before climbing into a taxi, she said we'd talk Monday because if we talked right now, she'd rip my fucking head off. Her words, not mine. But with her gone, much of the tension dissipated too.

The excitement was over. Neighbors went back inside. The fire truck, the paramedics, the police, and a reporter from the *Tucson Daily Sun* had finished their dutiful jobs and left—off to clean up other people's messes. Even my teammates had left.

Charlie took my hand and suggested I go inside to talk with my parents. But I didn't want to face them yet. Jet sat by my side and I scratched him behind the ears. He wagged his tail approvingly. Charlie was right. It was time. She stood and offered me her hand.

"You weren't driving," she reminded me.

"It still reflects poorly on me," I said. I didn't mention that we'd all been smoking marijuana, even as I spied the butt of a joint in the street.

"I think your parents will understand," she said. "It was an accident."

For the first time in our friendship, I lied. "Yeah, just an accident."

We hugged, parted ways, and I walked in through the front door with Jet in tow. My parents stood tall with their arms crossed, combatively.

"A word, please?"

Mom got right to the point. "Why was Piper driving your car?"

"Why did they arrest Piper?" Dad asked.

Now, it seems to me that human nature can be rather counterintuitive. I could lie to those I loved, but spill the truth to those who loved me. I couldn't tell Charlie that I'd been smoking weed prior to the car accident, yet at this moment, I locked eyes with my parents and said, "I was high and couldn't drive. It was a bad decision."

It also seems to me that there's an absolute time when a kid escapes the orbit of his parents. And I guess that time was now.

I launched.

"What I want to know is this…" I paused to make sure I had their attention, because heredity was their favorite subject. "Which one of you is to blame for my bad decision? Which one of you did I inherit this from?"

That shut them up. They were hurt. I'd hurt them. They wouldn't speak to me the rest of that day, or the next. I certainly didn't need to ask them if I was grounded. Some things were just that obvious. So, I stayed in my bedroom for the weekend, coming out only to eat—alone. When Mom didn't check on me or bring me sandwiches, I knew I'd really struck a blow. And through my bedroom door, I heard them discussing the point.

There was a time in my young childhood when they'd argue over whose eyes I first saw the world through, whose nose I'd picked, and on whose chubby legs I took my first steps. My parents said those were precious times. But then I began to develop a personality, or an attitude, as Dad would say. Things changed. Things were always changing. Mom tried to kiss me goodbye after dropping me off at school, and I turned a cheek. It hurt her. Dad asked me to go fishing with him, but I feigned illness instead. It hurt him. In their eyes, each year I did something worse. I think it's all part of growing up, a natural and necessary progression toward independence. Unfortunately, that road to independence is filled with jarring potholes that hurt the ones you hold closest. If I ever had another talent beyond running, it was that. I could hurt them, and did hurt them, and I was doing that now in my eighteenth year, as they discussed with heavy hearts who handed down the trait of a shitty attitude and bad decision making.

I couldn't see through my hatred. I'd lost so much over the past month—and now, my Malibu! As a self-loathing, teenage victim of the perilous evils of growing up, I laughed at my own discretion for causing them such heartache. I was being a horrible son and yet I didn't care. And for what it's worth, I took Charlie's advice and asked her Sky Daddy to explain things that weekend, but He didn't have any answers. So, I hated Him too.

* * *

If there was any good news that weekend, it's that Piper Cox's blood test came back negative for marijuana. No doubt a false-negative, but a negative is a negative, and he was released to his parents after spending five hours in isolation in a four-by-six jail cell, which, given Piper's reverent disposition, probably scared the bejesus out of him like no other.

Piper's parents were horrified when he was escorted to the lobby by the attending sergeant. Piper's left eye was purple and swollen. Blood had smattered, smeared, and dried on his Tweety Bird T-shirt, making Tweety Bird appear wounded as well.

The wound on Piper's forehead had not quite closed, and a syrupy, purulent discharge oozed from it. His mom, a meek woman with forgiving eyes, began crying when she saw her baby, tattered and ratty. This clearly annoyed the sergeant, who was busy trying to run a police station, not a daycare center. He rolled his eyes.

Piper's dad, who stood at only five-foot-two, pointed a finger in the sergeant's face, and like a barking chihuahua, threatened a lawsuit for denying the boy medical care, not to mention a false arrest of their clearly innocent child, who had never done anything wrong in his life."

Your son was at fault," the sergeant said. "It's in the report. Additionally, we had reason to believe your son had been smoking marijuana. My officers smelled it."

Mr. Cox was incensed. "My son is an athlete. He does not take illicit drugs and his blood test just proved that!"

Mr. Cox stomped his feet. "He is an ath-a-lete!" he repeated. "Look at the boy!"

And when the sergeant surveyed Piper's 110-pound stick-figure, dressed in a Tweety Bird T-shirt, who likely got his ass kicked at school daily, he openly laughed.

"Clearly, he was not at fault!" Mr. Cox continued. "Piper, tell the officer what you saw. Go on. Tell him what happened just before that crazy lady struck you."

Piper, still foggy from the marijuana and the blow to his head, stared blankly ahead and mumbled something inaudible.

His dad leaned in. His mom leaned in. The sergeant leaned in.

"What?" Mr. Cox asked. "Tell us what happened, Piper. We can't hear you."

This time Piper leaned it. He found his voice. "I-I…"

'You—what?"

"I twat I taw a puddy tat."

The sergeant pointed toward the door. "We're done here, Mr. Cox. You may leave and take Tweety Bird with you. Now!"

"Clearly, the boy is concussed! You'll be hearing from my lawyer," Mr. Cox threatened with absolute uncertainty. He gathered his family and made a quick exit.

* * *

By Monday, our classmates had heard about the incident. Some had seen a scathing newspaper article denouncing the character of the team. In the article, I was pointed out as the ringleader of this avoidable accident that nearly took the life of a promising, young attorney who was labeled as a rising star.

Jack Ash, once again, held a newspaper in my face. "Dude, we're in deep shit." Sure enough, he was right.

During third period, Principal Stevens' voice crackled over the intercom, calling the Fly Five to his office.

I was the last of us to arrive. He sat behind his desk, fixated on the newspaper article of the crash. He made horrible, contorted faces. On either side of him stood Coach Jones and Athletic Director Steven Strawbag, like two sentinels. A line in the sand had been drawn. We faced Principal Stevens like a chain gang.

Principal Stevens was a small man, who's threats were nothing without the weight of his position. He was balding, and had mastered the comb-over look complete with dandruf, though his perspiring forehead still shone through.

Tuba coughed to get his attention. "Is this where you ask if we're all right? We were in an accident, but nobody is asking."

Principal Stevens pierced Tuba with his eyes. He swept the room, giving the same look to each of us.

Piper blinked with his one good eye; his other eye swollen shut and grotesque. Principal Stevens stared at him with a look of disgust.

"What I don't understand," he started, "is why none of you helped that poor, old man who was attacked by Billy's dog," he said. "It says here that you sat in Billy's driveway and laughed while the dog mauled him."

"That ain't true, Mr. Stevens," Jack Ash spoke up. "They were fighting over his cane."

"Let me continue." Principal Stevens read on. "Witnesses said that a strong smell of marijuana was in the air as Mr. Ball's car burned to the ground. Care to comment, Billy?"

"Sir, that isn't accurate," I said. "There is no evidence of that to be true. We're athletes, sir. We don't take drugs."

"Perhaps. But none of you helped that poor, old man. You just sat there—and laughed."

"Jet is just a harmless old lab, Mr. Stevens," I said. "It wasn't like that. He was just trying to fetch a stick."

"Mr. Baldwin is quoted here saying he was in fear of his life!"

"It ain't true, Mr. Stevens!"

But of course, it was true. All of it. We'd sat in the driveway and laughed harder than we'd ever laughed before, high on marijuana, rooting for Jet to strip Old Man Baldwin's cane and run away with it.

"The man is ninety-two years old, for goodness sake," Principal Stevens said, incredulously. Coach Jones and Steven Strawbag shook their heads.

Principal Stevens addressed Piper. "Have you got anything to say for yourself?"

He avoided eye contact. Silent.

"Very well, then," Principal Stevens continued. "Ms. Dragenschits from AHSAA called this morning, wondering what kind of program we're running down here. It looks horrible for high school sports, she said. And you know what? She's right! She's damn right it does! My phone has been ringing off the hook from local reporters wondering what I'm going do about you all. The community is expecting that I take some sort of disciplinary action against the—what do you call yourselves—the Fly Five? And that's what I plan to do, boys." He took a deep breath. "Effective immediately you're all suspended indefinitely from the team. Be thankful I'm not suspending you from school altogether."

"That isn't fair," Jack Ash protested, looking at Coach for support.

"You shit the bed, Jack. You all did. It's out of my hands." Coach was no help.

"You should have thought about that before you disgraced your school and the program," added Principal Stevens.

Henry, Piper, and I looked on. Like pin cushions, we felt the pricks of Principal Stevens' words. And we played dead, because that's exactly what we were.

But Tuba was defiant. "Principal Stevens, sir. Henry has never done anything to disgrace this high school but wear his orange Polo shirt five days in a row and violate man law and fashion etiquette. Piper rarely speaks, and if he does it's in character."

"Character?"

"Yeah, like a cartoon character. You'd know that about him if you cared to know. I bet he has some good Tweety Bird tweets after spending Friday in jail. He may be a disgrace, but only to his parents."

Tuba continued. "And Balls? You want to suspend Balls? Balls is already suspended." He looked at Coach and Strawbag. "This ain't fair to Billy! He wasn't even driving."

"You're missing the point, Tuba. And I don't trust you." He crossed his arms and leaned forward. "I suspect you're defending your teammates because you had something to do with this. You're guilty as hell, aren't you? As for Mr. Ball...he may already be suspended, but now he's double suspended, once by AHSAA, and now by me." He turned to Strawbag. "I can do that, right?" His nose wrinkled, disgusted. "Enough of this, boys. You're all suspended from the team until further notice. I've got a school to run. That'll be all."

As we turned to leave Principal Stevens' office, Coach chimed in. "You all owe Mr. Baldwin an apology. Let's start with that."

On the way out, Piper finally spoke. "The-the-that's all folks!"

***

Meanwhile, my attorney, Diana Prince, was on the phone with Ms. Sommers.

"I'm afraid I've lost the tape," Ms. Sommers explained.

"You've lost the tape?"

"Yes, I've lost it. It's not in the camcorder."

This, of course, was nonsense. We had returned the tape to its rightful place.

"Ms. Sommers," Diana said. "Billy needs that tape to have the charges dismissed."

"I've looked everywhere."

Diana considered her next move. What she *wanted* to say was that she had seen the tape. What she *couldn't* say was that she had seen the tape. What she *wanted* to say was that she heard Ms. Sommers comment that Billy had a fine-looking bottom. What she *couldn't* say was that she heard Ms. Sommers comment that Billy had a fine-looking bottom.

"Ms. Sommers. Is there something on the tape that you don't want to share? I can assure you it will only be seen by myself and the prosecuting attorney."

"There is no reason, Ms. Prince. I lost the tape, and that's that."

Diana, at her wit's end now, pulled out her last card. "Ms. Sommers, I know you work for the church, and that you're a single mom of a teenage boy, but if you're withholding evidence in a felony case, I can obtain a warrant. I can have it this afternoon." This, of course, was a reach. And perhaps Ms. Sommers would not call her bluff.

But she did.

"Good luck to you, Ms. Prince. And God bless you." She hung up.

Diana wasn't doing a very good job at saving me.

And though I'd asked Him, neither was Sky Daddy. I guess He was still figuring things out, because the sky captured no colors on that Monday. It was simply gray and uninspiring as the sun set without fanfare.

16

Six Feet Under

The afternoon of our graduation I sat between Charlie and Jack on the infield of the Bald Eagles football stadium. Hundreds of white folding chairs aligned in perfect columns and rows like headstones in a cemetery. Apropos, since most of our graduating class had already peaked in life.

Without a cloud in the sky, we melted under the sun in our black caps and gowns, and wore dark sunglasses to shield our eyes. A hot, forceful wind swept down from the steep Santa Catalina Mountains, and I held my cap anticipating that it might blow off.

Charlie tied her hair back with an elastic band, and wiped beads of sweat from her forehead. She scanned the bleachers looking for her mom.

"Is she coming?"

"Probably not. She has an open house today," Charlie said. "Are your parents here?"

"Of course," I said. "They can't wait to get me out of the house. For them, this is like watching the coronation of a ship before it sails."

"And it's up to me to give that farewell speech." Charlie clutched a single sheet of paper with handwritten notes on it. Her hand shook, and the paper folded in the wind.

"Being named Student Athlete of the Year comes with responsibilities," I said. "You'll do great."

"I'm going to vomit."

Jack leaned in. "Just don't humiliate yourself."

"That's your advice, Jack? Don't humiliate myself?"

Jack was in a sour mood. "I had better grades. I had better race results. I should be up there delivering that speech."

"You were kicked off the team in November," Charlie reminded him.

"Reinstated in January," he said, brooding.

The ceremony began with Principal Stevens delivering a speech about exploration, leaving the confines of our dens, and going out into a brave new world to accept the challenges of responsibility and adulthood. It was the same speech he'd given the previous year, and every year prior.

When Charlie's time came, she approached the stage in high heels, walking through the deep infield grass, unable to see her steps beneath the flow of her gown. She tried to negotiate the stairs, tripping on the last one. She caught herself, but lost her grip on her notes, which took flight in the gusty wind. She pointed to her head, as if to say, *It's okay—I've got it up here.*

Principal Stevens stepped back, giving Charlie the podium, taking a seat behind her. All eyes were on Charlie now.

She cleared her throat, adjusted, and tested the microphone. It reverberated loudly, and she backed away before approaching again. She looked out onto her graduating cohort. *How quickly can I get this over with?*

"If anyone finds my notes, know that I didn't do well in English," she joked.

But no one laughed, and the joke fell dead. And so, awkwardly, she started…

Her cadence was slow and calculating. "I am truly humbled to be up here representing my fellow athletes from Oracle High. I'd like to thank Principal Stevens, Athletic Director Strawbag, and Coach Jones for this honor."

"As an athlete, you might think that I enjoy the spotlight. That is not the case. Thank God I'm a runner." She forced a laugh.

"When I learned of this honor, I thought Coach was joking. There were others, more deserving than me. My teammate, Jackson Ashworth, just reminded me of that." She paused, and shouts of "Jack Ash" rang out from the infield. Jack sagged in his seat and covered his face with his cap. "Plus, I swear too much," Charlie blushed. "I told Coach he could do better."

Someone shouted from the student section, "Hell yeah!" Principal Stevens rose quickly and yelled at the students to behave themselves. When the laughs subsided, Charlie continued. "I do. That is, I do swear a lot. I got that from my mom, who could not be in attendance today because she's too goddamned busy."

Principal Stevens stood again. "Ms. Simmons. Please."

"Oops, there I go." Charlie put her hand to her mouth. "My apologies, Principal Stevens. But I warned you."

"Now, where was I?" Charlie continued. "I asked Coach what I could possibly say to you. He said, talk about your time here, and how it changed you. And I said okay. I'll talk about time because, as a runner, I happen to know a lot about it. I chase time in every race."

Charlie took a deep breath and looked up at the cloudless sky, as if reaching for the words in her wayward notes.

"This is what I know about time. It doesn't exist in the singularity. It takes two." She paused and took a deep breath.

"It takes two objects for time to exist. Sound familiar? Einstein taught us that. The Special Theory of Relativity."

She spotted Coach, who gave her a thumbs-up. "You see, Coach Jones, I do listen. I did learn. All those races I won? All those races I lost? They wouldn't have mattered without you, the team, and the competition. Because time, in a vacuum, stands still. It simply doesn't exist." Several nerdy-looking kids wearing wire-framed glasses in the front row applauded.

"Two objects," she repeated. "You're one of them. If you're lucky, the other is alive. Yeah, let's start with that. If you're really lucky the object is a classmate, a friend, a coach, a teacher, an administrator, or even an adversary. These are the people that have guided us through our four years at Oracle High. Without them, our time here would not have existed. Appreciate them all." She applauded her audience.

"Fellow classmates, there are stars among us. We've spent time in the orbit of each other. Like Einstein's universe, we've gravitated toward some, and been repelled by others." Charlie paused to laugh. "Regardless of who, each defined your time here. And for that, you are lucky." She held the podium confidently with both hands now.

"Our time at Oracle High is over. We made it through this passage. Going forward, whatever you're chasing after today—whether you continue to pursue athletics, academia, or head straight into the workforce, accept others into your universe. Spend time with them. They will guide you on your next journey. Even if it's just one person, orbit that sun."

She stepped back, and raised a finger. "And hey, if you're really lucky, if you win the goddamned lottery, that person will be someone who loves you." She caught my eye. "That person might even be your best friend."

Another "Hell yeah!" shouted from the student section, accompanied by cheers and some illicit words. Principal Stevens rose again and tapped Charlie on the shoulder.

Charlie waved and exited the stage to a smattering of applause.

But I got it. I really did. Time was something Charlie and I cherished and revered. And when I heard her speak of it, my heart rose and sank, hanging on each word, fearing that our time together was nearly up.

If only I could turn back time. God knows I'd tried. I'd tried so hard that day in the desert by running so fast I might reverse it. If only I could go back to the state championship race in October. If I could do it all over again, I would have backed off that last turn and let Christmas Day outkick me to the finish line. I would have finished with my shorts on.

***

Back then, the tape was all the evidence I needed to have the charges dropped. The prosecuting attorney had said that. So, when Ms. Sommers refused to hand it over, I assumed the worst. Diana called to deliver the bad news. "That woman is awful," she'd said. "She'd rather see you go to jail than risk letting it be known that she thinks you have a nice bottom." Before I could reply, she got interrupted. "I'll call you back."

But days passed and she never did. Finally, I called and left a message, but it went unreturned. I convinced myself that Diana was busy, trying to work her caseload before the holidays.

Christmastime came and went and my anxiety kicked in. My imagination ran wild as I lay in bed at night. *Will I go to jail?*

It wasn't too many years ago when I lay in bed, unable to sleep, wondering what Santa would leave me under the tree. But now I wondered about life in a penitentiary.

I'd seen movies about it. I'd heard stuff. Would I be forced into a gang? Would any gang have me? Would I get a tattoo and start smoking? Maybe I'd be one of those contraband guys, roaming the hallways and cafeteria, selling cigarettes and narcotics hush-hush undercover. Would they let me out on weekends to pick up trash on the roadside? Maybe I'd bust a move and escape into the desert, and live my life as a fugitive. Or, maybe I'd lie in bed all day long and read novels, or textbooks, and come out educated and insightful—an actual intellectual. I'd be one of those rehabilitated criminals who authorities ask to speak with troubled youth to scare them straight. I'd gain weight, develop a permanent scowl, fake a hardened demeanor, and draw a tear-drop tattoo on my cheek for effect, and tell them to change their ways or they'd wind up just like me—damaged. Or maybe I'd tour high schools as a motivational speaker. I'd sit on a stool in the middle of an auditorium stage under a bright spotlight, look out at the students, blink at their youthfulness, knowing they viewed me as less than human. They'd be slightly afraid, but with space and security between us, they'd mostly be intrigued by this newly tamed animal who sat before them now, delivering life lessons. I'd start my speech: "It wasn't too long ago I was sitting right where you are. My life was good and I had time on my side. I was on the high school cross-country team. I had a girlfriend. My parents loved me. But then…"

Life in the pen was not going to be easy. I'd have a cellmate, a much older man covered with tattoos, a shaved head, who lifted weights hours each day. He wouldn't talk much but would grunt often. He'd take food from my plate and I wouldn't stop him. At night, he'd pass gas on the lower bunk while I lay above him trying to sleep, eyes wide, paranoid, and too terrified to ask him to stop. His name would be Bubba. Or maybe just Andy. But Andy wouldn't understand me. He wouldn't care too—this thin, naive kid from a pacified, gentrified town that attracted tourists. But I'd try to bridge our differences, strike up a buddy relationship, because hey, I was tough in my own right. The law said so. The law said I was a threat to society, just like him. They'd put me away for my crimes, just like him. I'd ask to compare notes on toughness. But I'd also want Andy to know me for who I used to be—a human being. I'd tell him about my life outside of the pen, that I used to be a runner, a good one. *Perhaps you read about me or saw me on TV?* I'd mention that I had plans to go to college, that I was a son, a student, and a boyfriend. All before the law caught up to me. We'd have a breakthrough and Andy would look at me insightfully, holding his chin in his hand, and finally speak. He would say that I could still be someone's boyfriend. "Welcome to Pen U, Billy."

It was all so horrible, this world I imagined outside of my house. I wondered if real adults lay awake with this kind of anxiety? I covered my head with my blanket and cowered, afraid of who knows what. And worse, I was even more scared when I woke the next day, fearful of the next development in my case. Fearful of Diana's next phone call and more bad news. Fearful that my parents had given me up to the wolves. Fearful that Charlie would stop being my best friend if she found out about me and Diana. *Maybe I should have told her. The canyons that divide.* I wondered if she would forgive me, even visit me in jail and bring me cookies and a cake, and if that cake might have a nail file in it so that I could escape the system—and Andy. I'd watched too many movies.

In January, I started back at school. My locker had been graffitied, and the words "Balls" and "loser" and "druggie" had been hastily written on it in permanent marker. But I was getting used to that sort of thing by now.

Shortly after, Diana called with exciting news. It was over. All charges had been dropped. Despite my doubts, she'd worked diligently during the holidays to interview witnesses and gather testimony. And during a deposition of the said victim-child, who was more interested in riding her brand-new bicycle—a Christmas gift—than wasting time talking to Diana, none of her initial testimony could be substantiated or confirmed. By this point, the kid's father had also lost interest.

Diana dumped my file onto the prosecuting attorney's desk. She postured, her arms crossed, and told him he didn't have a case. He didn't bother to open the file. "I've got too many cases on my desk to fight this one," he told her. "Had this happened anywhere but on the grounds of an elementary school, the young man would have never been charged in the first place."

I still had to appear before Judge Carol Bell so that she could formally dismiss the charges. She had a full docket, and the soonest she could do that was the second week in February. The legal system, I learned, moved at a snail's pace, and certainly not in alignment with the angst of a teenage defendant. But it did happen, and on a perfectly sunny day, I was set free just in time for lunch.

Diana said she'd treat, because we needed to *talk*. Ever since the car accident, she'd put space between us, leaving me confused about our relationship. During the holidays and throughout January there had been no mention of dinners, or hanging out, or anything else beyond the case. I assumed things were over between us, but I wasn't exactly sure. I didn't know much about adult relationships. Were they based on love? Sex? Money? Convenience? All of the above, some of the above, or none of the above? Was it normal to take time off from seeing each another? Was it normal to not talk? Was it normal to fight? Sometimes my parents sparred with words. Yet, they still loved each other. Mom says she endures Dad daily. That sounds like love…sort of.

Standing on this precipice of adulthood was terribly confusing.

In my dad's pickup truck, I followed her newly repaired BMW to the Mexican food restaurant where we'd first celebrated. We were seated at the exact table as the last time, where we'd had too many margaritas and lost our inhibitions to physical attraction and chemical reaction. But now, the mood felt guarded. I ordered a margarita. But she ordered a Coke.

"You're not celebrating."

She avoided my eyes. But only for a second.

Just as I didn't understand how adult relationships worked, I didn't know how they ended. This was my first experience at both. I thought about Rigby and how she'd just faded away. She didn't return my calls and avoided me at school. But this was different. Diana laid it all out there in an unemotional, unequivocal voice. At this moment, she was an adult and an attorney. I was a kid and a student. She sat poised. I slouched. She talked. I listened. The closest she came to showing any emotion was apologizing for her behavior after the car accident, and the cold shoulder she'd given me. But she also said the accident must have jarred something loose in her head, and that she'd come to her senses and that we couldn't see each other any longer. Then she cut lunch short, picking up the check, and said she had an arraignment in the afternoon. When I went to kiss her cheek—I expected that much—she stuck out her hand instead, and said in these exact words, "You've been saved, Billy Ball. I saved you." She stood and walked away.

Then, without a sound, she turned around, met my eyes, and winked goodbye.

That night, my parents took me out to dinner at a local steakhouse to celebrate. A pretty hostess wearing a cowboy hat and chaps greeted us. Above her, the head of a steer with horns six feet wide was mounted on the wall. He'd seen better days.

Dad took one look at him and said, "That could have been you."

I agreed.

"To new beginnings," Mom said, raising her glass.

Getting my life back. It seemed so easy. For the first time in a long time, I slept well that night.

But as it turned out, it wasn't easy to get back. The damage had been done. Sure, Principal Stevens, Athletic Director Strawbag, and Coach Jones invited me to rejoin the team, knowing I'd be the key to a state track and field championship.

Unfortunately, the bureaucracy of high school athletics did not move as fast. Two things had occurred during this time that would cement the end of my running career in high school.

One, the director of AHSAA, the Arizona High School Athletic Association, retired. It must have been an awful job because he left stacks of unfinished business on his desk, escaping to Yuma the same day. He bought a clapboard house in a retirement community frequented by Canadian snowbirds and began a new career of day-drinking on the front porch, waving pleasant hellos to other like-minded neighbors as they walked by.

Then, just as Deputy Director Ms. Dragenschits was to take over his position, she died. Dead dead dead. Just like that. Coach Jones called me to his office to deliver the news. As I was about to enter, I heard him speaking to Strawbag, rather jovially. I stopped short and eavesdropped from the hallway.

Coach was telling Strawbag that Ms. Dragenschits had died from constipation. "One week before she was to take the throne, she was sitting on a different throne. When she didn't show up for work, her co-workers knew something was wrong because Ms. Dragenschits had never missed a day of work in her life. When the cops arrived, they said her face was contorted like she'd been in some sort of awful struggle. Her eyes were bug wide, and she clutched onto something in death. When they bent back her rigormortised fingers, they saw that it was the AHSAA rule book."

"Now, there's a lady who loved her job," Strawbag joked.

Can humiliation be felt in death?

I was eighteen and therefore excused for an utter lack of compassion. Simply put, I was actually relieved. It seemed that good ol' Ms. Dragenschits would be out of the picture. And that was good news.

Unfortunately, Coach told me otherwise. After several calls to AHSAA, requesting my reinstatement, a hiccup appeared. Bound in the red tape of high school sports policy and procedure was the case of one William Ball. *Me.*

I didn't know anything about case management or the filing system of AHSAA, or any government agency for that matter. Maybe it was by alphabetical order, or maybe it was chronological. Maybe it was by severity or importance, or cohort, or the Dewey Decimal System, or some other fancy method that an excitable young bureaucrat once invented to efficiently bury paperwork.

Regardless, I guessed nothing ever got thrown out. I guessed that years of case files were crammed into deep rows of locked cabinets that time forgot. And when the file cabinets filled, they wound up in cardboard boxes stacked in hallways, under tables, in the break room, and behind the coffeemaker. Occasionally, one got left in the refrigerator under spoiled milk. I also pictured a basement, a catacomb of sorts, where the fat files wound up, the ones that regulators had long since given up on. Nobody went down there because they were haunted by the Ghosts of

Athletes Past, so screwed by the system they bellowed their grievances night and day, rattling ghostly chains like the medals stripped from them. I was certain, that's where my case was filed.

"It's out of our control," Coach Jones said.

He wasn't lying. Strawbag and I stood by his side when he called a third time.

"You have the kid's file, right?"

"Yes, we have the file."

"Did you read it?"

"Yes, I read it."

"Then, what's the problem?"

"I can't act on it."

"You're the acting director."

"Yes, but you see, I'm only acting. I can't make decisions."

"Why not?"

"It's above my pay grade. You'll have to wait."

"Until when?"

"Until then."

There were few things worse than trying to talk sense with a bureaucratic regulator.

"Coach, can they speed up the hiring process?" I asked with fading hope.

"It takes time to hire a director, Billy. They'll have to post the position. The posting will include a mandatory open period. Maybe six weeks or longer. We're already into track season by then. A committee will disqualify applicants who don't meet the minimum requirements. They'll narrow the search to a few distinguished applicants who've proven their mastery of leading by following—a necessary skill of regulators. Rounds of interviews, a decision, background checks, reference checks…. You get the picture. You'll be grown with kids before anyone overturns your suspension and lets you back on this team."

"That makes no sense," I said.

"As long as they follow their rules, they don't care if you're reinstated post-mortem."

Later that week I began reaching out to colleges that had shown interest. Some still questioned my character; others did not. But in the world of high school sports, athletes were soon forgotten. I was told to stay in touch and send results from track season. That's when I had to backtrack, and tell the improbable story about how and why I was not on the team. Interest waned. Interest lost. It seemed there were more runners out there than scholarships, and I'd been branded.

Yet, I held out hope, even as track season got underway. I went to the meets to support my ex-teammates.

The Fly Five were now the Fly Four. In cross-country it takes five runners to score, but in track relays, there are only four. So, I was not missed as much as I had hoped.

Coach was eyeing the state championship for the 4x800. And even with Tuba as the weakest link, they had a great shot of winning. And they did, but fell short of the state record.

Charlie just kept on being Charlie. She was even better on the track than cross-country. I'd sit in the stands at every meet cheering her on, providing the support that belonged to—but abandoned by—her absent mom. At the state finals meet, Charlie ran the 3,200. An assistant coach from the University of Arizona happened to sit next to me to watch her top recruit, and when she saw me cheering loudly, she asked who I was. "Billy Ball," I said. She asked, "Who?" "Billy. William Ball," I repeated. And she asked, "Do you run?"

"I used to."

Then she placed me. "Balls! Yes, of course I know you. Everyone knows you." I rolled my eyes, as she turned her attention back to the race. They were in the last lap, and Charlie was leading.

Charlie didn't win that race. She mistimed her kick, and her good friend and teammate, Jenny Ledge, caught her in the stretch along with four others.

"Maybe I should be looking at her teammate," the recruiter said.

This woman rubbed me wrong. I stood up and walked away without acknowledging her comment.

That was the end of track season, other than a notice I received a week later, stating that I had to return my uniform or my graduation might be delayed. What an insult, given the likelihood that the bottom half was still hanging in that cactus patch.

* * *

Now, as I stood applauding Charlie's speech as she walked off stage, I considered that I did not know what I was going to do with the rest of my life. I was as lost as I've ever been. I thought about my nemesis, Christmas Day, who's future was certain. After a lengthy tugawar between recruiting colleges, he had chosen to run for Colorado.

I had beaten him, but at this point nobody remembered. The only certainty in my life was what I was going to do that evening.

I'm not sure when the tradition started, but each year Oracle High's distance runners would gather ten miles out of town at a small abandoned mine in Cañada del Oro—the Canyon of Gold—to celebrate year's end. There would be a lot of drinking, singing, and general mischief, all under the hazy eye of the school. We slept in cars or tents. Parents lamented and worried, but went along with the annual ritual, because in all the years of this event, no one had actually died, become lost, or wound up pregnant, so it was said.

Oracle was surrounded by abandoned mines from the 1930s. Most were now overgrown with vegetation and decay. The shafts were sealed, and signs read "NO TRESPASSING." None of this deterred anyone. Instead, it only added to the thrill of adventure seekers. Rusted equipment littered them, and it wasn't unheard of to come across a gravesite marking the death of a miner. But these gravesites were typically rudimentary, marked only by wooden crosses.

At first glance, this particular mine looked no different than any other. But there was one thing, so odd and out of place that it was a magnet for the team to come back to every year—a granite headstone with an etching of a runner in full flight.

That headstone belonged to my great-grandfather, James Flynn.

I'd known about it ever since I was ten years old, when my parents took me to see it. But I'd never been back until I joined the track team my freshman year and heard about the tradition of partying on the grave of the Unknown Runner.

On that first trip back, I'd stepped out of the car and immediately recognized my whereabouts and the headstone. The stone itself was in pretty bad shape. Time had worn it. Its edges were chipped, and vandals had knocked it crooked. But there was no mistaking the scribe: "JAMES FLYNN. Beloved Father and Husband. Died April 10, 1934."

"I know this person," I'd said emphatically. "He's not unknown. He's my great-grandfather!"

My teammates collectively rolled their eyes, disbelieving. But I insisted, telling them the story of how he saved the lives of eight miners. They acquiesced, if only to shut me up.

At first, I was taken aback by this long-standing tradition, which until then I knew nothing about. But then I reconsidered. How could I be upset by this celebration? In a sense, I thought it was the coolest thing ever. James Flynn, my great-grandfather, was center stage amongst us runners once a year.

And I was eager to share what little I knew about his story. Cañada del Oro was a watershed, a deep canyon, that fueled runoff from the nine-thousand-foot top of Mount Lemmon. In the summer of 1933, a storm perched itself above the mountain for days, and when natural barriers gave way, a torrential runoff exploded down its steep slopes, causing a rockslide that blocked the entrance to the mineshaft. James Flynn saved eight trapped miners by running into Oracle to get help. The following spring, he met an untimely death of his own, and the mining company felt so compelled to honor him they'd buried him and placed his headstone on premise.

Not that this mattered much to excitable teenagers, sixty years later, and hours removed from the outing of school. We just wanted to celebrate.

Tuba was already there when I arrived in my dad's truck accompanied by Jack and Charlie. He said something about getting the party started, and within minutes we'd built a fire next to my great-grandfather's headstone and took our seats on plastic chairs.

Charlie was the first to crack a beer.

"Let's live it up tonight," she said. "Here's to your great-granddaddy!"

"The runner from down under!" said Jack Ash.

"Six feet under!" I laughed.

So, we cheered the iconic member of our brethren.

"I'll never be him," I said. "He saved all those miners. I can't even save myself."

"No, you won't be him. You'll do better than him," Charlie replied. She gazed into the fire as she said this, and her gold-flecked eyes sparked in the reflection.

I lost myself in those eyes for a second. And I said something sincere, but off the cuff. "I'm going to miss you, Charlie."

"I'm going to UA. It's thirty minutes away, dumbass."

Charlie and her shell.

"It's a new life—"

"That will include you," she interrupted, softening. "You can't get rid of me that easily."

I smiled and she smiled back, though both of us knew the truth. We were unwilling to acknowledge it. As she'd said in her speech, others will come into our lives, and we'll orbit them the way we do the sun. But in this moment, I felt merely like a familiar meteor that would only pass her by on occasion.

Hours passed, and even in darkness the bold shadows of the Santa Catalinas and Mount Lemmon fell on us, cast by a clear night sky and a waxing crescent moon.

And we continued to drink. And drink.

"A Wildcat," I nodded.

"A Wildcat," she repeated. "Billy. Whatcha gonna do? You worry me," she said, gauging.

"I'm holding out," I said.

"For what? For who?"

I looked directly into my beer bottle, peering in with one eye, like a peep hole, holding it to the light of the moon. The liquid inside waved like the Pacific Ocean. It was mesmerizing, kaleidoscopic. And I was drunk and didn't answer.

She asked a second time.

This time, I put down my bottle and said, "For you. I'm holding out for you."

I'd said this with such jest that we launched into a fit of laughter. Sure, I was fishing. I was testing our friendship. But even more so, our relationship.

Friendship is a strange thing. By its very definition, it has boundaries. For Charlie and me, the boundaries were set in our youth, as kids. Even as circumstances changed. Even as we changed. We were stuck in our non-written yet binding agreement. There were lines we couldn't cross.

We'd support, but couldn't touch. We'd listen, but couldn't say. We'd wish, but couldn't act.

When you're a kid those boundaries are small, like a stream you can't cross. But as you get older, as your emotions and maturity rise, and more is at stake, the stream turns into a river, and the river erodes its banks, and the banks become walls, and the walls become canyons, and before you know it, when you're bound in the grip of youth's desires, you're standing on one side of the Grand Canyon looking out toward the other side, waving to your best friend, wishing for more. Wishing for a bridge.

But there is no bridge. Not that you can see. Not as an eighteen-year-old. So, you smile at her, unable to find the words that live and breathe within you, but not yet exhaled. So, you nod, and play dumb, and pretend. You hold her eyes a second too long, and know in that moment that the friendship is a lie, and that you want more. Still, you cowardly accept the boundaries to preserve its shell.

But, you still fish…

"Hey, Charlie. Do you remember that time when we were ten years old? I was swinging on my tire swing in the front yard and you were running like the devil up and down our street. You told me you were looking for the Grand Canyon. You asked me to run it with you."

"I remember that."

"Why'd you ask me that—about the Grand Canyon?"

"I don't know, Billy. I was ten."

"Yeah, but why the Grand Canyon? Why not Mount Lemmon? We look up at it every day."

She thought about this, taking another swig of beer. "Perspective," she finally said. "I heard the lowest point in Arizona is the bottom of the Grand Canyon."

"So?"

"So. I was feeling pretty low that day. All year long, actually. My parents were splitting up. I figured if I could run from the bottom of the Grand Canyon, I could get through just about anything." Another swig. "I wasn't looking to run to the top of a mountain. I just wanted to get back to even. Level ground."

"I see."

And I did. And that's exactly how I felt now, after my senior year. I just wanted to get back to even. "We need to do that."

"What?"

"Run the Grand Canyon."

"You're talking crazy, BB. Why would we do that?"

"You know as well as I do," I said, still fishing.

I don't know what came over me next. Talking about our past made me yearn for our future. Charlie looked so beautiful sitting next to the fire, and I became lost in her presence. Tuba was off exploring, stoned and searching for miner's gold. Jack had since disappeared with Jenny Ledge. Piper, Henry, and the rest were all milling about, but somehow worlds away, their movements, the din of their talk, faded well beyond the frame of Charlie.

"Charlie?"

"Yes?"

"Oh, nothing."

"Are you feeling all right?" Charlie asked. "You're flushed."

And I was. The crescent moon was behind her now, illuminating her golden hair. The fire was before her, its flames casting contour and life onto her placid face. I felt helpless, surrendering to the pull of her being like that of the sun. But I'd fallen well out of orbit and was now on course for a direct collision. We were feet apart and I shuffled my chair to be closer. And in the boldest move of my life, I leaned toward her, my eyes trained on hers, my lips targeting hers. I was about to cross the bridge. I was going to kiss her. I'd risk it all—our lifelong friendship.

"Can I kiss you?" I asked.

Before she could answer, I made my move. A foot away. Now, six inches, leaning ever so close, and just as I closed my eyes and parted my lips, a leg of the plastic chair collapsed, and I toppled head over heels into the fire.

That's when I heard it. We all did. Jimmy Flynn, from six feet under, emitted a bellowed, lasting laugh that bounced and echoed from wall to wall of Cañada del Oro.

The humiliation tour continued.

PART TWO

17

Popcorn!
~ Arizona, 1995 ~

As it turned out, it wasn't my great-grandfather, Jimmy Flynn, laughing from his grave when I fell into the fire. It was a loud clap of thunder that echoed off the canyon walls, followed by a torrential downpour that sent us running for cover to our cars and tents, putting an early end to the evening. In a sense, the storm was Godsent. It saved me from having to explain to Charlie why I tried to kiss her, and allowed for a quick, convenient exit.

That was two years ago, and I'm in a much better place now. Although my mom disagrees. She still calls me a "pre-me," as if I still have some growing up to do before I drop the *pre*. I don't share her point of view.

Personally, I feel like I'm on the right path.

I'm the assistant to the assistant manager at a local movie theater with four screens. It's kind of a big deal. I make ten dollars per hour, almost twice as much as minimum wage. And Gus, the assistant manager, is leaving to accept a cashier job at Safeway. If promoted to Gus' job, I'll make three dollars more per hour, and feel good that

I've finally accomplished something worthwhile at only twenty years old.

Although, there are things that I miss.

I miss my Malibu. I miss the throbbing growl of its 305 V-8 Turbo-Hydramatic engine, and how it fishtailed every time I took a corner too fast. If Charlie was along for the ride, she'd scream in delight, and perhaps I'd do a donut in a parking lot and watch her smile grow even wider.

And of course, I miss Charlie. Every day. I miss our drives through the color-soaked desert at sunset, our backyard happy hours, and our fun trail runs at the base of Mount Lemmon. I miss that she'd put on her "I'm with Stupid" shirt only in my presence. Mostly, I miss the comfort of knowing she was always there. She had her sights on the University of Arizona, just down the road, but ended up accepting a better scholarship at Northern Arizona University, five hours north in Flagstaff. She rarely comes home.

I've replaced both.

I own a 1990 Ford Escort. I bought it for five hundred dollars with no help from my parents. It doesn't growl like my Malibu did, but it has four doors, gets great gas mileage, and shows that I am a responsible adult—something Dad said I needed to prove after my senior year.

And I have a girlfriend.

Her name is Holly Wodecki. She's eighteen and manages concessions. She hates her Polish name, and plans to change it to Holly Wood to be taken seriously when she becomes an actress. When I told her that was a good idea, she replied that the two of us will sit in this very theater one day and watch her do amazing things on the big screen. I have no doubt that will happen.

She's very outgoing. Her hair is cropped and dyed pink. She wears fake eyelashes that are long, thick, and curled. Red is her favorite lipstick color, though she'll apply orange or purple if it fits her mood. She leaves the top two buttons of her blouse open because she says working concessions is hard and that she overheats. Out of stress, she eats a lot of popcorn, but she says she's going to quit because it causes her to gain weight.

Popcorn seems to weigh on her in other ways, too.

She complains of smelling like it after an eight-hour shift. I tell her I like popcorn and that I don't mind. Then she says she's tired of handling the butter flavoring because it causes acne. I never know how to respond to that, other than to say I don't notice and that I think she looks pretty.

The other thing about Holly is that her eyes are the exact same color as dollar bills. I laugh and tell her how appropriate that is, because she's very creative at making money, especially when it comes to ripping off the theater.

Here's how that works: She barks at me when she needs more popcorn buckets. Literally, barks like a dog. The bark is our little signal that it's safe to bring out the used buckets to mix in inventory.

After cleaning a theater room, I'll wipe down and stash several in a broom closet. Then, Holly will send the concession girls on break, or to inspect the women's restroom, and I'll bring the buckets to her. Then she places them back in inventory, and removes their cash value from the register.

Holly justifies it. She says the theater doesn't pay us nearly enough for all the revenue we generate. She argues that the owner, Mr. Grant, owes it to us, and even expects it from us, because he factors employee theft into his pricing. "How else can you explain five-dollar buckets of popcorn?"

I'm not sure about that, but when I consider that an hour of my time is worth only two popcorn buckets, it makes a lot of sense.

Holly always makes sense, like the time when I asked her why she dropped out of high school. She said she didn't see the point of going to school when she already had a full-time job.

"You get an education to get a job, right?" she said.

"I guess so."

"Well, I have a job. School is for dumb people."

I saw her logic.

One other thing that's changed: I no longer run.

I don't think I miss it.

Maybe I do.

I don't know.

I ran some races after graduating high school, and often won prize money. It was easy money, especially when I ran against collegians who couldn't accept prize money since it violated their amateur status. So, the money would often roll down to me.

But when I couldn't shed the publicity of my past, and the chants of "Balls Balls Balls" accompanied me across finish lines, and at award ceremonies, I hung it up. I simply stopped, too humiliated to continue. I needed to reinvent myself.

That's what I'm doing now. Today is my performance review with Mr. Grant. There's so much riding on it, with Gus leaving.

It won't be a perfect review. I'm not perfect. Like Holly, I eat a lot of the company's popcorn, and consume excessive quantities of soft drinks. Being assistant to the assistant manager comes with perks. I hope I'm not docked for that. I'll apologize to Mr. Grant if he brings it up. Though, there are worse things that could come up.

For instance, I have the keys to the video arcade games. When Mr. Grant leaves at night, and the last movie lets out, I unlock them and add bunches of free games for the staff. I play them too—Ms. Pacman, Centipede, Galaga. They're all good games, but I love Asteroids the best. Using thruster and directional buttons, I propel my little triangular spaceship across the screen, navigating fields of asteroids with meticulous skill, firing on them, and blowing them to smithereens. For the most part I've mastered the game, and six months ago, I entered a tournament and won a hundred dollars. No one called me Balls at that tournament, and I decided then that this was going to be my new pursuit.

That's also when I started dating Holly. She says she loves winners. She says she noticed me back in high school before she dropped out, when I was a star runner. Then, when I was promoted to assistant to the assistant manager, she started flirting with me. But when I won that Asteroids tournament, she said she was drawn to me like a planet orbiting the sun. I scratched my head and smiled, because that sounded similar to what Charlie had said in her graduation speech. The next thing I knew we were a couple.

Holly is full of compliments. She likes that I've filled out. She says that it was hard to take me seriously as an awkward teenager, and that on the first day on the job she mistook me for a theater mop because I was nothing but a tall stick with sodden, ropey hair.

On busy nights, the theater pulsates to the ebb and flow of the showings. One minute, hundreds of moviegoers stand impatiently in line for concessions, checking their watches, urging those in front to hurry it up. The concession girls move at an impressive pace, but often bump into each other, spilling drinks and popcorn, and have to start all over. Minutes later, when the movies are playing, the lobby is eerily silent. The concession girls clean, restock the popcorn and candy, and repeat this routine three times throughout their shift. Holly tells me it's exhausting work. And I reply that so is being an usher.

The staff might include twenty of us, and most stick around after closing hours. Since girls work concessions or ticket sales, and boys work as ushers, we have a fairly even split between sexes. So, we flirt, and whisper behind each other's backs, especially when a new person comes on board. Most are still in high school, and those who aren't are not far removed. We stash beer in ice bins, and help ourselves to mouthfuls of popcorn taken with dirty hands, and mingle and smoke in the lobby as if it was our own personal lounge. Sometimes we watch newly released movies, but only if they're rated R and contain warnings for sex and violence. Occasionally, someone will bring a pornographic movie and we watch those too. I never know where these movies come from, but they are always amateur.

These are the things I hope Mr. Grant knows nothing about as I prepare myself for the performance review.

Well, that and the popcorn scam. Though if he knew about that I suppose Holly and I would be in jail by now.

***

The staff respectfully calls him Mr. Grant, because he's our boss and the owner of the theater. But his full name is Grant G. Grant. Nobody knows what the middle initial stands for. But one can only speculate. He likes to say that because of his size, the plural name suits him well.

Grant G. Grant is a large man whose favorite pastime is watching movies. Owning and managing a movie theater had been a lifelong dream of his that became a reality when the recession hit in 1990 and he retired from his position as a financial advisor at an investment firm.

He built an impressive theater that captured the spirit of Hollywood in his youth. The Oracle Theater's Art Deco design features a vertical marquee that bares its name in red neon that radiates above an inviting entrance; set back and decorated with gold, fluted columns, and black and white chevron-patterned tiles. Its facade glitters and sparkles and mimics the opulence and optimism of Hollywood's golden era.

Mr. Grant says the golden era was a time that he considers quintessential Americana, when a trip to the Fox Theater in Downtown Tucson with his nanny was a special, privileged event. He'd dress in his best clothing, part his hair, shine his shoes, and flock to grand openings for a chance to see his favorite movie stars on the silver screen.

His nanny would tell him stories about the glamorous stars, some of whom she'd met in person, when she had dreams of becoming one herself.

Every day, Mr. Grant pulls up to his theater with pride and purpose, but acknowledges its imitation. To look past its façade, one would see a large box, cheaply constructed with no hints of craftsmanship or fine materials. Slapped up in mere months, it was a sad replica of its aspirations.

"That's the movies for you," Mr. Grant says. "Nothing is real but the popcorn."

That's Mr. Grant's favorite saying. Because at five dollars a bucket, popcorn is very real. He calls it Theater Gold because it accounts for more profit than ticket sales.

Every Saturday a truck delivers hundreds of the pre-popped bags. Ushers stack them like bars of gold in the theater lobby, count them for inventory, and move them to a locked storage room that we call the Vault.

As I step into his office, ready for my review, I fully understand popcorn's value.

"Have a seat, Billy. You look nervous."

"I am." As a young man, I'm conditioned to fear for my life when called into an office. Plus, with Gus leaving, there is so much at stake.

"You've put on weight, Billy. Have you been eating my popcorn?"

Mr. Grant is joking, but I still worm in my chair.

"Popcorn sales are way off," he says. "It doesn't make sense because fountain drinks are steady. But hey, that's my problem. Let's talk about your performance."

"Yes, sir." I think about the past two years and the first time I'd walked into his office.

My dad had arranged the interview because he felt sorry for me. A few weeks after graduation, I'd received the long-awaited letter from AHSAA. They'd finally reinstated my eligibility to participate in high school sports. Coach was right. They were an idiot organization. I tossed the letter into the trash can and laughed like a madman, counting the days until I'd die. When I couldn't move off the couch, Mom said I needed counseling. But Dad said I needed a job.

"You haven't rebounded well," he said. "You can't lay around and brood forever. College is still on the table. Until then, you can work while you figure out your life."

And that's how I wound up in front of Mr. Grant. Dad insured his house, his car, and even the theater, and one day Mr. Grant mentioned to him that he was staffing up for the summer. I'm pretty sure Dad gave him a bundle discount if he agreed to hire me.

Even in that first encounter, Mr. Grant came across as a calculating, deliberate man. He sat behind a large, metal desk and analyzed me while steepling his fingers. Framed movie posters hung behind him. He was old—how old I didn't know, because as an eighteen-year-old kid, everyone looked old. But gravity had taken hold of his ears, nose, and jowls, which hung and clung like wax that had been heated and cooled too many times.

"Do I know you?" I asked. "You look familiar."

"You literally ran into me at the state cross-country meet."

"Did I apologize?"

"No, but I did."

"I'm sorry."

"It's okay. You ran a great race that day. Sorry about the outcome."

"Why were you there?"

"Your dad invited me. He's very proud of you. You know that, right?"

"He's a good dad."

"But a lousy insurance agent," Mr. Grant said. "Asshole charges me too much."

"Sir?"

He waited a long moment before exhaling a hearty laugh. "Just testing you."

"Why would you do that?"

"Ushers need thick skin." He pushed his chair back, resting his arms on his protruding belly. "Moviegoers are anxious. They fight traffic, can't find parking, and wait in line for overpriced tickets. Then they wait in line at concessions, pay for overpriced popcorn, and worry about finding seats."

"So?"

"So, they hate you for it," he said. "You're just another barrier that stands between them and the movie. You really want this job?"

"My dad says I do."

"Okay, then. What do you know about the movies?"

"I like movies, Mr. Grant."

"Everyone likes movies, Billy. What's your favorite movie?"

I'd watched a lot of movies with Charlie, but I didn't speak up in time.

"What about the classics?" he asked, pointing to the posters on the wall. "*King Kong, Casablanca, Citizen Kane*—"

"Citizen who?"

"Kane. You know. Rosebud. You know what I mean when I say Rosebud, don't you?"

"Rosebud?"

"Rosebud," he repeated. "You really don't know anything about the movies, do you?"

"I guess not, sir."

I thanked him, and rose to leave, but he motioned for me to sit back down.

"When can you start?"

Mr. Grant hired me because he liked building things, and thought I'd make a nice project, even if I was—just like his theater—a sad replica of its aspirations.

I know a lot about the movies now because every Saturday morning after the popcorn is delivered and stacked, Mr. Grant gathers the staff and speaks to the history of Hollywood, and why a trip to the movies should

275

be a special event. He does this because he wants us to impart this appreciation on his paying customers.

And I do. With the exception of ripping him off, I've become a great employee. I've had a lot of ideas in my time here.

Once, Mr. Grant observed me greeting an old couple who gingerly walked up to the podium with tickets in hand. But no concessions. I politely asked if they'd forgotten their popcorn and sodas. "Movies are so much better with refreshments," I said. To my surprise, they turned around and shuffled back to the concession stand, thanking me as they went. They returned minutes later with a small popcorn and a water. "We're going to split this," the woman said in a shaky voice.

Mr. Grant was impressed. He instructed all the ushers to adopt this practice. Concession sales shot up twelve percent after that.

Unless people were juggling five-dollar buckets of popcorn, four-dollar mega-cups of soda, and enough candy to cause a diabetic coma, we turned them around to the concession stand. Often, they'd return without enough hands to hold their purchase. We'd pluck a shirt pocket, or bend a pinky back to locate and remove a movie ticket. And for this, they'd thank us.

I remind him of this now during my performance review.

Now, tearing tickets, being polite, and suggestive selling is only one side of my job. Another side, the dirty side, is janitorial. It's why my white shirt is always stained, and my black bowtie askew.

When a movie lets out, a team of ushers descends upon the room with brooms and dustpans, mops and buckets, and large rubber garbage bins on wheels. The last one in blocks off the entrance with two aluminum posts and a retractable yellow belt, much like crime-scene tape. Because it is a crime scene.

In these moments I recognize just how deplorable humans are. I recognize that the floor of a movie theater is a mere reflection of humanity's worst, uncouth behaviors, and truly the underbelly of civilization. My shoes stick and suction and *pop pop pop* as I make my way up and down the aisles, picking up litter.

And I'd think, what in God's name happens to people when the lights are off?

Well, I can tell you. They turn into beings inhuman, who discard their trash with a flick of the wrist—because the ushers will pick it up, because as ticket-holding customers, they hold immunity to all things civilized.

What I saw when I walked into a theater room were strewn popcorn buckets, spilled popcorn, smashed popcorn, soda cups, candy wrappers, ice cream cups, hot dog wrappers, and hot dogs that had lost their wrappers. Half-eaten hot dogs. Uneaten hot dogs. Gum stuck to the back of chairs. Jujubes stuck to armrests. Ketchup tracked in the aisles, imprinted like a murderer's foot. And I'd think, why are we selling food to people who clearly can't locate their mouths?

Anything liquid was worse. There were sticky liquids, gooey liquids, coagulated liquids, and hardened, crystalized liquids. Liquids that ran the entire length of the sloped floor, liquids that pooled on chairs, soaked through chairs, liquids that splattered and stained the walls, and liquids that seeped into my shoes and wet my socks. And I'd think, why are we selling forty-eight-ounce sodas to children whose hands aren't big enough to hold the cups? Or to old men, who shook with palsy. Or to young men on dates, whose hands were interested in other objects. Or to anyone at all in dark theaters who can't see where they're going.

I'd find empty bottles of beer and rum and pills, and butts of joints. And, in partnership with the cockroaches that fed happily in the dark recesses, I'd clean up vomit, and urine, and once, a used condom. It would all meld into one hot mess of vile, human behavior that I embarked upon twelve times a shift. That is the job of a movie theater usher. And I'd think, wouldn't it be better if we left the lights on?

Finally, there is one other role of a movie theater usher—crowd control.

Stand here, form a line, don't move until I say it's safe to enter, because I'm in charge. I have a badge. It says USHER, which means I'm the sheriff. Don't enter until the cockroaches have had their fill and retreated to the dark corners and cracks of the room.

Then it's safe.

To enter.

One night I held the line for twenty minutes to disinfect and fan a theater that had been vomited in. Mr. Grant was hot when he heard the movie would start late.

"Our customers expect the movies to start on time, Billy. It's all part of the experience."

But I pointed out that while they waited, they would buy more overpriced shit to shove into their mouths. "That," he said, "is brilliant." He winked at me as if I'd just discovered a vein of Catalina gold.

"Let's hold the line for every movie," he said.

"Let's not," I pleaded. "The more shit they buy the more shit I have to clean up. They're disgusting."

"They're entitled," he corrected.

"Entitled?"

"Yes. Entitled to spend more money."

I saw his point.

And when we started holding the lines, concession sales shot up another twelve percent. That's when he promoted me to assistant to the assistant manager, which is just a fancy name for head usher. He said that I understood people.

"I understand that *lights-out* people are disgusting."

"Then you understand them perfectly."

"I do."

And I did.

I remind him of this as my performance review comes to a close. And as it happened, Safeway wanted Gus to start immediately and he had resigned this morning without my knowledge. So, Mr. Grant promoted me to assistant manager right there on the spot.

He high-fives me with an undersized, pudgy hand. "For the love of popcorn!" he says.

"To popcorn," I echo.

And this is how I reinvented myself and ascended to the greatest achievement of my adult life.

Meanwhile, living a very different life, Christmas Day had just been named to his second All-American team. I brushed it off. Uneasily so.

William Ball
Assistant Manager
Oracle Theater

18

Scatter
~ Pennsylvania, 1933 ~

On a brisk morning in Mount Lebanon, before the sun caught hold and the dew evaporated from neighbors' trees and manicured lawns, Paddy O'Donnell steadied himself on a stop sign three blocks from home. Bent at the waist, he held on with one hand, using the other to prop his barrel chest over his quivering knees. He wheezed and gasped for air, as his heart shuddered violently to escape to a kinder host. He shouldn't have tried to run. But Jimmy Flynn, that damn Jimmy Flynn, had gotten in his head. Paddy, old before his years, wondered what it might feel like to rise up on his toes and propel himself forward. And now he knew. It felt like death.

After the debacle in Boston, he'd retreated to his mansion to assess the state of his business. Congress had passed the Beer and Wine Act, which would pave the way to end Prohibition in the coming year. 3.2% beer was already legal, and real liquor would soon follow. He wasn't sure if things were blowing up or just crumbling, but either way his organization would soon be in ruins. The passage of the twenty-first amendment would destroy it all. Each day he spent hours on the phone with Franky, his consigliere, discussing finances and the end game.

Some of his bootlegger counterparts would hang on and reinvent themselves in other trades such as narcotics, prostitution, labor, and racketeering. He considered the transition himself. He had the means to do it. But pushing into new territory would invite violence, and in the end, he wanted no part of it. Not any longer. He had tired, and so, when the era of bootlegging came to an end he would simply disappear.

It would not be easy. Too many people relied on him. His money was in the pockets of politicians, beat cops, suppliers, associates, and his employees, which numbered in the hundreds.

He'd made enemies along the way. Disappearing would involve somewhere far-reaching, and forever. They'd come for him. But perhaps, if he ran fast enough, *poof!* He'd be gone and nobody would find him. That's what Jimmy Flynn liked to say. *If I run fast enough, poof, I'll be gone.*

A black Packard approached and slowed, coming to a stop just feet from him. In his line of work, it had the makings of a hit. Paddy, still holding on to the stop sign, flinched and momentarily cowered, before looking up to see an austere, gray-haired gentleman wearing a white fedora, posturing behind the wheel. The man rolled down his window and politely asked Paddy if he was in need of medical attention. Paddy took a couple deep breaths, gathering himself. He straightened, sneered, and told the man to keep driving or else *he'd* be in need of medical attention. "Wise guy, huh?" Perhaps the man recognized Paddy, because his expression shifted to fear, and he sped off.

It occurred to Paddy that in all the years he'd owned the mansion he'd never ventured beyond its front gate. He didn't know his neighbors, and they didn't know him. The streets felt as foreign to him now as the new world might have felt to Christopher Columbus. And so, he wondered, what else was out there beyond the horizon? What else was waiting for him, beyond...this.

Catching his breath, he placed both hands on his sides and walked home under a canopy of white-flowering magnolia trees, careful not to trip on the buckled sidewalk and unfamiliar cracks. He sneezed and his eyes watered. Everything was in bloom. Everything was changing and evolving. Including himself.

When he entered the house, the phone rang.

"Boss?"

"What is it?"

"It's Mike. I've been calling."

"I know your voice, dumbass."

"You sound out of breath."

"I *am* out of breath. I've been—running."

Big Mike let out a jovial, bellowing laugh. "Boss, you ain't no runner. No offense."

Paddy was in no mood. "Shut up. Why'd you call?"

"The Flynns are back. I'm sitting with them right now at the coffee shop. Johny's giving me the stink-eye. Says he still owes Jimmy Flynn a black eye."

"Tell Johny to shut the fuck up. Tell him he's fired."

"Fired?"

"Yes, fired. I'm tired of looking at his ugly, pockmarked face. He's bad for business. People look at that mug and they can't keep their food down."

"Will do, boss."

"What do the Flynns want?"

"They don't look so well, boss. A place to stay. Jobs. Says they've been kicked out of Wilmerding."

"Kicked out?"

"Kicked out. Locked out. The whole town is in an uproar over losing money on the kid. They've been ostra— ostra—"

"Ostracized?"

"Yeah, that's it, boss. Ostra—whatever you said."

Paddy thought about this.

"Give Johny's job to Daniel Flynn. Tell them they can stay in the upstairs apartment rent free until I figure things out. There. Problem solved."

"Will do, boss."

"One more thing. I'm going to be gone for a while. Maybe a long while. I need you to run the business. Are you okay with that?"

"You can always count on me."

"Good. But things are going to get messy, Mike. Don't fight it. There's nothing to fight. Just leave all the finances up to Franky. He knows what's going on."

"If someone asks where you've gone, what should I tell them?"

"Tell them I've gone fishing."

Paddy hung up.

Life was moving forward in ways he never imagined. In sorts, he was standing on a narrow, receding ledge, his back against a wall with his toes poking out over a great, clouded void. Peering out over this cliff, he saw nothing. The end of the world, perhaps? But he was ready to jump, a leap of faith. He removed a business card from his wallet and stared at it for a long while—O'Sullivan Loans—before picking up the phone and placing the call to Mike's cousin.

It rang several times before Sammy answered.

"Your boy lost fair and square."

"That's not the reason for my call, Sammy."

"Then—"

"It's all ending, you know," Paddy said. "Roosevelt is ending it. The wheels are in motion."

"Damned Roosevelt. I'm sorry, Paddy. It's a shame our government wants in on the action that good people like yourself built."

"I suppose," Paddy said. "Look, I no longer care."

"Then, what do I owe the pleasure?"

Paddy hesitated. "Remember the bar, the night before the marathon?"

"Sure, I do."

"Remember what you said?"

"I said a lot of things that night, Paddy."

"You said something about when this was all over, you'd go deep sea fishing off the Florida Keys."

"Oh yes, the Florida Keys."

"Well, that sounds nice...really nice. The Florida Keys, that is."

"What do you have in mind, Paddy?"

285

"Nothing. I mean, I just want to go fishing."

A cautionary, calculating silence followed. And Sammy answered, guarded. "I remember that conversation, Paddy."

"I was thinking—"

"About?"

"Doing some—fishing."

"Fishing?"

"Yeah, fishing. Off the Florida Keys. That's what I said."

"So, you want to go fishing off the Keys?" Sammy replied, circumspectly.

"Yeah, I want to go. I was thinking—"

"About?"

"Doing some fishing."

"Yes, you mentioned that. This feels like two sharks circling here."

"Well—"

"Are you inviting me to go fishing…with you?"

"Yeah. I guess so," Paddy answered. "I guess that's exactly what I'm doing."

More silence.

"I mean, I understand if now's not a good time," Paddy continued, hedging. "I just happen to have a lot of free time now, and apparently in the future…thanks to Roosevelt."

More silence followed.

Sammy broke first. "I need a few weeks to get things in order. To go…fishing."

"I can wait."

"We're just fishing, right?"

Paddy cleared his throat. "Just fishing."

"You realize, in our line of work, just how humiliating fishing can be if we got caught—"

"Fishing," Paddy finished.

* * *

Three weeks later, Paddy, Big Mike, Charles Finick, and the Flynns gathered under the dome of the coffered rotunda of Pittsburgh's Union Station. They stood in a loose circle, uncomfortable in each other's presence. There was so much to be grateful for, there was so much to be angry about, and there was so much still unknown.

Jimmy carried a small suitcase filled with his meager belongings. He was dressed for travel, in the same ill-fitting suit that he wore at the Boston Marathon reception. He also wore his canvas, rubber-soled running shoes. They squeaked on the white, marble floor of Union Station as he fidgeted in his surroundings. Sunbeams shot through the dome's skylight, spotlighting him.

"Ten minutes, Jimmy." Paddy glanced at his diamond-studded watch. "Boy, when things blow up, they really scatter," he said, adding some levity to Jimmy's sendoff.

"Sir?"

"You'll like Arizona," Paddy continued. "Charles says so."

"Thank you, Mr. O'Donnell."

"And your family will be fine here in Pittsburgh, running the coffee shop. Big Mike is going to look after them while I'm away…fishing."

"Thank you, Paddy," Daniel interjected.

The steam-engine whistle blew, an early announcement for passengers to board.

Charles Finick reached out to shake Jimmy's hand. "You've got the twenty-five-dollar advance?"

"In my pocket, sir."

"Don't get robbed."

Jimmy opened his suit coat to reveal his pocketknife. "I'll be fine, sir."

Charles nodded. "When you get off the train in Tucson, there'll be someone there to meet you."

Paddy, planning his end game and dishing out favors, had connected Jimmy and Charles Finick earlier in the week. Charles offered him a mining job at one of the company's new acquisitions north of Tucson. "It's a copper mine," he'd told him.

Jimmy scratched his head. "Copper?"

"Extracted from ore, Jimmy. Comes from the ground just like Pittsburgh coal. Didn't they teach you that in school?"

"I dropped out, Mr. Finick."

"Well, you'll learn," Mr. Finick said. "One more thing— it's hard work. But in the evenings, you can train for Boston, run in good weather instead of slogging around here in the freezing rain, choking on coal dust. That's what you want, right?"

"Yes, Mr. Finick. That's what I want. I made a promise to the dingers that I'd win Boston. I plan to uphold that promise, sir."

Jimmy turned to his family now, but not before Big Mike wrapped him in a bear hug. "Going to miss you, kid. I'll never forget that day you came into the coffee shop trying to rob us. You were a scared little shit. Now look at you. You're still a scared little shit." Mike turned to Shannon Flynn. "No offense, ma'am."

Mrs. Flynn nodded, but covered Maggie's ears.

The train whistle blew a second time.

"Wait, Jimmy." Paddy pulled out the *Arizona Highways* magazine that had been left behind by the flirtatious couple that day in the Wilmerding diner. "I've been holding on to this. I don't know why. Arizona's your future, not mine." He handed it to Jimmy.

On its cover was the huge saguaro cactus. Jimmy studied it for a second, trying to comprehend the green giant in an armored coat. "Thi-thi-this is Arizona?"

"Stay away from those things," Paddy said. "They look dangerous."

Jimmy admired the photograph. "I can't wait to see one up close and in person."

From the tracks: "All aboard!"

"I better get going," Jimmy said. He hugged Maggie and his mom. And without making eye contact, he shook his dad's hand. Then, in the scrum of other passengers eager to board, he disappeared from sight.

On board, he found his seat, and settled in for the three-day journey across the country. The train whistle blew a final time, a plume of black smoke released from its stack, steam shot from its sides, rods churned, and wheels churned, but like an old, stubborn mule, it fought to find its legs before inching away from the station. When it got up to speed, the rhythm and motion of its glide over the tracks rocked Jimmy to sleep.

When he woke, he was hungry. A black porter in a white jacket, who said his name was George, pointed him forward in the direction of the Pullman dining car. There, a white waiter wearing a long white apron and white gloves met him at the entrance. "We have one table."

The table was draped in starched white linen, adorned with polished silverware, fine china, and a vase with a single white rose. Red velvet curtains framed the windows. "Will this do, sir?"

Jimmy wasn't sure. It was *too* nice.

At the sight of Jimmy's canvas shoes, the waiter raised an eyebrow, viewing him with skepticism. Jimmy, seeing this, straightened his tie and apprehensively took a seat. The waiter then presented a menu in gold lace that was covered in protective plastic. He poured a glass of ice water from a silver craft and then excused himself for a moment.

In the fading light, Jimmy glanced out the window. The countryside passed by in frames—*Swoosh! Swoosh! Swoosh!*—with every crank of wheels and their exactness on the rails. It felt like riding in the belly of a beastly animal, calm and secure, protected from the snort and howl of living steel that thundered through tunnels, screeched on turns, and feasted on miles with a certain rabidness. In a sense, it reminded him of the veracity he felt when he raced.

He opened the menu and choked on his ice water when he saw the prices. *Nearly three dollars for a steak dinner!* He balked at the thought of treating himself, but for the first time since the eve of Boston, when he'd walked with Catherine Bechard along the Charles River, he felt alive, driven and resuscitated by the breath of the train itself. And so, when the waiter returned, he ordered it. The waiter, still skeptical, asked if he had the money to pay for it. When Jimmy pulled out a twenty-dollar bill, the waiter apologized and asked if he would care for a beer to complement the prime cut. "Sir, it's legal now," he said.

And Jimmy nodded his approval.

When the meal was served, he cut into the steak with savage abandon, uncouth and uncaring, as other diners looked on in dismay. But Jimmy was oblivious to their stares. He hadn't tasted anything this good ever. He took a long swallow of Budweiser to wash it down, then burped and smiled. He was living again, or maybe just for the first time. He wasn't sure. But he was happier than he could ever remember. He asked the waiter to bring him another beer, and when the waiter returned, he also brought with him a passenger looking to be seated for dinner. "It's the last seat available, ma'am."

Jimmy, still fixated on the steak, didn't bother to look up.

But the passenger, seeing his canvas running shoes poke out from underneath the table, gasped in recognition.

Startled now, he looked up. Their eyes met. She dropped her jaw. He dropped his fork and turned blue in the face, unable to chew, unable to swallow.

291

It was Catherine Bechard.

Catherine was striking, even more so than the first time Jimmy had laid eyes on her at the Lenox Hotel. She'd dyed her hair blonde and it fell to shoulder length, parted in the middle, and fashioned in waves that softened her appearance. She'd plucked her eyebrows and drew them on pencil thin, and higher. Later, she'd say all the movie stars did that to lift their eyes so that the camera could better capture their emotions. She wore pale ivory foundation in contrast to dark red lipstick, which accentuated her pouty, teasing lips. She was the image of her Hollywood idols.

When Jimmy asked how she'd come up with the money to travel and pursue her dream, she neglected to tell him she'd bet against him. *Those dingers were easy money*, she thought.

Catherine took her seat. She removed a cigarette from her purse and invited Jimmy to light it, but recalled that he didn't smoke. Instead, she lit it herself, exhaling to her side in the direction of other diners who looked on curiously. She told Jimmy that she'd secured a front-desk job at the Hollywood Roosevelt Hotel. "I'll be rubbing elbows and going to glitzy parties soon," she said. "I'll be discovered."

Jimmy's story was much different. He told her that he'd been ostracized from Wilmerding. "Being discovered isn't always a good thing," he joked. And that he'd secured a job in Arizona at a copper mine.

Both stood on the precipice of change, riding the rails into the unknown. But the very same train would deliver them to very different places: one chasing the spotlight, the other chasing spotlighted tunnels. And it was these differences that, once again, pooled their interests.

Unlike Boston, time riding the train was inviting and passed slowly. They ordered more drinks. Another beer for him, a second glass of red wine for her. Their conversation flowed freely and excitedly. Their eyes fixated on each other with no distractions. They talked of hope and better times that only youth can openly, palpably, dream of.

After dinner, they explored the length of the train. She, sashaying through the swaying cars with a certain grace that caught the eye of many interested male passengers. He, stumbling behind, finding hold of every other seat to steady himself, catching the eye of many jealous male passengers. How could *he* be with *her*?

They hopped from one Pullman car to the next. Each offered a new surprise. Some were for sleeping. One had rich, wood panels and an impressive library. Another was a cigar shop, and one offered a barber/valet. And in each car was a black porter who introduced himself as George.

Finally, they stopped between cars to breathe the fresh country air, cool now in the evening. Somewhere in Ohio? Somewhere in Indiana? They didn't know. They didn't care, because they were unburdened, and passing through at sixty miles per hour. Wind whipped their hair, and they gazed up at the stars that filled the night sky like fireflies hovering above the silhouette of endless cornfields.

The freedom was novel to both. They continued their push toward the back of the train, intoxicated on spirits, a keen fetish, and their very youth, until they came to the caboose, where they stood outside on a metal platform to view the tracks from which they'd come. Each rotation of the wheels, each tie passed over, distanced themselves from their pasts.

The train swept hard into a turn, rattling and lurching left, then right, then back to center. Catherine felt the bubbly lightness of speed that tickled her stomach. She held the iron railing tightly, and shook with laughter like a kid on a roller coaster, while Jimmy steadied her from behind with a hand on her shoulder, moving close enough to smell her perfumed scent.

He drew closer, his hand still resting on her shoulder. She allowed it to stay.

Beyond the transport of their physical beings, their emotional beings were also running fast.

"You look different, Catherine. You look so…happy."

She turned to meet his eyes.

"I *am* happy, Jimmy."

"You are."

"I'm happy to be on this train. I'm happy about leaving all *that* behind," she said, pointing on down the tracks.

"Is that all you're happy about, Catherine?"

She knew he wanted more. She wanted to give more.

So, she did.

"And I'm happy that I found you today, Jimmy," she said. "Tonight's been magical."

"Catherine."

"What is it, Jimmy?"

"I never got to thank you."

"For what?"

"For giving me that cocaine before the marathon. That was sweet of you. It almost got me to the finish line."

"I shorted you," she said, apologetically. "You'll finish next year. Just don't die again."

"Not everyone gets a second chance at life," Jimmy said.

"Or a second chance at death."

Catherine took a long drag off her cigarette.

"Catherine."

"What is it Jimmy?"

"Oh, nothing."

"You can say it, Jimmy. You can ask me anything."

"Ma-ma-may I kiss you?"

"No," she said, teasingly. "But I'll kiss you."

In a leap of faith that made no sense under any other circumstance, they drew closer. He touched her cheek with an open palm, and stared into her eyes that were ignited by the haunt of the evening.

The most beautiful girl on the train, perhaps in the entire world, was now in his arms.

She parted her red lips, slightly at first, before giving in to the moment and kissing his.

Just then the train whistle blew its stack. As if it knew. As if on cue. The two startled, and parted, and laughed.

"That was some kiss!" Catherine said, grabbing her heart.

"I always imagined it would be special, but not so loud."

They sensed the train was moving faster now, its wheels churning, heating up, an occasional spark, steam shooting from its sides, slicing through the unfamiliar and inconspicuous countryside like a bullet shot through the dark hollows of time.

There was no going back. For either.

19

You Can Fake It, But Can You Make It?
~ Arizona, 1995 ~

Every parent writes their kid's story far too soon. The kid sticks a landing, wins a spelling bee, completes a pirouette without falling on her ass, solos in band, solves a mathematical problem, scores a 1500 on his SAT, or wins a cross-country race. It's written just after the kid's fifteen minutes of fame. Parents' dreams are made from such moments. Dreams that their seed might sprout and grow and branch out to do something great, or good, or perhaps just worthwhile, so that when it's time to push him out of the nest and into the real world, they can do so without guilt, and proudly say they raised him well. That they, themselves, accomplished something worthwhile.

Please God, don't let him drown in our shallow gene pool. Don't let him fuck up, like us.

Inevitably, it never works out, because stories are best written in the first person, not by the parent, no matter how hard they try.

My parents had wonderful expectations of me, but not only did I edit the script, I rewrote it. I crossed out lines, entire paragraphs, ripped out pages, deleted passages, substituting them with my own watered-downed version. My story was written in a much smaller font, and included a footnote that read *Didn't go to college; kind of fucked up.*

Had I gone to college the scene of my leaving would have played out two years ago, and much differently. Mom would have stood in the driveway as I loaded my car, waving a pennant that read "STATE," and Dad would have sported the same college logo on a baseball cap. All smiles, they would have wished me good luck, and promised to visit often to watch me run. I'd turn the engine over, wave goodbye, but not before Mom told me to mind my grades, and Dad gave me some last-minute advice, whispering in my ear to respect college girls, but wear protection, just in case. He'd wink and I'd humor him by giving him a high-five. And I'd very slowly pull out of the driveway to appease them, looking both ways one last time, exiting stage left, leaving behind my childhood. I'd go on to receive a fine education, earn a bachelor's degree, and along the way, pridefully represent my future alma mater while winning a lot of races, substantiating my genealogy, my surname, and my great-grandfather's gift that fell him short. Everyone would have cheered for me. That's how it was supposed to be. That was my story, as written by my parents.

If my shorts hadn't been ripped off.

If I hadn't been accused of a crime and kicked off the team.

If I had gone to college.

Now, as Mom and Dad stood in the driveway to send me off, Mom was not waving a pennant; she was waving a tissue that she'd used to wipe away tears. Dad's shoulders slumped; his hands tucked in his pockets. There were no smiles. There was no cheering. They were sending me off into the real world as an assistant manager at a movie theater. In their minds, they had failed. Personally, I thought they were overreacting. After two years of happenstance, riddled with bouts of anxiety, I was happy with the direction. While it had veered from their script, and was certainly not the one I had envisioned, at least it was a direction of some sort.

My new job paid thirteen dollars an hour, plus popcorn benefits, as defined by Holly and me. I'd saved enough money to rent a nice apartment, and I was nearly a year into a relationship with her. One could argue that my life was justified and substantiated far more than my college friends who studied *general* this, and *general* that, none of whom held a job at the moment.

I loaded the last of my belongings into the trunk of the Escort. Mom kept crying, and Dad said to her, "Jesus Christ, Jean. The kid is twenty years old." Dad could be rather stoic when needed. But his body language suggested otherwise, and I sensed that this was not his finest day either. He looked...old. I reminded them that I was only moving fifteen miles south to Oro Valley, and that I'd come back often to do laundry.

"You've never done laundry in your life," Dad said. "Your mom does your laundry."

299

And for some reason this made Mom burst into another bout of crying—though she gathered herself quickly and forced a smile.

Jet looked troubled, his head hanging low. He paced back and forth, panting, and then jumped into the car to find his place on the passenger seat. Dad made a motion to stop him, but then refrained. He leaned in and petted his head, telling him to take care of me. Jet barked twice and wagged his tail. My parents were losing their only son and dog on the same day. I felt awful!

Mom raised her finger, and said, "Wait!" She went inside and came back minutes later carrying Jet's dog food and a leash in one hand, and a brown paper bag in the other. "In case you get hungry."

I peaked in to see a tuna sandwich and an orange. *Moms are the best.*

She smiled a thin smile and kissed my forehead. I could see more tears welling in her eyes; her pupils contracting now in the bright morning light, on par with her world that was about to get smaller with me gone.

And jokingly I said, "Don't do it, Mom! Don't cry. Don't you dare do it!"

Then, as I was about to drive away, Dad leaned in and gave me some advice—another edit from the story written years ago. He didn't advise me to wear protection. And we didn't high-five. He said something that made no sense at all. "Beware of imitations, Billy. And don't substitute for nothing. No replacements, no phonies, and no fakes."

I smirked and waited for the punchline. But Dad's face was stone-cold serious. These were his last words before sending me off into the world to fend for my own.

Then, from across the street, Old Man Baldwin appeared at his front door, wagging his cane, which flopped back and forth like a fish on land. In a voice that crackled, he yapped, "Good riddance to you and that horrible dog!"

Jet's interest piqued when he saw Old Man Baldwin coaxing him with the cane. He barked, saying hello, remembering the time when the two had had fun, wrestling with that stick. He thought Old Man Baldwin was the greatest biped ever.

"I guess it's time for me to go," I said.

Dad and I held back a laugh, and I very slowly pulled out of the driveway looking both ways, waving goodbye to Mom, just as the original script might have played out, exiting stage left, leaving behind my childhood. I was on my own now.

By the time I'd settled into my apartment it was dusk. I was tired from the day's move. I sat outdoors on a folding chair, with Jet by my side, and admired the shifting light and the panoramic view of the desertscape and Pusch Ridge from the second story balcony.

Pusch Ridge dominates the landscape of Oro Valley, and its deep crevices swallowed the failing light, leaving only it's bleached white, stegosaurus-like spine, to reflect the sun's last rays.

Jet sat attentively, drooling and eager to share the pizza I'd had delivered. Dogs are masters at communicating with their eyes. His were rheumy and focused, and told me I'll love you forever if you give me a slice. So, I did. He swallowed it whole, and those wanting eyes looked back at me, politely asking for another. "Tonight is special," I answered. "Two guys striking out on their own." So, I gave him another.

Then I opened a can of beer and offered it to Jet, but he snubbed it. "And you call yourself Man's Best Friend?" I stroked his head and rubbed behind his ears, and he licked the grease and pizza crumbs off my fingers.

It was still monsoon season, and as the sky faded to purple, cumulus clouds to the south stacked quickly to form a single, larger cloud that swept ominously across the valley floor, picking up steam as it spired into the heavens, pulsating, flashing heat lightning from its innards like muted beacons at sea. A sheer curtain of rain pushed out from beneath it. Twenty minutes later, the storm was upon us in its entirety. Jet moaned and cowered. But I loved this. The day's heat instantly smothered and erased. I absorbed the storm's punch, feeling alive and invigorated. This was happy hour in Tucson, and I savored every minute of it. I opened another beer, and still one more, enjoying the show and determined to ride out the storm under the protection of a low soffit that extended just far enough to keep us relatively dry. But when Jet's ears perked alarmingly and thunder rumbled and—*Boom! Boom! Boom!*—rolled directly above us now and lightning struck too close, we both tucked our tails and scurried inside. The monsoon storms were nothing, if not violent. "Smart dog," I said. "The Old

Pueblo is under siege. You're already doing a fine job of taking care of me."

Later that night, slightly drunk and definitely spent, I folded into my bed under cool sheets and lay awake listening to the storm cough and choke until it whispered and vanished like a ghost in chains that had rattled itself to sleep. The air in my room was stale, so I opened a window and the sweet scent of rain-soaked creosote bushes wafted up to my perch.

I lay back down and thought of the day with my eyes fixated on the ceiling. Moreover, I thought of the *significance* of the day. Nothing exists in perpetuity. Life's terms change and evolve. That's God's contract with us all. I'd never be that kid again in high school; the one my parents envisioned as achieving spectacular things, who could willfully throw himself into the depth of a running competition and come out the victor. Those days were gone. I'd never be that kid again who fried eggs on the sidewalk and threw pumpkins off cliffs with Charlie and howled at the moon. Those days were gone. I'd never be that kid again, period. "These things are gone forever, over a long time ago," sang Steely Dan.

My eyelids grew heavy, and Jet pressed against me, seeking warmth and security, curled at my feet and happily content, snoring. His presence was comforting and familiar. And as my eyelids fell one last time, I thought, some things in my story hadn't been rewritten. Some things stayed true to the script.

I understood now why Dad had let Jet come live with me.

***

A short time later I also understood why so many adults are miserable. As it turned out, the movie theater assistant manager hourly wage fell well short of supporting a nice apartment in Oro Valley, one that had sweeping views of the lush desert and Pusch Ridge. I complained to Holly that I wasn't making enough money.

But Holly had a solution.

She insisted that we expand the popcorn scam to include fountain drinks. When I objected, and pointed out that Mr. Grant already suspected foul play—since popcorn sales were not on par with fountain drink sales—she told me this idea was the perfect countermeasure. Placing the used fountain drink cups back in inventory would align the popcorn-to-drink ratio. Mr. Grant's suspicions would be satisfied. And, we'd make more money. It was a win-win, she said. I liked Mr. Grant. I liked Holly. A win-win sounded good. So, I agreed.

What I soon discovered regarding the issue with used fountain drink cups is that they became soggy if left to sit until the movie ended. Most had to be discarded, and our bump in income was barely noticeable. "That's it," I said after a few weeks. "I'll have to move back with my parents."

But Holly had another solution.

She showed up at my apartment a few days later carrying two large garbage bags stuffed with clothing. When I let her in, she rolled her eyes and motioned behind her. "Those boxes aren't going to move themselves," she said. So, I got busy, lugging her belongings upstairs. Jet circled nervously, and I tripped over him, dropping one of her boxes that had "fragile" written on it. "Easy!" she shouted blindly from the bathroom. "My bong is in that box."

Within an hour, we had moved her in. I excused myself to the bathroom. When I walked in, it was as if I'd stuck my head down a rabbit hole where a whole new world existed—a kaleidoscope of colors, scents, and foreign objects greeted me. The small one-sink vanity was cluttered with makeup, mascara, lipstick in eight shades, scented candles, scented soaps, scented lotions, hairbrushes, a curling iron, a blow-dryer, an assortment of toothbrushes, boxes of hair dye, a pint-size jar of Tylenol, razors, a plucking thing-a-ma-jig, and a box of tampons. She'd strung Christmas lights above the shower and hung colored loofahs. In the shower were scented oils and more lotions, scented soaps, and shampoos and conditioners with French names that I couldn't pronounce. And when I exited, completely traumatized, I asked, "Exactly how much time do you plan on spending in there?"

Then, in the bedroom, she'd placed a stuffed lion against the headboard. "It'll have to do for now," she said. "We need to make a run to Target and buy some decorative pillows." I raised an eyebrow, questioning. "Lionel needs pillows to rest on," she said without blinking.

The lion was indeed named Lionel. Lionel the Lion had seen better days; its mane was tangled and ratty, and one of its eyeballs had fallen from its socket, held on only by a few worn threads. She said she'd slept with Lionel since she was four years old and if I had a problem with that then she'd have a problem with me. I said that I didn't have a problem with that, and that I thought it was a cute toy.

Jet also thought it was a cute toy. He snatched Lionel from the bed, proudly showcasing the fetch in his mouth. Holly jumped from the sofa, but Jet was too quick and escaped through her legs. I laughed. But Holly was enraged, shouting at Jet to drop Lionel. When she finally trapped and caught him, she took hold of Lionel, and reminiscent of the scene with Old Man Baldwin, the two fought over the object until Holly, who'd had enough, smacked Jet hard on the nose, yanking Lionel from the grip of his mouth.

"Hey!" I protested. "That wasn't nice!"

She threw me a nasty look.

That first night, Holly had to work. I did not. She came home to find me fast asleep, with Jet curled at my feet. She shooed him off the bed, waking me, and when I asked in a groggy voice why she did that she told me dogs shouldn't sleep on beds. And I told her I'd slept with dogs in my bed since I was four years old, and if she had a problem with that then I'd have a problem with her.

And this was her response. She lifted the covers and crawled in beside me, removing her panties in the same motion. She ran her hand the length of my bare chest. She got on top of me and when I felt the brush of her on my thigh, I became instantly and impossibly aroused. She said I had a choice; I could either sleep with her or with Jet. So, guess what I did? We had sex as Jet whined from the floor. Lionel the Lion, still propped against the headrest, watched on with his one good eye, while the other hung and swung back and forth in rhythm with our joined motion.

Holly and I played house for the next month. We were barely adults, still figuring out how to live on our own, and with each other. More than once I'd forgotten to put the toilet seat down and she'd fallen in. She'd shout from the bathroom (I'm assuming in a compromised position) that I was an asshole. I'd apologize and agree.

We filled our days with the one thing we had in common: movies.

When we weren't working at the movie theater we'd stay home and watch movies. With Holly taking acting classes, she had a lot to say about them. Holly was very opinionated. We both enjoyed the ones that Mr. Grant recommended, the ones made in the golden era of Hollywood, though Holly said the women's roles were one-dimensional back then; that they all behaved too well, and only feigned love. "Vivian Leigh, Ingrid Bergman, Fay Wray, they're all phonies just waiting for the first man that comes along to sweep them off their feet."

"Fay Wray was swept off her feet by a big ape," I corrected her. "Quite literally. Was that not love?"

"That was love," she agreed. "That's the only kind of love that works; when a man keeps his mouth shut and is reduced to grunting. Now, shut up and watch the movie."

I grunted.

One evening we watched *The Wizard of Oz*, a movie each of us had seen countless times. We ate imitation crab meat and dipped it in imitation butter. When the scarecrow was disemboweled by the flying monkeys, and his innards lay scattered across the set, Holly rolled her eyes, and said, "This is so fake." And I replied, "It's Dorothy's dream, Holly. It's not real. Nothing in Hollywood is real."

"Actors are real. Acting is real," she replied.

"Acting is not real," I said. "Acting is acting."

"I'm myself when I'm acting," she insisted.

"Let me get this straight. You can only be yourself if you're playing someone else?"

"Exactly."

"So, the real you is someone else?"

"Yes."

"Well, that makes no sense at all," I said.

Neither of us worked much during the day. So, a few times a week Holly would attend her acting classes. She came home very excited one day, and said she'd landed a role in a commercial. She said it was for a new bubble bath, and that she'd have to seductively lay in a bathtub and rub bubbles up and down her arms and smile at the camera with fuck-me eyes. I raised an eyebrow, and Holly said, "Trust me, I'm good at it."

So, when Holly was out making that commercial, I spent time with Jet.

It was fall. The monsoons were gone, and we explored new, winding trails in the shadows of Pusch Ridge. Mostly we hiked, but occasionally the nostalgia of running sent me into a jog. We didn't go fast, or far. Jet was getting old, and

I was twenty pounds heavier than when I'd competed in high school against Christmas Day. If it was warm, Jet would stop at a stream crossing and lay in it, cooling himself until his tail wagged faster than his tongue. Getting to the top of a ridge, any ridge, was a victory that we'd celebrate by stopping to sit on a rock together, both of us panting. I'd put my hand on his head and stroke his ears, and he'd look up at me like I was his everything. "You love me, Jet?" He'd lick my face. "I love you, Jet." I'd kiss his head. And like two sentinels, we'd look out across the vast desert, and admire its form and color. Moments like this were real.

On one such afternoon, we'd returned from a hike-jog to find we had the apartment to ourselves. Holly had left a note that she'd gone to acting class again. When I sat down and opened a beer, my phone rang. It was Jack Ash.

"Dude! Did you hear?"

"Hear what?"

"Turn on the news. Christmas Day is on the news."

"Just tell me," I pleaded. "What did he win this time?"

"Dude, he was running on a trail outside of Boulder and was attacked by a mountain lion."

"A what?"

"A lion! A freaking mountain lion!"

"Was he…was he…." I didn't know to ask if he was injured or dead.

"He's fine. He's doing better than the lion," Jack said. "He killed the lion with his bare hands—strangled it to death!"

"Damn."

"Damn right. He's the man."

"He's always been the man."

"Yeah, but now he's a national news kind of man!"

When I hung up, I turned on the television. Sure enough, the story had made national headlines and he was shown in a hospital bed with a bandage on his forehead, being interviewed by an awestruck female reporter. I hadn't seen him in years, but he hadn't changed much. His black hair was longer and curlier now, and he still had that all-American charm about him, an impish grin, and a look so confident that I found it annoying. He told the reporter how the lion had stalked him before it pounced and how he'd fought for his life, managing to flip it and get on top before pinning it to the ground. He said the lion clawed at him, and took some skin off "right here," pointing to his forehead. But he managed to get his hands around the lion's neck and choke it until it lay lifeless. Christmas was all smiles, and I swear I thought the reporter, so impressed, so enamored, might blow him right then and there on the hospital bed.

My phone rang again and again. I heard from every one of the Fly Five. For some reason, each felt compelled to ask if I'd seen the footage of him gloating about having killed the lion with his bare hands. "Why are you calling me?" I asked, annoyed. "Why should I care?"

But I did care. Deep down, Christmas Day's success bothered me, and this news opened an old wound that festered the rest of the afternoon.

Christmas was not only living the story his parents had written for him long ago; he had added pages. A four-time state champion—one robbed from me—an All-American collegiate runner, a recipient of a full-ride scholarship, a free education, and now—drumroll, please—a lion killer. I was overcome with jealousy and bitterness.

From the bedroom, Lionel the Lion stared out at me with his one good eye. I asked him to stop, to please stop, but he kept staring, stalking my movements, mockingly, accusing me of a substitute life. I brought him out and placed my hands around his neck. "I know you're not the real thing," I said. "I know you're just an imitation yourself." But when his eye grew larger, more accusingly, I tightened my grip. Then, I thought about the charmed life of Christmas Day, and I squeezed tighter. I began choking him, strangling him, just as Christmas Day had done to his lion. "I'm going to kill you," I said. I squeezed even tighter, and twisted Lionel's neck, turning and pulling, and twisting harder, and he looked up at me with that one good eye in the pitiful way animals do when they want something—in this case, not to be murdered; his cheeks puffing, bulging with the polyester stuffing, as if he might pop, as if he was going to pop, until he did pop. I'd ripped his goddamned head clean off. Not even Christmas Day had accomplished that.

William Ball, Lion Killer. Stud.

This made me feel immeasurably better. "Who's bad now, huh? I'm bad!" I laughed like a madman and fed Lionel's body to Jet, who took him to a corner and began to slowly disembowel him. "Good boy," I told Jet. "Get to it."

I went to the bathroom to relieve myself, and when I came out, Holly was back from acting class. She stood in the middle of the living room, her eyes wide, disbelieving, following the trail of animal stuffing like blood to a scene of a crime. Her eyes stopped on Jet, who had Lionel pinned down with a paw, plucking his stuffing out in cotton ball pieces, oblivious to Holly's presence.

Holly shrieked and rushed to beat Jet over the head with her purse. She swung and missed, and Jet scampered away quickly, cowering as he went. I rushed forward to get between them.

With her purse already cocked and loaded, she took a swing at me and struck my head.

"Goddamn, Holly! That hurt!"

"How did you let this happen? Your fucking dog! Look at my Lionel!"

Lionel was no more. Lionel was in pieces. Lionel was disemboweled.

I didn't respond right away, taking a moment to weigh the evidence surrounding Lionel the Lion's death, seeing his stuffing strewn across the floor in little patches. "I think it was the flying monkeys that got him," I finally said.

"Fuck you," she replied.

But this time, I stood my ground. "And don't ever touch my dog again."

***

312

Holly and I made up in a few days after I surprised her with a new stuffed lion. This one was bigger and softer and wore a king's crown. I'd wrapped it in red ribbon and handed it to her as a peace offering. I was truly sorry for what I'd done to Lionel. And I was also guilty as I let Jet harbor the blame. "I know it's not Lionel the Lion. It's just a substitution," I said. "But he has two good eyes. Can you forgive us?"

Jet wagged his tail, understanding.

Holly rolled her eyes and reluctantly accepted it. I put it in her hands and she warmed quickly, bringing it to her chest, squeezing it, testing its softness. Then she held it at arm's length, examining it, straightening the crown, and finally saying, "I think I could love you—King."

I was relieved. "Then you forgive me?"

"I'll think about it," she said.

The phone rang, and Holly set King down to answer it. "Hello?"

No response.

"Hello? Is anyone there?" She hung up. "Nobody there."

We went to work later that afternoon. Holly was in a great mood. It was Saturday and the theater was abuzz. We anticipated a big payday.

Prefontaine, a movie chronicling the life of the legendary middle-distance runner, was premiering and had caused a big stir within the running community. Running geeks and their tolerant, eye-rolling loved ones had raced to the theater to pay homage to this idol on opening night.

Mr. Grant pulled me aside and put me in charge of crowd control. He poked my chest with his stubby finger and said with certainty that nobody could hold a line like me, and that we'd make a killing on concessions tonight. He coughed and went back to his office.

The line for *Prefontaine* snaked the entirety of the lobby like an agitated rattler about to strike. It was not going to be easy holding it.

My eyes ran its length. I recognized many. Some, I'd run against years back. Others, I knew from local road races, much older than me but still familiar faces. Then I saw Coach Jones and the Oracle High School cross-country team tucked three-quarters back. I was only two years removed from high school. Since then, my own legend had grown, mostly around fire pits and water coolers, in locker rooms, and at other such gatherings when people needed a laugh. I was always going to be remembered as the kid who'd finished the state cross-country meet pantless. No matter what I did, I would never escape those fifteen minutes of fame.

A voice rose above the din and I heard my name called out. "Billy Ball!" Fingers pointed my way. I played coy among this crowd of runners. But when shouts of Billy Ball turned into jests of "Balls Balls Balls," I swallowed hard. Chuckles turned into laughs, and laughs turned into bellows. How could I have not seen this coming? How could this be happening?

I stood before them, not on a podium like the champion I once was, but behind a podium, a celebrity askew, like a washed-up prizefighter, ready to ask for their tickets and thank them for coming.

When I finally released the line, it came at me like a procession of humiliation. I mechanically tore each ticket as I entertained comments and snickers and mentions that I was as famous as Prefontaine in these circles.

By the time Coach Jones and the team got to me, I felt like I'd been gut-punched a million times. Coach saw the hurt in my eyes, and he put a hand on my shoulder and told me not to let these jackasses get to me. "They mean well, Billy," he said. "They're just having fun." Then he motioned for me to call him, but not before asking if I'd heard the news about Christmas Day.

And that was it. A sucker punch to the kidneys. Down for the count I went.

Coach waved goodbye, and my eyes followed him and the team down the hallway as I blindly tore the tickets of those still in line.

Then, a hand reached out, touching mine. "Which theater is *Prefontaine* showing?"

"Just follow the—" I stopped short, placing the voice immediately. I looked up.

It was Charlie.

Her smile was radiant and her gold-speckled eyes were as lively as I remembered them.

"Hey there, stranger! Tough crowd tonight."

"Is it really you?"

She stepped around the podium and we hugged. I didn't let go. I couldn't let go. Until I had to let go.

"I can't believe it's you!"

"In the flesh."

Behind her was Jennifer Ledge, who'd stayed local to run for Arizona. Jennifer smiled, acknowledging me. "I'll get our seats," she said to Charlie. "You two can catch up."

By this point the line had dwindled. I tore the remaining tickets and pulled her aside. I didn't know where to begin. She looked older, more confident, and certainly as buoyant as ever.

"I've missed you, Charlie."

I didn't know what to ask. So, I asked it all. "How's school? Are you running well? How's your mom? What's college like?"

"Slow down, BB," she laughed. "We have so much to catch up on. I'm running with Jenny in the morning. Want to come?"

A run. With Charlie.

"Yes," I said. "But I didn't know you were in town."

"Just for the weekend," she said. "I called."

"You called?"

"This afternoon. But your parents must have given me the wrong number. A woman answered."

Then it hit me. Charlie had been the one who'd called earlier and hung up. She had no idea I was living with Holly. She probably had no idea that Holly existed. We'd grown apart in such a short time. Our paths, which years ago paralleled each other's like two sturdy legs, had splintered and split.

"Holly," I said. "My girlfriend—her name is Holly. She's the one who picked up the phone." I didn't mention we were living together. I pointed her out behind the concession stand.

"The one with the D-cup and the pink hair?" she said. "Impressive."

Charlie hadn't changed at all. She was still direct and a smartass. And I loved her for it.

"It's not always pink. She's an actress," I explained. "Sometimes it's blonde, and other times she's a redhead and..." And realizing how unimportant and silly this sounded, I stopped talking in mid-sentence. Here I was, trying to defend Holly and her hair color, passing her off as a real actress, as a real girlfriend, even as I watched her squirt fake butter onto pre-popped popcorn.

Holly happened to look up just then, and she and Charlie locked eyes. Both curious.

I stiffened and pulled back.

"She's pretty," Charlie offered. "I didn't mean to—"

"It's okay, Charlie. I should have told you. We've been dating for about a year now."

Charlie motioned that the movie was about to start. "I should be going." She turned to leave, but then paused. "I'm happy for you, BB. I really am."

"Really? I'll introduce you later," I said, calculating.

"It's okay, Billy." She paused again and carefully chose her next words. "I came to the theater tonight to see a great runner," she said.

"Prefontaine was the—"

She cut me off. "And I have. Here you are, in the flesh. I miss running with you, BB."

But before I could echo those sentiments another movie let out and we parted ways.

Like a murder of crows, me and the ushers descended on the room and picked it clean in mere minutes. I collected a handful of acceptable popcorn buckets (not stained by fake butter) and stashed them in the broom closet until Holly barked to bring them out.

We pushed our luck. I brought her twenty buckets after the first round of movies.

Mr. Grant called me into his office shortly after. I walked in with trepidation, thinking our luck had run out. But he coughed, told me he was feeling ill, and asked if I could manage things since he needed to leave.

"You don't look so well yourself," he said. "You're sweating."

"Well, I *was* sweating. I feel much better now."

"So, you can manage the theater if I leave?"

"I can absolutely manage things, Mr. Grant."

Ten minutes later Mr. Grant was gone.

I'm not sure why kids turn to bedlam with the absence of authority. It's like a permission slip to lose their minds.

We had a full staff that night; ten ushers, ten concession girls, two others who worked the box office, and a projectionist who was in his mid-forties, but he always left after he fed the last movie, leaving us animals in charge of the zoo.

I took thirty dollars from Mr. Grant's petty cash drawer, gave it to Thomas, and told him to buy a few cases of beer. He returned and stashed it in the ice bins.

318

An eight-hour shift on a Saturday night was exhausting work, and by the time the last movie let out, and I'd locked the doors, beer was already in circulation among the staff.

At this point, Holly had completed inventory and tallied the books, and I had removed the cash from the registers and placed it in the office safe, as instructed by Mr. Grant.

It was no secret that Holly and I were a couple. So, while the staff mingled, drank, and played video games, Holly and I found ourselves on a bench in the lobby. She removed a joint from her purse, lit it, and took a drag.

"Excuse me, miss. This is a no-smoking theater," I said.

"Want a hit?"

"I do." And I did.

"Who was that girl you were talking with tonight?"

"That was Charlie Simmons," I said. "She used to be my teammate."

"Is that all she used to be?"

"We are—were—friends."

Holly took my hand in hers, drawing me close, and kissed me. "I'm sorry that I've been such a bitch lately," she said. "We're a good team." Then she whispered in my ear, "We made 240 dollars tonight on popcorn buckets. I don't want you fucking that up."

"There's only one of you," I said, unsure of what to say. With Holly, I felt like I was one misplaced word away from trouble.

Then, Thomas yelled, "Who knows how to run the projector? I've got porn!"

Although I was in charge, I looked at Holly for permission.

"It wouldn't be the first porn movie shown in this theater," she said.

"If only Mr. Grant knew."

We laughed, and kept laughing. And for the first time in a long while I felt like all things were forgiven between us. I considered the possibility that it might work with Holly, that she might be the one.

So, I went upstairs to the projector room and loaded the movie, while Holly said she'd bring the popcorn and meet me inside the theater room. I joined her and fifteen of the staff several minutes later. The show was about to begin.

"Did you bring the popcorn?"

"I forgot," she said. "I'll be right back."

The opening credits rolled to cheesy music with wah-wah pedals and a minor 7 chord that sounded like a bad knockoff of Marvin Gaye's "Let's Get It On."

"Hurry up," I said. "You don't want to miss this!"

My eyes were fixated on the screen now.

Enter a woman with her backside to the camera wearing a red silk robe. She has platinum blonde hair that's cut and curled shoulder length. Beyond her is a large, bear-claw tub. A man with thinning, feathered hair and a pencil-thin mustache soaks in it; his eyes follow the woman across the white-tiled bathroom floor. She sashays toward him, letting the robe slip away mid-stride, her full bottom on display. She's wonderfully tan, except for her ass. Several staff whoop and holler. "Hell yeah," Thomas the usher yells out. "Show us what you've got, baby!" The woman stops at the tub and the man smiles confidently. She turns, but ever so slightly, to reveal large, pronounced breasts. Her face is still hidden. She reaches for a bottle adjacent to the tub. More oohs and aahs from the staff now. The woman laughingly pours bubble bath onto the man's chest, rubbing it in. The man moans and invites her to join him. She steps over the lip of the tub and slips into the bubbly water, taking a position on top.

Meanwhile, Holly is coming back with the popcorn. She makes her way across the long, dark aisle, careful not to trip, until she reaches me. "What did I miss?" she laughs. "Sounds hot!" She turns to view the movie, and her laugh instantly falls away. She drops the bucket of popcorn in my lap and screams, just as the woman on the screen reveals her face to the camera.

There are no oohs and aahs from the staff this time. There is only dead silence, as several turn to find her.

Once, when Holly and I began dating, she told me that one day the two of us would sit in this very theater and watch her do amazing things on the big screen.

Holly had not lied.

♪ *Let's get it on…Let's get it on…Let's get it on…* ♪

20

Stuck on You
~ Arizona, 1934 ~

For all the hot, stale sunny days that bake Tucson, the Sonoran Desert has its rainy season. Spring storms butted against the Santa Catalina Mountains, unleashing the heavens like a hammer to a well, turning usually-dry watersheds into swollen rivers from its nine-thousand-foot perch.

In a fading light, Jimmy ran with precision and purpose along the old mule trail that hugged the rugged base of Mount Lemmon. He bounded over nags and chutes where new streams had formed, carefully negotiating fields of scree and loose gravel, chased by a thunderous storm that threatened to engulf him altogether if he slowed. But he did not slow. He kept one step ahead, confident that he could outrun it, just as he had outrun his past back in Pennsylvania.

Just ten months ago, he'd stepped off the train in Tucson. It was like stepping onto the sun.

He was met by a blinding light, a cutting, hot wind, and fierce heat. He gripped a steel railing to steady himself, but it singed his hand and he pulled back instinctively. *Is this*

Hell? He squinted and shielded his eyes, making his way indoors to the depot. There, he spotted a large man with a round head and sunburnt cheeks, dressed in a lightweight, pinstriped gray suit.

The fat man held a placard that read "JAMES FLYNN." He forced a thin, welcoming smile, looking past Jimmy. That is, until Jimmy obscured his view, pointing to the sign.

"That's me," he said. "I'm James Flynn!"

"You're James Flynn?" His smile was gone now.

"In the flesh, sir."

He stepped back, surveyed Jimmy, and said nothing.

"Were you expecting someone else?" asked Jimmy.

"Someone who can swing a pickaxe," he said. "Damn that Charles Finick. There ain't nothing to you, son. You're just a pile of bones."

"I'm tougher than I look, sir. Before I got on that train my dad told me if I was going to mine, be the best miner I could be."

"That's all fine, son. But did your daddy ever feed you?"

"I'll work hard, sir."

"Fine then. I'm Horace Grant, general manager of the Oro Canyon Mining Company. You may never see me again, God willing. You'll be reporting to Otto Vokovotto at Number Sixteen Mine."

"I see." Jimmy nodded. "Thank you for picking me up, Mr. Grant."

"No need to thank me. I was in town to gather some supplies. So, here I am. C'mon now." He motioned for Jimmy to follow, then noticed his shoes.

"Jesus H. Christ! What are those?"

"They're my shoes, Mr. Grant. I run in them."

"You *what* in them?"

"I run. In them."

"You won't be running here," he said. "You'll be mining." Horace rubbed his unshaved chin, questioning the shoes. "Whatcha call them—running shoes? Is that all you brought, son?"

"Yes, sir."

"Well, you sure as shit can't work in those. I assumed you had experience working a mine, being from Pittsburgh," Mr. Grant said. "I'm not sure why Mr. Finick would send you out here."

"Mr. Finick thought the climate would be good for me to train in. He thinks I can win the Boston Marathon."

"The what?"

"Boston. The marathon."

"Did you come out here to work or run? If you came out here to run then you better run right back on that train."

"Never mind, sir," Jimmy said. "I'll work hard. I appreciate the opportunity."

They drove to Steinfeld's Department Store in downtown Tucson, and with the remaining advance, Jimmy bought a pair of denim jeans and leather boots with a top cap over the toe to protect his feet while working the mine.

When they exited, Jimmy spied the Fox Theater directly across the street. Its Art Deco design looked peculiarly out of place, juxtaposed alongside drab commercial storefronts on Congress Street. "FOX" was spelled out vertically on a towering sign that hung above a canopy marquee that showcased the current showing: *It Happened One Night*, starring Clark Gable and Claudette Colbert.

A half day removed from parting ways with Catherine, he was already missing her. After a heartfelt goodbye, she'd continued west to Los Angeles to pursue her dream of becoming an actress. He headed south to Tucson to pursue something entirely different: reality. He stood, staring at the marque for too long, romancing her name in place of Claudette Colbert's.

"Come now, Mr. Flynn. It's an hour's drive. That copper's not going to mine itself."

"Of course, Mr. Grant. My apologies."

"It's all right," he said, warming. "You like the movies, kid?"

"I guess so, Mr. Grant. I haven't seen many. There's a girl…" But his words trailed off.

They got in the car and drove off. Jimmy glanced back one last time at the theater.

"I like the movies," Horace offered. "After my wife died, I'd take my son to the Fox every Saturday. Then Mr. Finick bought the mine, and now I work on Saturdays. Says we've got to keep up with demand. Says Roosevelt is pushing the country towards electrification and it's driving copper demand through the roof."

They drove north on a single-lane road that made its way through the undulating foothills of Tucson. Despite the torrid heat, Jimmy craned his head out the window like a dog smelling new scents. Everything was novel. The view up the road, so hot, a mirage of water pooled on the asphalt, and Jimmy shook his head as if he was seeing things. "I'm seeing things," he shouted. Minutes later, he spied a stand of saguaro cacti and asked Mr. Grant to stop. "I ain't never seen anything like that except in a magazine!"

"You'll see them up close soon enough."

Jimmy stuck his head back out the window, energized as he set his sights on a mountain that stretched miles into the sky. "We've got hills in Pittsburgh," he shouted, his sinewy, long neck stretched for a better view. "But I ain't never seen nothing like that!"

"What?"

Louder: "I said we've got hills—"

"I can't hear you, son!"

Jimmy pulled his head back inside the car. "If we had mountains like that back in Pittsburgh, you couldn't see them with all the smog and coal dust."

"That's Mount Lemmon," Horace pointed out. "The mine is on the north side of it. Look, you're not a tourist. Don't fall in love, Jimmy. You'll be gutting it soon."

On that drive, something changed in Jimmy. He felt giddy. The recognition that life was about to change; that he could rewrite the story his parents had written for him. Sure, he'd be the best miner he could be, but he sensed that other opportunities awaited him. He'd been given a second chance at life.

He felt intentioned now, and by the time they arrived in Oracle, Jimmy was speaking openly like he'd never done, as if talking about his past self would free his future self. He told Mr. Grant about his family, and Paddy, and that his family was now managing and working Paddy's coffee shop in Pittsburgh, while Paddy had gone fishing with a business associate someplace south that he'd never heard of. He told him about Wilmerding and how the people had once laughed at him before they loved him, and when they fell out of love with him, they kicked him out of town. This led him to speak about the Boston Marathon again, and that he was going to return next year to settle things. Then he stopped mid-sentence when he saw the disapproving look on Mr. Grant's face.

"There you go again, Jimmy. You talk too much for your own good."

"Sorry, Mr. Grant."

"Look, I don't know much about running," Horace said. "What would I know? I barely fit behind this steering wheel. You're free to run after work, any time. The Boston Marathon, huh?"

"Yes, sir."

"You're a strange kid, Jimmy Flynn, but you're all right. Say, you got yourself a girl back home? You started to mention a girl earlier."

Jimmy told him about Catherine Bechard. "She's gonna be a movie star one day, Mr. Grant. She's the most beautiful girl in the world!"

Looking at Jimmy, who was anything but handsome, Mr. Grant doubted that was true.

They passed over Pima Wash on an expansive concrete bridge, piquing Jimmy's curiosity. "Where's the water?"

"There ain't no water. Here, in Arizona, that's what we call a river. Runs dry most of the time, but when the monsoons hit, stay away. The washes are watersheds from Mt. Lemmon. They turn violent. The runoff moves boulders as big as houses. Sweeps cars away, and people too."

They stopped in Oracle to fill up with gas before heading up to the mine. A man in chaps rode by on a horse, tipping his cowboy hat. *Right out of the movies*, Jimmy thought. He nodded back. All around him, the bustling, fledgling town was taking root. While the coal mines in Pittsburgh faltered and failed, the copper mines in Southern Arizona were thriving, buffering towns like Oracle from the harsher realities Jimmy had known back east. Newly paved streets and new construction was evident all around him.

He'd heard about the gold rush nearly a century earlier, and wondered if this copper rush was akin to it, attracting frenzied, unskilled laborers like himself from far-away places, perhaps as far as Europe and China.

They drove ten miles out of town on a rough, dirt road that ended at the head of a U-shaped canyon. Number Sixteen Mine was dug into the side of a steep wall face. On either side, granite spires towered above the opening, making it appear castle-like. The entrance was encased by sturdy, wooden beams that framed a steel track to move carts of ore.

"This is very remote," Jimmy said. "Where are we?"

"Does it matter? There's a vein of copper in there," Horace replied. Then, when Horace escorted Jimmy to the company-built bunkhouse, Jimmy's earlier thoughts were confirmed when told he'd be sharing it with three others—all immigrants.

The bunkhouse had two bedrooms, but it felt more like a barrack with no windows or indoor plumbing. It sat in a short row of similar houses.

He shared a room with a Fin, Ekke Kokko. Ekke had high cheekbones and piercing blue eyes like Jimmy's. He spoke with a clenched jaw and apologized for "Not knowing English so much." He was a powder monkey, prepping dynamite charges to take into the mine.

Jimmy's other bunkmates, like himself, swung pickaxes and shovels ten hours a day. Baldassare Guiluliani was Italian, and Yiannis Christodoulopoulos was Greek, and in their native languages they often quarreled about having to room with each other, given their country's differences. But at night, after their shifts ended, these things were set aside and friendships forged around fire rings. Each shared the mutual respect of sweat and labor in the mine. They'd pass whisky back and forth, tongue-tied in broken English, trying to pronounce each other's names. Baldassare became Baldy. Christodoulopoulos became Chris. But Kokko stayed Kokko, as did Flynn.

Each looked to Jimmy to teach them better English. "Let me get this straight," Jimmy would say. "You want me, an uneducated Irishman from Pittsburgh, to teach you English? Jesus, Mary, and Joseph. Feck off, ya bunch of eejits."

Laughter was a language they all understood. Most nights, the four went to bed drunk, happy, gassy, and dreaming of women, which were nowhere in sight unless they ventured into town. And even then, there were none that would have them.

Not only was Number Sixteen Mine isolated, it was the newest and smallest of all the mines belonging to the Oro Canyon Mining Company. Only thirty crew were assigned to it, along with the shift manager, Otto Vokovotto.

When Jimmy asked Otto Vokovotto how to pronounce his name, he was wishy-washy and said either way was fine. "Pronounce it forwards or backwards. It doesn't matter. It's the same."

Otto Vokovotto was assigned his own bunkhouse, which was no better than the others. However, he had one thing that the others did not—a company-owned vehicle. So, with few options to travel into town, the miners did their best to stay on Otto's good side.

It was possible to go an entire week without seeing anyone outside of the crew, especially if your job was to swing a pickaxe inside the mine. Administrators, geologists, and supply and hauling truck drivers were a welcomed sight. Life at the mine became a monotony of labor and drink, with an occasional evening gallivanting the bars in Oracle.

There was no time or motivation to run. The end of each shift left Jimmy sore and sometimes broken. His running shoes remained tucked underneath his bunk.

One day, Mr. Grant showed up unexpectedly. Jimmy was working inside the mine, mid-swing with his pickaxe, when one of the other crew yelled to him to hightail it out because Mr. Grant needed to see him right away; that Mr.

Grant was waiting for him in Otto's bunkhouse with some dame—likely an administrator.

"What does he want?" Jimmy asked. "Am I fired?"

"Beats me, Jimmy."

He exited the mine, walking stiffly, clanking metal, to Otto's bunkhouse. He didn't knock, but simply opened the door to find Mr. Grant standing squarely in the middle of the small quarters, his presence large and shielding.

Mr. Grant stepped aside. On a dirty sofa, in a clean floral-print dress, sat Catherine Bechard, looking out of place and troubled, biting her nails.

Jimmy made a move toward her. She was merely eight feet away, but her expression was distant. She was out of reach.

Catherine's lips were drawn before curling into a razor-thin smile. "Hey, Jimmy." She swallowed hard. He swallowed harder. "Looks like I'm stuck on you," she said, her hand resting on her belly. "I'm pregnant."

$$* * *$$

Now, heading back to Number Sixteen Mine on the mule trail, Jimmy swept through a turn too fast, remembering that life-changing moment. Catherine had appeared forlorn, but he was elated at the thought of becoming a father.

He passed through a thick stand of saguaro cacti, some forty feet tall with ten or more arms. They were ghostly, monstrous, and silhouetted in the fading light. His mind drifted to those first few months with Catherine.

On a Saturday morning, three weeks after she'd shown up, they were married in the Oracle Courthouse. Before an indifferent judge, the two stood as mismatched as pass and fail. Catherine wore an ivory satin, pared-back slip dress that hugged the contours of her budding frame. Jimmy wore his ill-fitting suit and his canvas running shoes that protruded from under the cuffs. She held a bouquet of desert flowers, freshly picked, and fought back a sneeze, while Jimmy nervously held an open box that contained a copper wedding ring. The ring was special, hammered from copper ore extracted from Number Sixteen Mine. "With this ring, I'm stuck on you," Jimmy said, mimicking her the day she announced she was pregnant. Catherine wiped away a tear, but for the first time since she'd arrived, she smiled, accepting of him and their fate.

Mr. Grant bore witness. As did Jimmy's bunkmates, Baldy, Chris, and Kokko, who were excited to see an American wedding, even as they sat many rows back dressed in their work clothing, unkept and unshaven. Each was taken aback by the ceremony; not for its sentiment, but for its lack thereof. It had only taken ten minutes. There was no organ music. There were no flower girls. There was no reception. Other than themselves, there were no guests.

Fortunately, a saloon stood across from the courthouse, and so, as to not waste the day, they made their way over after the judge pronounced Jimmy and Catherine man and wife.

Mr. Grant, on the other hand, thought the ceremony was splendid, even finding himself moved to tears by it. He'd taken a liking to Catherine since she'd shown up at his office looking for the whereabouts of Jimmy Flynn. "I don't get many visitors that look like you," he'd said, mentioning that Jimmy had described her well; that she *did* look like a movie star. "Well, plans change," she'd responded flatly.

After the wedding, Mr. Grant presented the two with a brochure of El Rancho Robles, a local, glorified dude ranch.

"What's this?" Jimmy asked.

"It's your honeymoon, Mr. and Mrs. Flynn," Horace said, smiling. "This place promises to make dreams come true. Says so right here on the brochure."

Horace Grant was a good man.

But each subsequent day brought new challenges. Catherine had roomed at an inexpensive hotel those first few weeks, and considered where they might live as man and wife. Where would they raise their child? She couldn't stay out at the mine. Jimmy couldn't stay in town. And when Catherine confided in Mr. Grant, he proposed that she nanny his young son. "I need the help," he'd emphatically said.

Raising the boy was a tall task for a widowed man who worked six days a week. Catherine happily agreed, and Mr. Grant put her up in the ranch's guest house.

At only four years old, young Grant was not old enough to attend school. Catherine's job was to watch over him and educate him during the weekdays. And on Saturdays, take him into Tucson for the matinee at the Fox Theater. "He likes that, Catherine. And you're perfect for the job," Horace told her. "Tell him all about those movie stars you mingled with."

Sundays were the only days Catherine and Jimmy would see each other. Jimmy would lace up his shoes and run the ten miles into town. But their interactions were awkward and complicated. Even as their unborn child grew inside her, they were still getting to know each other. They were barely older than kids, testing boundaries, losing hope, sparring, before finding hope again.

They'd spend time walking the grounds of the ranch, occasionally strolling into town, shopping for baby items without yet knowing its gender. She'd walk stiff-necked with purpose, while he shuffled behind, hands in pockets, as if not worthy of her company. For an unknowing observer, it was impossible to believe the two were together, much less married. He'd ask her about Hollywood, and her work at the hotel, and she'd say it was a disappointing experience, that it wasn't how she'd pictured, that she'd only met a few stars, and that they'd treated her with indifference. "And when my manager found out I was pregnant, he fired me. He wouldn't have me greeting guests when my belly grew fat."

"That was the end of the road for me," she told Jimmy. In turn, she asked him about life in the mine, and he told her it was hard work, but that any work was good work and that their baby would be well cared for. Then, she awkwardly asked if he still ran. With this, he fell silent,

335

avoiding the question, and placed his hand on her belly and pridefully looked into her eyes, anchoring.

"The baby is growing," he said. "I can feel it."

"The baby will be perfect. Be a dear now and hand me my cigarettes."

The Sunday visits passed too quickly, and when they parted ways, he'd run the ten miles back to the mine, yearning for the next chance to see Catherine and her bump, their unborn child.

He grew frustrated. He asked Otto Vokovotto to borrow the car on occasion. Otto refused, reminding him it was a company vehicle and that he was not authorized to drive it. But in the same breath, Otto mentioned the old mule trail that cut miles off the road route into town. The next day, Jimmy set out to find the trail.

What he found was overgrown, parts collapsed from the runoff of monsoonal storms that hammered Mount Lemmon. But Otto Vokovotto had been right. The trail cut the travel time to Oracle in half. From then on, Jimmy could run into town to see Catherine—if his spent body willed it—and still make it back before nightfall.

Distance is not only measured in length. It's also measured emotionally. The more time spent together, the closer they became. A greeting turned into a smile that turned into a laugh, then a hug, and a hug became a kiss, and a kiss beckoned a heartfelt moment. Along the path, there were nudges, retreats, sparks ignited, and sparks extinguished. But slowly, it happened. The distance between them grew shorter, until one day it was no longer there. Just in time for the baby.

* * *

Now, as Jimmy jumped a fat rattler that had been flooded out of its hole, he thought of the day Jacqueline was born. He held her in his arms and whispered in her ear, "I'm stuck on you." He kissed her forehead.

He continued along the trail, picking up the pace as the storm closed in. Spit hit his back, pushed by a kicking wind and claps of thunder, and he laughed at his maniacal push to run faster, for taking pleasure in something so primal that sane men wouldn't understand. But consternation had set in. The storm was swallowing him. He jumped a newly formed stream, landing on a soft patch that gave way beneath the weight of his footfall. Then, a larger runoff appeared before him, and he jumped that too, but just barely.

Still, he sped onward, giving thanks for the chance to train in earnest for Boston. Back in September, one near-tragic event had given him this opportunity.

Then, Southern Arizona had experienced an active end to its monsoonal season. With swords of lightning and drums of thunder the storms attacked every evening, saturating the ground and triggering rock slides. And because of its location in the canyon, the mining camp was in the crosshairs of flash floods and debris fall. This particular day, the crew joked that the safest place to be was inside the mine.

Then a massive slide occurred, knocking out a radio transmitter and covering the mine. Otto sounded an alarm and led the charge to help those who were trapped inside. Rocks continued to rain down, and he and others dodged injury and death while surveying its entrance. The team dug with abandon, but it was no use. The boulders were unmoving.

Otto hushed the crew and put his ear up to the pile of debris, hoping to hear signs of life, someone knocking, a cry for help perhaps. But he heard nothing. Kokko suggested using dynamite to blow a hole in the debris, but that idea was quickly abandoned; they believed the blast might trigger a second slide. Time was of the essence, and Otto ran to the company vehicle with the intention of driving into town for help. But when he turned the ignition, he was greeted by the clicking chatter of a dead battery.

Jimmy rushed to his side. "I'll run into town," he shouted. "I'll get help."

"The old mule trail will be impassible."

"Then I'll take the road." He rushed to change out his shoes, and in no time disappeared.

Ninety minutes later, Jimmy led a caravan of bulldozers and trucks back to the mine. On that day, Jimmy had been crowned a hero for saving the lives of the eight trapped men.

Mr. Grant, humbled in Jimmy's presence, had asked him how he could show his appreciation. And this is what Jimmy said: to spend more time with Catherine; to be there at the birth of their child; and to train for the Boston Marathon.

Horace Grant had agreed to the first two, but said he was in no position to gift time for a meaningless race. But Jimmy pushed, making a case that winning the Boston Marathon would be good press for the Oro Canyon Mining Company and cast Mr. Grant as a benevolent manager. "At least talk with Mr. Finick," Jimmy begged. "He'll tell you. He'll tell you I can win it."

Mr. Grant didn't budge. "Mr. Finick pays me to manage the mine, son. If the mine is profitable, then I profit."

Now this made sense. Mr. Grant was motivated by money.

So, Jimmy pivoted and mentioned that wagering took place, and that Mr. Grant could stand to make a substantial profit on the wings of his shoes. This, Mr. Grant understood.

For the next six months, Jimmy would only have to work three days a week.

* * *

Now, he was just a mile from the trailhead, but the sun had already set, and light was fading quickly under the cover of storm clouds. His shoes, the same shoes he'd removed in the wet conditions at his first race at Schenley Oval, found little traction on the slick granite slabs and cobbles. His dilemma was this: he could run cautiously, but risk not making it down before dark. The trail would be impossible to negotiate if that happened. Or, he could push the pace and risk injury.

And he thought to himself, the trail was such a metaphor of his life. It twisted and turned, and rose and fell, and shifted in speed and contour. Perhaps it would lead him to a victory in Boston. Perhaps it would leave him in the dark.

But anywhere was better than the life he'd left behind. The life of a kid who'd been made to sit in a corner wearing a dunce cap. A kid who got beat up during recess. A kid who ran away like a scared rabbit. A kid who played hooky so often the truant officer gave up chase. A kid who dropped out of school, couldn't find work.

His older version: a kid who'd botched a robbery, ran pantless, and eluded cops for thirteen miles to become the laughingstock of Wilmerding. A kid who'd gotten mixed up with a gangster to become a would-be savior of Wilmerding. A kid who'd died yards short of the world's most famous finish line. Ridiculed, even in death. Kicked out of town in life.

His story was long and connected by loss.

The rain pelted him now, coming down in sheets, but he pushed on as the light faded to purple. He slipped and caught himself from falling. Perhaps it was fitting, he thought. The challenges of his life's every step.

He couldn't deny, wouldn't deny, his past. Until he'd moved to Arizona, he'd met every expectation that had ever been levied on him, which was to say, none. But things were different now. He was rewriting the script. He'd crossed out lines and entire paragraphs, ripped out pages, deleted passages, and replaced them with his own enriched version. His story was being rewritten in the first person in a much larger font, and included a header that read: *Has a job, has a wife, has a child.* And in three weeks' time that header would also include this: *Won the Boston Marathon. Crowned with the laurel wreath.* His parents would be accepting—only then.

So would the dingers. They'd once again anoint him as their savior. They'd welcome him back with open arms.

Jimmy smiled as he sped along at breakneck speed in the storm.

It was fitting this was his last thought before the trail's saturated edge gave way beneath his next footfall. The saguaro cactus he launched into wasn't necessarily the grandest of them all. In fact, it was rather mediocre, rather young, with only two arms that extended straight out on either side like a cross.

The misstep happened so quickly that Jimmy couldn't bring his arms around fast enough to blunt the impact. Instead, when he hit, his arms were raised at his sides like a bird in flight, perfectly mirroring the arms of the cactus. A thousand two-inch-long barbed needles coddled him like a mother to a crying baby, pinning him to her chest. And for the second time in a year, Jimmy was dying. This time, in the image of Christ.

Hours passed. The sky pitched black. The storm passed. Stars came out. So did a crescent moon. Under any other circumstance, it would have been a beautiful night. He thought about his bunkmates, how happy they'd be, coming out of their quarters to look up at the diamond sky. He thought about his family, excitedly making travel plans to Boston; Maggie, packing her yellow dress for the trip, and his parents meeting their granddaughter for the first time. He thought about Big Mike, and Paddy O'Donnell, and how they'd be disappointed not to wager on him again. He thought about Catherine, laying Jacqueline down for the night, wrapping her in a warm blanket and kissing her forehead, telling her funny stories about Dada.

Nobody would come looking for him tonight. That wouldn't happen until morning when he was already dead. He wondered if the finders would mourn his loss, or laugh at the image of him stuck on the thorny cross like Backwards Jesus. It had been a life wrought with humiliation. Would he feel it in death, too? Mr. Grant's comment about the saguaros on that first day stuck in his head just as the barbed needles stuck in his body: *You'll see them up close soon enough.*

And now, fading to blackness, Jimmy Flynn was face to face with the Sonoran Prince and self-mockingly uttered his last words in a labored breath. "I'm stuck on you."

Not many people are given a second chance at life. And fewer are given a second chance at death. But finally, Jimmy had gotten something right.

21

Ghosts and Idiots
~ Arizona, 1995 ~

There's a ghost of a fourteen-year-old boy who lives in the attic. He's been there for fifty years and has been sneaking out lately to haunt the thoughts of the old man who'd locked him in.

The ghost has one job: to look after the shoes.

The shoes were a farewell gift from the boy's nanny, Catherine Bechard, who'd placed them in his hands with reverence, her telling eyes conveying their importance, explaining that she no longer had use for them. She'd told him they'd belonged to her late husband, and had seen the finish line of the Boston Marathon. "They're magic shoes," she'd said. "I hope they bring you joy one day." She and Jacqueline, her ten-year-old daughter, left for California, leaving the boy to wonder about the shoes. He'd never seen anything like them; the rubber soles with the white canvas upper.

Running? He didn't understand the importance, or how running could bring him joy.

He took the shoes to his room, knotted the laces, and hung them on the wall at the foot of his bed. He studied them with vivid curiosity. Their image stamped into his retinas each night when he closed his eyes and succumbed to sleep.

One night, he dreamt of winning a race. In the dream his body was light, and effortlessly floated along the path without a hint of effort. The dream left him exhilarated.

When he woke, the sun was peeking through his bedroom window, its rays spotlighting the shoes, casting them in a magnificent golden light. They beckoned.

It was time to put them to use.

He stepped into each one, anticipating what, he didn't know. A tingling sensation started in his feet, and it moved up through his legs until it tickled his stomach and set his heart racing.

He left the house with the intention of running an entire mile into town. His head was full of possibilities. But soon, his breathing labored, his large frame villain to his fantasy, and he stopped. He began the long walk home. His lungs burned. His sides split. It felt nothing like the dream. It felt…opposite. A passing car honked and a kindly man, seeing the boy in distress, offered a lift. But the boy turned his head, humiliated, and didn't acknowledge.

Horace wasn't surprised to see his son back so soon. "You're no athlete. You take after me," he said, patting his large stomach. "There's not enough magic in those shoes to do you any good."

Fooled by his naivety and dreams of running, he placed the shoes in a box and put them in the attic, burying the source of his humiliation along with the child that ceased to exist on that day.

Now, Grant G. Grant held the box in his hands, having brought it down from the attic. He brushed its dusty top and sneezed. Then he slowly opened it like a treasure chest that contained the riches of the world. The shoes were still there, exactly as he had remembered them. Nostalgia ran deep, warming him like an old blanket.

He mused at the silliness of his irrational fetish. Yet, he reasoned. Everyone has that one object that serves as a memento or token of their childhood. Grown men keep baseball mitts well after their playing days are over. Adult women hold on to ice skates years after their last toe jump. In his favorite movie, *Citizen Kane*, Orson Wells on his deathbed uttered the name Rosebud—his childhood sled. These ghostly mementos hide in the mind's recesses, drawn out in circumstance.

For Grant G. Grant, that object was the shoes. At first, they'd humiliated him, but as the years passed, he accepted his limitations, humbled. He cherished the shoes for reasons beyond Catherine's intentions. He cherished them because they'd been her gift. The shoes evoked a strong emotional connection to his childhood and the remembrance of the Saturday trips to the Fox Theater. He and his nanny, would escape the heat of the desert to sit in the cool, dark theater, side by side, sharing a soda and a tub of popcorn; his young eyes on the movie, and hers on him and her daughter.

The shoes—they'd be hard to part with, but guilt had eaten at him ever since curiosity had brought him to the state cross-country finals to see Billy Ball run. Perhaps Billy could have avoided the tumble if he'd been wearing them.

The shoes had to be returned. Billy was the rightful heir. But how? And when? There'd been times when he wanted to tell him. He'd come close in Billy's job interview, when he'd referred to Rosebud and how he had a "Rosebud" of his own. But he'd stopped short. The weight of their meaning was too great, and so he held onto the shoes for just a while longer.

But now, the time had come. He'd find a way to return the shoes and free the ghost.

* * *

Grant G. Grant wasn't the only one being haunted by ghosts. It was Halloween, and ghosts were everywhere.

I sat in my apartment with Jet, who curled next to me on the couch. We watched—of all things—*Ghost*. Demi Moore was kneading wet clay on a pottery wheel, as a shirtless—and very dead—Patrick Swayze approached from behind, wrapping her in his arms and seductively intertwining his hands with hers.

"Ghosts are from hell," I said to Jet. "Sure, she looks into it. See how she closes her eyes and leans into him. But I bet she's really pissed off that he ruined her pot."

Jet moaned and wagged his tail.

The doorbell rang. Jet barked. I stepped away from the movie. We were greeted by a small ghost in a homemade costume—a simple white sheet with cut-out eyeholes. It was holding an open pillowcase. My first thought: *Where do you plan on sleeping tonight now that you've repurposed your bed linens?* Jet scampered behind me and growled, scaring the ghost, who took a step back. But in a show of defiance, it continued to hold out the open pillowcase.

I hadn't anticipated any trick-or-treaters. "Sorry, little ghost. You'll have to haunt someone else. I don't have any candy."

The ghost turned and left without a word, as ghosts do.

It negotiated the stairs until it reached the last one, where its shoe caught the hem of the flowing white sheet, causing it to tumble forward, fall, and scatter its candy.

The ghost wailed, as ghosts do.

Before I could hustle down the stairs to attend to it, the mom—mortal, presumably—rushed to its aid and pulled the sheet from its head, revealing a little boy with pouting, sobbing eyes. The boy pointed up at me with a long finger and called me an asshole.

I didn't argue. I was a horrible mortal.

"Is he all right?" I shouted from above. But the mom ignored me, leading the boy away, leaving behind the white sheet and the spilled candy. It looked like the scene of a horrible accident, likely to be shown on the ten o'clock news, the white chalk of smashed SweeTarts outlining the ghost's body.

I went back to my movie. "Ghosts come and go," I said to Jet. With Jet's attention, I faked a chill, just for the thrill.

Speaking of ghosts, it had been two weeks since Holly had moved out. Her presence was not missed. She did not haunt me or my apartment, or sneak up behind to coddle me the way Patrick Swayze did to Demi Moore. She did not intertwine her hands with mine in the most inopportune time (dishwashing comes to mind), which I was thankful for. Instead, she'd floated away like an ethereal being, never to show up here, or at work, again. It was as if she'd never existed.

The phone rang. Another distraction.

When I answered, it was a familiar voice. It was Charlie.

"*The Great Pumpkin* is on TV," she said, without bothering to say hello.

"I'm watching *Ghost*."

"Isn't that about a woman who has sex with a ghost? Turn the channel."

I did.

"There. It's on," I said. Charlie Brown trick-or-treating, in his infinite ineptness, had somehow managed to snip a dozen eyeholes in a sheet, where only two were needed.

"I heard about Holly. I'm sorry."

"For the better," I said.

"You okay?"

"Jet's happy." He wagged his tail, hearing his name.

"And you?"

"Honestly, I thought I'd be humiliated," I said. "But it actually raised my status amongst the idiots I work with. They want to know my secret. They want to date an adult film actress too."

Charlie laughed. "That's one way to look at it. Look, I was just calling to say hello. You looked miserable at the theater."

"That was a tough crowd."

"You were supposed to meet me and Jenny for a run the next day."

"That was the night Holly and I broke up," I said. "I was going to call you."

"You were busy." She excused me. "Are you running the Pumpkin Challenge this year?"

The Pumpkin Challenge was an annual fundraising event for the Oracle High School cross-country team. It was held on Thanksgiving Day. It drew hundreds of local runners; however, a race within the race pitted past cohorts against the current team for pies and bragging rights.

"Doubt it," I said.

"Run with me, BB. I'll be in town for Thanksgiving."

"It will be great to see you, Charlie."

"Then you'll run?"

"I'll think about it."

"Coach will be disappointed. You didn't run last year. None of the Fly Five did."

"People call me Balls when I run."

"They're just idiots. They don't know—"

"It's humiliating."

An awkward, silent moment passed.

"Charlie Brown would do it," she said.

I had one eye on the television. Charlie Brown trick-or-treated in that butchered sheet, gathering rocks instead of candy.

"He'd run," she continued. "No one was ever more humiliated than Charlie Brown. But I guarantee you he'd run. He never stops trying, BB. Not even when Lucy pulls the football from underneath him."

Charlie Simmons never pulled a punch.

"Fine, then," I agreed. I didn't point out that Charlie Brown was just a fictional character. Besides, Coach's team could use a butt-kicking after how they treated me at the theater.

***

More ghost stories…

Earlier that day, Coach Jeremy Jones stood at the finish line of the last cross-country meet of a miserable season. When an apparition appeared of Billy Ball leading the pack, he shook his head and blinked, clearing the cobwebs and the slight of eye. But seconds later, cold air swept through him. It was easy to dismiss it as smoke and mirrors, a cold October blow, but he swore he'd seen and felt a ghost.

Billy Ball would have destroyed this field, he thought. So would have any one of the Fly Five. But they're all gone now. They're all ghosts.

He held a stopwatch and looked beyond the leading pack of runners for one of his own to appear. Not one was in sight. There wouldn't be one for another three minutes. They were ghosts too. Meanwhile, runners from other schools crossed the line in bunches. There would be no team or individual invitations to the state championship this year. He hung his head. It would be a long bus ride home.

Somewhere on I-10 between Phoenix and Tucson, Coach felt the need to address the team, as coaches do. He stood at the front of the bus and considered his words. He wanted to tell them that he was proud, and that next year they'd turn it around, because—as the tired cliché goes—it's not whether you win or lose, but how you run the race. The problem is that he didn't believe it himself. They'd given up, lost their fighting spirit when they'd finished dead last in each of their first few meets.

"The truth," he started, "is that you're not good. You're actually really, really bad. You *could* be good—really, really good—but you're not. You're the opposite of really, really good. You're really, really bad."

"Yeah, we get it Coach," a hidden face shouted from the back of the bus.

"Shut up. I'm not done yet."

The team groaned and averted their eyes to the window-dressing outside.

"And I don't mean bad, as in good," Coach continued. "That's what you say these days, right? I literally mean you're bad—as in fucking awful. Our boys scored a record-high 524 points. Just a little reminder, gentlemen, low score wins in cross-country. And the girls? Don't even get me started. Disqualified because Missy McMullan's tummy hurt and she dropped out. Jesus. Her tummy! Only four of you crossed!"

Coach sat down, hot, staring into the back of the bus driver's hairless head, remembering the conversation with Athletic Director Stephen Strawbag seven years earlier. *It's cross-country, Jeremy. How badly can you fuck that up?*

351

The team was defiant, and a few choice words were pitched at Jeremy's back. He stood, even hotter now. The bus rocked back and forth on the bumpy highway.

"Opportunities lost, kids," he said. "Life's lessons! And don't forget about the Pumpkin Challenge in three weeks. It's your annual fundraiser. You're required to attend if you want to run track this spring."

Several kids coughed and groaned.

"I invited the Fly Five. Remember those ghosts?"

But Coach was wrong. We weren't ghosts. Though, we *were* idiots.

***

It's Thanksgiving Day—race day—and we're running in the Pumpkin Challenge 10k.

Let's start with the bad. I'd been missing a sock, not just any sock, but a long, red compression sock that I'd worn all week to remedy a tight calf. The culprit was Jet, who had a penchant for eating socks. We drove to the race, and on the way, I twice asked him if he'd eaten it. He didn't respond, though he did burp. When we parked, he jumped from the car in full flight, which I took as a sure sign of his guilt.

Go play, Jet. Eater of socks.

In Jet's uncompromised passion to meet and sniff the crotches of everyone he's ever met, he ran from runner to runner looking for a friendly hand and a snack. Some might say I'm a bad owner, but I figured, who doesn't appreciate the love and affection of a dog? The plan was to put him back in the car for the thirty-some minutes it took me to run the race. However, minutes before the race started, as Jet worked his way through the crowd, I heard a woman scream, and then another, and yet another. Some ran backwards, as if they'd seen a ghost! But it wasn't a ghost. It was Jet, with my red sock hanging six inches out of his ass. He was chasing after those who ran from him, thinking it was a game of Catch Me. The screams soon turned into howls, and then into laughter, and lots of finger pointing. Then, Jet stopped and squatted on the starting line, trying to pass the elastic sock.

The sock hung, stuck. He pushed once, pushed twice, and pushed three times, to no avail. I turned to Charlie and said, "I can't do this."

"I've got this," she said.

Charlie approached Jet, who was still squatting. He raised his eyebrows and wagged his tail at the sight of his second favorite biped. She petted his head, smiled, and reached behind and pulled on the sock. It stretched. She pulled. It stretched again, but wouldn't dislodge. And then she leveraged her foot on his hind quarters to steady him, and pulled once more. The sock stretched to arm's length before it snapped and unleashed from his anus to the cheers and applause of three hundred relieved runners. Just in time for "The Star-Spangled Banner."

Let's move on to the worse.

Things aren't going so well in the race. Three miles in, I'm trailing Jack, Henry, and two girls—Charlie and Jenny

Ledge. Most of the current Oracle High School cross-country team are also in front, looking motivated. It's been a long time since I've raced, and the cobwebs are real. Plus, I'm wildly hungover.

After the Fly Five reunion last night, we all are.

Running somewhere behind me is Piper. He hadn't run in over a year. "Ironically so," he'd explained. After high school, he started reading books on how to run faster, but one book led to another, and then another. And by the time he was through reading all these books, which stacked two feet high on his nightstand, it occurred to him that he hadn't run in nine months. He lost interest, and to find motivation, he went back to re-reading the books on how to run faster. "It was a vicious cycle of binge reading and false starts," he said. I pointed out that he'd probably missed the advice that said *just run*. In any event, that was the end of his running career.

Tuba, and his burgeoning beer gut, which he'd named Champ, is also running somewhere behind me. I'd said to Tuba that he ate too much, and he responded that eating was more fun than running. I told him I liked to eat too, but that eating shouldn't be a consumption sport. He disagreed.

Disenfranchised, most definitely bitter, he said that running was stupid, though he'd agreed to run the Pumpkin Challenge because he wanted to reunite with us and party afterward. "And before," he added.

Up ahead I see Henry pull off the course. He makes a dash for a lone, inviting porta-john. If I wasn't in such distress myself, I'd laugh. In Applebee's, he'd said he was constipated from flying, and that he'd taken a laxative. After several drinks, he admitted to taking two, because "those pills are so damned small." Henry had been on the toilet all night and all morning long. He'd probably lost ten percent of his body weight in twelve hours.

Jack Ash is out of sight, but within the next half mile he's come back. He's fifty yards ahead and struggling. His gait is crooked, and I see him stiffen and lock up before his entire body lurches forward. I see a stream of vomit launch onto the head and back of a runner in front who locks up as if being drenched by ice water. By the time I pass, the two are stopped and throwing punches. Jack Ash swings and misses and takes a blow to the stomach, causing him to projectile-vomit again onto his attacker. He falls backwards and lands on his ass. The man, covered front and back now with Jack's spew, jumps on top to finish him off. I don't stop.

Out of the Fly Five, I'm the only one left that can challenge for a top ten placement. And even if I manage that, it will still be a humiliating experience for us, since we were rumored to sweep the top five spots. Sometimes humiliation is a shared experience.

But my head and heart are pounding so fast I'm afraid they might explode, and I doubt I can hang on. I'm sweating badly, and alcohol seeps from my pores. I want to vomit. Charlie and Jenny still run up ahead.

I push on, because I know not what else to do.

Now, moving on to the terrible.

Thanksgiving is a busy time for movie theaters. I was surprised that Mr. Grant was so accommodating when I'd asked for the holiday off. He was in good spirits and I assumed it was because popcorn sales were back up since Holly left. "I knew she was up to something," he said. "I have no doubt about that," I agreed, but not meeting his eyes. He asked why I wanted the days off, and I told him that my ex-teammates were coming in to race the Pumpkin Challenge. His eyes lit up, and he asked if I was going to start racing again. "I didn't know you cared," I said. "I do, Billy. You have a gift." I blinked. "I've been told."

Then he asked why I couldn't work the evening shifts, and I said that we had a reunion planned, and he nodded his agreement. I mentioned our plans to head up to my great-grandfather's gravesite and throw back a few beers because it's what we did in high school. "Up at the old mine?" he asked. "Where your great-grandfather is buried?" "That's the spot," I said. I thought he would lecture me on the inappropriateness of the act, but on the contrary, he said it sounded fun and made me promise to do that.

So, with plans in place, we kicked off our reunion at none other than Applebee's because Piper Cox was not so lucky in getting the night off. Piper was a bartender and had to work until closing time.

Piper had fared worse than me since high school. Not that he saw it that way. He'd dropped out of community college, but had worked his way up from busboy to bartender in a matter of months. Quite an achievement in his eyes.

The one thing we had in common is that while our teammates had scattered, the two of us had stayed in

Tucson. We weren't friends and didn't hang out, because, let's face it, he acted like an odd duck—quite literally. He'd graduated from lesser, easier characterizations like Tweety Bird and Speedy Gonzales to the venerable Donald Duck. He bragged that it had taken him just six months to perfect the buccal voice, where he produced an air bubble between his jaw and cheek, and like an extra lung, used it to push out sound. In doing so, he'd succeeded in becoming the most annoying person in the bar, the town, and alive. But he claimed the customers liked the voice and tipped him well, which if true was a good reason to never visit Applebee's again.

I was the first to show up, and in his presence I felt trapped. Other than a couple of middle-aged women in pantsuits who were deep into an alcohol-induced conversation about men being pigs and losers, I had the bar to myself, and unfortunately, all of Piper's attention.

"Is it always this packed, Piper?" I had no idea what to say to him. After two years I was still pissed off that he'd wrecked my Malibu.

Piper shrugged.

"It smells like stale beer and disinfectant," I said.

By the time Tuba showed up, I'd insulted Piper and his employer six times, drank three beers, and was looking for more of both.

Tuba, who hadn't seen Piper since graduation, surveyed him now. "Sorry, no kids allowed at the bar," he said. Piper still looked like a kid. His Applebee's embroidered shirt hung on his underdeveloped body like a burlap sack. But

Piper held his own, rubbing his belly and mocking Tuba's weight gain. "Does Champ want a beer?" he asked.

Henry Fly arrived next. Henry strutted in like a peacock, wearing an orange Polo shirt tucked into plaid shorts. He wore checkered Vans and tied a red sweater around his shoulders. Daylight was long gone, but his Ray-Bans adorned his head like a tiara.

I asked him if that was the same orange Polo shirt he'd worn every day in high school, and he said, "Don't be ridiculous. It's a *new* orange Polo shirt and I wear it every day at Stanford."

The two older women at the bar spied him, and considered. But their interest quickly faded when they saw Jack Ash.

Handsome Jack Ash surveyed the bar and high-fived us when he arrived, asking, "Is this the best we can do, gentlemen?"

Sadly, it was. There we were, the greatest high school cross-country team ever assembled in Arizona, reunited after two and a half years—in Applebee's.

As the evening wore on, Piper kept our glasses filled, and for free. There was a lot of catching up to do, and when Jack bragged that he'd earned All-American status running at Boston College, the two divorcees leaned his way. That's when we lost Jack to the divorcees.

He was on to more important things: getting laid.

Piper quacked. I eavesdropped. And Jack related a very believable story about being recently dropped by his girlfriend back in Massachusetts. The breakup had left him heartbroken. He lowered his eyes, focused on his beer, and produced a single tear, which landed like a soft raindrop in his mug. He said he was terribly sad because he'd been saving his virginity for her, and that he believed in the sanctity of love. "One love," he added. "Now what am I supposed to do?" Both swooned and swayed, caught in the web of his youthful, handsome looks and their need to make things right. They purchased his every word.

I pulled Jack aside. He winked at me. And I asked, "What gives?" In high school he'd been a prolific liar about having lost his virginity. Now, in college, he'd flipped the script and was lying about being a virgin. He laughed, and whispered that divorcees liked this charade because while their hearts had been charred, they still fought to rekindle the flame. He left shortly thereafter with both. We didn't see Jack again until the morning of the race.

At 11 p.m., we kept to our plan to move the party to the old mine. We were drunk, except for Piper, who'd clocked out and offered to be the designated driver.

"Your car. Not mine," I told him. "You only get to crash one car of mine in this lifetime."

That's when Tuba chimed in. "Whatever happened to your smoking hot attorney who hit your car?" he asked. I told him she'd gone on to save others in need.

We piled into Piper's Chevy Nova, and he revved the engine, which growled approvingly. Piper's small frame looked out of place behind the wheel of the Nova, but he reached behind his seat, grabbed a phone book, and propped it under his ass to see over the wheel. Then he quacked and punched the gas pedal.

When we arrived at the abandoned mine, a full moon rose from behind a high ridge, casting a ghostly light on dilapidated old bunkhouses that stood out like new haunts. Coyotes yipped and howled somewhere close by.

"Did anyone bring a flashlight?" Henry asked. We walked half blind, stumbling, tripping our way across the grounds that were littered with rusted scrap metal, tailings, and trash.

Tuba—drunk on tequila and high on weed—had a crazy idea about entering the mine. "There's gold in there," he said. "We don't have a flashlight," I told him. But he continued marching forward in a drunken obsession. When we got to the graffitied entrance it was boarded up as it had been for decades, and fortified several times over. Dejected, he said, "Fuck it, let's just go drink on your great-granddaddy's grave."

Piper produced a fifth of tequila. "Compliments of Applebee's," he said.

"We've got a race in the morning," Henry objected. "And I need to find a toilet."

"Fuck the race," Tuba replied.

From afar I could see the headstone silhouetted in the dim light. I approached it, feeling a sense of relief as it came into view. The mine had been vandalized so often over the years, I was always afraid it might go missing, or defiled or knocked over.

An object sat at the base of the headstone. I squinted to see it. But the moon slid behind a passing cloud, and my surroundings pitched black again. Behind me, Tuba let out a blood-curdling scream, causing Piper to trip and fall into

Henry, yanking on his orange Polo shirt to break his fall. Henry startled, and shouted that he'd just shit his pants. "Get off me!" Two of the three idiots snickered and giggled. But all had stopped in their tracks.

I continued on, moving closer to the headstone. My eyes dilated and adjusted to the diluted light. The object came into view. Closer now. Two objects!

Could those be? Was it possible?

Then, the moon re-emerged, and I could clearly see them. The hair on my back stood up. I blinked twice and shook my head. But even in my drunken state, there was no question what lay at the base of my great-grandfather's headstone.

Perfectly aligned—as if carefully set there, was a pair of white running shoes.

"Guys!" I shouted.

But the guys were well behind, with their dicks out, giggling and pissing, as idiots do.

I moved to pick up the shoes, but pulled up short as the moon slid behind another cloud and I lost the light. When it reappeared, my heart skipped a beat. Standing in the shoes was an apparition of a young man who mirrored my image. Wispy smoke, it took shape for just seconds before evaporating.

Later, I'd reason that I'd seen things, that it was just a trick of light caused by the moon and shadows. Or that I was too drunk to know *what* I'd seen.

But at that moment, there was no question what appeared before me: my great-grandfather, Jimmy Flynn, waving hello.

22

Charlie

I don't remember the day I fell in love with Charlie. I don't remember the month or the year either. But I do remember the journey.

I've been told that love sweeps you off your feet, and like a riptide it carries you helplessly out to sea. But as I sit on this raft far from shore, I disagree. I wasn't swept out to sea. I drifted here over time.

...and I am powerless to paddle back.

Charlie sits directly across from me at my parents' kitchen table under the Andy Warhol soup can print. Her eyes are lively. Her blonde hair falls straight, beyond the length of her shoulders. It's wispy and electric, and a few strands shoot straight up and sideways, matching her effervescent character. She's more confident than her younger self, and sits with a straight back and square shoulders, strikingly opposite of my slouched, heavier, intolerable self. A plate of cold, leftover turkey is set between us. I nervously pick at it. Jet rests under the table and I slip him a piece. He licks the grease from my fingers.

Thanksgiving dinner has left my parents in a tryptophan coma in the adjacent living room. Their labored breathing rattles the house, and if I cared or dared to look, I'd see my dad open-mouthed and closed-eyed, passed out on the same recliner where I was born. Mom lying next to him on the sofa, straight as a board, holding firmly onto an empty wine glass, snoring just the same. The television is on—a football game. But there is no need to peek in. This scene has played out many times over the years. "It's the same old circus in there," I say to Charlie.

Charlie picks up a newspaper which is open to the sports section. A photograph of Christmas Day is on its cover. "What's this?"

"An update on Christmas," I say. "The Arizona media still loves him. He won the NCAA Cross-Country Championship this week."

Charlie studies my face, looking for any emotion. "I'm sorry," she says.

"You're sorry Christmas won the meet?" I ask. "Or you're sorry that I no longer care?"

She looks down, and braces before engaging.

"What is it?" I ask.

"We've always been truthful with each other."

"Always."

"Thirty-five minutes?"

"So what? It's a fine time. I caught Jenny. I nearly caught you."

She looks at me incredulously. "You beat Christmas Day once. Now you're measuring yourself against Jenny and I."

"I never beat Christmas," I remind her. "Not according to anyone who matters."

I've hurt her. *She matters.*

"You can run a thirty-five-minute 10k hopping on one leg. You're at a low point, BB. I worry about you."

"I was hungover."

"It's more than that, BB."

"Probably."

"Definitely."

"I saw a ghost," I say, deflecting.

"You saw what?"

"A ghost."

"Now you're delusional too."

"I've got proof."

"Of what?"

"A ghost," I repeat. "Wait here and keep Jet company. Give him some turkey. He'll love you."

"He already loves me."

I excuse myself and go out to my car. When I return, I'm carrying the shoes. Jet has his head in Charlie's lap, and she's scratching him behind one ear. But Charlie is also staring up at the plastic-framed print of the soup cans.

"I've been wanting to ask this for fifteen years. What the hell is this?" Charlie asks, oblivious to the shoes.

"Andy Warhol."

"Andy who?"

"Warhol," I repeat. "You know, the pop-culture artist—the guy who coined the phrase "Everyone will be world-famous for fifteen minutes."

"He said that?"

"He did."

"Was this his fifteen minutes of fame?" she asks. "It's awful."

"I don't know, Charlie. Haven't you ever heard of Andy Warhol? Look, he made movies too. Made one right here at the dude ranch down the street. Or at least he filmed a scene there. I think it was a rape scene, but everyone forgets that little tidbit."

"Sounds like a lovely man," she says with a heavy dose of sarcasm.

"Just eccentric, like all artists," I say. "It's the Pittsburgh connection. The guy was from Pittsburgh. His father was a coal miner. That's why my parents took to him. Look, it's not important. Check out these shoes."

I tell her about last night, and how the Fly Five, minus Jack Ash, had gone up to the old mine to drink on my great-grandfather's grave.

"The gravesite where you tried to kiss me," she interrupts. "I remember it well because Sky Daddy threw you into the fire for that."

"Yes. We've been down that road before, Charlie," I say. And we *had* many times. But Charlie, true to form, liked to pour salt on the wound.

I continue with the story. "These shoes had been carefully placed on his grave. And standing in the shoes was a ghost, waving hello to me like he was riding on a float in a goddamned parade."

"A ghost—waving to you?"

"Yeah, that's what I saw."

"Did anyone else see the ghost?"

"Well, no," I say. "But that's not the point. Look at these shoes," I say again. "These are real. They must have belonged to my great-grandfather, Jimmy Flynn. That's why he was standing in them."

"You're seeing things, Billy."

She pulls them from my hands, turning them over, and sideways, studying them with a keen eye. They were rudimentary, clearly a prototype of today's running shoes; rubber soles, glued on to a canvas upper. There was no branding. They were worn, clearly very old, but in otherwise remarkable shape.

Jet takes notice. He sniffs them. Inedible, he lays back down in his spot under the table.

"Where did you find these?"

"I'm telling you. On my great-grandfather's grave."

Charlie looks skeptical.

"They were set there, waiting for me."

"What'd the ghost say?"

"What?"

"The ghost—Jimmy Flynn. Did he hand them to you?" Her eyebrows furled.

Charlie is still not buying in. She is simply humoring me.

"Look. Someone's playing a joke on you, BB. Probably one of the Fly Five. Probably Jack Ash. You said he disappeared halfway through the evening with those two women. Probably went up there and put these shoes on the gravesite as a practical joke. That's what you guys do, right?"

"I don't know, Charlie." I scratch my head, wondering. "I guess so."

"Who else knew you were going up there?"

"Nobody," I say. Then I think twice. "Wait! I'd told my boss, Mr. Grant. But that wouldn't make any sense."

"You try them on yet?"

"No."

"You've got to try them on, BB."

"I will. Not now. Look, you're the only person I've told this to, Charlie. Anyone else would think I'm crazy."

"You *are* crazy."

"Perhaps. But at least you know my level of crazy."

She hands the shoes back.

"At least tell your parents."

"They're busy," I laugh. From the kitchen we can still hear them snoring in the next room, a fluttering inhale followed by a whistled exhale. One coughs, the other chokes, but each resumes breathing.

"Turkey dreams," Charlie chortles, mimicking them.

"Look, Charlie. A few years back I was running the Arizona Trail and found a pocketknife that we believe belonged to my great-grandfather. Now these shoes. Something weird is going on. He won't stop bugging me."

"Why would he do that?"

"Unfinished business. Who knows? He was young when he died."

I study the shoes again, measuring them with my eyes. *I'll be damned. They're just my size.*

"Are we on for tonight?" I ask, changing the subject.

"Billy. You've got me all night long."

"Excuse me?"

368

She winks and purses her lips, teasingly so. "Yes, you'll have to put up with me," she clarifies. "Tom is at my house."

"Tom?"

"Tom. My mom's new boyfriend. She sold him a house. Now they're dating."

"Tom and Mom. Mom and Tom. Sounds simple enough."

"It's never simple. The point is, I feel like a third wheel in my own house."

"Pumpkin patch?"

"Of course. Where else would we go on Thanksgiving?"

"I'll bring the pie. You bring the wine."

***

The first frost of the season had come and gone, and while Charlie loved the idea of hanging out in the pumpkin patch, the ones that hadn't been harvested were left rotting on the vines.

"Stinks," I say. "Are you sure about this?"

"Yes, I'm sure." Determined Charlie spreads out a wool blanket and uncorks a bottle of red wine. To her side, Jet is already pawing at a large, rotting pumpkin that fell off a vine.

"We could have gone to a movie," I point out. "I can get us in for free, you know."

"What fun is that?" she asks.

369

So, we sit down amid a field of rotting pumpkins, and she fills my wine glass. Jet has clawed his way inside of a pumpkin, and when he pops up, he's wearing it. His head is stuck inside and he scurries toward us like the Great Pumpkin Himself!

"Jet! Over here!" Blindly, he walks my way. He barks, muffled. I remove the pumpkin from his head, and he scampers away to find another, unfazed.

"Should we toast to Jet, or us?"

"Take your pick. We've all survived—so far."

"Then, to us," Charlie says, holding up her glass.

"To us."

We touch wine glasses and sip.

"Charlie…"

"Yes?"

"What exactly is…us?"

Can we be more?

"Our friendship, of course."

"Yes, of course. To our friendship."

She doesn't want more. That's okay.

We clink our glasses again. Another sip. Behind her, the evening stars sprinkle the plum-colored sky like fairy dust.

"Charlie…"

"Yes?"

You're the most beautiful woman I've ever known. Why must we only be friends?

"Oh nothing."

"You can ask me anything, BB."

Can I kiss you?

But I say nothing.

"Ask away, BB."

"Fine then," I swallow hard. "Are you still waiting for a pumpkin to magically turn into a carriage and take you away?"

I pause. I've crossed a boundary. I bite my lip.

She says nothing. She stiffens, remembering.

There's a six-year-old girl who sits on a bed and switches on a black and white television set with rabbit ears. It's Thanksgiving. But there's little to be thankful for. In the dark room, the white static reflects in her eyes before she pushes a tape into a VCR. She pushes PLAY. It catches and the movie begins. Although it's well past her bedtime, she turns the volume up to drown out the ugly words that are volleyed between the two adults on the other side of her door. Her eyes are wide, focused and trancelike now, lost in every frame of the cartoon. Her head tilts as she watches Cinderella step into a gargantuan pumpkin that has been magically transformed into a beautifully adorned coach that will carry her to a better place; a grand ball— whatever that is. The six-year-old reaches out, touches the screen, and makes it real. The next day, she finds pumpkin seeds, dries them, and plants them in the garden just beyond her window, so that at night, as she's readying for bed, she can look out and wish.

But they do not grow. Seasons pass. Years pass. Her father is gone now. Her mother is neglectful. Other men enter the picture. Some stay for a while. But they all leave eventually. She's older now, and has given up on the fantasy of the pumpkin. But there's another way. There's always another way. She finds solace in an omnipotent being—she calls him Sky Daddy and He lives in Heaven.

He *is* Heaven.

She begs Sky Daddy to take her away, to deliver her to a better place; somewhere magical. He says she has it within herself to leave. He tells her to run. He tells her to run far, and to run fast.

"I'm not crazy," she says now to Billy. "I don't believe a pumpkin is going to magically turn into a carriage and carry me away."

She punches my arm.

"Sorry," I say.

"Then you also know why I started running."

"To get to a better place," I say. "And you have."

Charlie moves closer. She softens. "It's cold."

"It is."

Silence.

"How'd you know about my pumpkin fetish?"

Because you're stitched into my heart and the very fabric of my being.

"I've watched you try to grow that pumpkin patch for years. It was your escape. Why'd you think I taped that pumpkin to the vine that time?"

"Because you love me," she says, poignantly. It wasn't a question.

"I've always loved you," I say evenly.

Boundaries.

Charlie leans in and rests her head on my shoulder. Neither of us say a word. We don't have to. We sit side-by-side in the putrid smell, chuckling at the silliness of it all, warmed by the wine, watching the silhouette of Jet scamper back and forth between rotting pumpkins. I wrap my arm around her shoulder and pull her closer. I hug her, and wonder, is this pushing the boundaries? When does a hug turn into a caress? Are words unspoken heard? Are they understood? If I turn to look at her now will my eyes reveal more than they should? We gaze into the heavens and admire the stars that continue to *pop pop pop* over the ashen outline of Mount Lemmon. And we drink more wine.

I can sense that she's lost in thought.

"As friends?" she asks. "You love me like a friend, right?"

I give her the answer she wants to hear. "Sure, Charlie. Like friends." A pang kicks hard in my stomach.

And so, so very much more, Charlie.

23

Gravity
~ Arizona, 1998 ~

Like mystics, we stand at the edge of the Grand Canyon, our eyes dilated, absorbing, ethereal in reflection. The stars have faded in the muted, dawn light, but a crescent moon hangs bright and low in the western sky. We're anxious to drop in, but the moment is too precious, too valuable to rush. We need a minute longer to take it all in, to consider the scale of our journey. I rub my hands together to warm them, and laugh at the sight of Charlie's breath.

"Cold?"

She doesn't answer. She shivers.

"This was your idea," I remind her.

"Yeah, when I was ten."

She wears a cheap cotton beanie, pulled low so that her eyes are barely visible. Her blonde hair spills out beneath, frayed in the cold air. She's dressed in thin layers, knowing the heat will build quickly on our descent to the bottom—a vertical mile. On her back, she wears a hydration pack, with snacks and energy bars bursting from its side pockets.

"How long do you plan on being out here?" I jest.

She tells me to shut up, that she's thanking Sky Daddy, and to admire the sunrise.

And I see why. The sun has crept over the horizon. Light needles through the green pinyons and pines that dot the red rim, adding contour to the canyon, scraping its crusty shelves, which now stand out in relief. Hues of pink, purple, and red appear, brushed onto a canvas with the wide strokes of an impressionistic painting. "There is so much beauty here," she says. I turn. Seeing her, the maturity in her oval face, the freckles gone now, the beginnings of crow's feet from time spent in the sun framing her gold-flecked eyes. I nod in agreement. Then I turn back to face the canyon and agree again.

More light. More definition. A maze appears before us. Canyons within the canyon. Somewhere down there is the Colorado River. We can't see it. But we can see the north rim, ten miles straight across, and twenty-three miles by way of the trail. Across the void, lights from the North Rim Lodge flicker out. "We better get going," Charlie says. Even as she shivers now, she's worried about the heat later. "It's going to get hot." She high-fives me, and just like that, we throw ourselves into this painting and begin our descent on the South Kaibab Trail.

The canyon engulfs us, embraces us, and we disappear like grains of sand into a siphon. The trail is heavily switch-backed, scratched into near-vertical walls that fall away quickly beyond view. The dim light combined with the sharp-edged trail makes for a perilous descent. Charlie runs in front, navigating wooden planks that are placed horizontally to stay off erosion. We jump some, skirt others. The running is awkward, and despite our speed we're challenged to find our gait. Loose rocks and pea-size gravel cause our feet to slip out beneath us. Death by launching oneself off the trail is not unheard of. Cautioned, we slow.

Charlie's shoelace comes undone at Ooh Aah Point. She stops to tie it, and together we take another moment to admire the exceptional expanse that presents itself as grandiose. It is simply surreal. In a matter of minutes, the light has changed again, and a labyrinth of canyons before us grows wider, deeper. Colors pop, richer now, and the canyon's geology, timestamped in sedimentary layers, is on full display.

"We're literally running through time," I say.

"Ours is a celebration run," she says. "You've come a long way, BB."

This canyon is not absolute, I think. After six million years, it's still changing, eroding, each layer revealing its newer self. And for every layer there's a story.

It's a nice metaphor of my life these past two and a half years.

Two and half years. That's how long it had been since Charlie and I sat in the pumpkin patch and she'd confessed her concern for me, and that I needed to get my shit together. She didn't pull any punches—that's Charlie for you—and as she put it, that's what friends are for.

And so, I did.

I'm no longer a "pre-me." I'm finally just…me.

Not that the "me" could compare with my nemesis, the thought of whom would keep me up at night, wondering if my life would have been charmed like his, had our feet not tangled. Christmas Day went on to earn two more All-American titles, and most experts said he was a shoe-in to make the United States Olympic Marathon team.

Meanwhile, I'm still working at the movie theater, uneducated on most matters, save popcorn, ticket sales—and classic movies, as Mr. Grant had wished.

He'd promoted me again. This time to General Manager in Transition—not Training. It's a funny title, but Mr. Grant was getting on in years and sometimes said things that only made sense to himself.

He was looking to retire, and he was grooming me for his job when the time came for him to step back as a silent owner. Over the years, he'd catch me in low moments, once holding a sports magazine with Christmas Day's photo on the cover. My face was beat red. He knew this was not the life I had envisioned.

But the promotion had also come with a nice raise, and for that I was happy. I was no longer an hourly employee. I could afford to live in my Oro Valley apartment with views of Pusch Ridge without the financial assistance of my parents or a roommate. Jet was happier too. In his advancing age, he ate better than ever. Better than me, some nights. He got fat, even as I ran him daily.

I'd always had a good relationship with Mr. Grant. Years ago, he'd fist-bump me, joke about my weight gain. He liked my ideas to improve the theater. But until he'd confessed about leaving the shoes for me to find on my great-grandfather's grave, I'd never stopped to consider why we had a good relationship. Sure, he was a friend of the family, but that's all I knew. Teenagers don't dig deep. We're too caught up in ourselves. I'd never considered the whys and hows and whats of much of anything at eighteen. Like why he'd hired me in the first place. Or why he'd never questioned me about Holly stealing from the register, even when he knew we were dating. Mr. Grant had looked the other way for some reason.

But now I know.

Some of it was his doing. He'd felt guilty for keeping the shoes all those years. Hiring me, taking me on as a project, was his way of giving back, perhaps appeasing his own conscience.

Catherine Bechard, my great-grandmother, was indeed his nanny. My parents had known, of course, but had never gotten around to telling me. Perhaps they didn't see the importance of telling me. Or likely, I wasn't listening when I was told. So, when Mr. Grant mentioned his association to Catherine, almost as an afterthought to the shoe confession, I'd stood slack-jawed, trying to comprehend. I have to say it was a moment not unlike Darth Vader telling Luke he was his father. "I thought you knew," Mr. Grant said, his palms open. When I failed to respond, he added, nonchalantly, "Well, let's get back to work then."

But I didn't turn to leave his office. I sat down, anchored, and pressed him for more information.

He spoke highly of Catherine, saying she was as colorful and pesky as a yellow flower on top of a blooming prickly pear cactus. She'd also inspired his love for the movies. But he'd lost touch with her when she'd moved. He didn't know where she'd gone. "How would I know? I was just a kid." Many years later, Catherine's daughter, Jacqueline, returned to Tucson, and before her untimely death at just thirty-five years old, he'd promised to watch over the financial wellness of her own daughter, my mom, Jean. That's how he became a friend of the family.

Unfortunately, he had few memories of my great-grandfather. He'd caught glimpses of Jimmy when he'd visited Catherine on Sundays, and more often after the birth of Jacqueline. But the memories faded over time. "He was rail thin," Mr. Grant said. "Even as a young kid I had more fat on my bones than he did. And he was always dirty from working the mine. Not the kind of dirt he could brush off, but the kind of dirt that permeated his skin and became part of his fabric. Your great-grandfather was ashen."

When I pressed harder, he told me that Jimmy ran to the house from the mine a couple times a week. "There was never a car parked out front, or a horse, so I know this to be true," he said. "After he died, everyone talked about what a great runner he was. It was his gift that had saved the miners' lives when the collapse happened. But you already know that."

It was the one thing I did know.

Finally, Mr. Grant recounted that when Catherine gave him the shoes, she'd said they'd seen the finish line of the Boston Marathon.

I perked up. "Boston?"

"Yes. Boston. At that age, I wasn't sure what a marathon was. So, it struck me as odd. Catherine said she hoped the shoes would bring me joy one day. I hung them from the wall at the foot of my bed and studied them, unsure of what she meant. I'd never actually seen anything like them. They were soft looking, not at all like the work boots the miners wore, or the dress shoes my dad wore. Once, I even had a dream that I was a runner. Can you imagine, Billy? Look at me. Do I look like a runner to you?" He laughed. "I don't remember anything else. I wish I did, but I was just a boy."

The next day, I searched for James Flynn in the results of the 1933 Boston Marathon. His name was missing. Disheartened, I assumed Catherine had been mistaken, or perhaps Mr. Grant's memory had failed. Or perhaps the results were incomplete, or absolutely wrong. It was so long ago. There were so many possibilities.

On the phone, Charlie suggested that I ask the shoes. I did that and reported back that they weren't squeaking. Charlie called me an idiot.

Like Mr. Grant had done in his youth, I hung them on the wall at the foot of my bed. They were the last thing I saw when I closed my eyes at night, and the first thing I saw when I woke up. I questioned their origin, and what roads they'd traveled. Had they really seen the finish line of Boston? What other finishes had they seen? I wondered about the person who'd stood in them, my great-grandfather. What was he like? What was he *really* like? And why did he run, when back then, so few did?

I'd lay in bed each night and conjure up images of him running, winning races, spending time with Catherine and their baby, or roaming Oracle. Did he walk the same streets as me? Did he dine in the same restaurants, or drink at the same bars? In my dreams, he took on shape and identity, and the abstract became real. Jimmy Flynn had become much more than a ghost to me.

And perhaps my inheritance did not suck. My parents' favorite topic in my youth, as they pointed at me. *He has your eyes, he has your nose, he has your ears, he has your toes.* But in all their rhythms, and all their wrangling and discourse, they'd left out the thing that actually did pique my interest—Jimmy Flynn's lungs. Jimmy Flynn's speed. Did I inherit those?

Now, Charlie and I continue our descent of the canyon. I don't know how many miles we've covered—there are no mile markers—but the colorful sedimentary layers mark our progress. We pass through another, this one a dark purple. We pick up speed, our arms high, elbows out, flailing like two birds with clipped wings down the broken trail. Despite the poor footing, we descend quickly until we encounter a common site in the canyon—a mule train. It's long, perhaps twenty riders. We step to the side, our backs pressed against a smooth rock face to let them pass. The train moves slowly—after all, they're mules—and we grow impatient, but we also exchange pleasantries of a shared adventure. Chubby tourists ride atop the mules on unfamiliar saddles and hold onto reins and saddle horns with tight grips and white knuckles. One man, nervously perspiring, wears a safari hat and a collared shirt tucked into camel-colored khakis. He looks catalogued and out of place. But he also looks surprised to see us. He asks how on earth we got down here. I say, gravity. And he says, gravity. And then he adds, "Good luck climbing back up."

I chuckle. "I know a lot about climbing out of a hole," I say a little late, to the backside of his braying mule.

After the discovery of the shoes and thoughts of my great-grandfather's past, something inherently changed in me. A switch turned on. I became motivated to run. But the man on the mule was right. Climbing back up is not easy. I remembered back to when my obsession had kicked in.

The Christmas holiday season was in full swing. Which meant I couldn't turn on the television without hearing my nemesis' name—Christmas. I developed a nervous tic. My head would jerk to the right whenever I heard it, as if his spirit was resting on my shoulder, punching me.

It was also a busy time for the theater, and I worked nearly every evening. But this also allowed me to train every morning. Christmas was top of mind.

Tic. Tic. Tic.

Charlie was home again, on break, so we ran the familiar trails of Mount Lemmon, the Arizona Trail, and Sabino Canyon. The runs were no longer casual. I pushed the pace, and she responded. Each day I pushed harder, and by the time the new year rolled around, Charlie could no longer stay with me on the climbs. A week later she could no longer stay with me on the descents. It was a small victory at the expense of my best friend, but she slapped my back in appreciation and said good job. It had only been six weeks since she outran me at the Pumpkin Challenge.

I didn't stop running when she went back to college to start the spring semester. Instead, I bumped up my mileage. I ran in the mornings, and I ran in the afternoons, and when I wasn't running, all I could think about was running. I ran to work, and I ran home from work, even after midnight. And the after-work parties? Those stopped. I'd put an end to them out of my newfound respect for Mr. Grant, and myself. My priorities had changed. I started tracking my miles, which seemed like an obvious thing for a runner to do, but that exercise was new to me. They added up, surprisingly so. Five miles here, ten miles there, twenty in one clip, and a few more with Jet when he was up for it. All the while, my Ford Escort collected dust in the parking lot. I'd sweep my finger across its hood, marking each day that it sat. By the time February rolled around I was running a hundred miles a week and the hood of my Escort was numbered in the dozens.

In May, Mr. Grant called me into his office and asked if I was sick. By then, I'd dropped considerable weight, my body framed in adolescence again. My clothes hung loose and my face had thinned, evidenced by pronounced cheekbones and pocketed eyes. And when I told him I was not sick, he asked me point-blank, "Why the change?"

And my eyes bored into him. I answered point-blank, "Because I'm going to win the Boston Marathon."

And there it was—my admission.

The fat man laughed so hard he began to choke and cough. Tears welled up in his eyes before gravity sent them rolling down his cheek. When Mr. Grant gathered himself, he asked again, "No, really. Why the change, Billy?"

And I told him again. But I'd left out the part that I'd seen an update on my nemesis, Christmas Day. Killing the mountain lion with his bare hands years ago had emboldened him. He'd been quoted as saying how he could do anything, that collegiate running had bored him for lack of competition, and that his anything would include winning the Boston Marathon next year. That lit my fuse. That was the final push I'd needed to—as Charlie said—get my shit together. I'd had his number at the state finals cross-country meet, until the authorities had *my* number. It was time to settle things. And on the world's grandest stage.

Seeing the deadpan look in my eyes, Mr. Grant changed his demeanor, and apologized. But he also questioned the reality of my ambition. "Billy, you're a great runner—the best I've ever seen. But how are you going to win the Boston Marathon? Those are the greatest runners in the world. Maybe set your sites on something else."

It was the response I'd expected. Which is exactly why I hadn't told anyone until now. But I also felt the pang of disappointment, of his doubt. Mr. Grant had supported me in ways that I was only beginning to understand. Yet, he wasn't on board.

Then he said something that felt like a kick in my stomach. "Don't humiliate yourself."

I didn't answer him. Did I owe him a response? I sat, staring at his rubbery hands that were still open and postured on the desk. A wall of silence went up between us. I stood abruptly, flushed, upset with Mr. Grant for the first time ever, and left his office.

I can't humiliate myself. The shoebox is full.

Back in high school, after Danny Morales kicked me in the face in front of the girl I liked, and I lay groveling in the sand with a bloody lip, a swollen eye, and a bruised ego, my mom—being a mom—told me to keep a diary of my all my little failures. She called it a process of healing, saying that by writing down these events, it would help me cope with my feelings. And that when I felt better, I could tear out the entry and be done with it. I told her that was ridiculous, and that I wouldn't do it. But hours later I *had* done it—because Mom knew best. But I didn't write about the incident in a diary. I wrote about it on a plain, white sheet of paper that, once done, I folded and placed in an old shoebox. I took a black marker, and on the its top I wrote *My Little Box of Failures*, because I knew there'd be others to add to it. Then I placed it under my bed so that I could literally sleep on it, and if Mom was right, I'd feel better in the morning. But I never did.

The stack of papers inside the box grew thicker every year. Some of the obvious events—being led away from a school pep rally in handcuffs, losing my pants at the cross-country meet, falling into the fire trying to kiss Charlie, dating an adult-film actress. I could go on and on.

I'd even cataloged my birth. Born in a recliner, being mishandled and dropped on my head by Dad. It might not seem like a humiliating experience at the time—newborns can't feel humiliation—but when Dad began telling good friends and complete strangers about it as I was growing up, I relived that moment a million times over. There were at least twenty-five pieces of written paper dedicated solely to my birth in My Little Box of Failures. And many more referencing the catcalls and jeers calling me "Balls" in the hallways at school, at work, and in races.

Now, I'm focused on Charlie's footfall directly in front of me as we continue our descent on the South Kaibab Trail. We've reached Skeleton Point, named not for the number of humans that have died on the trail, but for all the mules that have perished in the canyon.

The trail flattens out here, and for the first time we feel the heat building. It's a good spot to take a break, peel off a layer of clothing, and eat before we flush into the inner canyon. Charlie removes her beanie, then fights back a laugh when she takes off her pink shell. She's wearing her "I'm with Stupid" T-shirt.

"I couldn't help myself," she says. She rests her hand on my shoulder.

"The shirt survives." I shake my head.

"It's the shirt that binds us."

The mood between us is light, whimsical.

I change it to something weightier.

"Charlie?"

"What is it, BB?"

"Do you think I can win the marathon?"

She pauses. "I think you can beat Christmas Day."

"Do you think *he* can win the marathon?

"No."

"So, you think I can win the marathon?"

She sucks from the nipple of her hydration pack and looks east to the climbing sun. "Let's get going, BB. The heat is building."

But I don't move. I want an answer. I prompt her. "So?"

She doesn't answer. She turns. She trots. She runs.

I follow.

I've followed.

The previous summer, Tucson had been typically hot. Temperatures rose above a hundred degrees nearly every day. The snowbirds were gone. The students were gone. And the trails were happily empty.

I ran early to escape the heat, often before the sun rose. But I also ran in the heat. Some days I returned from a run so dehydrated I looked mummified. I made a game out of it, rushing upstairs after a run to check myself in the mirror. The worse I looked, the better I felt. Few people were built to endure this kind of suffering. I was one of the brethren. I was as lean as a coyote and as mean as a javelina, putting in 150 miles a week now.

Jet, who used to get excited when I laced up my shoes, simply laid flat now, rolled his eyes, and wished me well. When your dog thinks you're crazy, you probably are.

Charlie called me one day. Now that she'd moved into an apartment, she had a phone and we talked often. I mentioned the heat, and she invited me to visit her in Flagstaff. At seven thousand feet, it was much cooler, and I could enjoy the benefits of altitude training, whatever that was. But Charlie explained it in very simple terms. "It forces your body to adapt to the lack of oxygen," she said. "When you return to sea level you run faster." Natural blood doping—that's what she called it. She told me that Flagstaff had become a popular destination for distance runners and that I'd meet training partners who could push me. I said that sounded good and that I was due some vacation time.

"But I doubt my Escort can make it. I no longer drive," I told her. "It just sits there collecting dust."

"Then, just run to me," she said, jokingly.

"I'll figure it out."

The next day, I dropped Jet off at my parents. He looked up at me with those big, soft Labrador eyes, but I sensed that he was happy to be rid of me for the time being.

Eight days later, by way of the Arizona Trail, I arrived at Charlie's doorstep, unannounced. I greeted her with a patchy beard and a crusty smile. My lips, so chaffed, so split, looked cheese-grated. My face flushed, sunburned.

She looked at me with dismay, arms crossed.

"My car wouldn't start," I said.

"Bullshit, BB."

"Don't make me laugh," I pleaded. "It hurts to laugh."

I carried no bags; just a hydration pack stuffed with basic necessities. I'd run four hundred miles from Oracle to Flagstaff—fifty miles per day. There were an adequate number of gateway communities along the route where I'd stop to refuel, resupply, and sometimes sleep. But just the same, I was happy to sleep under the stars if that's where I chose to lay down for the night. I was also happy to accept the generosity of others, mostly day hikers, who viewed me with both reverence and disdain when I told them my story, feeding and watering me like a stray dog, before shooing me away because of my stink.

Charlie shook her head in disbelief. "Have you lost your damn mind, Billy?"

"Yes. And my toenails."

"You ran all the way here, from Oracle to Flagstaff, on the Arizona Trail?"

"Yes."

"To me," she said. "You ran to me?"

"You told me to."

"I was joking," she said, incredulously. "You ran to me?"

"I did."

She pulled at my elbow to escort me inside. She winced, putting her hand over her mouth, pinching her nose.

"Good Lord, you stink."

I stunk.

"Roomies?"

She pointed to the couch. "Of course," she said. "But shower first."

Now, in just over an hour, we've nearly made it to the bottom of the canyon. The Kaibab Suspension Bridge comes into view a couple hundred yards beneath us. We step aside to admire it and to let a lone runner pass coming up the trail. We smile and wave. She nods, and without stopping, says to me, "Hi, Stupid." Charlie's T-shirt had prompted her.

We continue down the trail. There's a very short tunnel that's bored into the rock. We pass through and it spits us out onto the bridge above the muddy waters of the Colorado River. We're at the lowest point. We walk slowly, but we're also giddy with excitement. I'm behind Charlie, and halfway across I come to a dead stop. This moment is symbolic.

"Wait."

Charlie stops, turns to face me.

"Here we are, Charlie. Look around you. Look up."

She knows exactly what I'm getting at.

"We've talked about this moment since we were kids," she says.

"We still need to climb out of this hole," I say, looking up.

"We already have," she says.

She's right.

"We've come a long way…"

"Metaphorically speaking," she finishes. She looks up. "I can't see the top."

"Are you still talking in metaphors?" I ask.

"No. I literally can't see the top from here."

She's right.

From high above, we're nothing if not insignificant, two shapeless specks blown by wind, rolled by gravity. But we know otherwise. There's a moment of recognition, of awareness, that we share in this vast, impossible wilderness. We stand together on this bridge at the very crosshairs of our relationship with only one way to go—*Up*.

"Charlie?"

"What is it, BB?"

"You didn't answer my question back there at Skeleton Point."

She kicks nervously at the wooden planks of the suspension bridge, averting her eyes. "Because you already know the answer."

"Charlie?"

"What is it, BB?"

Jeffrey Recker

"Will you come to Boston with me? Will you watch?"
She pauses before answering.
"You need to promise me one thing."
"What?"
"You know."
"I'll win."
She looks up now, anchored, meeting my eyes. "I know."

24

Old School

I walk onto the University of Arizona's campus for the first time in my life. It's imposing, intimidating, so large that it takes up an entire square mile. I wander. I'm lost. But as a novel experience, I'm excited to be lost. My head is on a swivel.

I meander the mall, a narrow, verdant lawn lined with mature palm trees and esplanades that runs the campus's length like a central vein pulsating with student life. I pass by a large building, a city-block wide. STUDENT UNION. I walk by other modern builds before coming to a structure that looks out of place, a territorial design with a red brick façade, and an impressive, white staircase that extends to a second-floor veranda that wraps the entire building. If the mall is a vein, this building must be its heart. There's history here. In front is a placard: OLD MAIN. It was the first-ever building constructed on campus back in 1891. I wonder if my great-grandfather ever stepped foot here. In his line of work, doubtful. I drift to a large, concrete water fountain that is centered in front where dozens of students have gathered and socialize. I read another placard with the names of thirteen students who'd lost their lives in World War I. The fountain had been dedicated to them. Does the current cohort know? Do they have any appreciation of those who came before them?

They look different than me—these students. I feel very much out of place in their presence. They're dressed in bright clothing with ponies and alligators on the chest, with striped shorts and loafers and backpacks and Ray-Bans. They're confident and carefree and carry a swagger about themselves that comes with the privilege of belonging.

I'm a bit ratty, dressed in blue jeans that'd fall off without a belt, and a simple green, cotton shirt that has the beginnings of a small hole where a logo should go. Only my running shoes give me away that I'm any sort of something.

Apprehensively, I approach a small gathering of sorority girls wearing pink cotton shorts that have Greek letters written in black on their backside. One turns and smiles. She is freckled, and tan, and her eyes are lively and fixate on mine when I ask directions to the library. She asks if I'm a freshman. I'm so thin I could pass for one. "First time on campus," I skirt, thanking her.

Ten minutes later I find the library. I stand just inside the entrance of two ten-foot glass doors, and am overwhelmed by the scale of this place. It's the size of a large warehouse with multiple floors and departments and signage pointing this way and that way, and I have no idea what to do or where to turn. Fortunately, I spot a help desk to my right.

I approach a young woman with straight black hair and thick black mascara, a student-worker presumably, and she eyes my wardrobe judgingly. When I say hello and start to speak, she puts her forefinger up to her pursed lips to hush me. *What do I know about library etiquette?* I lean toward her and whisper, but now she can't hear me and asks that I step closer and speak louder. So, I do both, and she hushes me again. "At what decibel?" I ask. Without blinking, without expression, she says, "Forty-five, exactly forty-five."

She directs me to the third floor, where the microfiche is located. It's here that I begin my search for Maggie Flynn, my great-grandfather's younger sister. She'd be in her seventies by now, and if she is still alive—if I can find her—then perhaps she can tell me more about James Flynn. No one else could.

Mr. Grant had exhausted his memory, and Mom knew less. It seemed that the story of James Flynn was buried with him. Then, Mom called me days ago, and said she'd remembered something that might help. Her mother, Jacqueline, had once mentioned that James Flynn had a younger sister. She thought her name might have been Maggie, but that she definitely owned a diner in Pittsburgh. "I remember the diner part of that story," Mom said. "I love diners." It wasn't much, but it was a clue worth chasing.

So, now I scour the Allegheny County public records, but come up empty. By noon I've given up.

I rise to leave, and spot a row of computers tucked away in a corner. They're as foreign to me as the black monolith was to the apes in *2001: A Space Odyssey*. But just like those

395

apes, I find myself compelled, drawn to them out of curiosity. I take a seat in front of one. I don't know how to turn it on. But when I touch the keyboard it just magically comes to life. The bright screen shrinks my pupils, and my eyes reflect a future I know nothing about. And I wonder, is it going to start talking to me like HAL 9000? *No, of course not. Computers can't talk.*

But it does prompt me for a student identification. Dejected again, I moan, and mumble something under my breath. A student, sitting at another computer, hears me grumble, turns, and, of all things, recognizes me.

"Balls? Are you Balls?"

"Ball," I say. "No *s.*"

"Billy Ball?"

"Correct. Ball," I repeat. "No *s.*"

He's younger than me, and I can tell by his expression he's embarrassed. He's also rail-thin, and it's easy to spot him for a runner.

He introduces himself as Thomas, and I'm not sure if that's his first or last name, but before I ask, he says he's on the track team, and apologizes for getting my name wrong. He says this much louder than the allotted forty-five decibels. Then I tell him the mispronunciation of my name is okay, that it happens all the time. I laugh it off, and I call him Thomas Thomas to cover both bases. He also laughs it off. And I say my boss is named Grant Grant, even though this time I'm not joking around. He doesn't know what to say at that.

"You're a legend," Thomas tells me.

"For all the wrong reasons," I say.

"You beat Christmas Day. Nobody has ever beaten Christmas. Not even in college."

Tic.

"No, I did not," I say. "I impeded his progress and lost."

"Well, that's not what I meant, anyhow. You're back."

I understand his meaning. I'd come close to setting the American record in my debut marathon just months ago, a fine setup to the Boston Marathon. I'd become a national celebrity overnight. But no one, other than my parents and Charlie, gave me a shot at winning Boston. I'm too young, they'd said. Too inexperienced. No international competitions. Still, I'm widely considered one of the new, bright spots for American distance running, which had been in serious decline on the global scene since after the days when my namesake, Bill Rodgers, won.

After that debut marathon, I'd received dozens of calls from editors and reporters. They called night and day wanting to know all sorts of stupid things.

Who are you?
Who is anyone?
Why haven't I heard of you?
I don't know.
Where did you attend college?
HLU (Hard Luck University).
What do you do for a living?
General Manager in Transition at the Oracle Theater.
Are you married?
No.

397

Kids?

I don't think so.

Girlfriend?

I don't know. Maybe.

Are you a fluke?

Definitely.

What do you eat?

Food.

Do you take drugs?

I never inhaled.

How do you train?

Fast and faster.

Do you have a coach?

Coach Jeremy Jones. Taught me a life lesson: it's okay to shit my pants in competition.

You cheat?

Mom and Dad raised me better than that.

What's your pedigree?

I'm just an ordinary, average guy.

For two weeks I was praised, until a local newspaper ran what was supposed to be a feel-good story about me. The author interviewed Coach Jones, Mr. Grant, a few friends, and most importantly, my parents. But when the author dug, he'd discovered a new angle, something to exploit that would likely sell more newspapers. He painted me as a troubled kid who'd had a run-in with the law, charged with Public Indecency and Child Endangerment. The mention made my gut churn. *I guess it was fair. It was accurate. But was it necessary?* I tried to be objective about it. He did write that all charges were eventually dropped, and that I had persevered through troubled times. But I'll be damned, in every instance, he'd misspelled my name: Balls—with an *s*. William Balls. Billy Balls. *Always*, Balls Balls Balls. And even though the label of Balls had been circulated so often that people actually believed it to be my name, the misspelling was not okay, because when the article hit, it was picked up by the Associated Press, and so, the entire country now mistakenly knew me as Balls.

Humiliation casts a wide net.

So, I stopped taking phone calls, and stopped talking to reporters who wanted to know not about my running, but about the arrest, and how I had been rehabilitated, whatever that meant. Was I ever truly damaged? It was all negative energy that upset me. So, I focused on training, and the one thing that truly kept me up at night, the one thing that I found most inspiring even if I'd yet to understand why: James Flynn.

The pedigree question had haunted me. I purposely didn't mention James Flynn when it came up. I didn't know much about him, and didn't want to mistakenly say that my ancestor had run the Boston Marathon without knowing if it was true.

Now, Thomas and I chat for a minute and he invites me to practice with the team later that day. I decline, telling him I'm searching for a lost relative, but sadly, I'd given up after hours searching microfiche. "I thought this thing might help." I point to the computer and he sees that I can't log in. I admit that I don't know much about "these things."

Thomas scoots over and enters his credentials.

"Happy to help," he says.

While the computer is *thinking*, he says it will just take a minute to go online, but I don't reply because I don't understand the term. *What is online?* He says there's a lot of information on the World Wide Web, but I still have no idea what he's talking about.

Once his credentials are accepted, a message pops up that prompts Thomas to connect to the Internet Connection Wizard.

"A wizard?" I ask.

Then, another message pops up; something about trying to access my modem. "What the hell is a modem?" I ask, accompanied by a hushed laugh. But before Thomas can answer, the most amazing thing happens: the computer starts talking! Not in words, like HAL 9000 spoke, but in strange, eerie sounds as if from outer space. *Eeeh, oooh, aaah, blewww, churrr, bleep, blewww, churr, oooh, eeeh.* And it just keeps talking like that for a very long time. I push back from the machine, my eyes wide now. Thomas sees the disconcerted look on my face, settles me, and says it's just the modem. And I repeat, "What the hell is a modem?"

Only six minutes after inputting his credentials, we're online.

"It's the miracle of modern technology," Thomas tells me. "Fourteen-thousand bps."

"What is bps?"

"It's a car ride on the internet."

This time I find newer records from Allegheny County, and then hit a small jackpot when I find the birth record of one "Maggie Harriet Flynn. Allegheny General Hospital. 4/13/1921. Daughter of Daniel and Shannon Flynn. Wilmerding, PA." *Not Pittsburgh!* I'm excited by the likelihood that it's her. But where is she now? I search the death records. Nothing.

That's good, but I'm stuck again. I try a new approach, and search the business transaction records from Allegheny County. And I hit paydirt: "Maggie's Diner. Pittsburgh, PA. Purchased 1948. Former name: Paddy's. Sole proprietor: Maggie H. Flynn." A few lines down and I see that it was sold in 1978 by a Maggie H. McCollough. She'd been married. Still married? I return to the death records, and again find nothing. Good. But—where is she? I'd hit another dead end.

Thomas, finishing up his work now, asks how I'm doing and I tell him of my luck, but that I'm stuck.

"I'm no longer looking for Maggie Flynn," I tell him. "I'm looking for Maggie McCollough."

He scratches the top of his head and comes up with a brilliant idea. "Do you know this library houses a catalog of phone books from nearly every major city in America? There's this thing called a telephone—"

"Old school," I interrupt. We fist bump.

Minutes later I'm in the library's basement, and find what I'm looking for: the Pittsburgh phone directory. I open it to the Ms and scour the pages. McB... McC... McCo... And there it is: Patrick and Maggie McCollough. I'm both amused and somewhat saddened that old people still publish their phone numbers, beseeched for long-forgotten relatives, bill collectors, and telemarketers to call.

"Hallelujah!" I shout at exactly forty-five decimals—times two.

Later that afternoon, Maggie McCollough picks up on the first ring.

25

Dingers

The abandoned house pitches forward on the sloped knoll like an old woman hunched over a shaky cane, its bones frail and creaking under the weight of its age. Vines crawl the posts that support an off-kilter porch. They reach high, as if to pull it down, as if to reclaim the wilted structure as terra firma and erase sixty years of ruin and misfortune. Weeds overrun the lawn, poking through a broken, white picket fence, parts scattered and laying in disrepair.

I step back to double-check the address, to get an encompassing view of the dilapidated house where my great-grandfather and his family grew up. Maggie McCollough's words are fresh: *There were good times in that house.* But I struggle to imagine the probability, and question her recollection. I know that memories can be romanticized and filled with nostalgic feelings. But the reality is often much different.

The sidewalk is crumbling and I take another step back onto the street and into a rain-filled pothole, so deep that my running shoe disappears beneath its black, murky surface. I pop out, my shoe soaked. I look up to playfully curse God, against a low, gray sky. He responds with a bombardment of bird shit that sprays my shoulders and face. It's the sort of thing that Charlie would have laughed at if she were here, but she won't be joining me until I get to Boston.

This is Wilmerding, the town that ate itself, that relied on one thing and one thing only—the success of the Westinghouse Air Brake Company—for its sovereignty.

Rows of wood-framed, company-built tract houses, perfectly aligned like army barracks, run the length of the street and my sightline. Many are fighting a similar fate as my great-grandfather's house.

Dad used to say that time equals money. And I understand that. I also understand that if there is no money, time stands still. Because that's what I'm looking at here. With no upkeep, houses falling in on themselves, and a crumbling infrastructure, I'm stuck in the past.

I've seen enough and walk back toward downtown, toward the defunct factory. I find myself on Airbrake Avenue, following the street that Daniel Flynn walked sixty years ago, and other shift workers who answered the call of the company whistle each morning. They were inconspicuous figures, fettered and clonelike in overalls, flannel shirts, and flat caps. *Marching ants.* That's how Maggie had put it when I'd met with her earlier in the morning at her namesake diner.

She'd arrived before me, having walked down a flight of stairs one gingerly step at a time from the apartment she still owned above the diner. She took her usual spot in her usual booth, the last one in the row. She sat with her hunched, osteoporotic back to the entrance, facing an empty wall instead, hidden in her thoughts, but revealed in her posture.

A plump woman in her forties with the name Lilly stitched on her blouse escorted me to her table. She brought with her a piece of blueberry pie, setting it in front of Maggie. "She has a slice every morning," Lilly said.

Maggie sat across from me, wearing a yellow wool jacket. She was improbably small, shrunken and childlike, and her head rose barely a foot above the white laminate table.

She was more interested in the pie than me, barely acknowledging my presence. She bit into it, closed her eyes, and moaned ever so slightly. When her crepey eyelids opened, she asked, "Do you like pie, Mr. Balls?" *The* s, *the damn* s. I thought to correct her, but I simply nodded. Maggie motioned to Lilly to bring me a slice.

"It's free, Mr. Balls," she said. "I negotiated free pie when I sold the diner."

I did the math. "Twenty years of free pie," I said, amused. "That's brilliant, Mrs. McCollough."

This made her laugh. And choke. And cough. Her eyes bugged wide. And after a long minute and a sip of tapwater, she smiled again.

Maggie then pitched forward on the table, supporting herself on elbows that shook under the weight of age. Bulbous, blue veins crawled prominently up her neck, as if reaching up to pull her head down, as if to reclaim the wilted figure as terra firma and erase a lifetime of ruin and misfortune. She studied me with eyes the color of the pie, though opaque and obscured. She clutched a set of thick-rimmed glasses in her veiny and bruised hands. Her hair was heavily teased, so thin and fibrous, the redness of it appeared pink in the diffused morning light, its mass wrapping around the frame of her corrugated face like cotton candy around a thin, cardboard cone.

She tilted her head. "Do you like yellow?" she asked, touching her jacket, pleasingly. "It's not every day I get company." She spooned another piece of pie. And I said I liked yellow very much as she chewed. Then she smiled a stained, blueberry smile, broad and wide, launching lines drawn and intersecting on her cheeks like a roadmap to my past that I was intent to follow.

"Sorry I was late, Mrs. McCollough. The rain…"

"You don't like rain?"

"I like rain. But it made me late."

"I like rain," she said. "I like rain, blueberry pie, and the color yellow."

Mrs. McCollough oozed charm. And blueberries.

"But I don't like the cold," she said, noting my running outfit. "Aren't you cold?"

I told her of my plan to visit Wilmerding after our breakfast, that I was going to run there, retracing the steps of Jimmy on his butt-naked run through the streets of Pittsburgh and beyond. She'd shared that story with me on our first phone call. "Jimmy and I have more in common than you know," I'd said without explaining. Then I asked her for the address of the house. But she became still, and her lower lip dipped. When it became obvious that she couldn't remember, when she became flustered, I changed the subject and asked her what it was like to grow up in Wilmerding.

Her eyes sparked at this. She said that when times were good, the dingers were happy. And I asked what dingers were. She smiled even wider this time, and said they were a special kind of people. "The blue-collar type that worked hard. Fifty-five hours a week."

"That's a lot."

"What's a lot?"

"The hours," I said. "Fifty-five hours. That's a lot."

"Who?"

"The dingers," I said. "The dingers worked a lot." The spark had left her eyes.

"Did they?" she asked.

One second she was sharp and coherent, and the next she was something else.

"How many hours do you work, Mr. Balls?"

"Ball," I said, correcting her this time.

"Who?"

"Ball. My name is Ball, Mrs. McCollough."

She didn't acknowledge. But her eyes sparked again. She said that fifty-five hours was fewer than other mill companies required from their employees, that WABCO gave them Saturday afternoons and Sundays off. "It was a good place to live. It was a good place to work."

Lilly arrived with my pie. She eyed me warily, setting it down.

"Everyone loves pie," Maggie said. "Jimmy loved pie."

"Tell me about Jimmy. But first tell me about the dingers."

"The dingers were the type that bound together in good times and bad, their fortunes tied to the company's," she said. "That wasn't a bad thing. The company felt a strong sense of responsibility and took care of us. When my dad lost his job after the crash, they let us stay in that house for years after we stopped paying the rent." Then she averted her eyes. "Until they couldn't. Eventually, economics crushed the will of the company and its good intentions."

I sat listening, absorbing her every word, lucid and not.

"But it all came to a head after the Boston Marathon," she continued. "The economy had wrecked the town and the people looked for salvation beyond WABCO, which by now they had given up on. They entrusted a man named Paddy O'Donnell. He was a bootlegger from Wilmerding who'd made a fortune. A local hero, as they say."

"Yes, I remember you mentioned Paddy over the phone."

"Did I?"

"Paddy's Diner." I'd also remembered the name from the county records during my search.

"Yes. Same Paddy."

"Paddy—"

"Paddy O'Donnell," she said. "Paddy liked pie."

"Paddy's Diner," I repeated.

"Yes, Paddy's Diner. Didn't I say that?"

I said she had. Conversing with her was like playing ping-pong: hit, hit, miss, miss, hit, miss, hit.

She pointed at me with a crooked but assertive finger. "Until I bought it, and changed the name to Maggie's," she continued, proudly. "Paddy employed a lot of dingers who'd lost their jobs at Westinghouse. He had a good heart, lots of charisma, and the dingers took to him and called him Santa Claus. But eventually, they lost hope in him too, especially when it became clear that Prohibition would end after Roosevelt took office. Who needs a bootlegger at that point? But like I said, he had a big heart, and took Jimmy under his wing."

"Why Jimmy?"

"Paddy was a businessman. He recognized Jimmy's talent. Recognized the opportunity. He made a lot of money off of Jimmy's running."

"So, what happened?"

"We got kicked out of Wilmerding."

"Kicked out?"

"Got kicked out," she repeated. "Paddy too. Jimmy ran the Boston Marathon but came up short."

"You told me."

"Well, Paddy had backed him. Promoted him. Told the dingers to bet everything they had on him. Broke as they were, they lost a lot of money—money they didn't have. When hope dies…" Her voice softened.

"I checked the results. I couldn't find a James or Jimmy Flynn anywhere."

"You won't find his name in the results. He was disqualified because Paddy's right-hand man, an ape named Big Mike, dragged him across the finish line."

She shook her head and looked away. "I was there at the finish line in a yellow dress that Jimmy had bought for me, holding a bouquet of yellow flowers. I dropped the flowers, which were trampled in the melee that ensued when Jimmy was disqualified. I gathered them up, but when the dingers lost their money, they'd lost their minds too. I saw it all, Mr. Balls. Jimmy could have finished just fine if that big ape hadn't..."

I straightened. Maggie had a fierceness about her, fitting of a hard-luck upbringing.

She took a deep breath. "I apologize for swearing," she said.

"I didn't mean to upset you."

"It's okay. After all these years, it's good to talk about it."

And that's the thing about old people, I realized. You never know when you'll stir up something deep and rooted in their past, unlocking nostalgia and memories both true and false, or in the case of Maggie, a psychotic, delusional episode, which happened next.

We looked across the table at each other without speaking a word for several minutes. She seemed lost in her thoughts.

"Now, come closer, dear," she said. "Let me get a better look at you." She reached for her glasses, and with shaky hands slid them on. They were round and thick like the bottom of a Coke bottle, and magnified her eyes like two big blue orbs beneath cataract clouds.

I must have been a spitting image of Jimmy because she quieted, intently focused, squinted, and leaned closer to get a better look at me. I also leaned forward to meet her gaze. She put her hand to her mouth. And she gasped.

"Are you okay, Maggie?"

Her eyes bulged and her jaw clenched.

"Jimmy?"

"Billy."

"Jimmy!"

"I'm not Jimmy."

"We need to get home," she said.

"What?"

"We need to get home, now! Mama's gonna whip our asses."

"Maggie?"

"Jimmy!"

"I'm Billy, Mrs. McCollough. I'm not Jimmy."

Her voice pitched, drawing the attention of several customers. From her tiny, wasted body, her voice rose to a crescendo. "Stop playing games, Jimmy! Mama's gonna whip our asses if we don't get home before dark."

Lilly, who'd kept a watchful eye on us throughout, made a circular motion with her index finger to her ear, indicating Maggie was a bit touched.

I nodded, acknowledging. And, as to not upset Maggie, I played along.

"Yes, we need to get home, Maggie. To Wilmerding. Where exactly *is* home?"

And the address she couldn't remember ten minutes earlier in the here and now, she rattled off as if it was yesterday. Because, in her mind, it *was* yesterday.

Lilly stepped closer now. "Maggie, I don't believe you've introduced me to your friend," she said, extending her hand to meet mine.

Lilly's voice seemed to bring Maggie back to her senses. She removed her glasses, setting them back on the table. "Yes. How rude of me. Lilly, this is Billy Balls."

"Ball, actually. It's Billy Ball," I said. "No *s*."

"Balls, Mr. Balls. I know who you are!" Maggie said, indignantly, her voice pitching once again. "I'm not senile. Your name is Billy Balls."

Heads turned once more.

I acquiesced, lowering my head. "Yes. Of course, Mrs. McCollough. My name is—my name is…" I coughed. And then I said it quietly under my breath. "Billy—Balls."

Maggie put her hand to her ear. "Speak up, Billy. I'm old. My hearing is not so good."

I pleaded to Lilly, who hovered over me, amused. "My name is—my name is—Billy—Balls," I repeated, louder this time.

"What, dear?"

"Billy…"

"Who?"

"Balls," I said, even louder. More heads turned. And in a pitched, staccato cadence: "My. Name. Is. Billy. BALLS!"

"There's no need to shout, dear. I can hear you just fine."

Maggie turned her attention back to her blueberry pie. She ate quietly while I had a loud slice of self-inflicted humiliation.

I took a deep breath, calming myself. Those around us also went back to eating.

We sat for minutes without speaking a word. Maggie was lost in her thoughts, occasionally looking up, though not at me, but rather through me, at the empty wall.

"Guessing you'll be wanting this now," Lilly said, handing me the check.

"Hey," I said. "I thought this was free."

"Hers is free. Yours is three dollars."

I reached across the table, putting my hand on top of Maggie's veiny hand. This got her attention. She looked up from her pie and said, "It's wonderful to see you again, Jimmy."

And this time I didn't correct her.

"It's been good to see you too...sister."

I thought about my next words for a long moment before I said, "This time I'm going to win Boston. And, Maggie, you'll be there with me, wearing your yellow dress, holding a bouquet of yellow daffodils."

She smiled amiably and ate her pie, her blueberry eyes fixed on mine.

I left Maggie and paid my bill at the cashier's counter. On my way out, Lilly told me to keep my pants on, because the last boy in my family tree to run from this diner had not. "Maggie tells me everything," Lilly said, jovially.

I stepped outside into a damp chill. The rain had let up. I released into a slow trot along the busy sidewalk, weaving in and out of commuting workers in suits and ties who viewed me with indifference. Occasionally I looked skyward to appreciate the reach of the old granite skyscrapers, their tops disappearing in the low-hanging clouds that enshrouded the city. I was on my way, retracing Jimmy's infamous, pantless run.

Once outside of city limits, my pace quickened. I ran spirited, instinctively, following a sense of direction as if I'd run this route before, even though I'd only glanced at it on a map. I ran through Schenley Park, and spotted the oval. Its days as a horse racing venue were long gone. A college track team now stretched and performed drills on its infield. I thought to stop, but did not. The stands were empty, but from them, I heard the faint cheer of a crowd. I looked a second time. Nobody there. But as I passed, the cheering grew louder until I heard the crescendo: "JIM-ME! JIM-ME! JIM-ME!" I shook my head. My imagination was playing tricks on me, and I laughed at my mind's invention. I could still hear the voices miles later when I entered Frick Park.

I continued east along a cinder path under an umbrella of newly budded trees and the earthy, petrichor scent of this morning's rain. I jumped puddles and branches felled by the storm, and felt the splat of large water droplets dislodged from the canopy of saturated leaves. Jimmy could have disappeared in here, I thought. The cops would have lost him in the dense, forested trails. But instead, he'd continued onward to Wilmerding—to home—unlike the man he so wanted to be, but like the frightened child he was.

As I exited the park, my gut felt queasy. *The pie?*

No, the nauseousness was soon gone. I was on a paved road again, and I began a mile-long ascent that would eventually spit me out into Forest Hills. I ran with ease, cutting six-minute miles like child's play—because six-minute miles *was* child's play. Yet, my stomach knotted again. And without explanation, I glanced behind me. Nothing there. Then, a parked police car triggered my gut to drop again. I ran even faster now as I passed it, wiping my brow in relief. Though I couldn't understand why.

This experience. I felt light, lifted into the air as if by a desert-spun dust devil, free.

I saw myself from high above, covering the void in quick steps. I ran faster, yet I felt unencumbered by the pace. *Four days to Boston. Save it for the race.* Yet, I couldn't save myself—from myself. Something, or rather someone, had gotten hold of me.

Then, when I'd arrived in Wilmerding, I came to an abrupt stop in front of St. Aloysius Church, as if I'd hit an invisible wall.

I instinctively knew this is where Jimmy had flattened Father McClary, ending his run. A ringing in my ears. Someone is laughing. Someone is yelling. Others are pointing. A voice telling me to get the hell off him. But there was no one there. No one at all. I backed away from the church, onto the street, until the psychotic episode subsided.

And I thought of Maggie sitting in the diner with her thick, round glasses accentuating her fraught eyes and ghastly expression, calling me Jimmy. I assumed she was in a delusional state. But now I wonder.

He has your eyes, he has your nose, he has your feet, he has your toes.

415

I was my own being, but what traits had Jimmy passed down? Physical gifts, without doubt. Memories too? Was it possible? I'd run the thirteen miles without thought, as if every twist and turn, every anxious moment, and even the moment when I stopped was embedded in my genetic code. *Aren't we all just re-creations of our genealogy?*

I stood in front of the church, wet and exalted, my arms at my sides, then on my hips, looking up at the church bells that hung silent, yet rang in my ears. Jimmy's run might have started at Paddy's coffee shop. But his life's pursuit had been set in motion here at this very spot. I sensed it. I understood.

***

Now, after visiting the old house, I continue my walk down Airbrake Avenue that parallels Turtle Creek. On the other side is the plant, a half-mile long; so large, it takes five minutes to pass. I cross over the creek, and continue on toward the center of town. The turreted clocktower from the Westinghouse Air Brake Company headquarters peeks over the tree line.

Another two blocks and the entire castle materializes. It's a massive structure, stately amidst the surrounding urban decay. It sets back from the street, high on a hillside, with an expansive lawn that carries to an adjoining park in the town's center. This is the heart of Wilmerding.

There's no sign of life from inside the castle. No sound. No lights. It's a sleeping giant, a vacant edifice that once housed the administration of WABCO. Though it is not without care. The lawn is manicured, and the hedges are trimmed. There is little sign of neglect beyond the obvious: its age.

I stop to admire its architecture. But eventually I move on, and walk to the train station just a few blocks away.

I'm told the noon train to Pittsburgh is an hour late. I have time to kill, and spot a bar with a sign in the window: "Joe's Bar and Grill." Next to it is another sign: "CLOSED." But as I turn to walk away, it flips to OPEN. I'm hungry after the thirteen-mile run and the tour of Wilmerding.

Still in my running attire—black tights and a T-shirt—I reluctantly walk inside. When I do, the only eyes in the place are quickly on me. A grizzled, old man judges me from behind the bar as I cross the void on squeaky wood planks and take a seat in front of him. The old man sizes me up, and without saying hello, he tells me I've got bird shit on my shoulder. I say I know, that I'd been shit on. And, without expression, he says, "Haven't we all?"

He asks why I'm dressed like a fag, and I tell him I'm a runner. And he says that makes sense.

We're making progress.

Then he asks where I'm from, and I tell him Tucson, and he asks where the fuck is Tucson. And I tell him Mexico. And he says, "Your English is very good."

More progress.

Then he asks me what I'm doing in Wilmerding, and I tell him I'd run here from Pittsburgh, and I was waiting on a train.

"Covered in bird shit," he says.

"Yes, covered in bird shit."

"You runners are crazy fuckers."

And I agree.

He nods.

I've passed.

"What can I get you?" he asks.

I order a burger and water, and the old man disappears into the kitchen. I hear him and another man—presumably the cook—laughing.

I'm uneasy, and examine my surroundings. The bartop is a long, wooden plank perhaps fifteen feet in length, varnished and aged. An odor permeates from its being like a stinky, old running shoe. This creation is alive, and holds stories from Wilmerding's early days. On the wall, behind it, is a sign that reads "FREE BEER TOMORROW." I broaden my scope. On every wall are old, black and white photographs, cheaply framed, of Wilmerding and its people—the dingers.

The old man reappears and pours me a beer. I remind him that I'd asked for water, but he rolls his eyes and says, "Have a beer." And I agree. Then he asks, "Why'd you run here? Nobody runs here."

He's suspicious again.

I tell him that I'm on a tour to explore my roots. That I'm looking for answers, and that my ancestors had once lived here.

"You don't say." He pulls a pair of thick reading glasses from his shirt pocket and leans in, examining me, just as Maggie had done. "I've lived here my entire life," he says. "I'm Joe Jr. Who exactly are your ancestors?"

"It was a long time ago," I say.

"Then I was probably alive."

I take a long sip of beer. It's stale. I wince. "Daniel Flynn. He worked at the plant," I say. "James Flynn was his son. He was a runner."

Joe stiffens before leaning even closer this time. His face, a mere foot from mine. He squints, studying me. Then he grimaces, revealing teeth that are long and stained. His breath is rooted in rot, and I pull back.

I take another sip of beer, but I freeze when I see his expression. I don't swallow.

He backs away in recognition, as if he'd seen a ghost. He tells me my beer is going to cost fifty dollars. And I say, "What!" And he says, "That's how much my old man lost on Jimmy Flynn at the Boston Marathon!"

I spit my beer on the bar.

"Jesus Christ, kid!"

"You—knew—Jimmy Flynn?" I ask, disbelieving.

"Everyone knew that son of a bitch," he says. He points to a photograph hung on the wall to my side. "Him and his crooked promoter, Paddy O'Donnell!"

I stand and move closer to the photograph to get a better look. It's of a celebration on the lawn of the WABCO castle. Hundreds of people are gathered, nicely dressed, most sitting on blankets, picnicking. Their focus is on a fat man in a suit, wearing a white fedora. He has one arm wrapped around a much smaller man with a runner's build. *My build.* They stand on a wooden platform, and the fat man is smiling while the other is not. Draped behind them is an American flag. To their side is a small marching band in uniform. And hung from the platform is a banner: "GO JIMMY THE RABBIT. WIN BOSTON!"

My jaw drops and I ask Joe for his reading glasses. I need a closer look. I put them on and the photograph is magnified. Faces come into view. Even in the bar's dim light, I can see the image of the person in question. His hair is cut short, and his jawline is clenched and square. But so is his temple. *Square head.* He looks out at the crowd without expression, his eyes buried in deep sockets on a gaunt face.

I could be looking in a mirror. I remove the glasses and pinch the bridge of my nose. I'll be damned.

It's Jimmy Flynn.

26

Say My Name

M *onday, 11:50 a.m., Hopkinton, Massachusetts*
I still do stupid things.

I'm gathered with the other elite runners at the starting line of the Boston Marathon. I'm standing next to a brown-skinned runner, much smaller than myself. He's spirited and jumps in place, and wears the colors of Mexico. He smiles broadly, and nods. *"Buena Suerte,"* he says. "Good luck," I echo. We high-five. Then, he points to my shoes and asks: *"¿Que son esos?"* He looks puzzled. I look down and see what he sees.

I'm wearing my great-grandfather's shoes! He nudges a fellow countryman, still pointing at my shoes, *"¿Cual es su nombre?"* his fellow countryman asks. *"Su nombre es estúpido."* They laugh as I panic and recede to the back of the elite field.

The shoes! I'd gotten caught up in the excitement and forgot to switch them out after I'd put them on to pay respect to Jimmy.

I consider running back to the high school gymnasium to grab my racing flats, but it would take too long. These shoes, these prototype running shoes, some sixty years old with the uppers glued on to the rubber soles, would have to carry me all the way to Boston. My stomach turns.

Up ahead, a motorcade, including a large flatbed truck carrying a network crew and a television camera, sits idling, ready to lead us out onto the course at noon. I spot a clock to my left, on a white church steeple. Its mechanical arms click forward intermittently.

Tempe, Arizona. Tuba lies in bed with one eye open. He contemplates the effort of rising, and after a long minute he struggles to the toilet. When he's done relieving himself, he ambles to the living room in just his boxer shorts and turns on the television. He leans back on the couch, propping his feet on the coffee table that's littered with empty beer cans and an open pizza box. The feed from the Boston Marathon is from high above, and a reporter is shouting over the *thwop thwop thwop* of chopper blades, telling the viewers what a spectacular sight it is to see ten thousand runners lining the narrow streets of Hopkinton. The camera pans the length of them as proof.

11:51 a.m., Hopkinton, Massachusetts

I hear the buzz of helicopters. A half dozen hover overhead. Rooftops are littered with spectators, some holding signs wishing us good luck. Police, mixed with the National Guard, walk the perimeter. One holds the leash of a German shepherd, who pulls him along, sniffing for trouble. There's control in the chaos. My senses are overloaded. But my focus is on my shoes. *My damn shoes.* Over a loudspeaker that feeds back and pierces my ears, a moment of silence is requested for the singing of our national anthem. I remove my hat and locate the flag.

San Francisco, California. Henry Fly is running along a winding path in Crissy Field with the Golden Gate Bridge in the backdrop. He passes other runners with the ease and grace of a seasoned collegiate athlete that he is. He's impressed with himself. And he's convinced everyone he passes is equally impressed. He picks up the pace and races past a woman pushing a baby jogger. She startles. He laughs. He's unaware that the Boston Marathon is today. He runs his own race.

11:53 a.m. Hopkinton, Massachusetts

O say, does that star-spangled banner yet wave…
O'er the land of the free and the home of the brave.

It's beautifully sung, and cheers ring out from spectators and runners alike.

I'm relieved to put my hat back on. I search for clouds. There are none. It's going to be a hot day.

I'm sweating.

I'm scared.

Tucson, Arizona. Piper Cox has since moved on from Applebee's and tends bar on the patio of a Mexican food restaurant that overlooks the city. It's a perfect April weather day. Pink bougainvilleas frame the bar and two women talk passionately about legal matters while they sip on mimosas. One has pink hair and professes her innocence. The other is professionally dressed and scribbles notes on a legal pad. "What happened next?" she asks. Piper turns on the television that hangs above the bar. The Boston Marathon feed comes on at once. The camera pans the elite field as the commentators discuss the favorites.

The network lead has soft, doughy cheeks and wears a sandy-colored toupee. He's not a runner and never has been. He introduces himself as Bob Hall, and says to his co-host, "Who were you expecting—Bob Costas?" He calls her Ann because his tongue ties when he tries to pronounce her name, Ananya. "Say my name," she says under her breath. But he turns to the camera and covers his gaff with a smile that reveals perfectly aligned, white teeth, charming the audience. Ananya, of Indian descent, responds in an exaggerated, native accent. "It's a pleasure to be here, Boob."

Bob flinches, unsure of what he heard. "What do you make of the Americans this year?"

"The Americans have no shot today," she says.

"Perhaps they do," Bob counters. "There he is, folks!" The camera stops on a handsome young man with a chiseled jawline and a black flock of hair. "The lion killer, himself. Christmas Day. America's best hope."

Distracted by the banter on the television, the pink-haired woman looks up from her mimosa. "Fucking runners," she says. "I used to date one." "So did I," her attorney says. "Mine had a square head." "So did mine!" They laugh. Pinky continues... "His name was Billy Ba-ba..." She doesn't finish. She points at the television, stupefied. The block-headed runner comes into focus. "Balls!" the women say in unison, staring at his image. Their jaws drop. A long second passes before Diana Prince turns to Holly. "Sorry, Ms. Wodecki. I can't save you after all."

11:54 a.m., Hopkinton, Massachusetts

I spot Christmas. He's not wearing a hat. There's no mistaking his black, wavy hair, a view I'd seen a dozen times in chase back in high school. Even from my vantage, I can sense his confidence. He stands taller than the other runners. I glance down at my shoes again, still disbelieving. *I can't run in these things.* I take a long swallow of a sports drink and toss the bottle aside. I reach down to touch my toes, stretching my hamstrings one last time.

Oracle, Arizona. Mr. Grant sits at his desk holding an envelope with his name on it. Inside is fifteen hundred-dollar bills and a note: *For the love of popcorn. I'm sorry – Billy.*

He places the envelope back in the desk drawer and leaves the office to manage the activity in the lobby. Right away he spots Coach Jones, who has pulled his track and cross-country teams out of school today for the show. The kids wait impatiently in line for popcorn and soda. The marathon is about to start and they're anxious to find their seats in the theater.

Coach Jones takes time to thank Mr. Grant. "Redistributing content without consent of the network is highly illegal," Mr. Grant says with a chuckle.

"Yeah, you better keep this quiet," Coach Jones says, laughing. "Nothing conspicuous outside."

Outside, the flashing neon marque reads "BILLY BALL RUNS BOSTON. 10am. Free Show."

The minute hand bucks forward.

11:55 a.m., Pittsburgh, Pennsylvania

Maggie sits in her apartment above her namesake diner. She wears a yellow dress and is perched on the edge of a worn, floral sofa and tells her husband to hold it. "Hold it right there!" He's adjusting the rabbit ears that sit atop an old black and white television console. He's bent from age and tells her to put her glasses on, that she can't see a damned thing without them, and that he's not going to stand here all day adjusting the picture. She does as he says and agrees that the picture is better. She tells him that Jimmy is going to win this time. He rolls his eyes and says, "Sure he is, sweetheart."

11:56 a.m., Wilmerding, Pennsylvania

The owner of Joe's Bar and Grill flips the "CLOSED" sign that hangs in the window to "OPEN." He's not expecting many customers. Not on a Monday. He stands behind the bar and riffles through a stack of mail, mostly bills. There's one that stands out among the rest. It's a letter that's simply addressed to Joe. No last name. No return address. He tears it open to find a hundred-dollar bill. Attached is a note: *Sorry your dad lost fifty dollars on Jimmy Flynn. Please accept this as a debt paid, plus interest—Billy Ball.*

Joe smiles for the first time in a while. He remembers that the kid is going to run the marathon, and wonders if it's on television. He finds the television remote, calls for the cook to join him, and locates the race. A few regulars walk in.

11:57 a.m., Boston College, Massachusetts

Jack Ash is tailgating with other students on Commonwealth Avenue, about four miles from the finish line of the marathon. He works a grill, flipping burgers and hot dogs, while drinking beer from a keg. He boasts that on a good day he could beat Billy Ball, but admits he hasn't had a good day in a very long while. His buddies sit on a sofa, dragged to the sidewalk from their brownstone apartment. They stuff their youthful faces with potato chips and beer. It's Patriots' Day, and it's their duty.

"Billy who?" one asks, wearing a baseball cap with the letters BC.

"I told you," Jack says. "Billy Ball! He was my teammate in high school."

"Oh yeah, Balls," the guy says. "I heard about that dude."

"Because I told you about him, dumbass," Jack says.

11:58 a.m., Boston, Massachusetts

Near the finish line, Richard and Jean Ball sit in the bleachers awaiting the start. They sit in view of a Jumbotron that feeds the pre-race commentary, cutting to scenes of the starting line. But Richard isn't paying attention. He's proudly telling anyone who will listen that his son is running. He adds that he'd dropped him on his head at birth but look at him now, running in the Boston Marathon, Jesus Christ! A lady sitting next to him is unimpressed and points out that nearly everyone watching has someone in the race. And he says, "Yes, of course they do." He rolls his eyes, turns, and whispers in Jean's ear that not everyone's *someone* is going to win.

Just then, Charlie appears and scales the bleachers carrying a tray of cold sodas and snacks. "There you are!" she says, all smiles, beaming as only Charlie can. "Ready for the show?"

11:59 a.m., Hopkinton, Massachusetts

Another ear-piercing announcement: "One minute, runners. One minute!" A few runners stride out in front of the line, jog back, and squeeze in between others. They extend their elbows, widening their stance, fighting for an

428

inch, fighting for the protection of space and a clear lane for when they're unleashed.

I take a deep breath, and then another, tunneling my vision, corking my energy. My heart slows. I settle. *This is the calm before the storm.* All around me, objects blur, sounds mute. On a windless, hot day, flags hang lifeless. I look to my left at the clock tower one last time. The hour hand clutches twelve, the minute hand a fraction behind. Animated spectators holler from the sides, fists high and pumping. I step forward, taking a position next to another runner whose odor is strong, feeling the sodden skin of his arm on mine. He pushes his elbow out ever so slightly, keeping me at bay. Capped energy percolates among us, fueling an impending eruption. My mouth is dry—so dry I can't swallow. Above the stand of runners, I see the raised starter's pistol. I lean slightly forward, anticipating. A drop of sweat falls from my temple. My eyes follow it the length of my body, as if in slow motion, until splat, it lands on the top of my great-grandfather's shoe at the exact moment the pistol fires.

A shot heard around the world.

Go. Go. Go!

***

The pack hits the first mile in 4:50. It's not particularly fast, given the adrenaline and the downhill start. The favorites check each other, calculating, respecting the looming heat.

I tuck in comfortably toward the back of them. Leading the charge is Christmas. He's intent to stamp his mark early on.

But I settle in. And my mind goes elsewhere.

Charlie once asked me what I thought about when I ran. Right now, I'm thinking of her.

We met in the lobby of the Lenox Hotel last night. She wanted to wish me good luck and, in the process, told me to break a leg. Then she laughingly rescinded. We sat in red leather chairs by a fireplace set against stately wood panels that shot fourteen feet high, and pretended that we belonged, that we were comfortable in our lavish surroundings. A large, ornate vase filled with fresh spring flowers sat atop a mahogany pedestal next to her. She said the Days Inn was exactly like this, and I laughed and told her to run faster.

"Run faster?"

"This is how invited runners are treated," I said, humbled. "You should see my room."

"Should I?"

She followed me upstairs to the fourth floor. We stopped at room 423. Under the numbers, a placard read "Judy Garland Suite."

"You're staying in Dorothy's room?" Charlie said, round-eyed.

"I got lucky. They had a cancellation," I said, unlocking the door. "She lived here, off and on, for thirty-five years. Come in."

The door opened up to a sitting area, elaborately decorated with high-back chairs and heavy-textured, gold-leaf patterned wallpaper. A vintage chandelier hung from a high ceiling that was wrapped in crown molding. Charlie stopped directly beneath it to look up into its crystals. As she did, they sparkled on her face. But then, Charlie always sparkled.

"Come," I said. "You've got to see this." Beyond the sitting area was the bedroom and a wood-burning fireplace encased in an opulent, arabesque mantel. As a hotel prop, a replica of Dorothy's ruby slipper sat atop.

"It's all been remodeled," I told her. "Except this fireplace. It's original."

"You've done some remodeling, yourself," Charlie said, seeing my great-grandfather's shoes set next to the slipper.

"I brought them for good luck."

"Tap your heels together three times and win the marathon?"

"That's funny, Charlie," I said. "There's no magic in these old shoes, but I'm going to wear them in the morning and switch them out when I get to Hopkinton. As a tribute to Jimmy."

* * *

It's very early in the marathon, but I feel at ease with the pace that's being set by the frontrunners. *Perhaps there is magic in these shoes.* Though, I keep my distance, calculating the others, staying out of the chum and hanging cautiously toward the back.

We enter the quaint town of Ashland. I see a tattered, wooden sign that's nailed to a tree. It reads, "It all started here in 1897." It's a reference to the original starting line of the Boston Marathon. It's yet another cast that reels me into history. And I wonder if Jimmy Flynn had seen this same sign.

It's also here that, for the first time, I see a hint of crowds that this race is so famous for. On this state holiday that commemorates the battles of Lexington and Concord, families are out in full support, picnicking and cheering us forward. Kids wave American flags, and some hold their hands out in the hope of high-fiving a passing runner. But they'll have to wait. None in this elite field offer theirs.

These early miles speed by quickly. Surprisingly, a few of the elite runners have dropped back. The heat is already taking its toll.

We enter Framingham at mile seven, and shortly thereafter, I see my reflection in a glass-pane storefront that stretches a half block. My posture shoots straight and pitches forward ever so slightly. My stride is long and purposeful and shaped like a crescent moon laid flat on its tips. There is no hitch. There is nothing but fluid motion propelled by long, sinewy legs. In one stride I cover an entire glass panel. I pass in seconds. And I wonder, is this how others see me?

I know that Charlie and my parents are watching the live feed at the finish line. Though, since I've been running toward the back, do they know I'm in the mix, and that I'm just hiding? I consider pushing to the front to give them a peek, to give them something to cheer about. But I hold back for one very big reason: doubt.

In my suite—the Judy Garland Suite—I'd told Charlie that I didn't belong in this race. I told her I couldn't win, that my one and only marathon had been a fluke, a sub-two-hour and ten-minute lucky draw. I wasn't on anyone's radar as a favorite, and at no time in Boston did one reporter address me. I'd already been cast as an also-ran.

And in typical Charlie fashion, she told me to screw off. She said she didn't come all this way to watch me give up before the race even started. Charlie was nothing if not full of tough love.

"I'm serious," I said. "I can't beat these guys."

And then she said something that surprised me; something out of character.

"Then just run to me."

"Run to you?"

"Yes. Run to me, BB. I'll be waiting."

Charlie gave me a lasting hug. I held on for a moment too long, feeling the coolness of her wispy hair against my flushed cheek, feeling the years of friendship in our embrace, and feeling the want of something more.

When we finally broke from our hold, our eyes met, locked in uncertainty and conveyance. *Where was this going?* She looked away, avoiding my eyes.

"Just don't keep me waiting too long," she said, making light of the awkward moment.

She left me with my hands at my sides, standing beneath the chandelier, its crystals mirroring my spotted mood.

433

Alone, I paced the suite with nervous energy, stopping to open every closet and dresser drawer for no reason whatsoever. I removed a hotel terry-cloth robe from a hanger, put it on, and slipped my feet into matching slippers. I walked in circles.

I settled onto the bed, on top of the duvet, and turned on the ten o'clock news. The main story was the marathon, as expected. The weatherman said it might hit ninety degrees. And I smirked because ninety degrees in Tucson is a cool front.

Then the story switched to clips of the earlier press conference. Christmas Day stood in front of a microphone. My nervous tic came back, and my head shuttered left. A caption under Christmas read "AMERICA'S BEST HOPE." "Are there any other Americans to watch for?" a reporter asked him. And Christmas shook his head. "No."

I couldn't deny that.

I was too wired to sleep, and so I called room service and asked for a bottle of beer. *One beer will relax me.*

Minutes later there was a knock on the door. A tall, thin man in a bellhop uniform greeted me and presented the beer in a silver ice bucket on a silver platter.

"What's this?" I asked.

"It's your beverage, Mr. Balls."

"It's just a beer," I said. "You didn't need to go to all this trouble."

But he didn't understand.

"Would you like me to pour it for you, Mr. Balls?" A tall glass rested on top of the platter.

"No," I said. "And there is no *s*."

"Very well," he said. "Then, would you like me to turn down your bed, Mr. Balls?"

"I don't even know what that means," I said.

"Sir…"

"And there's still no *s* in my name," I said. "Say my name."

But he left before he did.

I went back to sitting on the bed, with my back against the headboard and still wearing the terry-cloth bathrobe and slippers. I sipped the beer—from the bottle, not the glass—and tried my best not to think about the race. I turned off the television and watched the flames flicker and dim in the fireplace. Thirty minutes passed. The beer was long gone now.

The ruby slipper. *Judy slept here.* I imagined her lying in this same bed, feeding her narcosis with pills and wine, fixated on the fireplace as flames sparked and crackled as she weighed her next performance. *How apropos.*

I stood and took the ruby slipper in my hand. I tapped my head with it three times and said, "If there's any magic in this slipper, then let me sleep." Then I ran my hand the length of the mantel, admiring its craftsmanship and the hand-carved, golden overlay. I moved to its side, examining every inch. My finger hit a depression, a flaw in the wood. With my curiosity piqued, I leaned close to examine the flaw. Underneath a thick coat of paint, something was carved into the mantel's side. I knelt to get a better look. Initials of some sort…

J –

J – G.

Judy Garland must have carved her initials into the side of the mantel. *What a find!*

I ran my fingers over it again, to be sure. The J. Then the—wait. It wasn't a G. I examined it closer now. It wasn't a G at all! It was an F. My first thought was one of disappointment. She hadn't carved her initials in it after all. Why would she? And with what—a butterknife from room service? But if not her, then who?

The initials: J – F. The letters were edgy, likely carved with a pocketknife.

And in that second, I shot straight. A pocketknife. Jimmy's pocketknife. J - F. James Flynn.

I called down to the lobby, and the same bellhop who'd delivered the beer picked up.

"Yes, Mr. Balls?"

"The room…" I began.

"Everything was remodeled except for the fireplace," he confirmed. "That's been there since the early nineteen hundreds."

I hung up.

It was 11:30 p.m, but I dialed the phone without hesitation, or consideration.

Maggie McCollough picked up on the first ring—again.

"Mr. Balls. Of course, I remember. Of course, I'm sure," she said. "Jimmy stayed at the Lenox."

***

Ten miles in, we charge through Natick where we're greeted by the biggest crowds yet to a parade-like atmosphere.

And just a couple miles later we hear a shrill so high-pitched that Jet would have cowered and run the other way. As we close in, the fever pitch grows louder. And then we see them: Hundreds of screaming young women from Wellesley College welcome our presence. They push in from each side, creating a tunnel of noise we shoot through. They hold signs that say "KISS ME," "MARRY ME," "I'M HAVING YOUR BABY!" Several of the runners hold their fingers to their ears to block out the ear-piercing shouts. But even at a five-minute-per-mile pace, I'm not immune to humor. I wink and smile.

It's also here that I surge and pull alongside the frontrunners. And for the first time, I'm finally within view of the press truck.

At the makeshift press booth near the finish line, the two broadcasters spot the move.

"Who's that?" Bob Hall asks.

Ananya has to check the roster. "William Ball. From Arizona," she says. "Goes by Billy."

"Billy Ball?"

"Yes," she says. "Billy Ball."

"I don't have much on him," Bob says.

"Wait—I know this guy," Ananya says. "He was a former high school standout, overshadowed by Christmas Day, but clearly one of the best young runners in the country. He disappeared from competition—until recently. Certainly, no one expected him to be here this far into the race."

"A true underdog," Bob chimes in. "He certainly looks comfortable running in today's heat."

"Yes, he does, Boob."

In Oracle, Coach Jones and his team are howling at the mispronunciation of Bob Hall's name. But they're also howling at seeing Billy for the first time. He's on the heels of Christmas Day, who does a double-take when he sees Billy.

In Tempe, Tuba is joined on the couch by his girlfriend, who has just woken up and is also nursing a hangover. He lights a joint, takes a hit, and hands it to her. He coughs when he exhales. "Billy is in the lead pack," he says.

"Who's Billy?"

"I told you last night," Tuba says, perturbed. "He's the dude!"

In Pittsburgh, Maggie McCollough leans closer to the television, her eyes magnified by her thick lenses. She can't believe what she sees. But there's no mistaking it. There's no mistaking her *brother* running in the lead pack. "Get in here," she shouts to her husband. "Jimmy is winning!"

In Wilmerding, Joe has the television on in the background and has mostly forgotten about the race as he tends to a few locals who sit at the bar drinking whisky and beer, while complaining about the price of whisky and beer. Nobody is paying any attention to the race. But when Joe hears the name Billy Ball, his ears perk up and he tells his customers to shut the hell up, that this Billy Ball kid has ties to the town. Joe points to the old black and white photo hanging on the wall of Paddy O'Donnell and James Flynn. "That's his great-granddaddy, for Christ's sake," Joes says. Suddenly, all eyes are on the television.

At the finish line, Richard and Jean Ball sit restlessly under a cloudless sky, still watching the coverage on the Jumbotron with Charlie. When they see Billy pop out from the pack, Richard shouts, "That's my boy!"

Charlie stirs. Her heart jumps. "Run to me," she whispers under her breath. "Come on, BB!"

We reach the start of the Newton hills at mile seventeen. The heat is breaking the field, and the pack is strung out now. But to me, it feels like just another day in Tucson. By the time we crest Heartbreak Hill at mile twenty-one, only five of us remain in the lead pack, and it's Christmas that still leads the charge.

I've simply forgotten about my shoes, but now my feet are beginning to ache in their unfamiliarity. The beginnings of a blister form on my heel. It grows quickly. My gait compromises, and I fight to stay with Christmas and the others at this pace. I drop by ten yards. Then twenty. Five miles to go, but I'm fading.

Run to Charlie!

On the broadcast, the co-hosts continue to discuss the enigmatic runner, Billy Ball. They find more information: a troubled youth, run-ins with the law. And they air it all. But seeing that Billy is struggling with the pace, Ananya picks up a slight hitch in his stride as the camera focuses in on his shoes.

"What are those?" asks Bob.

"They must be new technology," says Ananya. "I don't see a logo. But clearly, there must be magic in them, Mr. Boob."

"Hall," he says. "Just call me Hall. Say, isn't it time for a commercial?"

At the finish line, Charlie can't believe her eyes at the sight of the old shoes on the Jumbotron. "Billy—you didn't!"

At the Oracle Theater, Mr. Grant G. Grant sees the same thing. "Rosebud," he says under his breath. "I'll be damned."

In front of Boston College, Jack Ash is following the broadcast on a transistor radio. It won't be long before the lead pack passes by. He pours another beer out of pure nerves. He takes a mouthful, but spits it out when he sees them coming. He screams at the top of his lungs, "Jesus Christ! Balls is in the lead!" Sure enough, despite the hitch in Billy's stride, he's worked his way back and is a shoulder in front of Christmas Day.

His friends match his enthusiasm. "Balls is in the lead!" they echo. Jack corrects himself and shouts, "Ball, I meant. Say his name! His name is Ball. No ₰!" But it's far too late, because those celebrating alongside repeat what they'd heard, and before long the name is passed along the chain of fans, a hundred feet wide, then two hundred, and a quarter mile, and then a mile, as quick-moving as a cough and a sneeze, until "Balls" is shouted from every mouth along the course.

Tightly bunched, we slingshot onto Beacon Street, picking up speed. But almost immediately two others drop off. Within a minute, it's just Christmas, a runner from Kenya, and me. The sun is directly overhead and beating down on us without mercy. I'm struggling with the pace and doubting that I can hang on. The hitch in my stride is being caused by the blister that is hot and ballooning now. But then—it pops! It feels like I've been shot in the heel! I arch my back and blood oozes on my sock and shoe. Raw tissue rubs against the old shoe now, but oddly, my gait comes back and I'm running well again within minutes.

My body has responded, but now it's my head I question. I'm hearing things—at least I must be—because the crowd is cheering for me, but they've got my name

441

wrong. They're calling me "Balls, Balls, Balls!" And I think that's impossible. Who is responsible for this?

Miles back, Jack Ash is high-fiving his friends, chugging a beer.

Am I really being mocked by a hundred thousand spectators at the Boston Marathon?

I'm also hallucinating—at least I must be—because the giant Citgo sign comes into view and seems to hang in the distance, dancing on waves of heat, like a desert mirage that doesn't get closer. Once I reach it—if I can reach it— there's only a mile left to the finish line.

Hang on. Hang on.

Run to Charlie.

"Balls, Balls, Balls," they chant at Coolidge Corner.

In the Oracle Theater, Coach Jones and his team are throwing popcorn, hollering at the big screen, "Balls Balls Balls!" A steady stream of townies has filled the theater now, as word has spread that Billy is in the lead.

Fifteen miles south, in the foothills of Tucson, Piper Cox has his back to the lunch-goers sitting at the patio bar. He's in character, again, mimicking Speedy Gonzales and shouting, *"¡Arriba, arriba! Andale, andale!"* Up, up! Go on, go On!

In Joe's Bar and Grill, the dingers don't chant. But they drink, and watch, curiously intrigued as they listen to the old man brag that he knew the kid's great-grandfather. "Spitting image," Joe says. "Fine kid, that Jimmy was." The bar is filling up with more dingers. Word has spread.

Above her namesake diner, Maggie McCollough is now joined on the sofa by her husband. He tells her she looks pretty sitting there in her yellow dress. He takes her hand in his, but her eyes are fixated on the television. "Go, Jimmy," she says.

But I'm not hearing things, and I'm not hallucinating. We pass the giant Citco sign and Fenway Park and enter Kenmore Square. The Red Sox game has just let out and the crowds are the largest of the day so far. And there's no mistaking it; they're calling me Balls. A boy wearing a Red Sox hat reaches out to high-five me and shouts, "Go, Mr. Balls!"

Say my name, kid.

But I have no time for that. I'm focused on the race now—or what's left of it. I look to my side. The runner from Kenya is gone. I don't turn to see where he is. I instinctively know he's been shot out the back by the tempo that Christmas has set.

It's just the two of us now and we're flying well under a five-minute pace. I'm step for step with Christmas Day, once again, after all these years. The crowd, rows deep at this point, shouts and raises their fists, cheering us on— the two Americans. But we're running so fast, and I'm so focused now, that they appear dreamlike, as if in slow motion with their mouths agape and their movements forced.

I'm on Christmas' heels, but I'm not content to let him lead. I'm not just hanging on now, and I want him to question me. I pull alongside him. "Say my name," I say between breaths. But he doesn't acknowledge. I don't expect him to. So, I push on and pull in front, and now it's he who locks on *my* heels.

We enter a short underpass at Massachusetts Avenue. It's dark and cooler here, a short reprieve from the direct sun before the final push to the finish. It's also quiet, a reprieve from the manic crowd. Christmas is fighting for breath, but so am I. We're at our limits, squeezing every inch of speed from our bodies, locked in on each other in rhyme and reason, in step and breath. Our footfalls are heavy now. *Slap, slap, slap.*

But my shoe slaps harder than his. As we exit the underpass, I see why. The upper of my shoe has torn away from the sole. *The damn shoes won't make it the final mile!*

We take a hard right onto Hereford Street, and the shoe completely disintegrates before my eyes. Somewhere behind me I've left the sole, and I run on a blood-spotted sock while the upper flops around my ankle.

Just before we make the final turn onto Boylston, I step on a pointy rock with my shoeless foot, and my reflex is to pull up, just enough that Christmas, still locked on my heels, pushes into me.

Our feet tangle. And down we go…once again.

I hear the gasps of the crowd while I check myself for injury. I'm fine, and rise, but Christmas has fallen hard and struggles to get up. He screams, calling me names that are not my name. And I don't dare ask him to say my name this time. But I have no interest in sticking around. The finish line is too close, and I know the Kenyan must be closing in.

I lurch forward to right myself, but Christmas has a hold of the one shoe I'm still wearing. He's not going to let me escape. I try to free myself from his grasp, and when I yank, the shoe comes off. But now he's quick to latch on to my leg, clawing, pulling himself up, climbing me, and in the process, grabs hold of my shorts. I push him back with both hands, but he holds tight against my forward motion, and the shorts yank to my ankles. I kick, and I kick twice, and with the one free foot, I manage to free them and tear away, leaving Christmas on the ground holding my shorts and one shoe.

I make the famous left turn from Hereford Street onto Boylston Street, the world's grandest stage, butt-naked and shoeless. *Six hundred yards to go.*

Joe's Bar and Grill erupts. The dingers, after sixty years, finally have something to cheer about. Joe flips the "FREE BEER TOMORROW" sign around and shouts, "Free beer today!"

All along Boylston Street, the fans are ten deep and maniacal. I'm running shoeless. I'm running without shorts. They scream what they believe to be my name:

"Balls! Balls! Balls!" And somehow it all makes sense. My penis flops back and forth from right to left, and left to right, and they have my name wrong, and I don't care. *I no longer care.* I embrace their collective voice, and raise my hand to my ear, beckoning them to shout my name. "Say my name!" And they do—"Balls, Balls Balls"—and nothing, absolutely nothing, has ever sounded so good in my life. One last glance behind, and I see Christmas giving chase with a pained expression, still clenching my shorts in his hand, and I laugh as I sprint, and I can't stop laughing—my gut wrenches and it hurts, and it hurts so good that I bend at the waist I'm laughing so hard, knowing he's seen this view once before of my naked ass running away from him.

The finish line draws closer—three blocks, then two—and I hear the race announcer calling me in. I look for my parents in the stands and spot them—my dad standing, taller than anyone, both in physics and stature, shouting my name with his arms raised; my mom with one hand covering one eye, peaking out with the other.

And Charlie. Where is Charlie?

I don't see her. I've run to her. I've run to Charlie, but she's not here, and I'm swept with sadness when I cross the line.

And then…I see. It's her. She's here! She's waiting for me just beyond the finish. She's beautiful, golden, and luminant in the sun. She's laughing, and she's taken the shirt off her back to cover me, standing unabashed in her bra.

"I ran to you," I tell her.

She's fighting back tears of joy, wiping one away as it rolls down her cheek. She looks up, our eyes fastened on each other, and in typical Charlie fashion says, "What took you so damn long?"

26.2

The Humiliation Tour

Charlie is back home, visiting her mom after graduating college. It's been a full month now since Boston, and a celebration of our accomplishments is in order. I drive to her house in a newly purchased, classic Malibu convertible that I've custom-painted pumpkin-orange. It's Charlie's favorite color, and I know it's going to make her laugh. I pull up to the curb and Charlie is outside waiting for me.

Jet sits in the passenger seat. He sees her and leaps from the car. He douses her with kisses, and in turn, she strokes his head and gives him a long hug. "I've missed you too, Jet!"

Lucky dog.

Charlie opens the passenger door, and I tell Jet to get in back. But Charlie won't have any of it.

"We'll share," she says. "It's his seat."

She gets in first, and Jet takes his place on her lap. "Pumpkin-orange?" she says.

"Your carriage, Cinderella." I smile and tell her to buckle up. She does, and holds onto Jet tightly. We drive west, melding into the sunset, which is also pumpkin-orange.

A mile out of town, I punch the gas pedal and accelerate. Charlie's head lurches back and her wispy, blonde hair shoots straight behind her, riding the curl of the wind. We take a hard left onto a choppy dirt road that points us toward the silver-laced silhouette of Mount Lemmon. The Malibu fishtails and the three of us howl in delight.

Ten minutes later we arrive at the old mine. I pop the trunk and remove two folding chairs and stand them up next to a makeshift fire ring and Jimmy Flynn's headstone.

We're here for a reason.

From my pocket, I remove the token finisher medal I'd received at Boston. It carries weight in both ounces and meaning, and I hold it in the palm of my hand, taking a moment to admire its logoed image of a unicorn. It's a wonderful piece of hardware, and something my great-grandfather would have been proud to wear around his neck. His time has come and I place it on top of his headstone as Charlie looks on.

I knock three times on the stone and tell him, "Thanks for the shoes, Jimmy. There was magic in them after all. This medal is for you."

Charlie pulls two beers from the cooler and hands one to me. Then, she pulls a rawhide from her knapsack and hands it to Jet. "You're such a good boy, Jet." His eyes grow wide as he takes it from her. He lays between us, content with his new chew toy.

I light a fire and we settle in, admiring one of Arizona's great treasures: its night sky. The city lights are somewhere distant, luminescent above and beyond Mount Lemmon. A full moon climbs a wall of diamonds as the stars *pop, pop, pop*.

I tell Charlie of my plan to buy the Oracle Theater with my race winnings. "Mr. Grant is retiring," I say. "He says I should hire a general manager until my running career is over. And he says I need to invest in an electronic register so little shits like my younger self can't rob my older self."

"You're lucky you're not in jail," Charlie reminds me.

"I've thought long and hard about that," I tell her.

We tap our beer bottles to my good fortune.

"Hold on." I walk to the Malibu. When I return, I'm holding an old shoebox.

"What's that?" Charlie asks.

"My life," I say.

I show it to her. "MY LITTLE BOX OF FAILURES" is written on its top.

I open it and take out a piece of scrap paper that's been scribbled on hastily.

"Oh, this is a good one," I say, reading it from just the light of the flickering flames. "Dad dropped me on my head at birth." I pause for effect. Charlie raises an eyebrow and says that explains my square head, among other things. "I've had to relive that moment a hundred times." I toss the paper into the fire and watch it ignite.

"Over it," I say. I offer the box to Charlie. "Pick one."

The game is fun, and Charlie reaches in, pulling out another note. She unfolds it and reads aloud. "I swung with all my might at Danny Morales. I missed, and all my momentum spun me full circle until I lost balance and fell on my ass. And then Danny kicked me in the mouth."

"That was a memorable day," I say. "Right in front of the girl I liked."

"Who happened to be his girlfriend," Charlie reminds me. She glances in the box. "BB, there are so many notes in here!"

"It's been quite a tour," I say. "But not for you. Don't you ever feel humiliated?"

"I do," she says. "I've been hanging out with you my entire life."

"Good point."

"Your turn," she says, handing me the shoebox.

I remove another note. I read it without speaking. I move to place it back in the box. "I can't read this one out loud."

"C'mon, BB, don't hold out on me. What does it say?"

"Nothing."

"BB!"

"Nothing," I say, holding the note high now, out of her reach. But she snatches it from my hand just the same. I fight to pull it back, but I'm too slow.

She reads. "Fell into the fire while trying to kiss the girl of my dreams."

She surveys me, but she too is speechless. Our eyes lock and we see each other through a mature lens now. We're vulnerable to the truth. Nothing is guarded.

I break the silence. "Charlie…"

"What is it, BB?"

"The box is full."

"It is."

"Charlie…"

"What is it, BB?"

I swallow hard. "Can I kiss you?"

She's still holding the note tightly, and places it squarely in our sightline. She crumples it in her hand and blindly tosses it into the fire. Peripherally, we see it catch and flame. But she still doesn't say anything. And this time, neither do I.

I move closer.

She leans in.

Just then, rolling thunder bounces back and forth off the canyon walls. We pull back, startled. "Strange," I say, looking up. "There's not a cloud in the sky."

We don't know what to make of it. But then our eyes gravitate toward Jimmy Flynn's headstone.

"Do you think?" Charlie asks.

I shake my head yes. "Jimmy's found his voice."

And we laugh a bellowing laugh. And when we stop…

"Where were we?" I ask.

Jet barks, telling us it's time. He backs up to give us space.

This time it's Charlie who leans in, and I'm quick to meet her halfway. Our lips are a foot apart. Hers curl at their edges. We're six inches apart now. Her gold-flecked eyes shut.

And for me, time stands still. Einstein was right. I'm moving at light speed now, lost in the cosmos, and everything surrounding me simply stops. I'm flooded by a

453

thousand memories. A sensual wish teases me. Our lips brush once, and then again. Her touch is therapy.

This time the chair leg does not collapse.

This time it holds firm against my weight.

This time I do not fall into the fire.

This time, the humiliation tour has ended.

Dear Reader,

THE HUMILIATION TOUR existed only in my mind until April of 2020. And only in bits and pieces; a fragmented outline of what it could be, and what I might find once I shed my skin to expose the connective tissues that held the story.

In July of 2021, I finished the book—all except for the last sentence. I penned that in a desolate cabin, high in the mountains of Colorado. It was the perfect James Caan moment from the movie, Misery. My wife was with me, and together we celebrated by uncorking a bottle of champagne.

In my hands, I held a manuscript which I felt was worthy of my ambition and intention. I held the lives of characters, not yet born fourteen months ago, who talked, laughed, loved, fought, and even ran. They were fully baked, and ready to be devoured by whomever wanted to feast.

Time is our most valuable asset. It's an exhaustible, finite resource. So, I want to thank you for taking your time to read THE HUMILIATION TOUR. I am hopeful that it captured your interest and kept you entertained throughout its pages. Your reviews and recommendations go miles in helping the story find its audience. So, if you are inclined, I truly appreciate the mention.

Best Regards,
Jeff Recker

The Slummer: Quarters Till Death (Slummer - Book 1)
by Geoffrey Simpson

An impoverished runner, from an era of prolific genetic engineering, chases his dream of the 5000-meter national title.

The Farmhand: Dante's Ladder (Slummer - Book 2)
by Geoffrey Simpson

Coming Soon – 2023

The Humiliation Tour
by Jeffrey Recker

A humiliated cross-country runner makes a redeeming comeback in this hilarious coming of age story.

Acknowledgements

Inspiration is knocking on my door, but I've got other things on my mind. It's one month after the country shut down. I've been laid off. I'm emotionally spent following the exhaustive news about the pandemic. My wife encourages me to start writing. She knows that writing grounds me and will act as my crutch during this anxious time. She's right. I have a bit of exploration to do of my youth, my roots, and my imagination. I have a platform in mind on which to build things. And I have questions that can only be answered through careful assiduity. I open the door and let inspiration in.

The Humiliation Tour would not have been possible if it were not for the influence, guidance, and help from so many.

So, here's to…

My wife, Kathaleen, who has a habit of kicking me in the ass when she knows I need it. Much of her character can be found in the words of Charlie. She knew this story had been brewing in my head for years, and encouraged me to start the journey.

Kevin Koch, the inspiration behind the character of Billy Ball. We were running in the Las Vegas Marathon. He was wearing his favorite—and very tattered—shorts, when the crotch ripped out mid-stride. On a very windy day the frayed fabric lifted in the stiff crosswind. He happened to be running alongside of the lead woman, and a television crew was filming her from an accompanying vehicle. My guess is that buried somewhere in a production company's vault is a clip of my buddy's penis flopping around in the wind, unedited, uncut.

Geoffrey Simpson, author of THE SLUMMER. When many large, established publishers passed, Geoff was there for me. I am forever grateful.

David Aretha, my editor. I handed him the manuscript, and naively, shamelessly, said, "I think it's pretty clean." He's probably still laughing. Thank you for the corrections, and offering so many great suggestions on how to make this novel better. I took them to heart.

Bob Diforio, my former agent, for taking a chance on an unknown author, and putting the manuscript in play.

My beta readers and proofreaders, especially Shanna Miller and Suzanne Sgroi. Thanks for sticking with it.

Chuckie, my late, and very loved, black Labrador, who was my running partner. Your antics live through Jet in this book.

Champ, my beer belly, and lifetime sidekick who I try to kill every January. He makes an appearance as Tuba's burgeoning beer gut in this novel. I always knew you'd be immortalized. Drink up, my friend.

And to the towns of Wilmerding, and Oracle.

I knew nothing about Wilmerding before I began writing this story. I chose it because of its proximity to Pittsburgh. When I began to research the town, I realized I'd struck gold. It has a rich history as America's first company-owned town, and was a perfect representation of difficult times during The Great Depression.

As for the small town of Oracle—it sits at the base of Mt. Lemmon, and holds a special place in my heart. It is here that I ran my first race—a 10k in 1989.

But I did not accurately describe Oracle. Purposely so. I used plenty of poetic license in my description. Oracle High School does not exist. Neither does the Oracle Theater. And, surprisingly, there are few saguaro cacti in this town of less than five-thousand residents. I chose Oracle as the setting for this novel because of two things: its proximity to Tucson, and the fact that it was once a thriving mining town. And let's not forgot the sunsets; those amazing sunsets that God wrings from the sky each evening. They're simply magical here.

Finally, I'd be remiss if I didn't acknowledge the Boston Marathon as the bearings for this novel. For runners, all roads lead there.

Ever since I was a kid, long before I became a runner, The Boston Marathon has intrigued and found a special place in my heart. For many runners, it is the pinnacle of a life well lived. When you run Boston, your fabric is stitched into history. Just ask Jimmy Flynn and Billy Ball. Of course, neither will answer. And neither ran the race. They're fictional characters. But I think it would have meant something to them if they had. I think it would have been a path worth chasing.

About the Author

Jeffrey Recker is a two-time recipient of Road Runners Club of America's Outstanding Club Writer's Award for Journalism Excellence, and a past contributor to Colorado Runner Magazine. Born in Pittsburgh, raised in Phoenix, he now lives in Grand Junction, Colorado, with his wife, two daughters, and three rescue dogs. He's an avid runner, and has competed in more than thirty marathons, including the famed Boston Marathon on five occasions. He's also a seasoned triathlete, and has competed in eight Ironman competitions. Inevitably, he's experienced his fair share of humiliation.

BarkingBoxer Press

The Future of Sports Fiction